FORGOTTEN WITNESS

Novels by Patricia L. Stebelton

SUSPENSE. MYSTERY. ROMANCE.

*

The Sleeping Matchbook

Watched!

Inherited Danger

Henri's Ghost

Uncharted Storm

The Forgotten Witness

Forgotten Witness

Patricia L. Stebelton

OakTara
www.oaktara.com

The Forgotten Witness

Published in the U.S. by:
OakTara Publishers
www.oaktara.com

Cover design by Yvonne Parks at www.pearcreative.ca
Cover images © thinkstockphoto.ca: old graveyard/Jag_cz, 186236066; © shutterstock.com: portrait of beautiful young woman close up, isolated on white background/BestPhotoStudio, 12525284
Author photo © Patricia L. Stebelton

ISBN-13: 978-1-60290-201-5 ▪ ISBN-10: 1-60290-201-1
eISBN-13: 978-1-60290-406-4 ▪ eISBN-10: 1-60290-406-5

Printed in the U.S.A.

* * *

TO MY GRANDDAUGHTER,
VANESSA STEBELTON, BSN, RN.

I run to her whenever I need medical information,
and she points me in the right direction.
Thanks, Ness.

"When you pass through the waters, I will be with you.
When you walk through the fire, you will not be scorched,
nor will the flame burn you...For I am the Lord your God."
ISAIAH 43:2-3

Prologue

1994
Seventeen years earlier

TIRED AND FRUSTRATED, KAREN COTTRELL CALLED FROM THE KITCHEN, "Ellie, finish your homework! There won't be time to bother going to Stevie's house if you don't hurry. Though, as far as I'm concerned, you're together too much as it is. How often have you come home dirty, with torn clothes from climbing trees, playing baseball, and what all? I've told your father time and again, you should have a nice girl friend—someone you could do girl things with. Ellie, are you listening? What's taking you so long?" She turned from her position at the sink to stare at her dark-haired daughter with deep blue eyes mirroring her own.

Eight-year-old Ellie Cottrell squirmed in her chair, her face broodingly troubled. "I'm listening, Mom, but I just can't think about homework. My mind won't stick. Don't you ever feel that way? I've got this scared feeling about Stevie." Worry lines formed across her small forehead.

"Scared feeling! What prompted that? Did something happen at school?" Now concerned, Karen walked to the doorway.

Rising from the table, Ellie scurried to the front room to look out the window. "No. Nothing happened at school. Stevie said he would call, and he hasn't. Can I go over there now? I promise to finish when I get back. Please, Mom!"

Karen jammed her hands on her hips. "Enough of that, young lady! You are going to sit right there until that homework is done. If you want to go to Stevie's house, get busy."

Ellie was still working at the dining room table when the phone rang. Karen grabbed the kitchen phone. As she listened, she felt the blood drain from her face. Turning away from Ellie's view, she closed the door between them. Moments later she walked zombie-like, hands trembling, from the kitchen to sit next to her young daughter.

"Ellie, something terrible has happened." She took hold of Ellie's hands. "There's been an explosion at Stevie's house." Her raised hand stopped Ellie from asking questions. "I don't know anything. Nobody does, but it doesn't look good. Both Stevie and his mother were inside the house when it exploded...."

*

Horror-stricken, Ellie pulled away from her mother. With tears streaming down her face, she tore toward the front door, only to be blocked by her mother.

"No, Ellie, you can't go over there! I don't want those images in your mind." She pulled Ellie into her arms and held her tight until she quit struggling.

On the living room floor, mother and daughter prayed for the Turner family. Ellie's eyes were squeezed shut, but the tears wouldn't stop. She prayed fiercely for Stevie. *Make him be all right, God. Make him be all right!* She determined to sneak away and ride her bike to his house. *I've got to see for myself! God wouldn't let Stevie die.*

1

Late Appointment

Seventeen years later

THE FORLORN HOOTING OF AN OWL echoed hollow in the dense night air. Lacy Eleanor Cottrell squinted a short distance beyond into the black forest and shivered. The quarter moon she'd noticed while driving had been swallowed up in fast-moving dark clouds. She commended herself on her foresight to carry a small flashlight. Although she had no wish to cause notice of her arrival, the darkness was impenetrable beyond the city limits devoid of street lights. And if her vague recollections were accurate, the ground in the old cemetery was dangerously uneven. She could break an ankle.

The walk from the old church parking lot had been cold and damp. Lacy carefully picked her way in designer snow boots over mud puddles and around bunches of dirty snow. Drawing her lined, off-white trench coat around her slim figure, she lifted the hood to protect her from the sharp wind. Why hadn't she thought to wear those old farm boots she kept in the closet for hiking at this time of year? Early spring weather always oozed mud. If it hadn't been for the note she would be home now. Reading it had thrown her off center, and she hadn't thought anything clearly through since that moment. Her fingers tightened on its wrinkled form inside her pocket.

She didn't need to read it again to know what it said: *Meet me where Stevie lies on the 31st of March, at 11:30 p.m.* The fact it was unsigned made the hair on the back of her neck prickle. That and it had been addressed to *Ellie.* Lacy hadn't been called *Ellie* since she was fifteen, when she'd declared she would answer only to the name of *Lacy* from that point on.

Eleanor was her middle name, a name her mother preferred, and the reason she was called Ellie as a child. This year would mark the seventeenth anniversary of Stevie's death. Who might remember their childhood names? Memories ran long in a small community. But the bigger question remained: *Who knew about the purple feathers?* When the purple feather first fell from the note, she gasped.

Was it one of their original purple feathers—hers and Stevie's? The chill in her spine had not left since she'd stared down at that fallen feather. A purple feather in a message was a coded SOS—their personal signal for help. *Who knows about our code?*

The catch on the wire gate was worn through. She pushed it open, hearing it creak loosely in the wind, and gazed at the wrought-iron sign above the gate. It was too dark to see, but she knew what it read: *Gladden Hills Methodist Cemetery.* Its oldest residents dated back to the early twentieth century.

Lacy gathered her courage as she stared skyward. Had she asked for prior wisdom, she might not be standing at the gate of an old cemetery shortly before midnight waiting to meet a stranger. *Have I lost my mind?* As her left hand groped for the flashlight in her pocket, her fingers brushed the small pepper spray canister. *Just in case I'm making the mistake of my life.*

Lacy followed the thin beam through the gate to find her way toward the extreme back of the small cemetery. Bypassing several molehills, she worked to keep to the narrow makeshift path off to the side of the headstones. The rate of her heart increased two-fold even as her focus shifted from the footpath below to ghost-like headstones to the left, searching the surrounding areas for any unusual shadow formations or unexplained movement. When that owl hooted a second time, she fought to regain her fragile composure.

Lacy worked her way to the last row. Stevie and his mother, Terri, resided in the final two gravesites in this cemetery. After they were buried, the cemetery was officially closed. They occupied the remaining plots held by the Turner family. Stepping carefully along that last line of graves, she lifted her small beam from headstone to headstone, scanning the names. With each quiet footfall she listened, but only the wind responded. Was she the first to arrive?

Thinking she heard a twig snap, Lacy spun around, aiming her light in the direction the sound had occurred. The blackened forest lay at least fifty feet beyond the natural stone hedge bordering the cemetery at the back end. Seeing no one, she swung the beam erratically from place to place. No sign or evidence of anyone. She wanted to think it was the work of a bird landing on a weak branch, but doubts remained. Her chest heaved with fear of the unknown.

What am I doing here? Biting her lip, she pivoted back to focus on the headstones.

Lacy suddenly wanted to be done with this place and back inside her car, but her curiosity and the feather SOS alert wouldn't allow her to leave—not yet. *You're a reporter, Lacy Cottrell. Start acting like one and summon some of that gumption you've prided yourself on having for so long.*

As she lifted her beam to the next headstone, everything came to a halt inside. So many years had passed she thought her senses were dulled to the impact of the tragedy. But one glimpse of his name on the headstone wrenched her heart open and raw, as if it happened yesterday.

Steven Thomas Turner
Beloved son of Terri and Matthew Turner
1985-1993
August 25

Only eight years old! He was my best friend. She swallowed hard. *Is that the lump sum of Stevie's young life? Four chiseled lines on a cold marble slab?* Her heart filled with new grief. She had never forgotten her childhood playmate and had thought of him nearly every day since.

Moving the light to the next headstone, she was prepared for what she would find there:

Terri Elayne Turner
Beloved wife of Matthew Turner
Mother of Steven Thomas Turner
1963-1993
August 25

She was a nice lady. Lacy remembered the day it happened. She and Stevie were supposed to play soldiers on his front porch. He was going to call her when he was done with his homework. But when the phone rang, the call wasn't from Stevie.

The bombing of a neighborhood home and the killing of a mother and child was big news in the small city of Gladden Hills. The whole town was thrown into confusion and grieved the loss, but none more than little Ellie Cottrell, who lost her best friend that day.

At what point had she promised Stevie to find justice for his unsolved murder? *Lord knows I've tried! Every direction I've followed has reached a dead end.* The memories of that day were brutal. She couldn't think on them now.

Shivering from the rawness of the night air, Lacy shone the light on her watch: *11:40 p.m.* Whoever she was supposed to meet was late. She stamped her feet to keep warm. Five more minutes and she was out of there. *Meet me where Stevie lies,* the note read. Shining her light back to Stevie's headstone, she dropped the beam to its base where limp, partly frozen flowers lay. Someone had visited this grave recently.

Lacy stooped to look closer at the flowers. They were spring daisies. Lacy had carried spring daisies to the gravesite service to lay on Stevie's coffin on the day of his funeral. They had always been her favorite flower. She shivered, not liking any part of this arrangement. Her black gloved hand lifted the flowers at the base of the stems, where something white peeked out from underneath. Pulling out a soggy envelope, she withdrew a folded paper and stood, unfolding it under the weak beam of her small flashlight. The battery was almost shot, and she had to steady her shaking hand to draw it close.

The note was for her, Lacy knew without reading the words—so were the wilted flowers. Her gaze moved across the messy scroll:

> I know you are searching. Come back to Gladden Hills. The answers you seek about their deaths lie here, where the danger remains—a slumbering giant. I need your help.

Just like their childhood game, the purple feather carried an SOS message…but who was doing the asking? With the note was another purple feather…and an advertisement: *Wanted: Experienced reporter, apply at Gladden Hills Gazette.* Did the unknown writer want her to apply for the position? Incredulous! How much did they know about her? *They'd known enough to send the first note to the Chicago office,* she reminded herself. Were these notes merely a hoax or a solid lead? Someone was counting on her need to discover the truth. Could she afford to ignore the offer or the request for help? Who knew her that well? Who had followed her discreet investigation these past few years? Goosebumps formed on her arms. She scanned the area. It was time to leave this ghostly place.

Lacy placed everything back into the plain white envelope and stuffed it in her pocket. The beam from her flashlight was almost nonexistent. She turned slowly, peering into the dark woods behind the cemetery. Someone was out there in those woods watching her; she could feel it. Was it the same person who had left the envelope? One thing she knew for sure. There would be no face-to-face meeting tonight. It appeared the writer of the notes did not want to be known at this time—but why? Two questions remained: Could she trust the writer? Did she want to know the answers to Stevie's death bad enough to take a longshot chance and come back to Gladden Hills, Michigan?

And what might it all lead to?

Turning back, Lacy directed her steps away from the gravesite, her fingers cradling the small canister of pepper spray, just in case. Something told her she would get no sleep this night. She had heavy thinking to do. Before she made her decision concerning Gladden Hills, she needed to determine the source of the purple feathers. Were those feathers authentic? Were they actually Stevie's and her feathers? Lacy needed daylight to find the answer.

*

The cloud cover of the previous night ripened into a full-fledged spring rainstorm by morning. Lacy had taken an unpretentious motel room on the edge of town for the night so she could be back at the old church promptly after breakfast and from there on her way to Chicago. Otto's Country Café in town was in the same location as when she left as a child, nestled in the middle of Main Street. Only the décor had been altered. Table decorations were small appliances made into lamps, an iron here, an old-fashioned coffeepot on the next. Quirky, she thought—original, but quirky. When you entered the small shop, the horseshoe lunch bar lay but a few steps away, sparsely occupied at this early hour.

Her eyes roamed the familiar café, searching for what she wasn't sure...perhaps the joy of her childhood that ended with Stevie's death. Shifting, she noted the row of booths to the left and right in their original positions and found it strangely comforting. It was to one of these booths on the right that Lacy made her way early the next morning, eagerly anticipating hot coffee and its energizing effect on her lethargic system.

Nursing her coffee cup, she removed her wet trench coat, laying it off to the side. The rain beat steadily against the windows, wave after wave rolling down in heavy sheets. Nothing had been easy this trip. It made her feel strange, sitting in this café as an adult. She and Dad had shared many a hamburger and fries for a Saturday lunch when her mother was away on business.

Discreetly she combed the cozy interior for anyone who looked familiar from her childhood...not that she was anxious to make it known she was visiting. In fact, quite the opposite. Her plan was to slip in and slip out, but after her unusual appointment the night before, she'd altered her plans to do further research.

Just about the time she felt confident in her anonymity, the shop door popped open and in shuffled a familiar, sharp-featured face—older, but definitely someone she'd known well. *Miss Pruitt!* Lacy cast a covert glance from side to side, afraid she'd voiced the name out loud. Her old piano teacher stood but a few feet away, but any words Lacy might have spoken were swallowed in indecision. She was hesitant to reveal who she was, and Miss Pruitt was the least likely person she would chose to do so.

"Morning, Gladys, come in and dry off with some hot chocolate," said the tall, wiry waitress behind the counter.

"BLAST!" the high-volume voice boomed. The small-framed woman wrestled with her wet umbrella, clearly unaware she'd been spoken to. She shook her body like a newly bathed puppy. "There are buckets of cats on one side of the street and buckets of dogs on the other!" Her voice was known for carrying across a two-block radius and now, with her obvious hearing problem, the volume was piercing.

"Gladys!" The waitress spoke louder. When the woman turned toward the counter, the waitress lifted a coffee up and grinned. "Chocolate?"

Closing her black umbrella, the old woman squinted and frowned. "Did you say coffee? You know I don't drink coffee, Wendy. Make me some hot chocolate. Surely you know that by now! I've been coming here for years," she said crossly, shuffling away. "I'll be in the first booth like usual."

Wendy, the waitress, rolled her eyes before turning away. Gladys Pruitt crossed to stand in front of the booth where Lacy was seated and frowned again. She was clearly not happy to see her usual booth occupied.

Lacy tried a warm smile to soften the effect of her presence in the coveted booth. Curiously the woman's frown altered into puzzlement, as if Miss Pruitt was straining to discern something troubling. Seeing this, Lacy glanced away before the old woman could recognize her. Although she gravely doubted Gladys Pruitt could make the connection after so long a time. Lacy Cottrell had done much changing in seventeen years. Still, she desired not to chance it, and made a pretense of studying the menu. The older woman wagged her head in clear irritation and passed by to the next booth.

Finishing her light breakfast, Lacy paid the bill and left quickly without a last look at one of the few people who might remember her from childhood days. When she crossed the street to her car, she spied the *Reporter Needed* sign in the front window of the *Gladden Hills Gazette* and recalled the advertisement in her note.

The small city newspaper was housed in the same 1800 Victorian brick building where it had always been since its original début. Pausing on the sidewalk, she stared again at the front window. Right next to the first sign was another public announcement: *Under New Ownership—Jason Gardner.* Now that was news. The *Gladden Hills Gazette* had been in the same family for fifty years at least.

Hurrying to get inside her car and out of the rain, Lacy raced to open her door while holding to her hood. Shivering, she slid behind the wheel and adjusted the heat on high. The dampness penetrated through to her skin. While stylish, her off-white trench coat didn't hold up to a driving rainstorm. Its strongest feature was the black pile removable lining that did an adequate job of buffeting the cold. Rain or no rain, she had no choice but to follow through with what needed to be accomplished.

With one last glance at the signs in the *Gazette* window, she turned left out of town and followed County Road 10 out past Madison Orchards for almost a mile, passing the farmers' granary to the crossroads where the old site for the Gladden Hills Free Methodist Church stood like a sentinel. It had been the proud home of several denominations over its eighty-year life, but now looked out across the cemetery empty and silent.

The vacated building was primarily used for private bazaars, small concerts, and the like in the last ten years. She and Stevie had come often with his grandparents as children. Most days now, it sat dark and lonely except for an occasional visit from a custodian. Lacy hoped today was not one of those days. She had no desire for her presence to be noted.

Behind the wooden church addition, she paralleled her car with the front of the cemetery. She turned off the engine and sat quietly observing the wrought iron fence surrounding three sides of the old cemetery with the natural stone hedge bordering it across the back. Beyond that, the grown-over path threaded its way into the woods. Though thoughts of the woods continued to nag her memory, Lacy lifted her focus to the high hill running upward behind the woods. The hill was just one of many noted high spots interspersed throughout Gladden Hills' rolling terrain. It was also an area of adventure from her childhood.

Observing the rain had slowed, Lacy took advantage of the opportunity to exit the car and pick her way to the cemetery gate. When she had rushed from the cemetery the previous night, it was swinging free and open. Now it was closed and secured with a piece of loose wire. Turning where she stood, Lacy searched for any sign of a custodian but found none. It was not surprising, considering the early hour. She moistened her lips. Someone had indeed followed her out of the cemetery last night. Would they know she returned today?

Her fingers lingered on the wire. It would unwind easily, but she paused to consider what she might be getting herself into. Who was sending those notes? Who was the wizard behind the curtain? If she left now, she could be back in the big windy city in five hours. Her logic told her to leave and move on with her life, to let go of her life-long desire to know the truth about Stevie. Then stern determination grew. *Whether I leave for good or chose to return, I must know about the feathers.*

Unwinding the wire, she pushed open the gate and hurriedly made her way over the slippery, uneven ground, chancing frequent backward glances. Passing the last line of gravesites, Lacy proceeded to the corner of the natural stone hedge mostly hidden by tall, unruly, wet grasses and low-hanging limbs.

Checking one last time to make sure no one was observing, she stooped down and worked her fingers around an irregular wedge-shaped stone that was deep into the base of the corner section.

It had been so long, she expected to find the ground around the rock packed tight, yet the mixture of clay and dirt was fairly loose, allowing the large stone to be removed easily. The conditions of the hedge in this one area indicated a strong possibility that the stone had been recently tampered with. Inserting her gloved hand into the slot where the rock had been extracted, she reached deeper into a dugout pocket of earth.

Slowly removing her hand, Lacy held tight to the square-shaped object and brought it forth to the light. She brushed loose dirt from around the child's plastic lunch box that bore the barely discernible picture of The Littlest Mermaid. The clasp opened freely, which puzzled her even more. Lifting the lid, she saw the green washcloth she and Stevie had yanked from the garage rag bucket. The unfolding of the faded cloth caused her chest to grow tight.

There they lay—the collected pigeon feathers, dyed purple by two children who experimented with a box of purple dye one hot summer day. Altogether the feathers had numbered fourteen. She counted them slowly so as not to make a mistake. No more than twelve feathers remained. This confirmed the feathers inserted in her notes came from the lunchbox. But how and by whom?

Who knew about the feathers or our secret hiding place in the stone hedge? Had Stevie told others about their special secret? He'd had two other close friends, Chuck Walden and Jerry Collins. Then there was Cindy Bradford, who was always running over to the Turner house. Cindy's mother and Terri Turner were good friends, and the Bradfords lived next door.

Lacy thought back to that time of her life with sober thoughtfulness. She'd been jealous of Cindy Bradford's close proximity to Stevie. But Lacy and Stevie always had a special connection between them. It was like they came in on the same sunbeam and knew instinctively what the other one would like to do or if one of them was sad. Stevie was imaginative and bright; his sharp wit had kept her laughing. She smiled, remembering how his dark brown eyes would dance with red highlights. They could twinkle with mischief at the drop of a hat.

Lacy brushed aside memories that now brought her pain. Perhaps she, herself, had told someone about the feathers, though her childhood friends were limited in number. Even now, only one came to mind, and she had moved away a few years ago. Stevie had been the center of Lacy's world. Still, it was possible in their childish enthusiasm that either she or Stevie had told others about the feathers.

The back of her head ached from strain. It was too many years to recall and this was no time to research her past. The rain was picking up once more. Replacing everything as she'd found it, Lacy wedged the pie-shaped stone back into place and packed mud all around it. Once the sun came out, it would harden and look no different than the rest of the hedge. Standing, she brushed off her gloves and looked back toward the parking lot. It was time to leave.

*

The drive back to Chicago was long, giving plenty of time to think. Lacy drew an exhausted breath when she pulled into her apartment parking complex. All those miles and nothing had been decided. She'd be working long, hard days the remainder of the week to make up for the time she'd spent in Gladden Hills. After downing an easy bowl of cereal for supper, Lacy unpacked and sorted laundry before she began assembling notes and reference material needed for the office the next day.

Each moment she worked toward a time she could afford to stop for the night and curl up in bed, frequently checking the clock. She loved her job, but it was unrelenting, tense work, with hardly a break between assignments. She expected a dressing-down from Goff first thing in the morning, dealing primarily with her unexpected two-day leave.

When finally she was allowed the luxury of readying herself for bed, she lay awake for a long period before drifting off to sleep. Lacy had reached a plateau of weariness too dense to further consider the pros and cons of returning to Gladden Hills.

Yet when she awoke in the night, thrashing and soaked in sweat from her dream, she was still able to visualize Stevie's sweet face: *"You promised me justice, Ellie."* There was the crux of her conflict. She had made a childish promise to a dead playmate in a slurry of tears and rage. Now she was an adult with responsibilities. Was she still bound to that promise? Changing her wet T-shirt, she drank a tall glass of water and went back to bed.

*

But in the morning, the conflicting thoughts were still there. Was it pride or a wild fantasy to think she could uncover what the police had been unable to find? The writer of the notes didn't think so. Somehow this person knew she'd been investigating on her own. He'd written: *I know you're searching.* The mystery writer had sent the purple feather and asked for help. That statement had the connotation of someone who was investigating on his or her own. How did he know she'd been searching secretly? Her mind churned with troubling questions.

Did he mean for them to work together? Could she trust him? Did he have an angle of his own? And...why didn't he meet her face to face in the graveyard? Lastly, Lacy questioned why she'd begun to think of the note writer as a man—yet she had, for whatever reason. After three years of beating the bushes for a scrap of information or a new theory to follow, she'd come up empty.

Now this.

Walking out the door to go to work the next morning, her eyelids were heavy with the need for sleep. Still she was no closer to a decision. There was no use in calling and talking it over with her parents. They'd lived through the tragedy along with the town but had disassociated themselves as quickly as they could from the cruel impact of Stevie's death—mostly for Ellie's sake. When a job opportunity for her father had popped up in mid-Illinois, the decision was made to move.

If Lacy now told them of her lingering interest in the unsolved crime, she knew what their reaction would be—let the past stay buried. Whatever she learned would not change the past or bring Stevie back. Lacy knew it clearly enough. She also knew that God was the great leveler who would someday right all the wrongs. Was it possible she was meant to be part of righting the wrong done to Stevie and his mother? *Could God be leading me back?*

She was unsure where that idea had sprung from. For years God had been on the outer fringe of her thinking. Was she now feeling a stirring in her cold heart? Her tired brain gave her no rest. Lacy sensed she was at a crossroads. But, then, hadn't she been locked in a time warp for seventeen years, never quite able to leave that portion of her life behind her? Would going back to Gladden Hills help her to finally be able to do that?

*

After four grueling days at the office, Lacy tidied up her desk and wrote herself a memo for Monday morning. Collecting her purse, gloves, and coat, she started toward the door, only to pause outside the editor's office.

J.T. Goff glanced up. The man's ability to zero into the heart of a matter was uncanny. It was like he knew what was going on inside her head. His brows narrowed. Lacy sucked in a breath before entering.

*

The endless highway stretched out like an unwinding ribbon in the bright sun of the cold March day. Lacy propped her head up with her free hand while the right hand guided with the wheel of her black pearl Challenger. Its Hemi engine hummed like a fat cat curled up by a fire. Driving east in the morning was a bear with shards of the rising sun piercing the dirty windshield. She'd meant to get the car washed before leaving town, but there'd been no time with everything else she'd had to arrange.

I must be insane, going off half-cocked like I am. What am I thinking?

Asking for a leave of absence had been difficult, not to mention tense. J.T. had reluctantly granted her a one-month leave—no more. Would that be enough to learn the truth? It had to be!

Her foot tapped the brake, disengaging the speed control as a semi suddenly switched lanes and slowed down ahead of her. Her other hand took instant hold of the wheel; traffic was getting tight and hairy. Still her thoughts were prone to wander. *Did I miss doing anything?*

She'd made phone calls for two hours the night before. Her cousin, Kelly Larson, was expecting her to stay with her during her time in Gladden Hills.

Kelly had openly accepted her explanation for coming to Gladden Hills. *"Sure, come ahead. I'd relish the company. Everyone needs a time to get away from the rat race they know. Though we usually can't wait to trade it in for the rat race we don't know."* Her cousin had laughed heartily at her homespun philosophy, assuring Lacy there was plenty of room in the old family house.

Lacy thought back on her phone call with her parents. They were thoroughly confused, almost bristly, as why she would take a leave of absence from her high-paying newspaper job in Chicago to go back to stay in Gladden Hills for a month. It had taken five minutes to assure her mother she wasn't having a nervous breakdown.

After a break for lunch, she was back on the road. For the first few days in Gladden Hills she would play everything by ear, getting reacquainted with the town and its people. A nervous tingle ran through her, wondering about acquaintances she might run into. She didn't want to arouse suspicion. Pulling into the far right lane, Lacy reduced her speed and allowed herself to unwind. There was no good reason to hurry. Why should she beat the miles down the road? When she arrived there would be time enough to go into high gear.

She didn't have to check in to the *Gladden Hills Gazette* until Monday morning. Last night's phone interview with Jason Gardner, the new owner, had been somewhat disjointed. Newspaper publishers were often that way, she told herself. He'd seemed indifferent about her calling at such a late hour concerning a job with the paper.

Waving away her apologies, Mr. Gardner was direct. "The point is, Miss Cottrell, I have a job opening and you're looking for one." His attitude would take a little getting used to, but J.T. Goff had prepared her for almost anything.

Mr. Gardner had warned her up front that, although her credentials sounded impressive, he'd have to put her on a trial basis. Their conversation put a whole new meaning to little enthusiasm. Lacy hadn't expected a warm, fuzzy exchange with her prospective boss, but his stoic manner had been most irritating. After all, he was the one in need of a reporter. She wasn't in dire need of a job. Maybe she'd just forgo the position altogether. It wasn't a necessity, was it? She chewed on her lip thoughtfully.

It was true. Lacy didn't require the money or experience a small-town newspaper could offer, but she did need cover for her investigation. A job at the paper would act as a perfect blanket for her snooping, unless Gardner proved to be an obstacle. She'd sensed during their short interaction that behind his ambiguous manner lay a steel-like personality. He might fire her in a heartbeat if he became suspicious of her motives or smelled a problem situation.

I'll have to prove my worth in short order. Perhaps there was a way to get on this publisher's good side. If not, she would be back in Chicago quicker than she thought.

2

The Lay of the Land

SLOWING, LACY TURNED THE CAR UP INTO THE DRIVE. The last time she had been inside this stately, old, white-sided Victorian was also the last time she'd seen her grandparents alive. Wanting the home to stay in the family, Ella and Frank Mayborne had willed the entirety of their home and its contents to her older cousin, Kelly. The young woman had anchored her life in her hometown after her husband, Grant, was killed on duty in Afghanistan.

Upon her approach, Kelly Larson pushed open the front door with gusto and rushed to stand on the wide expansive porch. Her honey blond hair was flung casually over her shoulder as she stood rubbing her arms. She was clothed in a bulky, dark blue cardigan covering a white T-shirt and jeans. Waving wildly, she beamed spontaneously and gestured for Lacy to pull further up in the drive.

Kelly met Lacy as she was exiting the car and clutched her in a bone-crushing embrace. "Welcome to the old homestead. Just look at you—a sophisticated knockout! Weren't you in your last year of college the last time I saw you?" A cloud covered her animated face. "What am I thinking? It was at Grant's funeral. Sorry. I was more or less in a fog at that time." She took another long look at Lacy. "Now you're on your own and working for a big, exciting, Chicago newspaper."

Cocking her head to the side, Kelly searched Lacy's face, a slight frown twisting her attractive features. "I'm thrilled to have you stay, but I can't help but wonder what's up, girl?" She shrugged. "Whatever your reason, it's my gain, and we'll have a fabulous time!" She grabbed Lacy and hugged her again.

Laughing, Lacy drew back, reading her cousin's confused thoughts. "You're wondering why I'd leave *that big city job to* come back to Gladden Hills." She heaved a sigh. "Like I said on the phone, I'm plain worn out, Kelly. You talked about a rat race. Well, it's worked into a nonstop schedule, and I haven't had a break since college. This rat is worn thin. Besides, I'm looking for small-town background for an article I'd like to write. I appreciate you taking me in on such short notice."

"Not a problem. It's not as if I'm cramped for space, and I love the idea." Kelly shivered. "I can't believe we're standing out in this cold. Let's get you inside and settled. We've got lots of time to catch up at dinner. Supper's in the slow cooker and won't be ready for a few hours." She reached for one of Lacy's soft-sided suitcases and a duffle bag. Situating her purse strap over her head, Lacy grabbed up the last bag as well as her computer satchel and followed her cousin up the wide stairs, across the gray-painted wooden porch, and into the house.

Behind the tantalizing aromas of simmering meat and vegetables lingered the base smell of the old family house, a smell she remembered well and associated with her loving grandparents. It was the aroma of aged, well-oiled oak doors and wood paneling. She thought of the large mantle in the old parlor. Assorted antiques added their own scent with their rubbed spiced lemon oil. Lacy allowed her senses to fill with the smells and memories they created. Up the creaking stairs she trudged to the large second story, which mainly was comprised of four bedrooms, a sitting room, and a spacious upstairs bath.

Kelly paused in the hall, shifting to address Lacy. "Well, take your pick. You know the layout as well as I." She tossed her hair away from her face.

Tilting her head in the direction of the room across from the bath, Lacy crossed the hall and walked into the spacious front bedroom, noting it was still decorated with the fragile feel of delicate wallpaper and old lace. She placed her computer on top the four poster bed and sat the smaller bag near the luggage holder where Kelly was even now lowering the large suitcase.

Scanning the room, Kelly placed her hands on her hips. "Unless I'm mistaken, isn't this the same room you occupied as a kid when you came to stay with Grandpa and Gran? I was always down the hall."

Nodding, Lacy chuckled. "I was the youngest. You were three years older. They didn't want to risk me not being near the bathroom at night." The women laughed, bringing back the times they'd spent together as children during summer vacation. Aside from a few faint lines in Kelly's face, there was a striking family resemblance in their features. The difference showed itself in Lacy's stark coloring with her deep umber hair set against the remarkable blue of her eyes. In this she favored the Cottrell side.

Backing casually toward the door, Kelly wiped her hands on her jeans and pulled a card from her pocket. "If you're all set here, I have to leave for a couple of hours. I'm showing a client a few houses outside of town. My cell phone's on this card. Call if you need me. Otherwise, I'll be back in time to finish up supper."

Dropping her purse on her bed, Lacy turned. "Hey, tell me what I can do to help."

"Well, I guess I should treat you like a guest at least for the first night you're here, but since you asked, if you want to put together a salad, that really would be great."

Lacy nodded. "Consider it done. I'll rummage in the refrigerator and find the fixings."

"Just promise not to look at all the mess. I'm not the best housekeeper—never was—but I try. I have to hurry and change." With that, she whirled about and headed out into the hall and down the stairs.

Lacy smiled, remembering from earlier years. She knew her cousin had most probably taken over their grandparents' room off the front room downstairs. She'd heard the old couple had put in a new combined bathroom and shower adjoining their bedroom in the last years of their life. Scanning her room, it didn't look as if the redecorating had reached this level—everything was much the same as always. But it was clean and held her childhood memories in limbo as if the years had never passed.

Checking her watch, she looked longingly at the puffy gold and ocher tinted bedspread. Pulling off her long black boots and trench coat, she tossed them to a nearby chair. Lacy flipped her smooth, dark hair out of her sweater collar and climbed up on the bed, drawing the cream comforter from the end of the bed over her weary form, burrowing into the thick pillows. The salad could wait.

*

Kelly stretched and pushed her chair back from the well-used, square oak table. Pulling out an empty kitchen chair, she propped up her feet. "This is the good time of day. It's almost as if the day itself pauses to savor a moment of quietness when all of the pressures fade with the sun."

"That's almost poetic," Lacy said brightly. She lifted her coffee mug in salute, staring with envy at her cousin's obvious relaxed manner. Slowly she sipped the lukewarm liquid. Why was she finding it so hard to let down her guard and turn back the years? *Is it me...am I afraid to slow up?* She searched her feelings. Shortly after rising from her short nap, she'd felt the tenseness in her body immediately return. How long had she been this way, keeping her system on ready alert, always trying to prove her worth to her boss, her parents? And when had that feeling first begun to drive her life. *Is this who I am, or has it become a way of life?*

At the paper, J.T. Goff thought nothing about handing back an article with no explanation and telling her to redo it and take a different approach or calling at odd times and demanding she leave on a moment's notice. Her vacation time had been cut short every year she had worked thus far. *Whatever got into me to walk into J.T.'s office and ask for a leave of absence?* Lacy shook her head in disbelief at her rashness. Now she had a month with no clear mandate, unless you called searching for an impossible truth a clear mandate. *Who do I think I am, J. Edgar Hoover?* Her fingers combed her silky hair away from her troubled features.

Centering her focus on her cousin, she brightened, redirecting the conversation into a safer realm. "Dinner was awesome, Kelly! What all was in that dish?"

Kelly uttered a sound that was half between a cough and a chuckle. She leaned forward to grab her coffee mug, a teasing smile curving her mouth. "Oh, I don't know if I can share such a complicated recipe. Now listen real close. You take meat, potatoes, vegetables, a little water and one package of measured spices. Then you turn it on low and let it cook all day. Any cooking I do anymore is easy fare. It's not much fun cooking for one. Now when Grant and I were first married, I tried a new recipe every week." Her face sobered. "It was worth it to hear him *ooh* and *aah* over any new attempt. But after Grant..."

Seeing the raw grief spring to her cousin's face, Lacy looked quickly away, not wanting to intrude on such a personal moment. She'd been in college when the news came about Grant's death, and though sad for her cousin's loss, she'd felt oddly inadequate, even awkward in her attempt to offer consolation. But here, sitting at this table, she realized her cousin's longing wasn't something that disappeared with the closing of the burial service. Once again she felt out of her realm.

She inclined her head. "I'm so sorry, Kelly. I-I didn't know what to say at Grant's funeral and..."

Kelly was quick to interject. "Listen, Lacy, it's not necessary. I was in too much of a fog at the funeral to think about people's responses...oh, maybe, one here or there, but people as a rule don't know what to say, so please don't worry about it. Besides, you were just a kid, and what does a kid know?" She looked up and grinned, her eyes brimming with moisture. "I haven't thought back on that time for months now, but every once in a while something will come up that brings back the memories and off I go."

"I know," Lacy murmured. "It happens so suddenly. Sometimes it's a smell, like coming back to this house or an object you haven't seen in a long time." *Like a purple feather.* Standing, she set down the mug and started clearing the table. "Did Gran ever get around to having a dishwasher put in?"

"No. But I did." Kelly pointed to a chrome-faced appliance placed agreeably to fit between the white-painted pine kitchen cabinets. It occupied a space next to a bottom corner cabinet sitting against the outside wall. "You know better than anyone how I hate to do dishes," she said, wiggling her brows. They both laughed.

When the kitchen was made right, the women poured fresh coffee and moved into the smaller front room off the hall leading from the kitchen. Gran used to call it her "cozy parlor" and kept a constant fire going three-fourths of the year. By the time Lacy sank into the dusty rose, overstuffed sofa, Kelly was busy assembling the makings of a fire.

"After two days of rain, this big old place begins to hold the dampness." Kelly moved from the hearth to unhook the heavy drapes and allow them to swing closed. On her way back to a matching chair, she switched on a couple of reading lights causing a soft glow to filter across the room and mingle with the mellow light of the fire.

At that instant Lacy's muscles felt like Jello. She allowed her head to rest easy on the chair back. "I must say, you've settled into this old place like a glove. You seem completely at home."

Flopping into the chair, Kelly focused on the small flames gaining momentum as they licked at the dry kindling and loose paper. "You think so? I guess it's comfortable enough, and it certainly has been a source of steadiness and security for me these last five years since Grant was killed. I was adrift for a very long time. Maybe I still am. I moved in with Grandpa and Gran the day after the funeral and never left, but I can't seem to put down roots."

She looked over at Lacy. "It's as if I'm waiting for something to occur. You must have noticed that I haven't changed a thing in the upstairs. I sorta feel like I'm not the designated one who's supposed to do the job. It's weird. I don't know if that makes any sense to you?"

Lacy thought on her statement. "Maybe it's not that so much as it is that you're waiting for something or maybe waiting for someone?" She chuckled to herself. "Listen to me, the wise philosopher. I don't have a relationship or even a boyfriend in the wings. What do I know?"

Kelly studied her curiously for several seconds. "Yeah, what does a kid know?"

"Technically, Kelly, I don't think I qualify as a kid any longer. Though some days I wish I did." Meeting her cousin's gaze, she asked, "Do you still pray about your life? You know, like we did that last summer I was here? I only ask that because, right now, I'm floundering. I haven't thought much about God for a long time—my own problem," she added sheepishly. "But now, I've got the weirdest feeling that God has thrown up a huge detour sign in the middle of my express highway. How else can you account for my being here instead of Chicago?"

Shifting to prop her head on her arms across the wide arm of the chair, Kelly looked up at her. "I can't. Did I hear you mention you've *already* taken a position as a reporter at the *Gazette?* I thought you are here on leave from your home paper for a relaxing change?" Her eyes were filled with question.

Lacy chuckled. "Yes, I have. Even while I'm trying to get away, I still can't lay aside a chance at a good article. Remember I said I was looking for *local background.* I figured a small-town newspaper was the best source of information I could find—running down the urban stories. And I guess I'm hoping it will be slow-paced enough to allow me to get a line on my own direction at the same time. This town is where I started, Kelly."

Kelly frowned. "I guess I'm not sure if you're here for research or to figure out your life."

"Both. My life has become a treadmill without purpose. It was time for a change." Lacy sobered. There was more truth in that statement than she'd realized…until now.

"Well, I hope it's possible for you to accomplish both. Hopefully one doesn't cancel out the other." Kelly's gaze probed her cousin.

"So do I," Lacy said softly. She knew she wasn't being completely honest by leaving out her *main* reason for coming back to Gladden Hills. Though, strangely, everything she'd said had been the truth, even the part about gathering material about the inner workings of small-town America. She'd wanted to do such a story for a very long time, but her childhood recall was too vague to rely upon. The gulf between living a child's life in a small community and observing it from an adult's perspective was vast.

Part of her wasn't sure if she was ready for the adult's perspective. Would it destroy what good memories she had of Gladden Hills? *The danger remains,* the note said. Someone in this town had killed Terri and Steven Turner in a vicious, horrendous manner seventeen years ago. Lacy was in town to discover who that person or persons were…and somewhere, not far off, under a hidden guise, she had an accomplice—someone who claimed to be as interested in finding the truth as she was. If this person had a hidden purpose for luring her back to Gladden Hills, that was something else she needed to discover.

Lacy refocused on her cousin, realizing they'd strayed from her original question about prayer without receiving a reply. It had been an easy subject between them when Lacy was eight and Kelly eleven. Now she sensed tension when the subject was mentioned. Kelly had drawn herself up into a ball in the oversized chair with her legs pulled underneath her in little girl fashion. It reminded Lacy of when they were children and Kelly was unusually troubled.

Lacy was uncertain which way to proceed. The reporter instinct within her was inclined to be pushy with unanswered questions. But she purposely shied away from that tactic with Kelly and decided to allow the matter to pass.

Kelly stared broodingly into the fire. "Not so much." Her uncertain voice startled Lacy. "You asked me about prayer—if I continued to pray about matters in general—more specifically my life. I have to say, not so much. I'm not proud of it, but that's the way it is. In college I was easily drawn in with the crowd. You know me, always anxious to please!" Pain flickered across her features. "That's where I met Grant. He was a senior and quite the opposite to me. He taught me to be my own person." She looked up at Lacy. "Something you never had trouble doing.

"Grant was accustomed to going to church prior to our marriage, but sadly the issue of faith never came up between us until he deployed to Afghanistan. By that time I was an emotional mess. I tried to pray, but my prayers never seemed to pass the ceiling. And then Grant was gone. I guess I figured God gave up on me after that." She walked over to stoke the fire before returning to her chair.

Lacy watched her. "And I wasn't much help. My family basically came in for the funeral and then left the next day. But you were living here with Gran, and I know she would have pressed you to hold on to God and pray." She blinked in puzzlement. Their grandmother was a firebrand when it came to her faith. Grandpa was more low-key, but not Gran. She would have met the issue head-on.

Kelly's laugh was hollow. "You remember well. She tried, but I wasn't very responsive. More than once Gran urged me to keep my heart soft. She'd quote, *'The same sun that hardens the clay will soften the wax.' In time the good Lord will heal a softened heart.'* "

Lacy nodded. "That sounds like her." She had no further words of wisdom for her cousin. Lacy was working on her own issues of faith. Her thoughts and feelings in this area had been as erratic as the stock market. The basics were there, but little else. Though lately she'd felt as if an unseen hand was nudging her in unlikely directions. At night, late before turning off her light, she'd found herself reaching for her Bible.

Kelly's eyes met hers. "I heard you were pretty straight in college, but then you were always steady—more controlled and determined than I ever was. You would fix your goals. I was afraid to dive into the waters down by the willow at the river, but not you. You first walked the stream to see where the rocks were hidden and where the bottom was sandy, solid, and sure. Once you were sure, then you would dive and always land on the mark. You were kind of a strange kid—little sister on one hand, Wonder Woman on the other. Anyway, that's the way I saw you." She smiled warmly. "It's so good to have you here with me now."

Lacy laughed. "Oh, yes, steady and sure, that's me, never do anything wild and uncertain." But her thoughts boiled with contradiction. *This move back to Gladden Hills is anything but steady and sure and might cost me my job, if not my life.* The warning—"The danger remains"—echoed in her mind. *Oh, what am I doing here? I have no idea where the hidden rocks lie in this stream.*

She pushed away her fears. "Kelly, if you remember, Gran fostered those feelings of sisterhood between us from the time we were small. Since we're each an 'only child,' I think she desired a solidarity between us to give us a sense of family."

"Your thoughts go much deeper than mine, Lacy Cottrell. I'm afraid my thinking process dwells more on the here and now, shying away from self-analysis. I shall have to start looking below the surface, won't I?" Kelly teased.

Lacy inwardly groaned. *Please don't look too deep, Kelly, not yet. I have too much to hide.* Pushing up from the comfort of the sofa, Lacy straightened her sweater and slacks. "I think I'll turn in and try to shake the cobwebs out of my brain before I start my new job on Monday. What do you say we drive around tomorrow, and you can refresh me on some of the landmarks I might have forgotten?"

Kelly arched her neck backwards to look up at her cousin. "I have a couple of showings in the morning, but I'm free after lunch. If anything comes up, I'm sure Jerome can handle it. He practically lives at the office anyway." There was disapproval in her voice.

"Jerome?" Lacy questioned.

"Jerome Collins. He took over the business from his father after the elder Mr. Collins had a heart attack.

Lacy stared at her cousin incredulously. "Jerry Collins? I remember him from school. He was a couple of years older than Stevie and me, yet he always hung around more with Stevie and Chuck than boys his own age. Is Chuck still around town too?"

"Oh, yeah, Chuck Walden is *very much* in town. He owns his own mechanic shop and towing business. I haven't really kept up with him, but I think there was a period when he left town for a while after graduation. Some rumors flew that he'd spent that time in jail." Kelly lifted one shoulder. "While I have no way of knowing for sure, I gotta say, he's grown up rough around the edges. I think...well, never mind what I think."

Lacy tilted her head, wondering what meaning lay behind her cousin's innocuous words. "That's very interesting. I'm sure I'll have a lot of catching up to do, getting reacquainted with everyone." She looked across at Kelly, cheeks flushed from the fire, her relaxed form sprawled loosely in the chair. The cozy effect warmed Lacy. "It's good to be back. While I appreciate your hospitality, I expect to pick up my half of expenses while I'm here. I just might even remember some of my mom's recipes and dust them off."

"If mac-and-cheese is one of them, it's a deal. It was fabulous! Sleep well, Lacy Cottrell."

"Sleep well, Kelly. I might sleep in some in the morning, so don't look for me early."

"Everything is pretty much the way Gran kept it, so make yourself at home and I'll see you when I get back from work."

Each step up the staircase filled Lacy with a sense of wonder. Here she was back in the home of her summer vacations with her cousin Kelly. Her memories were scattered everywhere and out of control. Dealing with the past while trying to make sense of the future was a tricky matter. She saw no way for her emotions to be sidelined. Perhaps she would continue to search the Scriptures for absolutes—something to sink her teeth into. There were certainly none in her life at present. Her steps continued to lead her upward to the four-poster bed.

*

He stood in the shadows across the street, hidden between the foliage of bushes and beneath the tall oak. Staring up at the softly lit upstairs room that he knew to be the bedroom of Lacy Cottrell, the man peered around the quiet old neighborhood to make sure he wasn't being observed. His jaw was set.

"So, Ellie, you've decided to come back home. It just might not be your wisest decision. Tread lightly, little Ellie," he said, backing into the foliage that would give him cover to the next street that lay directly behind Cloverdale and then slipping into a small, gray sedan parked at the far end of the street with no outlet. Backing around, he drove through the sleepy neighborhood.

Pausing at the end of the street, the man pulled his hat low over his shadowed features and rested his foot on the brake. *From now on I'll have to be careful of my movements. Lacy Cottrell is a reporter and clearly no dummy. Until I know how perceptive she is, I'll monitor her actions.*

Lifting his foot, he coasted around the corner. The coming weeks would definitely prove interesting. He had a feeling the cover of the hidden past would soon be blown off this little town, and it worried him. Everything he had was resting on what would be revealed. He gunned the engine and headed for home.

*

Lacy was ready and waiting when Kelly returned from work around noon on Saturday. After a hurried lunch, they had gathered their coats to leave when Lacy rushed back up to her room. *I almost forgot my camera. I might want to collect a few photos for reference.*

They began their tour by coasting through the main area of Gladden Hills. At the first stoplight, Kelly pointed out two of the town's oldest structures. "Remember the library and courthouse?"

Cruising the quiet, picturesque streets, Lacy spied an older home on the edge of town that appeared to have been renovated. It now boasted a large wooden sign on the front lawn. "Slow up, Kelly. Am I reading that sign right? *Attorneys at Law—Cynthia Bradford and Morgan Streeter?* Don't tell me that is Cindy Bradford?"

"We all grow up, even Cindy," Kelly explained, rolling her eyes. "Yeah, Cindy came back to town after law school and a year in a big firm out east. She lost no time in hanging out her shingle. I guess the old hometown was too much of a draw. I also heard that her parents had health issues. They've resettled in a condo at the edge of town and let Cindy take over the old place."

"Interesting," Lacy mused. It was beginning to appear that anyone who could possibly have knowledge of the purple feathers was ready and available in Gladden Hills. It only made her job of finding out who sent the notes more difficult. While Kelly continued pointing out new businesses, Lacy asked, "Who is this Morgan Streeter that Cindy's in partnership with?"

Kelly chuckled. "You know small towns. Morgan just happens to be the nephew of Mr. Heyworth, the bank president. I don't know how or when Morgan met Cynthia—probably at one of those movers-and-shakers get-togethers. One day they hung out their law shingle for business. I only heard about his being connected to Heyworth through our Wendy at the café."

"Wendy, the waitress?" Lacy asked, slightly taken aback. As she thought on it, she realized a waitress in a popular gathering place in town was a perfect source of information. "Well, well..." She filed that bit of knowledge for when it might become useful.

"Like I said, small towns."

Exchanging glances, they shared a laugh.

Lifting her right hand in a sweeping arch, Kelly pointed to an upscale separate building kitty corner from the courthouse on the town square. "Do you remember the Old Toy Maker Shop and Emerson's Bookstore? When they closed down a few years back, Harold Shaw snapped up the property and building and turned it into an office."

"Harold Shaw?" Lacy looked puzzled. "I remember that name, but I can't place it."

"Harold Shaw has been around Gladden Hills for a long time. He was district attorney for several years before he ran for judge."

Lacy frowned. "He was the DA during the investigation into the bombing."

"Yeah, I guess he was," replied Kelly, casting a furtive glance at her cousin. No one needed to explain what bombing. Gladden Hills had only had one, seventeen years earlier.

"So, Mr. Shaw is now a judge. He couldn't seem to ever collect enough information about the bombing for the police to make an arrest," she said critically.

"Be fair, Lacy. By the time the firemen were done, there wasn't much evidence to find—only fragments of the bomb and not enough to determine anything. I was eleven and remember some. It was a scary, traumatic time for everyone! I know for you it was personal, but you were young—too young to take note of evidence." She took a right at the end of Main Street, heading out of town.

"Yes, it was personal." Lacy crossed her arms across her chest. "But putting that aside, I remember reading that nearly a year ago, some DA in Ohio got a court order to have the bomb fragments reexamined using modern forensics, but they didn't name the DA. Naturally, I followed the story. They were actually able to determine that the bomb maker was a known arsonist, Clem Browning, already serving time in an Indiana prison on another arson sentence."

Kelly's forehead wrinkled. "Yeah, I guess I do remember something about that, but I never heard anything afterward. Whatever came of that situation? Do you know? I'm also curious why a DA in Ohio would ask for a court order dealing with a cold case in Michigan?" She slowed the car and searched Lacy's eyes.

Lacy contemplated her cousin's last question. As hard as she had tried, she hadn't been able find information on that Ohio DA. "Beats me. Maybe this particular DA thought it was a high-profile case that would get him exposure for advancement. Nothing more was heard about it because the whole episode screeched to a halt. The day before the authorities were scheduled to question the arsonist, Clem Browning, he was knifed in a laundry room inside the prison."

"You're kidding? That's a weird coincidence!"

Lacy looked out the window. "If you believe in coincidences." Taking note that they were beyond city limits, she inquired, "Where are we going now?"

Kelly pointed further down the road. "I thought I'd take you by some of the places I'm currently handling. And then," she grinned, "for old times' sake, I thought you might like to drive down by the river in the park where the Grans used to take us for picnics."

When Kelly stopped the car in front of a large log home nestled high within a copse of pine trees, Lacy studied it. "Is this one of the places your real estate firm handles?"

"Yes. Unfortunately, the young couple who had this built were way over their heads with mortgages, and it took both of their paychecks to make the payments. Then he got sick, real sick, and they could no longer swing the payments. It was really sad."

Lacy noted the dreamy warmth that crept over her cousin's face as she studied the lines of the log home. "Kelly! You really like this place, don't you?"

"Yes. I've dreamed of a place like this all my life, ever since my parents and I spent a vacation at the lodge in the hills of Georgia."

"Why don't you buy it? If this is more your style than the house on Cloverdale, then sell it and purchase this one. It's not written in blood that you have to hold on to the family home." Yet even as she said it, the thought of selling Gran and Grandpa's home struck a blow in Lacy's heart. She quickly dismissed such sentiments. The house belonged to Kelly and was hers to do with what she wished. If this log house was what she wanted, then so be it.

"Even if I could bring myself to sell the old homestead," she said wistfully, "it wouldn't be enough. As much as they've discounted this place to get it off the bank records, Gran's house wouldn't cover it. But a girl can dream." Sighing, she looked at Lacy. "To be honest, it would be no fun to live there alone. Now if Grant was still alive or…"

Lacy wondered what her cousin's next words might have been. Was Kelly interested in someone new? It was a subject that bore interest and gentle questioning. Lacy determined to ferret out the information in the days to come. For now, her focus swung back to the log mansion on the hill.

"Why don't we head up to the river spot? I'd like to get a few shots of the area in the spring." She lifted her camera and snapped a quick picture of the log house before Kelly pulled away. "I'll print you a copy to give you something to dream about."

It was late afternoon before the girls returned home.

"I'll build a fire," called Lacy, throwing her coat to a nearby chair. "If you don't have anything planned for supper, maybe we could go out to the café and make it an easy meal?"

"I was hoping you'd be up for something like that. There's Marnie's, an upscale supper club a few miles out of town if that's your style? It's a nice enough place if you want a quiet night out with a date or special night out for yourself or family."

"Actually, I think I feel more like the café tonight, if that's all right with you. If their burgers are as yummy as I remember, it will give me something to dream about too." She heaved a huge, melodramatic sigh, bringing laughter from Kelly, who joined her in the cozy parlor.

"Sounds good to me. Keep working on that fire while I make cinnamon apple tea and round up that special cake I picked up at Mona's Bakery."

"It's a deal. I remember that tea blend. Gran always had it on hand for our tea parties."

*

Lacy followed Kelly into the warm, slightly steamy country café, secretly hoping that the mystery writer of the notes might reveal himself once he saw she was back in Gladden Hills. The time for her anonymity had passed. The news of her returning would get around quick enough, though it was her desire to keep her actions as low-key as possible. The fewer people who took note of her, the more she would be able to dig around for the truth.

As always, it was casual style in the café, with everyone seating themselves. Almost as soon as the door closed behind them, Kelly turned abruptly and walked with purpose toward the line of booths on the left. Lacy kept close on her heels. When her cousin stopped as abruptly as she started, it was all Lacy could do to not plow into her back.

The booth Kelly stopped beside was occupied by a slender, well-built, medium-tall man. The occupant seemed totally absorbed in a thick leather volume. His large, heavy-rimmed glasses seemed to suit him. Under a gray-striped suit coat, he wore a navy blue V-neck sweater and under that a light blue dress shirt. His light brown tousled hair fell carelessly over his brow.

"Jerome! How nice to see you. I didn't know you ate at the café. Do you come here often?" Kelly had amazingly combined four sentences into one without hardly a breath.

It was obvious the startled man hadn't noticed the two women blocking his reading light. He was trying to adjust to their presence and having difficulty processing all of her questions. He blinked and adjusted his glasses.

"Kelly! Mrs. Larson. I-I, ah, often come here. I frequently grow tired of my own cooking efforts. I-I don't believe I've seen you here before."

Lowering her head, Kelly chuckled softly. "I'm inclined to be lazy. It's too easy to snack on something and vege-out. I splurge once in a while and cook up a storm, then have to eat off it for a week or more. You know how it is with only one eating on a whole casserole?"

Lacy stood there feeling as welcome as an ant at a picnic. She cleared her throat to remind her cousin she was still beside her.

"Oh, sorry!" Kelly turned sharply, giving Lacy room to move up beside her. "Mr. Collins, my cousin, Lacy Cottrell. She used to live in Gladden Hills with her family. Lacy, my employer, Jerome Collins."

Jerome lowered his glasses. "Lacy Cottrell? I have recollection of someone named Ellie Cottrell. Are you somehow related?"

Lacy smiled. "One and the same. I chose to be called by my first name, Lacy. Eleanor is my middle name. And I remember you as Jerry Collins. Though I believe Jerome does suit you better." She searched his serious features, trying to discern if he was as surprised to see her as he appeared.

"Welcome back to Gladden Hills, Lacy. Are you here for a visit, or do you have plans to stay?" His hands folded over his book in a more comfortable pose as he spoke, but his eyes seemed to probe her for deeper answers.

While she considered his question and how best to answer it, Lacy wondered if Jerome was thinking of Stevie as she was. The last time they saw each other, Stevie had been with them, always the focal center of their group.

"At this point I'm only visiting, but I plan on staying around for a few weeks. Kelly and I have a lot of catching up to do." She winked at her cousin.

His hazel eyes looked from one girl to another with a flicker of surprise. "I never realized you two were cousins. But seeing you here together, I can now see a definite family resemblance." His eyes lingered on Kelly an extra couple seconds; then he looked away, as if self-conscious.

Jerry Collins had always been something of a loner. Lacy wondered if that was why he had sought out Stevie as his friend. Stevie never made demands on anyone but Lacy. With her, he'd play mind games, expecting her to know what he was thinking.

A plump, brown-haired young woman edged her way to his booth. "Sorry, ladies, but it's the café's policy to serve the food while it's still hot," she said with a sassy smirk.

Lacy and Kelly quickly backed up to give her room. "We didn't mean to block the aisle, Amy." Kelly glanced at Jerome with an embarrassed smile. "I'll see you on Monday, boss."

Jerome snatched up his large book and set it aside. He nodded at Kelly, while trying to make hasty room for Amy to set his dinner in front of him. "Ah, yes, on Monday at work. It was nice to see you...Kelly." Her name came out with hesitation, as if he debated if it was proper. Jerry Collins always had a sense of what was proper and just. His mother was something of a socialite. Lacy thought it funny she should think of that now. Was it possible that Jerome was her contact in Gladden Hills?

Feeling Kelly nudge her, Lacy started to sidestep the energetic waitress when Jerome's words caught her off guard. "Good to see you again, Lacy Cottrell. Perhaps we could talk more about our memories at another time?" There was a wistful feel to his words that brought a catch to her heart. *So...he is thinking of Stevie?*

The intensity of Kelly's sharp gaze rested heavy on Lacy's back as they made their way to a booth further down the aisle. Had Kelly gotten the wrong impression about Jerome's last statement when he spoke of their memories? It hadn't taken long to determine her cousin's new love interest.

The silence was unusually dense while the young women selected their entrées. Closing her menu, Lacy regarded her older cousin. "Does Jerome know how you feel about him?"

Kelly's jaw went slack. "I—excuse me! I-I—he's strictly my boss. There is nothing going on between us," she fairly sputtered.

"Yeah, right! I don't doubt everything is strictly business at work, but it's clear to me how you feel about him, Kelly. And it's equally clear that just *being* in your presence outside of a work atmosphere flusters your Mr. Collins. That fact in itself is interesting, don't you think?"

"Don't play that big-town reporter tactic on me, Lacy. You're getting no information from me. This is a small town, so please keep your exaggerated opinions to yourself, cousin dear."

Peering under Kelly's lowered head, Lacy grinned at the lifted corners of her cousin's mouth. "Oh, I consider romance to be family business," she whispered playfully. "Just don't get the wrong idea about Jerome's reasoning behind wanting to talk over memories with me. I sense that seeing me has brought back thoughts of Stevie's tragic death."

Looking up, a sober expression covered Kelly's attractive features. She leaned across the Formica tabletop and said in a low voice, "Don't be surprised if you encounter the same reaction in other people. When your family left town after Mr. Turner pulled up stakes and relocated, I think the town sighed with relief. It gave them an avenue to forget about what had happened, and they desperately needed to forget. Be careful what you stir up, Lacy. "

Lacy shivered, thinking of the reason she had come back to Gladden Hills. She also wondered about the reactions her return would cause in the days to come. Glancing up at Kelly, she nodded. "I'll be careful."

3

The Game Begins

MONDAY MORNING LACY SAT SHARPLY UPRIGHT, staring at her alarm clock. "Oh great!" she sputtered, bounding from her bed. Grabbing a black pinstripe pants suit and a bright fuchsia blouse from the closet, she tore for the shower. Her first morning at the paper and she was going to be late—*wonderful!* Once dressed, she hurriedly toasted a bagel while pouring black coffee into her thermos cup. With the bagel jammed tight in her mouth, she wiggled into her trench coat and slammed the front door behind her. Racing down the stairs, she prayed she wouldn't catch a red light driving the six-block distance into town.

The railroad tracks ran through the west side of town right across Lacy's route. And here came a train—of course! Slamming on the brakes, she banged the steering wheel in frustration with her palm. She didn't want to say something she would have to repent of later. Living on the ragged edge of her faith didn't leave her with a strong sense of security.

Naturally she had excuses to justify her position. At first there was the crush to establish her career. At what point the career became her life she wasn't sure. When she wasn't working, she was beating the bushes for information on the Turner Bombing, coming up empty time after time. The hollowness within her had grown to a place of desperation. It was in the sludge of that desperation she'd sent out panic prayers, not even knowing what exactly she needed.

Were the recent events the result of those prayers? Lacy wondered. If so, God had a sense of humor. She had no feeling of solidarity with the Almighty. What few prayers she'd offered rang hollow in her ears. Yet she kept experiencing the silent nudging within. What was that all about? She slammed the steering wheel again in irritation for everything she had no control over, beginning with the stupid train.

When the last commuter car whizzed by and the gates lifted, she sped across the tracks, hoping the police chief wasn't anywhere near. Pulling into an open parking place behind the old publishing building, she raced around to the entrance. Arriving at the front desk slightly askew, she aimed a bright smile at the woman behind the desk. "Hello, I'm Lacy Cottrell. I have an appointment with Mr. Gardner. He asked me to come directly in to him when I arrived."

The plump woman of medium height with short, dyed red hair eyed her disapprovingly. Her nose and cheekbones were pronounced and unyielding. Her focus shifted from her watch back to Lacy, clearly drawing attention to her tardiness. "I believe your appointment was scheduled for 8:30 a.m., Miss Cottrell. It is now 9:00 a.m."

Lacy bit her lip.

The woman, somewhere in her fifties, had clearly come to her own conclusions concerning Lacy's work ethics. "Mr. Gardner is a very busy man. I'll ask him if he can still work you in," she said condescendingly before moving with authority toward the glass-fronted office about forty feet behind the entryway counter. Rising on her tiptoes, Lacy could barely make out the back of a dark head bent over a desk. *Mr. Gardner, I presume?*

The red-haired woman reminded Lacy of a bulldog guarding the master's den. Lacy was still trying to understand how she could have slept through to 8:00 a.m. Perhaps sitting and talking with Kelly by the fire had relaxed her to the point her system crashed, craving the rest she'd needed for months. Unfortunately the timing was poor. Late on the first day of her new job wasn't a good beginning.

As she waited, she scanned the interior walls, predictably lined with framed copies of headlines from years past. Drawn by one framed headline in particular, Lacy made her way to the wall. It was dated the day after the bombing of the Turner home. Lacy had combed the internet for stories and old newspaper reviews of the incident. Her eyes locked on the article. She read it eagerly, hoping for something in this account that hadn't been noted in other write-ups.

"Miss Cottrell!" The sharp voice jarred her attention.

Lacy spun around. "Yes?"

The plump woman shot her an irritated look. "I called you twice! Mr. Gardner will see you now." She lifted her hand in the direction of the office and turned abruptly as if she assumed Lacy would follow her through to the back.

The woman swung the door open and stepped aside, indicating that Lacy was to proceed inside to sit in one of the two chairs facing a worn oak desk. The dark-haired man facing away from her seemed to be concentrating on an open file spread out on a back table. When Lacy glanced back at the red-haired bulldog, the woman exited and returned to the front counter, leaving the door open.

Lacy tried to collect her thoughts, wondering what she might say to this new owner of the *Gladden Hills Gazette.* Her situation was unique, maybe even unorthodox. As long seconds passed, she tapped her fingers nervously on top of her purse. Hearing the squeaking of a rotating office chair in need of an oil job, she glanced up into the stern face of a man about her own age or older. His short dark hair made his strong chin and features look all the more severe, and his shaded, wire-rimmed glasses obscured eyes of an indeterminable color.

What she could see of the man's eyes seemed adept at thoroughly scanning a person in an overall glance. Had she imagined his curious gaze lingering on her face? It all happened so quickly, Lacy wondered if her observation had been accurate.

Lifting a printed form from his desk, he spoke quietly, his voice controlled and cool. "Miss Cottrell, were you held up in traffic this morning?"

She rolled her eyes, glancing away. *Here we go! There's no way to avoid this opening blunder.* "No, Mr. Gardner, I wasn't held up in traffic." Suddenly, the bizarreness of the situation struck her as funny. Too late she pressed her lips, unable to squelch a small chuckle.

"Do you find the issue of your tardiness a laughing matter, Miss Cottrell?" Gardner's sharp tone brought her concentration front and center, and Lacy braced herself for the fallout. "I assumed I'd find a person with your background with a more professional attitude toward work...unless you believe that we take less than a professional approach toward our work. If that is the case..."

"Not in the least, Mr. Gardner, I assure you," she interjected. With Gardner's eyes fixed sternly on her, she lifted her right hand, as she was prone to do while attempting to explain an awkward situation. "To be honest, Mr. Gardner, I simply overslept. Something I have not done since my early college days. I can't explain it...perhaps being back in my grandparents' home, I don't know. I mean no disrespect. I laughed only because your comment about traffic struck me as humorous, in lieu of the fact I did catch a train on my way to work, compiled with my late departure from the house, and of course, the gates took forever to lift." She grimaced.

From her peripheral viewpoint, she thought she'd seen a vague semblance of a smile touch Jason Gardner's mouth. She blinked to clear her vision. Whatever she'd seen was gone in an instant.

"Now that we've established the reason for your tardiness," Gardner said in a businesslike tone, "can you tell me, Miss Cottrell, what exactly you want from this newspaper? We are in need of a reporter and your credentials are excellent, but I need to know I can count on you to be around long enough to establish a pattern to your paychecks. As I understand the situation, you are currently on leave from your Chicago newspaper and wish to take a position with us."

"Simply put, Mr. Gardner, I need a change. I came back to a place I remember fondly, where I spent summers with my grandparents. I saw your sign and decided to see what it would be like to work at a slower pace. I'm looking for a new perspective for my life. That is the truth. Right now, I can't promise you more than one month." She met his eyes without flinching. Whatever other reasons she had taken the job, this much was the truth. She waited, wondering if the new owner of the *Gazette* would take a chance on her.

Jason Gardner continued to study her. "All right. The one month will prove a suitable trial arrangement on our part as well. We will soon see if we are right for each other, Miss Cottrell." He closed the file cover on the printed paper in front of him and was in the process of standing when Lacy spoke.

"Mr. Gardner, my integration into the workings of this paper might go smoother if you were to lay out what you will expect from me during my probationary period. What areas do you wish me to handle, or will I be assisting other reporters?" Her eyes followed his easy movements as he pushed away from the desk and rose from his chair.

Gardner unfolded to his full height of six feet something and fixed her with a steely return gaze. "I hired an experienced reporter, not a gopher. I expect you to ferret out news that would be of interest to our community. We have a couple of freelance writers on the payroll, myself included, but you will be our only full-time reporter. Write-ups have to pass my inspection and final okay. I expect at least one to two quality stories per week, more if they have merit. Internet news has taken over in many areas, but in this town, the people look for their daily paper. The longer you are here, the more familiar you will become with the area, the people, and vice-versa. The paper carries a good deal of advertising. It's what pays the bills. Anymore questions?"

Lacy stood, silently questioning why everything would go through him and not the editor, but she pushed her concern away for more pressing matters. "Until I know the area and its people, it would be beneficial if you could start me off with a few potential stories or directional leads." She glanced around. "I think that about covers everything…unless you'd like to alert the lady watchdog at the front desk that I'm working for the good guys now." She cocked her head, speaking with wry humor.

Gardner's expression tightened. "I'll have Maxine show you to your desk. You will find a sheet of possible leads and reference material laid out for you, and I'll need your write-ups by Wednesday noon at the latest. I know it's a short week for you, but I think you can handle it."

He drew himself up. "A word to the wise, Miss Cottrell. It would be worth your effort to cultivate Maxine Flanders, the lady at the reception desk. She's our office manager, a jewel in the rough, with more fingers in the community than anyone I know. Not only is she related to half the town, but she has secret dirt on the other half—not that she would use it. Besides, she's been with this paper for about twenty-five years. If she acts like she owns the place, there's no one who has a better right. Wait here. I'll send her in."

Grabbing up a smooth black briefcase, Jason Gardner paused at the office door to add, "Welcome to the *Gladden Hills Gazette,* Miss Cottrell. Your addition to our little family should prove interesting."

Lacy winced. Her attempt at humor had fallen flat as a broken egg. She'd allowed her tongue to run wild, a fall-out from her nervousness. *Take a memo, Cottrell. Keep your mouth shut until your brain has time to engage! No points awarded for getting on the boss's good side this morning. Interesting?* she thought with an inward sigh. Instinct told her not to bother trying to explain. She stepped toward him. "Excuse me, Mr. Gardner. How can I reach you if I need to speak with you personally?"

He studied her as if making a decision. "Maxine will give you a number known only to a selective few. Don't use it lightly and keep it in a discreet place. It is my private number. I trust you understand."

Lacy nodded. *Take another memo, Cottrell: Don't use the boss's number without a darn good reason...and under penalty of loss of blood, never give out his private number! Obviously, the ramrod of this newspaper has a definite list of dos and don'ts.*

With no time for her to contemplate a meaning behind his stringent warning, the self-assured newspaper owner turned to leave.

She hurried with one last question. "Mr. Gardner. Who is the editor of the *Gazette?"* She found it odd that such an important element of a newspaper should not have been mentioned in her interview.

"I am," he answered without looking back, his easy rolling gait moving him toward the front counter.

Like standing on the edge of a train wreck, she was unable to prevent herself from continuing to observe. Gardner stopped at the counter to converse with the red-haired woman, who then pivoted to regard Lacy briefly. He smiled down at the loyal office manager as she looked up at him like a favored, adoring aunt. When he lightly patted her arm, the little bulldog fairly melted. Lacy exhaled like a deflated balloon. She was out-flanked.

Well, well, it looks like our Mr. Gardner has charmed his way into the dragon lady's devotion. He certainly hadn't wasted any of his charm on a lowly beginning reporter. There was clearly a bond between the boss and his receptionist. Lacy had blown it with her out-of-place humor. *Way to go, Cottrell!* she chided, knowing she needed to back-pedal fast to improve her image. *Third memo: New boss is on the short side of humor.*

When she saw Maxine Flanders striding toward her with purpose, Lacy wrapped herself in a contrite mantle and applied her open, appreciative smile. *I can do humble and sweet,* she told herself determinedly.

*

Lacy had discreetly covered several yawns and forced attentiveness to Maxine's detailed instructions. In the twenty-five years at the *Gazette,* the woman had obviously devised a workable system and outlined it in gold-plating. Being a big-city reporter had actually lost Lacy points in Maxine's eyes. She sensed the little bulldog would be watching their newest reporter for any sign of a *Know It All Big City Attitude*, and Lacy was resigned not to show even a whisper of such. *God, help me. This woman is a formidable force. If I blow it with her again, it could cost me unnecessary grief.*

Lacy chuckled when she saw lunch indicated down the list on the new employee instruction form. The form was included with her lists of suggested news items and possible background material for one of several leads. Finding a pile of manila folders in her metal desk, she inserted her paper pile and locked it inside her middle drawer. Apparently locking one's drawer when an employee was away from their desk was standard operation procedure at the *Gladden Hills Gazette.* It made her Chicago paper seem like a big unruly metropolis in comparison.

Get your back behind the plow, Cottrell. They run a tight ship here in Gladden Hills. And to think I was hoping for a less stressful atmosphere in the workplace.

Carefully placing her desk key in a small inside pocket of her purse, along with Jason Gardner's private phone number, she pushed away from her desk and looked to an old fashioned coat hanger where Maxine had earlier deposited her trench coat. In doing so, Lacy caught the woman observing her. The sharp-eyed manager had missed nothing of her actions. They regarded each other briefly. The woman's curt nod of approval took Lacy by surprise.

Turning away, Maxine returned to her high-backed stool in the entry, concentrating on the thick pile of paperwork laid out across the counter. Shifting her ample form on the padded stool, she raised her head as Lacy's heels clicked on the entrance tile.

In passing, Lacy paused. "Do you not take lunch, Miss Flanders?"

The hawk-like eyes considered her thoughtfully, as if deciding how to answer. "You may call me Maxine, Lacy. And I take my lunch break on the half hour to cover the office for a longer period of time. That way the paper will not be closed more than a half hour to forty-five minutes. Many of our contributors use the lunch hour to come by and conduct business. I try to keep to a schedule that gives them the maximum opportunity."

Lacy caught herself from giving this office manager a rousing "Atta Girl" and patting her on the arm. This woman was clearly committed to this small-town newspaper and held its interests before her own. She wondered if, like her, the paper had become the main focus of the woman's life. Lacy nodded in understanding and would have passed by if her reporter's intuition had not stopped her.

"Maxine, as you probably already know, I lived in Gladden Hills as a young girl. I don't remember any family by the name of Gardner. Is Mr. Gardner not originally from around here?"

Lines crinkled around the older woman's eyes in obvious consternation. Seeming to accept her as trustworthy, Maxine answered, "Mr. Gardner arrived in Gladden Hills almost three and a half months ago with a fair bid on the paper. Mr. Handleman had put the paper on the market only a few days earlier. After his wife, Gretchen, died, his heart wasn't in the business anymore."

"Does Mr. Gardner own other papers?" Lacy inquired, curious about her new boss.

Again, Maxine took time to weight her words before speaking. "He spends at least half of every day right here at the paper, so I doubt that he has other interests. In the short time since he arrived, Mr. Gardner has shared little of his background, although he's been quite open about his limited newspaper experience. First thing he did was put me in charge of the daily operations. I can tell you he's a man of character and great vision. Today he is having lunch with some of the town leaders, Judge Shaw, for one," she stated proudly. "Our Mr. Gardner means to make great strides in this little town. Mark my words—a man of vision."

Feeling slightly dazed by the woman's sterling impression of their employer's abilities, Lacy made a mental note for further reference. Her new boss might have just the right contacts for her to find out some long-buried information, especially if he was hob-nobbing with a judge. If Jason Gardner ever decided to run for office, Maxine Flanders would qualify for campaign manager. Lacy thanked the office watchdog before making tracks across the street to the Otto's Country Café.

Her underfed stomach had been marking time and dreaming of one of Otto's specialty burgers. Instead of taking a booth, Lacy purposely took a seat at the far end of the horseshoe counter on the left where the least amount of people congregated. If the opportunity arose, she would try to plug into the waitress, Wendy, and her notorious knowledge of the town.

The café hummed with lunch traffic. Orders were called out and hot plates shuffled so quickly that Lacy stared with admiration at all the harmonious interaction. Obviously, it wasn't the first time this cafés workforce had handled a busy lunch hour crew. Lacy waited for a thinning of clientele. She'd written down a few pertinent questions concerning her upcoming articles for the *Gazette.* One was a human interest story with plenty of heart. A gal like Wendy might eat that stuff up, if Lacy was any judge of human nature. It might also give her the "in" with the waitress she was looking for. She cringed at the thought, realizing her big city tactics sounded cold in light of this friendly community. But the fact remained, she needed information.

When Wendy paused by her counter assessing her empty plate, Lacy took this advantage to introduce herself as the new reporter at the *Gazette* and pleaded for the waitress's help for her first writing assignment about the Morrison family. The slim waitress appeared surprised and pleased that Lacy would ask for her help for such a special story. Watching Lacy write notes, the freckle-faced woman with a pert nose and pinned-up, blond pigtails stared at Lacy with open interest. Her curious gaze indicated she had a few questions of her own.

"Were you by chance the little girl who was best friends with that poor little Turner boy who was killed in that bombing years ago? Amy said you and your cousin Kelly were in the café over the weekend. Seems like you've got people talking about your return." The eager, light blue-eyes held Lacy captive, and she could hear the waitress inhale in anticipation of what juicy information she might hear.

At that moment, Lacy knew she'd been check-mated. There was marked intelligence behind that wide-eyed look.

Lacy sighed. "Yes, Wendy, but I do wish you'd keep that to yourself. I don't relish hordes of people bringing up unpleasant memories. That's the main reason my family pulled up stakes and left town years ago. Do you think you could block some of those memories being brought up again and again? I don't think I could bear it." Her eyes pleaded for the protection of the precocious waitress.

Wendy slapped the counter quietly. "You got it, honey! If you have trouble or need someone to run interference for you, just let me know. I've got your back. It's good to have you home, little Lacy." Gathering the empty dishes, she swiped at the counter with her wet cloth and gave her a sly wink, easing Lacy's uneasy feelings. She liked this young woman.

Exiting the café, Lacy watched for her chance to cross the busy street. Her little town was a lot more active than what she remembered as a child. As expected, she found Maxine still on lunch hour when she popped in to the *Gazette.* Writing a short note explaining she was going to run down a couple leads for the Morrison story, she stuck it on top of Maxine's giant desk planner and reminded herself to follow up with a phone call in a half hour. Maxine was a stickler on rules, and right now Lacy needed to play by them.

Following Wendy's sketchy directions, Lacy weaved her way out the back roads to the more rural areas. Reading names on mailboxes, she turned into a long snake-like drive back to a modest farm. Mrs. Morrison led Lacy into a large living room to find Mr. Morrison tucked into a comfortable recliner recovering from his multiple surgeries. It didn't take Lacy long to discern the gist of what their major problems were. After months of being unable to work and tend his farm, the Morrisons were now in danger of losing their farm to back taxes. It was a family farm intended for their son, who was now away at school.

Lacy talked with him at length and took quick, accurate notes, including who Mr. Morrison had talked with at the tax office. Closing her notebook, she smiled tenderly at the middle-aged couple and told them she would do her best to portray their situation accurately, without picturing them as objects of pity. "I'll write the facts as they are. From what you've told me I believe you have a good case for tax review and just perhaps this story will help to speed up the process."

Leaving the friendly homestead, she looked to the farm directly across the way. Wendy's information had given Lacy another slant on the Morrison story, and Lacy's instincts were leading her to follow where they would take her. Two stops later, Lacy had the story she wanted. Leaving the neighbors with a couple of suggestions, she extended an offer for a free public service advertisement. Back in the car, she pushed her starter button into action and headed the Challenger toward town. With any luck she would have time to write up the story and have it ready for Gardner's review before she left work this very day.

On the drive back, she compartmentalized her first assignment, releasing her thoughts to review Wendy's earlier remark: *"Seems like you've got people talking."* Lacy cringed afresh, thinking that was just what she didn't want to occur. People talking could cause unwanted attention and interference for her real assignment.

It was obvious that Amy, the sassy waitress who worked the café on weekends, had listened in on their conversation. *I will have to be more careful about public conversations.* It appeared there was no way possible to keep a lid on the awareness of her presence in Gladden Hills after this. It would take more than Wendy watching her back to keep her from potential danger.

The note writer said: *The answers you seek are here, where the danger remains—a slumbering giant.* Would the slumbering giant see her return as a possible threat? Would they sense she was here to uncover the truth? The very fact she was a reporter was a threat.

*

All around her, people in the large open area of the *Gazette* building were shutting down their computers and various machines, but the distant sounds of an office calling it a day didn't penetrate Lacy's concentration—except perhaps as a mild distraction. She was accustomed to working her own hours. Her job depended on meeting a deadline. Lacy's policy was to stay until the story was finished.

Maxine Flanders' commanding tone shattered her wall of concentration. "Lacy, the office is closing. You can finish up tomorrow."

Lacy kept typing on her computer, her tongue slightly visible between her lips. "I'm sorry, Maxine, but I simply can't stop now. This write-up needs to be okayed by Mr. Gardner first thing in the morning for other aspects of this project to be put in action. It's a community project that might hopefully save the Morrison farm before tax date. I realize this might be confusing to you without additional information. But I can't take the time to give that to you now. Time is essential. I will need to contact others as soon as it's okayed." A sidelong peek caught the force of Maxine's piercing stare.

All Lacy's desires to follow the office manager's plans to the measure went out the window with the pressing needs of her story. It was always that way with her—the story and people took precedence over anything. She looked up into the stern face of the little bulldog, who was not used to having her orders countermanded, wondering if she might possibly be unemployed by supper.

"How much longer do you need to complete the write-up?"

Maxine's unexpected question took Lacy aback. She released her pent-up air. "Fifteen minutes to a half-hour max."

"I'll take supper at the café and return to check back with you. You'll be locked in the building. Mr. Gardner won't have anyone here alone without the doors locked. Is that all right with you?"

Lacy nodded. "That will be great! Thanks, Maxine!" Refocusing on the computer screen, she didn't even hear the front door close. She was laying the last printed sheet of her write-up inside a new manila folder when she heard the front door open. Checking her watch, she realized it had been a full hour since Maxine had left for the café. Additional time had been awarded than originally promised. Her eyes followed the manager's approach.

"You finished?"

"I'm finished. Once it's on Mr. Gardner's desk, I'm gone. I appreciate your understanding. I think this could be important to quite a few people. It's a chance for the community and Morrisons' neighbors to pay back some of what this man has done throughout his life to help others."

Maxine studied Lacy. "Put it on his desk and I'll follow you out."

As Lacy stepped through the front door, the little bulldog threw out a parting quip. "I hope you won't make a habit out of last-minute crusades that keep me overtime. I'm an old woman, the sole supporter of three cats who expect their dinner on time. We'll look for you to be on time tomorrow morning, Lacy Cottrell. Good night!"

Before Lacy could reply, the front door was closed and locked. All she saw was Maxine's broad back marching back into the bowels of the building. Drawing her coat collar around her, Lacy made her way around to the parking area. Before climbing into her black car, Lacy squinted at the back of the *Gazette,* where a metal door opened and Maxine emerged, complete with pocketbook. Lacy watched the bent figure make tracks to an economy-sized, American-made car. Without a look to the right or the left, the stoic office manager settled inside and started her engine.

Lacy viewed the car proceed from the parking lot to merge onto the village streets. *So there is a rear entrance to the building. I wonder why Maxine didn't let me out the back way?* Perhaps it was a private entrance for management only. She started the car to head home, happy that it wasn't her night to cook. *Today was a poor start to a more leisurely lifestyle.* She shrugged, trying to organize her hazy thoughts.

*

When the last of the supper dishes were stashed in the dishwasher and Kelly was busy sorting her laundry, Lacy took her phone up to her bedroom, propped up pillows against her headboard, and settled herself comfortably upon her bed. She shook off the jitters before dialing. Her first day on the job, and already she was rocking the boat.

"Miss Cottrell?"

Lacy blinked. "Mr. Gardner!" She hadn't expected him to have caller ID.

"I assume this is a *necessary* call."

"It is. I need an okay to authorize a free Public Service Advertisement, belated as it is," she said, biting her lip.

"Belated? Do you care to explain?"

Lacy explained how a group of the Morrisons' friends and neighbors would host a benefit spaghetti dinner at the fairgrounds building on the upcoming Saturday—the proceeds to be used to pay the Morrison's tax bill for this year. She paused, then said carefully, "I okayed a free advertisement from the paper as a goodwill gesture. It was a spur-of-the-moment decision, and I took a chance. They really needed the advertising, and..." She added quickly, "The story is on your desk waiting for your review."

Long seconds of silence followed.

"I see," he said, slowly. "When you interviewed Morrison's neighbors this afternoon, this event was in the making?" His mellow voice was seemingly not satisfied with the completion of her explanation.

Lacy took her time in answering. "Ah, let's say it was in the incubation period. Close, very close!" she finished with emphasis and went back to biting her lip. Having no background with this man, whose shielded eyes she had yet to clearly see, Lacy had no idea what course of action to expect from him. She'd acted from her heart and sense of community unity, but would he see it that way? *It will be what it will be!* she told herself with a fatalist attitude.

"Incubation period?" he reiterated.

"So to speak, Mr. Gardner, but it has taken a surprisingly aggressive turn since this afternoon."

"It has? How so?"

"Apparently one of the neighbors I spoke with just happens to be in charge of the Fairgrounds buildings. He said it would be no problem to set the main area up to be used as a dining area, and of course, the kitchen is connected. So you can see how convenient it makes everything, especially with the help of another neighbor who heads up church suppers on a weekly basis."

"Yes, I can see now how it all came about," he said dryly. "I'll read the write-up first thing tomorrow morning, and you can consider the Public Service Advertisement compliments of the *Gladden Hills Gazette.*"

Exalting in what she heard, Lacy briefly closed her eyes in gratefulness. She was even thinking of easing her head in the direction of her pillow when Gardner's following words caught her up short. "Next time, Miss Cottrell, I would prefer to have a heads-up prior to hearing about our community generosity. You know, a short phone call beforehand?"

"Yes, sir!" She sat straight up on the bed as if saluting a commanding officer. The thought occurred to ask if such a call would have been merited "a necessary call," but common sense held her tongue.

"Miss Cottrell, were you this much trouble at your last employer's?"

"I-I really don't know quite how to answer that question, Mr. Gardner."

"Tomorrow, Cottrell, on time!"

Lacy heard the click of his phone.

*

Later, while the cousins relaxed in Gran's parlor, the fire crackled brightly. Its warmth penetrated the small room. Lacy closed her folder of notes and stared across to Kelly. "What do you know about my new boss, Jason Gardner?"

Kelly moved not one iota, as she stared into the blue and yellow flames shooting upward. "Only what I hear from town scuttlebutt. About three months ago he drove into town in his expensive, executive-type automobile and bought the *Gazette* before it officially hit the market. I was still waiting for the complete specs when I heard it was sold. Somehow he had gotten hold of prior knowledge concerning the sale. He comes from somewhere in the Midwest I think, either that or the east coast. There are two or more theories floating around."

"Any family?" asked Lacy.

"Not that anyone has seen or heard about. Some speculate he is a business mogul living out his dream to run his own newspaper. Others say he's kin to old money and is dabbling in enterprise. What it all boils down to is no one knows why or how your Mr. Gardner is here, but his money spends like everyone else's, and he's supplying jobs for the local people. That is, until his newest reporter arrived from the 'big city' and took a good-paying job away from townspeople." Kelly gave her a sly smile.

"Is that what people are saying? That's not fair. After all, I'm originally from Gladden Hills. I'm technically a hometown girl."

Kelly looked over at her cousin. "Yes, I believe you are, Lacy, but I'm not sure you know it yet. In fact, I'm not sure of the real reasons you *are* here."

"Kelly? What makes you say that?"

The keen-eyed blond tilted her head. "A feeling deep inside, like an itch you can't scratch."

Lacy rolled her head back and maintained a calmness she didn't feel, purposely not making eye contact with her perceptive cousin. Kelly was bluffing—not actually sure, but hoping her comment would cause Lacy to fill in some of her "itchy questions." It was a tactic her cousin had used even as a child and one Lacy had fallen for on a regular basis, but they were no longer children. "Kelly, I'm trying to figure out a few things in my life, like I said—just feeling my way through. And from the boners I'm making on the new job, it might be more prudent to keep my bags packed," she mused more to herself than Kelly.

Kelly lifted an incredulous brow. "Surely not? You're too good at what you do, Lacy Cottrell. Tell me, how are you getting along with the little general, Maxine Flanders? I've heard rumor that she was a Marine Drill Sergeant in a previous life."

Throwing her head back, Lacy laughed freely. "Marine Drill Sergeant? That thought hadn't yet occurred to me." She was careful not to mention that she had secretly dubbed Maxine the dragon lady or little bulldog. "To be honest, I had just enough common sense to realize it would be good policy to play nice and not buck the system for my first few days on the reservation."

Kelly's eyes narrowed suspiciously. She angled her head to get a clearer view of Lacy's face in the firelight. "Really? And how is that working out for you?"

"As long as I kept to that policy, it worked fine."

Kelly chuckled. "And how long was that?"

"The better part of the day, actually…until closing time, and then I blew it big time! I had a story to finish, and I couldn't let it go." Lacy shook her head at how she'd broken her own goal to secure a solid position with the newspaper manager.

"Well! I haven't heard that you were fired."

"Oh, no, I wasn't fired, but Maxine clearly was not pleased. That's why I'm still puzzled as to why she went out of her way to give me an extra half-hour to finish everything up. Apparently it's her job to lock up each night, but she waited. Gardner comes in early most mornings, but more so on Tuesday and Wednesdays before the paper comes out, and I wanted the article on his desk."

"That's curious. I'd say the little general has taken a liking to you, cousin dear. She must have thought your article warranted the extra effort on her part—definitely unusual!"

Recalling Maxine Flanders' parting words of warning gave Lacy sufficient pause to doubt her cousin's vote of confidence. What did Kelly call her—the general? *Major General* was a better title. Long minutes passed as the two women sat silently lost in their own thoughts.

Looking over at Lacy, Kelly broke the stillness with a request. "How about meeting me at City Bank during lunch hour tomorrow?"

Lacy frowned. "Why?"

"Why? You know why. You've been avoiding signing the bank forms for months. It's time to take care of the matter. I got the house and the Grans set up a joint bank account with you for a certain amount of funds. Now that they're gone, you have to reestablish the account in your name. It won't take you long."

Lacy grimaced. "I never wanted the account, I wanted the Grans. Look, Kelly, I've waited this many months, so surely a couple more days won't make that much difference. I'd rather meet you on Thursday after the paper is out. This is a short work week as is, and I need to do a good job. Besides, I've been warned against any more crash articles."

"Thursday at noon it is. Now don't try to wiggle out of that time. Bear in mind this is what the Grans wanted."

"Thursday it is." Lacy gave her cousin time to settle back in her overstuffed chair before saying, "So how are things at the office—you know, with Jerome?"

"Don't start, Lacy. Jerome is my employer."

"Why don't you invite the poor man over for a home-cooked meal? I mean, you couldn't have a better chaperone than me. Use this time I'm here to the best advantage. A nice, relaxed time with the three of us around a table—no pressure." A square-tasseled pillow hit her in the side of the head. "Hey. At least think about it, okay? He's always been a shy person, even as a kid. Stevie was younger, but he'd speak for Jerry more often than not. Jerome's smart, just shy. He was even hesitant to go up to houses on Halloween."

Kelly's face grew earnest. "But he's not like that at work. He comes alive when he's with a client talking about real estate. He's a wonderful salesman and has a great head for business."

Hearing the adoration in her cousin's voice, Lacy rolled her eyes. "Think about it, Kelly. That's business—not personal."

"Well, I'm used to guys who make the first move. I'm uncomfortable with the tables turned. I just don't know..."

Lacy picked up the tasseled pillow. "How badly would you like to spend time with Jerome?" She aimed the pillow back at Kelly and laughed.

Catching the pillow, Kelly held it close. "How did you become so wise about romance, young cousin?"

"I have no idea." Lacy recalled all too well the four or five almost relationships that never got to first base. *My fault.* "Remember the old saying, 'Do what I say...not as I do?' Just promise you'll think about it," she said, brightening.

Kelly sighed. "All right, I'll think about it."

4

Finding Who's Who

THE NEXT TWO DAYS WENT BY QUICKLY with Lacy sequestered mainly in her three-quartered partitioned office. She had more privacy than most of the employees. With short runs out and about she was able to collect enough information to complete two additional articles for Thursday's edition. She'd heard nothing further about the Morrison article other than it had been okayed by Gardner early on Tuesday morning.

As soon as Maxine related the news, Lacy made several phone calls to help advance the Morrison Spaghetti Benefit for Saturday night. She couldn't wait to see the community impact. Almost from the start, she began to feel as if she were somehow invested in the Morrisons' life. She'd suffered the same feelings in her work whenever she dealt with people on a personal level. Finding that occasionally the outcome brought her heartache caused Lacy periodic pause to reevaluate her *modus operandi,* but there was no help for it. Right or wrong, it was her emotional makeup. At present she was straining to get past this short week where the news articles were driving her life. It was time to get on with the reason she was here.

Finishing the last article, she stared at the computer screen, organizing her thoughts. Now that she had a better idea of where the various village offices were situated and a line on a few connections, she could plan a course. She thought about Jason Gardner, though Lacy doubted he would willingly use his influence with town leaders to obtain information for her. Still, if she were to word a question in the right manner...just maybe? She formulated various scenarios.

Arching her neck, Lacy felt suddenly uneasy. Her neck muscles tensed. One eager young helper at the paper had taken to loitering by her desk whenever an excuse provided her opportunity. It was unsettling the way Lacy would sense a pair of eyes watching her from the edge of the office partition. "Chloe, may I help you with something?" she asked.

"Ah, no. I mean, I was in the area and I just love to watch you work, Miss Cottrell. You know I want to be a reporter in the worst way, and when I heard you'd worked on a big paper in Chicago, well, that's the big leagues. Everyone knows that. I was…hoping to learn from you. You know, pick up a few pointers. Of course I wouldn't want to be a *nuisance."* Her wide, greenish brown eyes added color to the pale face haloed by wispy blond hair.

The way Chloe had accented the word *nuisance* made Lacy cringe. The girl couldn't be more than twenty or twenty-one, thin and slightly slump-shouldered. "Chloe, I'll be pleased to work with you, but it might be better if I set up the times. And right now *isn't* a good time. This is my first week and…" She lifted her hands in frustration.

The youthful face exploded in a smile. "You just let me know. I will be happy to help you with anything—anything at all," she said, backing away.

Lacy pushed away from the desk. Scooping up the two finished articles, she stifled a yawn on the way to Jason Gardner's office. She rapped on his partially opened door and pushed the door open in one smooth motion.

Gardner's head snapped up even as he rotated his office chair from the back table to face the door. "By all means, come in, Lacy Cottrell." He indicated one of the chairs in front of his desk.

Her focus gravitated to his darkened glasses. She could see the merest hint of the strength that lay behind the gaze, creating an extra aura of mystery to his persona. She vaguely wondered if he might have a serious eye problem. Many people wore dark glasses for that very reason. But Lacy liked to see a person's eyes. They often mirrored truths that mouths seldom did. Those dark glasses of Jason Gardner were like a padlocked bridge holding her at bay across a vast body of water.

Strangely, it was his mellow voice that brought her thoughts up sharply.

"Miss Cottrell? You wished to see me?"

"Yes—sorry! I finished these and thought you might like to check through them." She released the pages into his waiting hands.

Instantly he began scanning the first paragraph of the top page. She saw the quick movement of his head as his focus moved rapidly down the page. Without looking up, he murmured, "Please sit down, Lacy."

Having entered his office with no intention of lingering longer than it took to pass him her articles, she hesitated, though it now seemed she had no choice. Lowering her body into the nearest chair, she restlessly surveyed Gardner's sparsely decorated walls. The new owner clearly had more important items on his mind than beautifying his office.

Without realizing it, she started transmitting her thoughts. "You really should put a few pictures up…if not for yourself, then for other people of the community who might call on you." Her eyes lingered on a watercolor of a farm scene before lifting to an outdated calendar advertising tractors that hung slightly off-center on an opposite wall.

"Excuse me?"

With the instant realization of what she'd said came a flush of warmth to her cheeks. "Sorry. I should never have—I mean, whatever you choose or don't choose to put on your walls is really *none* of my business."

He nodded. "You're right. It isn't any of your business."

She tensed, waiting for the fallout. She wasn't sure what to think of his comical smirk.

Lifting his chin, Gardner scanned the walls and rotated his chair to take in all four walls. Whipping his chair back in line with his desk, his lips pursed in thought. "To tell the truth, I've never really looked at the walls. You're right. Something should be done. All right. You're in charge. Do whatever you think suitable." He waved his hand, his concentration returning to her articles. "When I've checked these through, Maxine will let you know if there are any needed corrections." His tone told her she was dismissed.

"What?" she said with a thin voice. Flustered, Lacy ran her fingers through her hair. "Mr. Gardner, am I understanding you correctly? You want me to pick out some pictures or decorations for your office?"

His head shot up again. "Certainly! Who better? You're the only one who's noticed. Why wouldn't I pick you? If you purchase something in town, have it charged to me. If not, bring me the receipts. Anything else?"

"But what if you don't like what I pick out?" she sputtered. "Art is subjective, you know!"

Gardner rescanned the walls. "If I haven't noticed that out-of-date calendar until today, what makes you think I'll care?"

Baffled, Lacy threw up her hands. "Fine! I'll look around. If I find something, I'll bring it by for your approval."

"Whatever makes you happy, as long as I don't have to do it." His head lowered to the articles.

Making her way to the doorway, Lacy hesitated. "Ah, Mr. Gardner, in case I need to check into some old town records, would I find them at the police station or over at the old courthouse?"

The muscular shoulders of the new owner bunched beneath his fine-textured sky blue shirt. "Town records? Let me think." Seconds ticked by before he replied. "Speaking without knowledgeable authority, I'd chance an opinion that files older than the last couple of years would most probably be found at the old courthouse." Slowly raising his head, Jason Gardner asked curiously, "Are you working on something I should know about?"

"No," she said with a hint of hesitation. "I just have a few vague ideas that I might like to sniff around about."

"Let me know if you need any help or run into a snag, Lacy. I have the feeling that you have a 'nose for news,' as the old saying goes."

"Is that why you hired me?" Her quick comeback was accompanied with a slow smile. She could feel his eyes studying her features and wondered what was going on behind those glasses.

His face remained stoic, without expression. "I needed a reporter, Miss Cottrell. It's as simple as that."

Feeling as if she'd been put in her place, Lacy cocked her head curiously. This man not only puzzled her, but he had the ability to spark her anger. Twice now her attempt at humor had been shot down. *Maybe rule #3 was: Do not joke with employees.* Closing the door as she left, she strode with long legs toward the front of the building, her heels clicking hard against the tile floor. *What I need is a strong cup of café coffee.*

As she passed Maxine at the front counter, the woman shifted to stare at her. "Is something up?"

"I recommend never voicing an art critique in public. In fact, I may give up art appreciation altogether." Lacy flung her parting words over her shoulder, her hands striking the opening bar to the outside door with more force than needed.

Crossing the street in record time, Lacy entered the café and slid into her favored seat at the far end of the horseshoe counter. "Coffee," she said in a moody tone as Wendy drew near.

"Got it!" Wendy said brightly. "Anything to go with that? You look like you could use a 'pick-me-up,' and there's nothing better than a taste of something sweet. We got six French Silk chocolate pies in today. Greta Hostettler is renowned, her French Silk pies legendary. Mona's Bakery keeps them on hand at a premium if you want a whole pie."

Lifting her eyes to Wendy's bright blue gaze, Lacy said, "Actually, I think one full piece of Greta's French Silk ought to do the job just fine. You've got a sale…as long as it comes with a helpful hint."

Wendy's golden freckles seemed almost to dance on the bridge of her perky nose along with her rise of interest. "You need info for a new story?"

"Calm your pigtails, Wendy. What I need is much more domestic. Where can I find reasonably priced decorating items? You know, something to brighten the décor of an outdated area."

"You're redecorating your grandparents' old place?" she asked with obvious interest.

She sighed. "Nope. The boss's office...and Wendy, that is off the record also. That is, if you want me to keep my job."

Leaning close to her ear, Wendy whispered, "I got an idea. If you've got a minute, I'll ask around and get back to you." Whipping about, the slim waitress glided toward the kitchen, returning with both hands loaded. Placing Lacy's pie and coffee in front of her, she slid a folded piece of paper under the pie plate and lowered her voice. "Just mention Shirley's name. It's her cousin's place on the second road out of town. Tonya will treat you right." With a nod her blond pigtails bobbed off in another direction, and she was off.

All Lacy's viable senses were invested in the yummy slice of French Silk pie until she caught part of another conversation. It was something in Wendy's tone. She laid down her fork.

The waitress had cranked up her usual warm greeting at least two notches. "Judge Shaw, *how nice!* It's been a few days since we've seen you. I'll bring your usual order *right over.*"

Through thick lashes, Lacy viewed the extremely tall, well-dressed, middle-aged man as he followed the horseshoe to the right and progressed to a far booth. Raising the fork to rest on her tongue, she reviewed everything she'd heard or read about the judge that dated back to when he was Gladden Hills' eager, upcoming district attorney. His name had been in the papers and on the daily news during the tedious months following the bombing.

On one side Shaw was praised for his "around the clock" diligence during the frantic days of the investigation. On the other, he was highly criticized—something about an undisclosed controversy dealing with possible contamination of stored case evidence. Nothing had ever come of it, but many questions remained unanswered, and questions foster doubts. Lacy might have felt some empathy for his earlier plight, but apparently the DA used the publicity to his advantage. It appeared the whispered doubts hadn't kept his career from rising to that of a judge in the fair young city of Gladden Hills.

From her position on the counter stool, Lacy could see only the top of the man's brown hair with grayed temples. He looked every inch the picture of an honorable, prestigious judge. *But is he honorable? If the rumors have all faded into obscurity, then why is it I can't dismiss all the doubts?* She felt like she was clutching at straws.

Wendy rushed from the warm kitchen, her cheeks pink and becoming with her pigtails pinned up on her head. She carried a tray as if it was the queen's best silver service. It was laden with a steaming mug of cinnamon hot chocolate with buttered English Muffins, and she lowered it with care in front of Judge Shaw, most prominent citizen. Straightening her sturdy shoulders, she glided away like a long-necked swan. Impressed with the whole presentation, Lacy noted the grin that enhanced Wendy's attractive features. The judge sipped his chocolate, seeming unaware of anything out of the ordinary.

Surveying the café and noting its lack of customers, Wendy ambled back to lean on the counter in front of Lacy. She glanced covertly at the judge, sighing softly. "Now there is one *handsome* man! Yes, sir. Perhaps a mite older than the norm. Nevertheless, a handsome man!" She cocked her head. "He's a great tipper too." Looking around as if making sure no one could hear her, she bent her head before continuing.

"Now that banker man, the new la-de-da president, I can count the times he's ever stepped foot inside this café with his haughty manner. Prefers to take his meals at the Valley Country Club about five miles out of town. My friend's husband has worked there for years, and he says the man squeezes every quarter down to the size of a dime before it ever leaves his hand. I just hope he takes as good care of our money as he does his own," she said with a grunt. "You met him yet?"

Lacy shook her head slowly, savoring every creamy bite of pie and not missing a word. A person can learn much from just listening, as long as they are careful to verify the information. Being an outsider, she viewed herself as a sponge, thirsty for insight—any insight. She could shift through whatever she learned later. There was much to learn if she were to make any headway into the bombing. She remained quiet, hoping Wendy might continue with her small-town rundown of who's who.

She was totally unprepared for the girl's next comment.

Casting a sly wink Lacy's direction, Wendy moved her head closer to Lacy's ear. "Of course, that new boss of yours at the paper, Jason Gardner…" She whistled low. "Now there is *a total fox!* When he looks my direction through those shaded glasses he wears, my heart palpitates like a tiny bunny rabbit." Her tinkling laughter rang like a small set of chimes. "If you find you need any help decorating his office…," she offered.

Lacy swallowed hard on a gulp of coffee and coughed several times, her eyes watering. "Wendy!" she spurted out, restraining her laughter, then took a fast water chaser. "Tell me, who else is on your dream list? You seem to have the run-down on every eligible guy in town. There just might be something a single gal could use." She chuckled softly. This delightful young woman was a deep well of research material in every respect.

Moving quickly and gracefully to the left, Wendy hefted a freshly brewed pot of fragrant coffee. She gave Lacy an affirmative nod. "I've got to make the rounds, but I'll be back." She refilled Lacy's cup as if giving her reason to remain before making her way to the few customers dotted across the restaurant. Nearing the booth where Judge Shaw was seated, she offered another cup of chocolate. His mumbled response was too low to be heard.

Obliviously drawing the steaming liquid to her lips, Lacy stared across the café, buried in thought. It wouldn't hurt to check out available information on the handsome Judge Shaw. Lacy jerked away from the offending cup and rubbed the tip of her singed tongue against the inside of her teeth. Glancing up, she discovered Wendy had returned with a glint in her eyes. The perky waitress efficiently scanned the quiet café before bending eagerly over the counter. "Are you ready for those 'man tips'?

Lacy covered her mouth. "Sure!" she whispered, suppressing a giggle.

"Actually, there has been a surprising influx of attractive men finding their way to our little city the last few years." Lowering her voice in a secretive tone, Wendy asked, "Have you encountered our Eric Greer yet?"

Lacy shook her head in the negative, and Wendy rushed on. "Eric is Manager at the bank and quite the ladies' man, or so I hear. He hasn't hit on me yet." She grimaced. "With his surfer good looks and fabulous job, he's rated high on the eligible hit list. Some of the women have even joked about asking him out just for a chance at him." Pausing for effect, Wendy threw Lacy a wide curve. "Some say Eric's been buzzing around that pretty cousin of yours lately."

Chuckling, Lacy sipped more coffee, quickly concealing any noticeable interest in Wendy's final comment. She would definitely question Kelly about it later. Lifting her gaze to Wendy's watchful eyes, she redirected, "So...who else has recently moved into town?"

Wendy was about to speak when both women caught the stealthy movement of Judge Shaw leaving his booth. He was working his way toward the checkout counter by the door where an older woman sat reading. Even as Wendy lifted a hand in a parting wave, the judge's penetrating stare swung their way, resting unexpectedly on Lacy. There was something in that cold look that made Lacy shiver. Did he know or remember who she was? Lacy was only eight years old at the time of the investigation, but Shaw had questioned her. *What exactly did that look convey?* she wondered.

"Well, the judge certainly noticed you. First time I've ever seen him react that way with someone." Wendy studied her with curiosity.

Shrugging off a shiver, Lacy forced a laugh. "I probably remind him of someone he sent to prison. I certainly wouldn't call his glance a 'come on,' would you?"

Wendy's expression twisted into a perplexed frown. Together they watched the café door swing closed behind the judge. "No…no, I wouldn't, but there was definitely something…"

"You were saying," Lacy prompted.

Wendy shifted her attention back with amazing precision. "Yes," she whispered. "The newest guy in town—besides your luscious boss, of course—is the serious type, nose to the grindstone and all that. The man acts like the job is everything! I guess that's why he's reported to be among the *best in the country*—or so I've heard. Don't get me wrong, he's a real looker, but definitely the studious type. One day he wasn't here, the next he was seen all over town asking questions. He ruffled quite a few people, which is too bad because he really is very nice from what I can tell."

"He was asking questions…what kind of questions? What's his name, Wendy?"

Wendy explained, "Mr. Darling was appointed to come in and take over for our belated district attorney. Ralph Wagner died sudden like, so *Michael Quinn Darling* rode in to save the day," she said with emphasis on his name, chuckling. "Isn't that a handle? In all honesty he can be a little frightening at times. His eyes pierce right through a person. The first time I tried to make him laugh, he stared at me kinda funny. I can tell when a guy's being rude, and Mr. Darling wasn't like that. He's just…well, sorta distracted sometimes. I kept trying. After several attempts, I finally got him to smile, and he grinned up at me like a little boy with a shoe box full of speckled frogs." Her eyes looked dreamy. "Mr. Darling is real smart. I think that's part of his problem."

Lacy laughed at Wendy's description. "Sounds to me like you've got a crush on the very intelligent Mr. Michael Quinn Darling," she said gently.

Wendy blushed. "Oh, I have a crush on half the guys who come in here, but it does me no good." When she giggled, one pigtail broke loose from its confines and bobbed on her shoulder like a spring robin on a branch.

Grinning at the comical picture, Lacy decided Wendy was an exceptional young woman, one capable of deep caring and strong character. She had a tendency to talk too much, but it was part of her charm, along with her flare for spontaneous honesty. Strangely, Lacy felt if she made the request, she could trust this lady to keep her confidence. It was something she had sensed from the first time they'd talked. Wendy George was much more than she appeared on the surface.

With the influx of new customers filing into the café, Lacy used the opportunity to impart a hasty thanks and farewell before grabbing her bill. She headed for the checkout counter and the door beyond.

Wendy called after her, "I can't wait to read your articles tomorrow."

The shadows were growing long with the lowering of the afternoon sun, and the brisk chill of spring air tingled Lacy's cheeks as she rushed back across the street to the *Gladden Hills Gazette*. A glance at her watch told her there remained only enough time to clean up her desk area before quitting time. The front counter was glaringly void of Maxine's presence. While common sense told her the major general could merely be visiting the ladies' room, experience had also taught Lacy that changes in established routines could equally indicate trouble. Her footsteps increased in momentum.

Approaching Gardner's office, she paused. His drapes were drawn, the door of the publisher/editor's office was slightly ajar, and a light shone through the opening. She moved ahead with the thought of proceeding on to her desk until the clear, cutting voice of Maxine Flanders caused her to swerve back around in the direction of the door opening.

"Miss Cottrell? Did you enjoy your long coffee break?"

The door widened, revealing the erect figures of Maxine Flanders and Jason Gardner standing in front of his desk. They observed her with keen interest and perhaps an additional element of expectation—or was it censure? Lacy couldn't tell.

She dropped her head to conceal her uncertain feelings. "Yes, Maxine, I did, and I found it especially beneficial for gathering information." Looking up, she forced a confidence that was at best dubious. Their eyes locked in a tense gaze. Was that a hint of a smile at the corners of Gardner's mouth?

Maxine cocked her head at her. "Really? Would you care to share?"

Directing slow steps in their direction, Lacy lowered her voice. "You know yourself that a good reporter *never* reveals her source. But if you'd care to know anything specific, I'll do my best to comply." Glancing from one to the other, she asked, "Were my articles acceptable?"

"And if they weren't, it's somewhat late to make any adjustments. Don't count on my benevolence a second time, Miss Cottrell. The editorial portion of this paper will close *on time* tonight even as the paper goes to press."

Lacy felt a sharp twinge of wrongdoing and professional regret. She knew it was her responsibility to be available to make changes on her articles. In the midst of listening to Wendy's ongoing rundown of new residents in Gladden Hills, it had completely slipped her mind.

As she opened her mouth to offer an apology, Jason Gardner intervened. "Your articles were quite acceptable, Lacy. You've done an excellent job your first week at the paper. Wouldn't you agree, Maxine?" His tone indicated her compliance was expected.

Lacy heard a small intake of air expressed from the throat of the ample-formed manager. Following a slight hesitation, Maxine replied stiffly, "Certainly, Mr. Gardner."

It wasn't the warmest of compliments, but Lacy was exhausted and didn't intend to look a gift horse in the mouth. "Thank you both. I'll say good night then." Spinning about, she quickly made her way to her desk. *How can I ever get in Maxine's good graces if I keep messing up by breaking her established rules of good procedure? Next time, Cottrell, cut your coffee break short.*

She was still reading herself the "riot act" while readying her desk. Gathering her trench coat and black purse, she locked her desk drawer and turned to leave. With her head down and her thoughts entrenched on her own failures, Lacy's feet carried her straight into a body collision with her new boss. Gardner had just turned away from his closed office when the impact occurred. Both heads jerked up in surprise.

"Oops! Sorry! I wasn't..." Lacy sputtered. Too late her right foot shot backwards to steady her balance. She felt her body plunging backward and down.

"Steady there!" Gardner's hands shot out like lightning to grab hold of her shoulders. Her dissent came to an abrupt halt, and her thoughts raced in that split second. His wedge-shaped face was so close to her own it was impossible not to get a clear view. His eyes looked to be brown or dark blue behind those glasses and the slight olive-tint to his complexion struck a nerve of recollection, reminding her of an amorous freshman back in college. Ironically she recalled Wendy's description of Gardner: *"Your boss is a fox!"*

A warm flush rose to her cheeks. Their bodies were still positioned awkwardly at best.

"Are you okay?" he asked, raising her to a stable place.

Suddenly the whole situation struck Lacy as humorous. "I'm fine. Thanks, boss, but that was the worse rendition of a tango dip I've ever experienced." Her words rushed out, followed by an unexpected ripple of nervous laughter.

In a flash Gardner's laughter erupted, echoing her own. "You have a gift of humor that will carry you far, Miss Cottrell. Now if you can only learn to watch where you are walking, there will be no stopping future achievements." His grin was infectious.

Working to straighten her disheveled clothing, Lacy was in partial shock. She couldn't get over Gardner's response. It was the first time she'd ever heard him laugh. "Actually, Mr. Gardner, that sense of humor you speak of has often placed me in hot water with both friend and foe."

He tilted his head. "I don't doubt that for a minute, Cottrell."

Behind those dark glasses, his eyes were mocking her. Lacy could feel it, but she held her tongue, determined to keep herself from further embarrassment if at all possible. Though only Wednesday afternoon, it was the end of her first week of working for this paper. She'd completed a full week's assignments in three short days—the beginning of her investigative vacation. What a joke!

With a cocky salute, he turned and walked toward the outside doors. "See you in the morning, Lacy." His voice echoed slightly off the hard entry tile floor. She heard the palms of his hands strike the bar opening the door.

Please, God, let me walk through those doors to freedom without encountering the redheaded major general.

*

Every beat of her heart on the short drive home longed for a quick meal and early bed. Her weariness went clear to the bone. Each foot dragged up the broad steps leading to the stately old family dwelling. Finding the storm door open, she entered the house, easing her briefcase into a niche by the stairs that led upward to the second level.

Lacy heard the clatter of hard heels strike the dark wood flooring between the kitchen to the front room and entryway. Turning, she encountered the anxious, heat-flushed face of her lovely cousin. "Oh, Lacy, I'm so glad you're home. Hurry! Ditch your stuff and come to the kitchen. I need you now!"

The half-frantic look in Kelly's eyes caused her alarm. Lacy lifted her chin and sniffed the air. Was there a fire? Then she caught the aroma of something. Not fire. Garlic and other spices—Italian spices. She gave her cousin a hard look. "What's going on, Kelly?"

Kelly intertwined her fingers nervously. "I took your advice and asked Jerome to come to dinner tonight." She raised her hands in obvious distress. "I don't know what came over me. I mean, I should have planned things out better, but there I was, saying, 'Would you like to come to dinner tonight?' And he said yes! Would you believe it?" She giggled as if she didn't believe it.

"Then the office got crazy, so it wasn't until I was driving home that it hit me we had absolutely nothing to serve! I raced back to the market and the only thing I could think of that I could do quickly was your mom's spaghetti sauce. I've got it started, but you've got to finish it, Lacy. I'm so nervous I'll blow it for sure! I did have the foresight to pick up dessert and garlic bread," she added in a more hopeful tone.

Lacy stared at Kelly, hoping it was all a weird practical joke and, at any second, her cousin would scream out, "Only kidding!" But she didn't. Gradually it sank in that Lacy was staring at cruel reality. Inhaling, she closed her eyes to give herself a moment of peaceful silence before rushing to her cousin's rescue. After all, it had been her idea to invite Jerome to dinner. But with her eyes closed, her equilibrium became dangerously compromised. She felt her weary body sway to the side.

"Lacy! Are you all right?" Kelly guided her with a steady hand toward the nearest chair. Once seated, she removed Lacy's coat and purse. "You sit here while I get a glass of cold water. Just relax now," she called, hurrying away.

Relax is all I wanted to do. Lacy leaned her full weight against the support of the ladderback antique chair, hoping it would hold her weight. If the chair should give way, there was nothing she could do to save herself from an abrupt fall to the hard floor. Her body was in limbo. Her half-opened eyes spied her cousin rushing toward her with a bottle containing a colored substance of some kind. It was definitely not water.

*

Standing at the stove, Lacy gave the simmering meat a quick stir and held up her hand. "Crushed tomatoes," she called out like a short-order chef. Kelly hurriedly pressed a large opened can of tomatoes into her cousin's hand.

"Careful!" Lacy exclaimed, swiping at her tomato-spotted apron with her left hand as she poured the can into the simmering meat and onions.

"Sorry! I'm just so nervous. I never expected him to accept. I haven't even thought of dating anyone since Grant. I'm worried that we'll sit at the table and not find anything to say to one another. What'll we talk about? Be prepared to fill in the blanks, please, Lacy!" She wiped furiously at the salt and pepper shakers.

Shooting a glance at her anxious cousin, Lacy soothed, "Relax. Technically this isn't even a date. You're asking a café-weary man to your house for a home-cooked meal. And as far as conversation goes, you two talk every day of the week. What's different tonight?"

Kelly patted Lacy's shoulder. "Thanks for the pep-talk. You're right. I just need to try to pretend we're at the office." She surveyed the room for something to do.

Shaking the oregano container over the bubbling pan, Lacy laughed. "Kelly, do something useful and set the table. The salt and pepper shakers are fine!"

"Boy, I'm glad I gave you that potassium junk." Kelly ran her hands through her slightly mussed hair. "I couldn't do this without you—not tonight. One of us needs to be on our game. And don't worry about the clean-up. I'll take care of all of it after he leaves. All you have to do is stay long enough through dinner that Jerome doesn't get the idea he's been set up. I know him. He's so shy he'll panic and freeze up. Then the whole night will end horribly."

"Kelly! Set the table!"

The stunned blond raised her eyes to meet Lacy's, and both women laughed.

*

Lacy rose from the table and moved to the counter to serve dessert, doubtful if Kelly or Jerome noticed her action. They'd talked nonstop about one thing or another from the moment they'd sat down to the table. So much so Lacy found it difficult to inject word or thought into the conversation. It amused her to remember her cousin's anxiety prior to his arrival.

As she set a dish of cheesecake in front of Jerome, he looked up at her with sudden interest. "Did Kelly tell you Cynthia Bradford was in the office today?"

Lacy lowered the other dish in front of Kelly, her gaze moving from Jerome to her cousin. "No, we haven't had much time to talk. Was Cindy looking for a house or land to build?"

His face appeared almost pinched. "I thought so at first, but then she seemed more interested in questioning Kelly about you."

"Me!" Her mouth fell open. "Wonder what's behind that? What did she want to know?" Lacy asked casually, sliding down in her chair, her eyes never leaving his.

"Kelly would know better than I," Jerome said, glancing up at a flushed-cheeked Kelly who'd quietly left the table.

When she returned with the remaining plate of dessert, Kelly stopped in place when both heads swiveled toward her.

Kelly shrugged. "It wasn't that big of deal, really. At first Cindy pretended to be interested in possible property for a building site. But as soon as I started laying out potential areas, she hemmed and hawed a line of excuses, then switched directions smooth as butter. Cindy said she'd heard you were back in town and staying with me. Before I could comment, she pressed to know how long you were going to stay. Not knowing, I said as much."

Kelly's delicate chin tightened. "By this time, I'd pretty much surmised that Cynthia had come by solely for the purpose of pumping information about you, so I walked away. Then she hit me with one last question. Why had you taken a job at the paper?"

"Really?" Sparks of anger flashed. "Cindy always was…" Lacy allowed her words to drop away for fear she'd say something nasty.

"Don't worry, Lacy," Kelly urged, placing the cheesecake by her plate. "I simply told her you wanted a change. I don't think she believed me, but it shut her up. You two never did get along well, did you?"

Lacy's nose wrinkled in distaste. "I haven't seen or spoken to her since our family left town seventeen years ago. Why the interest in me now?"

"It's hard to tell, but I can understand why you didn't get along." Kelly's gaze hardened.

The intensity behind Jerome's glasses never wavered. "Years don't transcend all the questions and drama still cloaking the tragedy of Stevie's death, like why he and his mother would be targeted by a bomb? Terrible things like that rarely happen in small, quiet suburban areas. Your close relationship to Stevie was such that some people may still wonder if by chance you knew something of importance about the incident."

Kelly stood to her feet before Lacy could reply. Obviously shocked by his comments, she stared at her boss. "Jerome, what are you saying? Lacy was only a child and nowhere near that boy's house. Everyone thought his mother, Terri Turner, was the object of the attack. Either that, or it was all a cruel mistake of some sort. Nothing was ever found that indicated she or her husband had any questionable connections."

Jerome's face colored. "I'm just saying what I've heard expressed upon occasion throughout the years. Unsolved crimes leave doubts in people's minds and cause imaginations to run rampant."

"Well, surely they don't concern Lacy," Kelly said indignantly in clear defense of her cousin.

Lacy held up her hand. "It's all right, Kelly. I understand what Jerry is saying—sorry, Jerome," she corrected. Turning to face him, she briefly wondered again if he could be her secret contact in Gladden Hills. He was part of the close circle of Stevie's friends and knew Ellie was the name she answered to as a child. *What else did he know?*

She held his gaze without flinching. "I was questioned at length by the police and the DA until my parents made a formal complaint. I had no clue why something like that might have happened. Stevie had never mentioned one word to indicate that he knew anything was out of the ordinary."

Yet, even as the last words left her mouth, her recall flickered a picture of the previous afternoon before the bombing. She and Stevie had been sitting on a lawn swing in his backyard. *Stevie had gone into the house and...*

She couldn't remember beyond that.

"What is it, Lacy?" Kelly injected.

"Ah...nothing. You know how it is." She forced a smile. "Whenever you start to turn back the years, your mind has small explosions of memories."

Jerome shot her an unsettling look as Kelly poured coffee in all their cups. Lacy averted her eyes and concentrated on her cheesecake.

"There's been altogether too much talking about a tragedy that happened years ago, especially since there's nothing we can do about it now. Lacy doesn't need bad memories to plague her during her stay in Gladden Hills. She's here for a rest," Kelly said with such punctuation that the subject was dropped.

Nevertheless, Lacy worked to recall those last forgotten moments she'd spent with Stevie. Why were they plaguing her now?

Later in bed, as she allowed her weary muscles to unwind, Lacy set aside the Bible she'd been reading of late, the comfort of its written words ringing in her troubled thoughts. Bible reading was once again becoming a part of her daily activity. God had allowed her to wander for the past few years, but now, it seemed, He was drawing her back to Himself—to Gladden Hills and the tragedy that had lain fallow the last seventeen years.

Lacy felt the pull back to her faith like the force of a giant magnet. It was all God's doing, and she could no more deny the strength of that force than breathe. She sensed His presence was with her, energizing her with fresh purpose. Turning out the light, she lowered her head to the pillow. "Bring back those lost memories, God. I think I can handle them now," she whispered. A sliver of moon shone a shaft of muted light across the dark room.

Noises from the kitchen filtered through the heat registers where Kelly was efficiently cleaning up the kitchen as promised. It had been a very good evening for her cousin. Lacy had noticed the first spark of hope for a new love for Kelly. She thought back on Wendy's comment that the young bank manager had eyes for Kelly, and wondered how that might play out in the days ahead if the gossip were true. Interesting happenings were afloat in Gladden Hills, and Lacy sensed it was only the beginning.

5

The Power of the Press

LACY DRUMMED HER FINGERS ON HER STEERING WHEEL IN FRUSTRATION. Every single day she had been caught by the morning commuter train. It didn't seem to matter what time she left. She shook her head in dismay. This day of all days, when she was so anxious to see the Morrison article in print. She gunned the engine as soon as the guard rails lifted.

Grabbing a copy of the paper from the front counter of the office, Lacy proceeded toward her cubicle, eager to read her article in print. Pleased to see it positioned on the front page, she read as she walked. "Good morning, Miss Cottrell," spoke a curt voice nearby.

Stopping in midstride, she jerked her head up to encounter the nondescript expression of Maxine Flanders. Lacy groaned inwardly. *So...one late coffee break and we're back to Miss Cottrell!* It didn't bode well for the rest of the day. Forcing a pleasant smile, she looked into the steel, cold gray eyes of the redheaded bulldog. "Good morning, Maxine. My thanks again for staying after that day and allowing me to finish the Morrison article. Hopefully it will be of some help to them. They're nice people."

The eyes softened in the lined sockets of the older woman. "Yes, I hope so too. The article is fine work." The statement was matter of fact with no frills. Once the comment was declared, the matronly, stout-figured woman turned on her heels and marched back to the front counter. Their brief exchange left Lacy feeling slightly off center.

Lacy's eyes lingered on Jason Gardner's closed office door as she passed. The blinds were drawn, and there was no light beneath the door—curious. Normally Gardner was in the office earlier than anyone. Did his routine differ on the mornings that the paper came out? Puzzled, she continued toward her cubicle and immersed herself in the article. Lacy's reading had progressed to other articles when Chloe's little-girl voice sounded in her ear.

"I *loved* your articles, Miss Cottrell. They're amazing!"

Lacy looked up into the eager face of Chloe Camry. The girl was so earnest and so open in her admiration of Lacy's ability that she felt guilty for the frustration that overwhelmed her whenever Chloe swooped into her cubicle. Lacy sent a prayer heavenward for a right attitude.

"Please call me Lacy, Chloe. Really, I am *just* one of the employees like yourself, but I do appreciate your kind remarks. Thank you."

"Is this a good time for you to give me pointers, Miss—I mean Lacy?" she pressed.

Lacy looked down at the paper. She hadn't had opportunity to get past the first page. Glancing at her watch, she sighed. This girl standing expectantly in front of her had a penchant for putting Lacy on the spot.

"Not this morning, Chloe," she said firmly. "I'm sorry. When I finish scanning the paper, I have an appointment in town." She took a moment to phrase her next words. "Chloe, remember me saying, it would be better for me to contact you when a good opportunity arises for mentoring. Trust me, the timing needs to be right. Sometimes I need concentration, and not everything I work on is easily conveyed."

Even as the girl's head bobbed in agreement, her eyes wavered nervously, indicating her mind was darting elsewhere. Then Chloe blurted, "Maybe tomorrow would be one of those right times." As her slim form backed away on silent-soled shoes, Chloe's overly bright eyes remained on Lacy until the partition blocked their view.

Exasperated, Lacy felt like she was watching a lithe Indian fade away into the forest, where she would hide, stalking her, watching for new opportunities to strike. Shaking her head free of her paranoia, Lacy continued reading until she found herself interrupted again and again by well-meaning employees who stopped by to encourage her on the articles—something that would never have occurred at the large Chicago paper. She was surprised and flattered by their display of thoughtfulness, but it also made her uneasy. She wasn't used to the pressing attention and it drained her emotionally.

Suddenly she experienced a powerful urge to escape the building. It was accompanied by a pressing desire for strong, dark coffee—caffeine to booster her increasing tiredness. Rechecking her watch, she decided on impulse to finish reading over at the café. She wasn't expected at the bank to meet Kelly for yet another forty-five minutes, and it would give her a few minutes to herself. Folding the paper, she reached for her purse and lifted her coat from the back of the chair before heading out.

Lacy stopped briefly, preparing to encounter Maxine at the front desk. Their earlier, amiable greeting wasn't sufficient to fill her with lasting confidence. Pausing, she clearly and succinctly apprised the dour-faced woman of her morning schedule, then squared her shoulders and hurried toward the door.

Once outside, a balmy wind caught up her shiny dark hair in its playful dance. She raised her head, enjoying the wonderful feeling of freedom. Buttoning her coat at the waist, she mused on the ironic situation with Maxine. Surprisingly, the watchdog had seemed perfectly agreeable to the idea Lacy would be gone most of the morning—without even a noticeable hint of censure in her bearing. Once again, it had put Lacy off-center, having expected a short grilling session, especially after yesterday's set-to over the late coffee break.

Lacy reexamined the situation. What had taken place back there in their verbal exchange? *Is it possible Maxine doesn't care where or what I'm doing…that the woman just wants to be kept in the loop?*

Her surmising might not be 100 percent accurate, but it bore consideration. Chuckling to herself, Lacy found a similarity in the situation that paralleled previous dealings with her mother. Mom had always trusted her as long as Lacy was upfront with her and kept her in the loop. It saddened Lacy that she now felt it imperative to keep her own counsel concerning the real reason she was in Gladden Hills.

Entering the café, Lacy scanned the noisy interior, taking an empty booth on the left side for a little privacy. It was the busy time of the morning and Wendy and her early morning helper, a broad woman with bleached hair and an air of efficiency, were waiting on two and three customers at a time. It surprised Lacy to see Wendy appear so quickly at her booth.

"Morning, Lacy. Anything besides coffee?" Wendy asked brightly.

"Just coffee, Wendy, thanks. I only have a few minutes, and I'm trying to read through the paper."

"Understood. I read it earlier. That article about the Morrisons was sensational! It made me proud to know you. I've heard people all excited about the Spaghetti Benefit on Saturday. The Morrisons are well thought of in this town."

Lacy smiled warmly. "Good! I couldn't have done it without your help that first day, Wendy."

The waitress blushed and lowered her eyes shyly. "Glad to be of help." She nodded. "Coffee coming right up." She whirled about in the direction of the brewing pots.

By the time she neared the end of her second cup of coffee, Lacy had worked her way to the back page of the paper, where she was engrossed in a piece by a freelance writer, specifically an article about the discovery of several boulder formations in the area that simulated natural caves. Holding the coffee mug to her mouth, Lacy immediately thought of the base of the mound behind the old Gladden Hills Cemetery at the back of the woods. It had been a secret hiding place for Stevie and Ellie to play after church on Sunday mornings. Was ours one of the discovered caves? She wondered. There was much to discover in the area. Would she be here long enough to check out those boulders? The question bothered her for a reason she couldn't identify. This town was getting under her guard.

Her thoughts were distracted by the formidable personage of Gladys Pruitt in front of her booth. The sternness on the old woman's face caused Lacy to sit upright. "Mrs. Pruitt?" she exclaimed. In an instant she was eight years old again, anticipating a lecture from her piano teacher.

"Ellie Cottrell! Why didn't you make yourself known to me last week?" her voice boomed out across the crowded café. "I worried with my memory all day long. I *knew* there was something familiar about you, but I couldn't place it. I'm an old woman, you know."

Lacy's gaze darted across the room to see if anyone was listening to the loud words of her former teacher. Suddenly she was glad for the noisy busyness of the café. Only a few heads turned at the sound of the old woman's voice, but they quickly lost interest and turned back.

"How are you, Mrs. Pruitt? It has been a long time. You're looking good." Lacy babbled on nervously.

"Yes...well, never mind all that foolishness," said the wrinkled-face woman, waving Lacy's comments aside. Her diminutive arm thrust outward, and in her hand was a copy of the *Gladden Hills Gazette.* "I heard tell you were a reporter and, I admit, I had my doubts at first. You were always a fanciful child and easily distracted from your piano studies. Not to say you didn't have talent. I hated to see you waste it." The woman paused as if to allow her words to sink in.

"The point is, I read your article on the Morrison family and revised my opinion." She raised her tiny fist. "It was a good thing you did with this story. You portrayed them as they are—independent, proud, outstanding community residents, descended from a strong family. Why, their family roots go back over one hundred years. Now they need to be supported, paid back so to speak. I want you to know you can count on me to support the Spaghetti Benefit on Saturday night, and I'll start calling around to all my friends."

Almost speechless, Lacy groped for the right words. "Ah, Mrs. Pruitt, that is so kind. I'm sure the Morrisons will appreciate your efforts."

"Well, people need to stand up for neighbors, that's what community life is all about. You did your part. Now we'll do ours. Keep up the good work."

The woman turned to leave.

"Thanks, Mrs. Pruitt," Lacy hurried to add, grateful Gladys Pruitt was wearing her hearing aids today.

The steel-eyed woman regarded her with interest, nodding curtly, her gaze lingering on Lacy's features. "Well, you're pretty enough, I'll say that. You grew up well, Ellie Cottrell, or whatever you call yourself now. Do you ever play the piano anymore?"

Lacy grinned. "Some, Miss Pruitt, when time allows, but I'd like to get back at it again in earnest. I find it comforts me when I'm trying to relax."

"You do that, Ellie. You do that. You had talent, and that comes from God—not to be wasted." Her chin bobbed.

"Yes, ma'am," Lacy answered in the same tone she'd used doing her piano lessons.

Stretching to gaze around the edge of the booth, Lacy watched the woman lift her head and trundle through the peopled area to the checkout counter. *Whew! She hasn't changed.*

*

Lacy arrived inside the bank with three minutes to spare, searching for her cousin. Kelly was rarely late and most often the first to arrive. Shifting to view the clean, fresh interior of Gladden Hills National Bank, she noted the brightness of the lighting. *Better for keeping an eye on our money,* she mused sarcastically.

"Lacy, sorry I'm late. I got hung up on a last-minute phone call. Jerome finally took it from me so I could leave." Kelly's face was flushed with exertion and her frustration of straining against the clock. "Well now, let's find someone to help expedite the matter as quickly as possible. I know how you hate to waste time on matters such as this." She scanned the large, busy room.

"Don't worry yourself, Kelly. Today I've got the time to get this issue straightened out once and for all. It's my fault it has been pending for so long. It bothered me to think on the whole situation of the Grans being gone."

Kelly touched her arm in a gesture of comfort. "I know, Lacy, I know." She still scanned for an appropriate person to help them. "I was hoping to see Eric, but...well, let's talk with this clerk at the first desk."

The cousins were about the same height and build, but the stark difference in their hair coloring—Ellie's a dark umber and Kelly's blond—was striking. The youthful clerk stood as they neared and addressed them eagerly. "How can I be of help, ladies?"

Before Kelly and Lacy were able to sit in the two padded seats offered to them in front of the young man's desk, a man's command from one of the inner offices jarred their attention. "I'll take care of this, Ryan. You may go back to your work."

The clerk's good humor faded immediately. "Certainly, Mr. Greer. Let me know if I can be of help," he offered with soulful eyes.

Lacy observed the tall, aggressive-walking man who was fast closing the distance between them. His shock of blond hair and sunglasses gave the appearance of a Hollywood celebrity. So much so, a fleeting thought occurred to Lacy to wonder if his hair was bleached. She immediately threw off the idea as ludicrous. His narrow face and even features contributed to his good looks and caused Lacy to remember Wendy's description of someone of up and coming importance at the bank, someone who matched the image of this man. Lacy knew instinctively who he was—the well-proportioned, dashing bank manager.

Kelly turned with a warm greeting. "Eric! I was hoping you might be in. There isn't much left to complete the distribution of our grandparents' estate. How nice of you to leave your busy work for such a small matter. This is my cousin, Lacy Cottrell. Lacy, this is Eric Greer, newly appointed bank manager."

Fascinated by the man's dark glasses, Lacy had to force herself away from staring. *What is it with the men in Gladden Hills and their penchant for dark glasses?*

"It's hard to believe two such lovely women in one family." His admiring gaze shifted to Kelly with an ample supply of warmth. Suddenly his expression altered, and he turned to consider Lacy with more keen interest. "Did you say Lacy Cottrell? Are you by chance the new reporter for the *Gladden Hills Gazette?"*

Lacy flashed an uncertain smile. "Guilty as charged. News gets around fast."

Eric's expression turned frosty. "Especially when said reporter uses the press to publicize a private cause. I'm afraid your well-crafted article on the Morrisons has pictured the bank as 'the heavy' in your little family drama, Miss Cottrell." His tone was light, almost as if he were teasing—but not quite…"Why, I would be surprised if anyone in town or in the general vicinity will miss attending that spaghetti dinner on Saturday night to benefit the Morrisons. That sterling write-up of the couple's community contributions and importance was a *nice touch.*" His final words had a sharp edge.

Fire sparked between them, and the tension in the air increased.

Kelly looked confused, then anxious. She edged closer to Lacy.

Squaring her shoulders, Lacy chose her words carefully. "Eric, as a new member of the community, I would naturally have thought the bank's foremost concern is to protect the monetary interests of their clientele, to help their contributors navigate rough times, not take advantage of them at the first turn of trouble. And I'm sure your presence on Saturday night at the Spaghetti Benefit will help to reinforce that public image of your support."

If it was possible, his features tightened more so than at first. Their eyes met in a brief challenge of wills. Then he said, "Naturally, as the bank's representative, I'll put in an appearance of goodwill. I wouldn't want my absence to be noted in next week's issue of the *Gladden Hills Gazette.*"

Lacy sobered. "I wouldn't do that, Eric. That's not my style. I only did what I could to help an effort of goodwill for good people in a hard place. And I hope you'll view it as such."

Her softened manner seemed to thoroughly disarm him. In an instant, his face altered. "Of course," he murmured. With averted eyes, he bowed slightly before turning back to a much-relieved Kelly. "Now you were going to tell me how I can best help serve you today."

*

Sitting at a small comfortable table in Eric's office, Kelly looked on as Lacy signed the last official paper. Laying down the pen, Lacy reread the amount of funds transferred to her personal account. It gave her no pleasure to know it signified the finality of ever seeing her grandparents again. Eric Greer stood looking over Kelly's shoulder, off-handedly teasing her in whispers. Observing his schoolboy actions, Lacy determined Wendy was right. The debonair bank manager was definitely hitting on her cousin, and though Kelly appeared not to notice, Lacy doubted she was that dense.

The abrupt opening of a door leading from Eric's personal office drew the attention of all three. "Eric, could you come into my office as soon as you're able?" the medium-tall man called from the doorway.

"Certainly, sir, we are almost finished here. I'll be right in."

The vague focus of the well-dressed man in his forties sharpened as he took in the presence of the two women. Holding a stack of papers, he ventured further into the room. "I'm sorry I wasn't aware you were involved in something, Eric."

"No problem, sir. As I said, we are finishing up." Eric's stature took on a new stance of professionalism.

As the smooth-moving, gray-suited man came closer, Lacy realized he wasn't nearly as tall as she'd first estimated. His straight shoulders and features gave him a sense of largeness that was deceiving at a distance. He extended his strong, manicured hand outward toward Kelly, who was the nearer of the two. "Kelly Larson. How nice to see you. How long has it been?"

"Mr. Heywood. I believe it was a few months ago at the hospital committee meetings."

"After four grueling weekly meetings, I believe it's permissible to call me Connie." His eyes moved curiously to Lacy.

"My cousin, Lacy Cottrell. Lacy, this is Mr. Conrad Heywood. He was recently named bank president," Kelly said proudly, as if she'd promoted him herself.

A look of puzzlement formed on the lightly lined face, strikingly framed by a styled salt-and-pepper haircut. "Cottrell? The name sounds very familiar, and I have the peculiar feeling I know you somehow."

Before Lacy could comment, Kelly spoke up. "Lacy's family used to live in Gladden Hills."

"Really? That probably is the answer. It's one of those things that will nag at me until I remember." He dipped his head. "Nice to see you again, Kelly. I'll look forward to seeing you at the next committee meeting in mid-May, if not before. Eric is anxious to attend as well. He's becoming my right-hand man," he said, looking with brief admiration at the young assistant. "Miss Cottrell." He nodded pleasantly and returned to the room beyond the door.

Lacy pushed through a maze of memories but was unable to place this man, yet something rang familiar. Was it his name? Her previous research into the bombing had indicated someone by the name of Heywood was connected with the bank during that period. In what capacity she couldn't recall.

What reports she'd read were vague about any connection or relationship between him and Stevie's mom, Terri Turner. Still, something about Mr. Heywood remained at that shadowy place in her memory. Noticing Eric Greer collect the signed papers, Lacy reverted her attention to the situation at hand.

While the women donned their coats, Eric took advantage of the time to steer Kelly's focus back to him. Lacy couldn't hear all of what he said to Kelly, but she saw her cousin's face flush slightly. Kelly countered by offering her hand to say thank you. After they'd voiced their appreciation and good-byes, Lacy and Kelly were gallantly escorted out to the main area.

Lacy's feet couldn't carry her fast enough toward the outside doors. It had been a stressful morning, and she needed space and quiet. But since Eric had first commented on the Morrison article, Kelly had been withdrawn. Lacy sensed her cousin was biding her time to question her about the matter. It had been an uncomfortable moment with Eric. Clearly, the man was a bore and had over-reacted. Hopefully he wouldn't continue to prove that difficult. After all, Mr. Heywood spoke highly of his young bank manager. Perhaps her own attitude needed some adjustment.

Maybe I overacted and became defensive too quickly, she mused, anxious for the outside cool air. As they reached the doors and would have exited the building, a forceful duo entered to stand opposite them in a direct face-off. It was a startling moment, and no one spoke. Lacy swallowed hard in disbelief as she confronted her childhood enemy. It was turning into a banner day!

In a flicker of an instant she'd recognized the striking blond woman in the stylish, well-tailored, aqua suit. The tilted nose and light blue eyes hadn't changed much in seventeen years—they still irritated her. Lacy juggled the small possibility that the woman had not recognized her. Perhaps they could simply pass by. At least she could hope.

"Ellie Cottrell!" The well-shaped arm raised as the woman's fingers touched her mouth in astonishment. "Wait! Excuse me! If I'm not mistaken, I believe it reads Lacy Cottrell on your byline." She glanced briefly at the imposing, muscular man to her right. "You be the judge, Morgan. Tell me, why would a reporter feel the need to change her name?" the sugary voice challenged teasingly, probably more for Lacy's benefit than the man she called Morgan.

Lacy gritted her teeth and forced a matching, light-hearted manner. "Cindy? What a surprise to run into you, so to speak. Actually, Lacy is my proper name on the birth certificate, and I prefer it." She tried to move to the side and edge her way closer to the door. "Forgive me for blocking the entrance. I'm sure you must have important business, and I wouldn't want to hold you and your friend up."

"Oh, we've no pressing engagement that can't wait for an old friend, do we, Morgan? Would you believe that this young woman in such a hurry is Gladden Hills' newly celebrated reporter, Ellie Cottrell—or Lacy, as she prefers to now be called. And, of course, you already know her cousin, Kelly Larson, of Collins' Real Estate. Lacy, my law partner, Morgan Streeter."

The sing-song cantor of Cindy's speech had always rubbed Lacy the wrong way, for her words were habitually double-edged. Cindy's humor as a child was often tainted by a tongue dipped in nasty, especially directed toward someone she viewed as a rival. Unfortunately, Lacy was her primary target. Trying to distract herself from Cindy, she glanced to the handsome man before her, whose presence could not be denied.

Thick auburn hair and compelling features were enhanced by his ruddy complexion, now deeply tanned. It gave evidence that Morgan spent much time out of doors. There was an energy about the man that quickened her heart. Leaning forward, as he was now, to extend his hand, Morgan's penetrating gaze was poignantly serious, yet his crooked smile caused Lacy to question his sincerity. These conflicting messages emitting from his body language threw her in a tizzy. *Yes, this could be a dangerous man in many areas.*

Lacy gently withdrew her captive hand. "Mr. Streeter," she said, her tone politely reserved.

"Lacy, I hope you'll call me Morgan. May I dare to also hope we might become friends in the coming days?" His eyes held a definite invitation.

"Oh-oo-o! Watch out for this one, Lacy! His wolf fangs only show up at night," Cindy said laughingly, with the merest hint of a bite. "I should know."

Her last words were accented to what purpose Lacy wasn't sure. There was obviously more than a law partnership between them, and Cindy wanted her to know it. The glance Morgan shot his partner was pointed, but he offered no rebuke.

Hearing Kelly heave an anxious sigh, Lacy nodded. It was time to go. "It was most interesting to run into you again, Cindy. I'm sure we'll see more of each other. It is, after all, a small town," she said amiably, turning away. Even as she and Kelly made their way to the side of the couple to exit, Cindy's cynical comment followed her out.

"Morgan and I will be at the Spaghetti Benefit on Saturday night. After reading your article, we couldn't possibly not attend and be supportive, now could we?"

At last Lacy and Kelly passed through to the freedom of the beautiful spring day. But they hadn't walked more than a few steps past the front of the bank when Kelly placed a restraining hand on her arm. "What in the world did you write in that article?" Before Lacy could reply, Kelly muttered, "Never mind. Whatever it was sure has stirred people up. I'm going to pick up a paper on the way to the office and read it for myself." When she tried to veer off toward her parked car, Lacy caught up with her.

"Kelly, what's going on between you and Eric Greer? I thought Jerome was the only one in your sights?" Her lowered voice was meant for her cousin's ears and none other.

Kelly glanced around. "Nothing on my part...and I honestly doubt anything on Eric's part. He's a flirt! Ask several of the young professional women in Gladden Hills. I don't doubt but that he's probably hit on Cindy

Bradford as well. Did you get a load of her? Nearly the whole town has speculated on her relationship with that partner of hers. After her remark today, I would almost bet on it." Kelly's eyes grew serious. "She doesn't like you, Lacy, and she didn't like Morgan Streeter making advances in your direction. Watch out for her!" A worried veil settled over Kelly's features.

Lacy regarded her sharply. "Why?"

Hesitating, as if considering whether she should answer, Kelly spoke quietly. "I hate to repeat something for which there is no real proof, but a friend of mine—one I'd trust with my life—believes Cynthia Bradford might have been behind a series of unexplained attacks. Indirect, insidious attacks that undermined the honesty of this person and attacked her character."

Kelly checked her surroundings once again. "An anonymous source gave my friend's name to various city agencies, implying she was involved in illegal activities. Eventually this friend was found to be innocent in all areas, but not before she'd spent a ridiculous amount of money and time, not to mention worry and lost sleep. All these situations occurred after she'd had a couple of serious run-ins with Cynthia. Now there may be nothing to it, but all I'm saying is, be careful."

Feeling a sudden chill, Lacy recalled a childhood incident of her own, one she'd almost forgotten. *That nasty occurrence in the early part of second grade when a stolen book was mysteriously discovered in the bottom of my locker—a book I'd never seen before or had any idea where it came from.* Thinking back, Cindy's locker was conveniently right next to hers, and Lacy had questioned more than once if it might have been Cindy—the golden-haired princess with the musical voice and sweet face. How hard would it have been for the girl to watch her open her locker and remember the combination.

After that episode, Lacy had asked for a new locker and kept a safe distance from Cindy.

Lacy vividly remembered being on the hot seat with school officials for several days, but it was the suspicion from classmates and teachers that had hurt so much. One special teacher came forward to vouch for her character, and gradually the episode faded with no assigned punishment. But there were some who might doubt her still. Childhood memories have long shadows.

"Lacy!" Her cousin spoke her name sharply. "You looked like you were a million miles away. I need to get back to the office. Jerome is covering for me, but I hate to put too much on him. Remember what I said about that Bradford woman—watch your back!" Pulling her keys from her purse, Kelly turned toward the driver's side of her car.

Lacy's initial decision to walk the distance from the café to the bank had been a good one. She used the return walk to her advantage, time needed to clear her torrent of thoughts. This town seemed to be tumultuous with hidden secrets and dark passions. Could there be those in town who knew what happened the day of the bombing—those who were fearful someone might find out? Her unknown contact contended there were. Lacy didn't have much time to find the truth, and somehow her memories intertwined with all of it.

I need to discern what is real and dangerous from petty, distant feelings. Cindy has been a thorn in my side since we were children, but I can't let her muddy my thinking. She wasn't part of what happened seventeen years ago. So if I can just keep her off my back...

But to keep Cindy off her radar, Lacy knew she'd have to stay clear of Morgan Streeter, and Streeter looked like a man who wasn't easily dissuaded. She walked faster to release pent-up anxiety. Cindy had definitely put a wrinkle in her outlook for the day. *Just like old times.*

Breezing through the front door of the *Gladden Hills Gazette,* she waved at Maxine on her way through the front area and was passing Gardner's office when she heard him call out, "Miss Cottrell! A moment, please."

Backing up, she turned into his office in time to see her editor reposition his chair upward. Had he been sleeping? His fingers adjusted his dark glasses before looking up at her. "Have you already taken your lunch, then?" he asked, glancing at his watch.

"No. Actually I was just coming back to the office for that reason. I brought my lunch with me today. There was some personal business at the bank that needed my attention this morning," she said with displeasure.

"Was it all that bad?" His focus zeroed in on her negative waves.

"I've had better mornings. Disagreeable people have that effect on me," she said tersely.

Gardner's head inclined. "Someone you just met?" he asked casually.

Lacy inhaled before answering. "One of them. The other was someone I knew a long time ago."

"That's right. I remember you lived in this town years ago. Anything I can do to help?"

Lacy could feel his eyes study her, sensing immense energy in this man, something she'd not picked up on before. Fleetingly, she wondered what would happen if Morgan and Jason ever collided. Dismissing the ridiculous idea, she wished she could see his eyes. People's eyes often revealed insight into their character, and there was much about Jason Gardner she wished to know.

In reply to his offer, she shrugged. "I don't think either of my disagreeable people was planning to do bodily injury—although *she* might be considering it."

"She?" he inquired.

"Forget I said that. But I will give you a heads-up that some people who've read my article seem to feel they are being pressured into attending Saturday night's banquet…afraid if they don't attend, they'll lose community image and be considered less than supportive…and they are not pleased."

The small smile grew in length. He folded his arms. "That's their problem. Your article was sensitive to the feelings of the Morrisons, yet you artfully gave the community a chance to repay good people—people who have repeatedly in the past been there for their neighbors. I'm not too concerned about those few who are a little uncomfortable or feel pressured to attend."

"Fair enough." As Lacy turned to leave, a nagging thought caused her to turn back. "I met the new bank president, Mr. Heywood, today. Do you know what his position might have been at the bank some years back?"

Gardner's head lowered. "It is my understanding that Mr. Heywood has come steadily up through the various stations over the years. How many years back are you talking?"

Lacy hesitated. If she stated seventeen years, would this man connect the bombing with the time frame? "Oh, maybe ten or twelve?"

Jason Gardner crossed his arms. "I can find out for you. Any particular reason?"

"Yes," she said vaguely. "A very uncertain memory. I used to live here, as you say, but I have memory gaps that trouble me." Her tone was wistful.

"It happens. Sometimes the mind blanks out times and occurrences to protect the person, but I will search out your information for you if you wish."

Lacy eyed him curiously, wondering if he knew about her closeness to one of the bombing victims. If he didn't, someone in town was sure to inform him. Lacy refused to worry about that now. "Thanks, Mr. Gardner, I appreciate your willingness to help me in that area."

She took his nod as her cue to exit. As she passed through the doorway to her cubicle, her thoughts were already on her plans to ferret out old records at the courthouse after lunch. Next week's columns could wait. She had some investigating to do.

"Miss Cottrell?"

"Yes." She whirled to await his remark.

"You *are* planning on attending the Spaghetti Benefit Saturday night?"

Her expression blanked for an instant. Actually she'd not given it much thought. Flashing an impulsive grin, she answered, "Well, it would seem I have little choice. Besides, I wouldn't miss it for the world."

"Good. I will see you there."

He was going?

She must not have covered her surprise well, for he leaned forward on the desk. "What? You don't think I would miss being there after that article appeared in our paper?" he said, chuckling.

As warmth spread up her neck toward her cheeks, she turned swiftly back toward the door.

Perhaps I've underestimated my new boss. Maybe he has more of a sense of humor than I first thought.

6

The Inner Workings of Gladden Hills

THROWING THE REMAINS OF HER LUNCH IN THE TRASH, Lacy hurried from the office to the courthouse on the first leg of her efforts to check out the old files. She was politely turned away, redirected to a certain office official in the newer building of City Hall and told she was required to have signed authorization. One hour and five offices later, she took the elevator to the third floor, where she entered an office comprised of one person at one main desk.

Approaching the desk with false confidence, Lacy glanced at the name plate on the desk. "Vicky Subert?"

The dark, curly haired young woman looked up at her and took off her glasses. Her fair skin and wide blue eyes accented her pleasant, plump face. At first glance, she looked like a large baby doll. "May I help you?" she asked, smiling.

Lacy liked her immediately. "Oh, I do hope so. I need signed authorization to review some of the old files at the courthouse. I've been all over City Hall trying to get a pass—one place sends me to another. Nobody seems to know who is in charge," she said, frustrated.

The cherub-faced woman nodded. "Yes, there has recently been a major change-over of duties, and people are still feeling their way around. Actually, they should have sent you to me first off. I can write out a pass, but it needs to be okayed by a major official. Judge Shaw generally okays such passes, but he is out of town today. Perhaps…" And the woman went on.

Lacy recalled the way Judge Harold Shaw had stared at her in the café. The judge was the last person she wanted to know she was prying into the old files when he was district attorney. She cut off Vicky's next words. "Excuse me, but with the judge out of town, wouldn't an okay from the district attorney be just as legal?" Her eyes grew eager with hopefulness.

"I don't know why his authorization wouldn't be sufficient. Actually, even the chief of police has the authority to sign off on such a pass according to the rule book, but Judge Shaw has always been a hands-on sort of person, you understand?"

Lacy nodded. "How would I go about getting the pass okayed today?"

Vicky opened her side drawer and ripped off a sheet from a small pink printed pad. Without a word, she scribbled on the paper. "Your name, please?"

Hearing Lacy's name, she stopped writing. "Miss Cottrell, I loved your article in the paper about the Morrisons. I lived with them for over a year when I first came to town and had nowhere to go with very little money. They just took me right in like family." Seeming to remember the official form in front of her, Vicky quickly signed off on a side line and extended it to her. "I'll buzz Mr. Darling's office and see if he can spare a moment."

After waiting a few minutes, Vicky stood up from her desk. "Mr. Darling would like to see you in his office. This way, please."

Lacy checked her watch. Another two hours and it would be too late to get into the courthouse files today. Mr. Quinn Darling's office was not pretentious, but it was comfortable, cool, and decorated in earth tones. As she crossed the room, the man behind the large desk glanced up at her with a no-nonsense stare. Wendy had told her he was handsome, but Lacy saw him differently. Darkened skin stretched tight over his strong cheekbones gave him the look of a rugged Western frontier man. His discerning eyes examined her thoroughly behind wire-rimmed glasses. He was a tense, serious man who immediately intimidated Lacy. It amused her to think Wendy was the only one who had brought cheerfulness to his stern face.

He directed her to a close chair as Wendy exited. *He wants to watch my reactions to his questions,* she thought, feeling like a criminal being brought in for interrogation. Mr. Darling rolled his chair closer yet. "So, Miss Cottrell, tell me why a new reporter in town is interested in going through old files in our courthouse."

All of her prepared, memorized reasons faded. Instinct told her this man would know if she lied. "Personal reasons, sir. I used to live in this town many years ago."

Mr. Darling raised his hand. "I already know who you are, Miss Cottrell, and your prior association to the Turner family many years ago. What is it you expect to learn by going through the old files? Unless, of course, you are working on a story *about* the unsolved crime itself?"

"No, sir," she answered quickly—too quickly. "That is not the idea behind my wish to examine old files. At least not at this time."

Mr. Darling glanced down at the pink form, then back up at her. "All right, I'll sign your pass. But I warn you against investigating this cold case on your own. It may be as cold as a campfire on a winter morning, but there are dangerous embers beneath the coals. Check with me if you think you have uncovered the slightest bit of new evidence—me only, do you understand?"

His gaze held hers with steely determination, and she nodded.

His focus shifted back to his desk. "It's my belief you'll not find anything to warrant the loss of your time, but it's your time, Miss Cottrell." His decisive fluid hand signed the pass in quick order and handed it back. "Good day."

Feeling like she'd aged in one interview, Lacy rushed from the building, her vision locked on the discolored brick courthouse in the square across the street. She had an hour and a half, hardly any time at all, but still she could get her bearings and establish the best source of information. She kept walking.

Everything moved quickly forward at the courthouse. She was directed to the basement area where the fluorescent lighting, though adequate, was less than desirable. Since her time was short, Lacy took little notice of the older man in charge of the file room, whose nametag read *Nicholas.* He took her pass and led her through the maze of file cabinets to the back aisle.

She pulled out the police reports dealing with that time sequence and took them to a bare wooden table, using a nearby metal chair to sit on. Laying her notebook on the table with a ready pen, she filtered through the various legal forms beginning with the week before the bombing. Reports had been written up on everything from attempted robbery to a complaint about a Peeping Tom. Combing her hair with her fingers, Lacy read on.

The day of the bombing was unusually light of police complaints and nothing to raise any flags. She lifted the thicker file dealing with the bombing itself and laid it alongside. There were pages of personal interviews. Too many to read through today. She would have to come back. The pass was open dated, which would give her that time.

Hearing the closing buzz sounding throughout the courthouse above her, she collected the files and returned them to the towering metal cases lining the wide room. Lacy wiped her hands on a tissue from inside her purse and wearily left the old building. Aiming a vague thank you at Nicholas as she passed, Lacy rode the elevator up to the main floor and walked outside, squinting at the startling brightness of the afternoon sun. Lacy felt like she needed a bath, but the fact she'd taken the first step in her search for Stevie's killer gave her an inner source of accomplishment.

With your help, God, we'll find the answers. She'd begun talking to Him as she had before her spirit had grown cold and distant, though somehow things weren't quite the same…as if there was a blockage. Unsure what was wrong, she chose to center on the positive and decided it was a good start.

Lacy threw her head back and let the wind caress her face and whip free through her hair. She hadn't felt so alive for several years. That constant stirring within her was bigger than life. In the intense exuberance of her feelings, she sensed the unrelenting awareness of Jesus. He was wooing her back. He had never deserted her. Lacy now knew that. An immense shame consumed her heart—shame that she'd pushed Him away for so long. She looked up to the sky. *I need You so desperately. Forgive me!*

Tears of forgiveness and refreshment mingled with the basement dirt of the courthouse. Even her steps felt lighter as she crossed the street to the newspaper office. Had that elusive blockage broken free?

*

As Lacy entered the house early evening, she paused in the entry to listen to the familiar sounds emanating from the kitchen. Kelly was once again energetically preparing food, and Lacy chuckled at the new homemaking trend that had lately overtaken her cousin. Hopefully Jerome would not be coming to dinner yet again tonight. Lacy wanted to get off by herself after dinner. She had a lot to think over, including her initial introduction to the new DA, Michael Quinn Darling. It wasn't something she would soon forget.

Quinn, as his close associates called him, was much more of a forceful personality than she'd expected to encounter. He certainly was no dummy. *Does he know my real reason for coming back to Gladden Hills? It seemed almost uncanny how he zeroed in on the area I would be investigating when he found out who I am. He was obviously well advised about the seventeen-year-old unsolved crime. Either Quinn had done incredible research on Gladden Hills, or he had knowledge from another source. How much does he know? And who is my secret contact? Have I met him?* She thought over everyone she'd come in contact with since arriving and drew a blank.

There have been no further notes from my contact containing purple feathers since I arrived. Lacy's thoughts drifted into wispy trails with no substance as she entered the kitchen to face her flushed-faced cousin. "What's for dinner?" she asked, grinning at the domestic scene before her.

Her cousin's reply was a tossed apron. "Get out the fixings for a salad. What kept you so late tonight?"

"My conscience. I used a good portion of the day on personal business and decided to remain as late as the major general would allow to line up potential articles for next week's paper. I can't rest on my laurels, you know—be they good or bad," she said wearily.

Kelly turned toward her, her hand slowly stirring the pot. "I read the article, and I liked it! I can't imagine Eric going after you the way he did." Her faced screwed up in an unpleasant expression. "I take that back…maybe I can. Eric doesn't like to be put on the spot unfavorably. He came to town with a goal, and he's been pushing his way toward it ever since—almost obsessive at times. He has hinted at connections, but nobody seems to know much about where he came from. I do know Mr. Heywood has promoted him at an accelerated rate. According to Heywood, Eric pretty much handles all the trust fund accounts at the bank."

"Really? It sounds like Eric's background and rapid rise at the bank is cloaked in mystery, and my reporter background wonders what he might be hiding," Lacy said in a mysterious tone.

Kelly rolled her eyes. "Honestly! This is a small city with a small-town mentality—normal, quiet people who lead nice, uninteresting lives."

Lacy sobered. After gathering the salad fixings on the cutting board, she stared over at her cousin. "There are secrets in this small town, Kelly, dark secrets about the bombing that killed Stevie and his mother. Time hasn't erased the crime. Don't underestimate small towns." Her tone was heavy.

Kelly shifted from the stove. "You won't be free until you let go of the past, Lacy. Maybe it wasn't good for you to move back here—not if it stirs up all those sad memories." She let her words stand, leaving the meaning hang in the air between them.

Lacy wanted to tell Kelly her real reason for returning but was afraid of revealing too much. What if she told the wrong person? "You're a wise woman, Kelly Larson," she said lightly, then changed the subject. "Do you know why Eric Greer wears sunglasses? It seems like a town epidemic. My boss wears them too. It drives me nuts when I can't see his eyes. Plus, it makes it harder to know what he's thinking."

"Your boss? No kidding? I've heard he's a sharp dresser and ruggedly handsome, but I've never had the pleasure of meeting him. You'll have to introduce me." She wiggled her eyebrows, making Lacy laugh.

"Right…so what about Eric?"

Clicking off the top burner, Kelly opened the cupboard and drew out two large dinner plates. "I only know what he said when I kidded him about being Mr. Hollywood. He said he had a skin condition and the medication made his eyes super sensitive to light. Did you notice how bright the lights were in the bank? But what's up with your boss?"

Lacy took the filled plates from Kelly and carried them toward the table to find silverware already set up. "I really don't know. Maybe he has the same problem as Eric. Speaking of Eric, have you tried telling him you're not interested? I sensed he was beginning to get on your nerves today. He's pretty obvious in his attentions toward you."

"I don't take him seriously. I'm just another challenge. He's dated half the women in town, and like I said, possibly even Cindy."

Setting the drinks on the table, the two sat down and bowed their heads. Lacy hurried to ask the blessing ahead of her cousin. After her illuminating walk from the courthouse, she couldn't wait to speak a blessing with a sincere heart. For too long she'd been going through the motions whenever it was required of her. When the girls lifted their heads, Lacy saw her cousin regard her with curiosity.

"So you think Cindy went out with Eric?" Lacy prompted. "That's interesting. The possessive way she acted about Morgan Streeter, well…it just surprises me, that's all."

"Rumor has it she's a bit of a player. But then, the same rumor says the same of Morgan Streeter. Maybe it was just you, Lacy, that brought out that possessive streak. You two were never close. And if body language is a recognized form of communication, Cindy was screaming her dislike for you. I meant what I said this afternoon. Stay away from her."

The tasty stir-fry hit the spot, so well that both women took an extra helping. As Lacy crunched into a piece of warm baguette, Kelly mentioned, "Jerome asked me out to dinner tomorrow night. Thought I'd give you a heads-up that you'd be on your own."

Fork in hand, Lacy took notice of the heightened color in Kelly's face. "A thank-you gesture for the home-cooked meal—or something more?"

"Don't know yet. Time will tell," Kelly said, taking another bite. But the upturned edging of her mouth told Lacy more than her words.

Both women made it an early night, each secluding themselves in their room. Comfortably situated on top of her bed, Lacy opened her large scrapbook. It was filled with newspaper clippings and typed research she had accumulated over the years about the bombing in Gladden Hills. She'd traced Stevie's father, Matthew Turner, from Gladden Hills no further than to Traverse City, where his sister lived. There he was reported to have stayed two or more months following the tragedy of his family, and then he had seemingly disappeared off the face of the earth. *People don't just do that without help. Did the FBI give him a different identity?*

Three years ago, she'd tried to convince Matthew's sister she was a close friend of the family and wanted only to talk with Matthew, but she'd gotten nowhere. It was frustrating. When she tried to approach the FBI about what information they had gathered, she'd been repeatedly turned down or put on hold. *Zilch!* So, when Lacy spied that small newspaper article about a district attorney somewhere in Ohio, she'd taken notice. The man had somehow stumbled on information that might have bearing on the cold case bombing in Gladden Hills, Michigan. It was the first real clue in seventeen years.

By the time she'd followed up on the news and was revving up a full engine of steam, the trail went dead again. Lacy found out that an arsonist by the name of Clem Browning, currently serving out a second sentence for arson, was thought to be the one who'd built the Gladden Hills bomb.

The Ohio article reported a private detective had somehow gotten hold of fragments from the exploded bomb and exposed them to new technology methods based on cold case evidence. Two days after the private detective visited the jail to speak with Clem Browning, the detective was viciously struck down by a hit-and-run driver. Shortly following, Clem Browning was mysteriously found dead in the prison laundry. Lacy groaned in dismay and closed her scrapbook.

That district attorney in Ohio who initiated the new research on the old bomb evidence was an anomaly she couldn't figure. Why would he take an interest in a seventeen-year-old Michigan cold case? Her thoughts wandered to Quinn Darling, the new intermediate district attorney in Gladden Hills who was extremely well-versed in the Turner family bombing. Could there be any connection between the two?

Leaving her bed, she gravitated to her upstairs window that overlooked the quiet street below lined with stately older homes. The people or persons behind the bombing had done a great job of cleaning up loose threads, anything that could point a finger in their direction. Was there nothing left for her to find? The headlights of a passing car threw its beams into the dense foliage between two houses, revealing the stark, undeniable form of a man. She jumped back from the window.

Lacy's heart pumped wildly with fear. *Someone is watching this house—watching me?* Moving across to the bed table, she lifted the phone and dialed 9-1-1, asking for the police department. "There's a strange man standing across the street in the shadows staring up at my bedroom window." Her lips thinned at the responding question. "No, I wasn't undressing! Could you send a squad car around to check?"

Turning on the table light, she crossed the room and flicked off the overhead light. She carefully made her way back to the far side of the window and peered out into the blackness. Was he still there? Another passing car told her he'd moved further back, but the outline of his lower torso was still visible. Had he sensed she'd spotted him? In that first brief illumination from the headlights she'd thought she'd seen a large hat on his head, shaped similar to a cowboy hat, though she now doubted it was such. *Who wears cowboy hats in northern Michigan?*

Long minutes passed. *Where is the patrol car? Hopefully they won't come with sirens blazing.* Fewer and fewer cars were moving down the street. Seeing highlights turn the corner at the end of the block and drive down the street, she held her breath. Reflected lights from the house two doors down revealed it was not a patrol car, and Lacy was about to walk away when she saw there was a second car close behind the first. Her eyes darted back to the foliage between the houses.

The oncoming car's highlights were strong, piercing the shadows. She squinted, trying to make out plant shadows from human form. She spotted men's pants just as they turned rapidly from the sudden glare and disappeared into the foliage behind. The second car slammed on its brakes and two uniformed men jumped out into the night, their forms merging into the blurred, distorted lighting of crossed headlights. They too disappeared into the foliage.

Lacy moved into the full window and stared after the forms. Discovering she was a backlit target, she moved quickly from the window and raced out of the bedroom and down the stairs. "Kelly," she called out. "Kelly!" She rounded the base of the staircase and watched the hall as her cousin's bedroom door flew open. They stared at one another in dismay.

The two women stood out on their front porch as others in the neighborhood had migrated to theirs. They'd heard the commotion, seen the lights, and come out to watch the excitement. Kelly stood in the dim lighting, draped in a quilted robe of questionable vintage and vague coloring. She turned to her cousin. "Tell me again, Lacy. You saw this man across the street from our house out your window?"

"Yes," she whispered, "and I want you to keep this to yourself. Tell no one, okay?"

Even in the shadowed darkness, Lacy could see Kelly's troubled, confused expression and hated the fact she didn't feel free to explain completely.

"Why do I have to be so secretive? You saw a prowler, that's all."

"I don't want a lot made out of this incident. I'm a reporter. I write news. I don't want to be the news. My reputation is spread about enough at this point." She wrapped her arms about her, more from nervousness than fear or cold. Yet not for a second did she believe the stranger in the shadows was a random prowler or Peeping Tom.

"All right. I'll play it close to the vest, but this little city still has its small-town mentality. You can't muzzle the neighbors. They're going to wonder why the police are coming to our house." She pointed to the men who had emerged from the foliage across the street and were even now approaching their walk.

Later that night, when the neighborhood was dark and void of light save for the Victorian globe street lights at the end of each lane, Lacy stared blindly toward the locked bedroom window with the lowered blind. The man had gotten away—lost in the intense growth in the vacant lot between the houses. The patrolmen had pursued him all the way through to the street beyond, where he'd disappeared without a clue, but they'd shown enough foresight to record all of the license numbers of parked cars on the street at the random chance one of them didn't belong to local homeowners. It was a long-shot, but a chance they might get lucky.

The bottom line was, the man in the shadows was still out there somewhere. *Will he dare come again now that he knows he's been spotted? No one besides my secret contact supposedly knows the reason I'm here.* She paused to consider the uncanny perception of Quinn Darling before dismissing it as unsupported. *Yet, if no one knows outside of my contact, then it could only mean that my presence is making someone here uneasy.* Drawing the covers close around her, she knew it would be a long time until sleep would come this night.

When Lacy tired of wrestling with endless questions—questions that seemingly had no answers—she finally allowed the concerns of her heart to be lifted in prayer, wondering why she was so slow to learn that it was easier to go to God first. *Too many years of practicing bad habits,* she mused.

*

With too little rest to bolster her sagging energy, Lacy rose early and carried a large thermos of coffee into work on Friday morning. Her sunglasses balanced midway on her nose and her steps varied in steadiness as she entered the lobby area, where she stopped to take a gulp of the strong dark brew from her thermos.

After Jason Gardner had purchased the *Gladden Hills Gazette,* he had established a routine that initiated the necessity of the building being opened two hours earlier each morning than its regular schedule. Lacy decided to make use of that time. The bulk of the building lay silent and dark as she tiptoed lightly past the closed door and lighted office of her boss and settled into her quiet cubicle. His drawn blinds didn't invite company, which was fine with Lacy. It was too early for conversation, and she didn't want to lose a valuable work opportunity.

With the thermos uptilted to her eager lips, Lacy struck the start button on her computer. If she made good use of the extra time this morning, she could take time for her investigating in the afternoon. There were more files to wade through at the courthouse before she looked elsewhere. And she'd been thinking about the old man at the sign-in desk named Nicholas. He'd looked closely at her pass before admitting her to the file room. Did he recognize her name? *Relax, Cottrell, not everyone remembers.*

The woman at the information counter in the courthouse told her that Nicholas had been there for twenty-five years and knew everything concerning those files. She was told to ask him for help, if needed. Lacy had bypassed the idea the day before, but the more she thought on it now, it appealed to her. The man's eyes revealed that there wasn't much he missed in individuals as well.

Nicholas's gaze had lingered long on her features, almost as if lost in thought. And though he didn't appear to be the warmest of individuals, she hoped he might prove helpful. If she asked nicely, just maybe...

Her mouth slid easily into an impish smile. Gulping more coffee, she directed her energy to next week's articles.

When all the lights came up in the building and *Gazette* workers filed through to their respective areas, Lacy noticed the all-too-familiar form of Chloe Camry peering around the partition at her. Lacy motioned the girl forward. In the minutes following, she laid out a simple assignment for the girl and sent her off, troubled by the unnatural brightness in Chloe's eyes. She'd noticed it on several different occasions—a brightness that went beyond exuberance. Too busy to dwell on it, Lacy pushed her concerns aside, focusing back on her own assignment. She had some creative ideas about the subject matter for her next articles.

On her way to the copy machine, Lacy passed Jason Gardner in the hallway talking with Maxine Flanders. "Lacy, a moment, please," he called. She turned and looked from one to the other expectantly.

It was Maxine who spoke. "Would your afternoon schedule allow for a special errand for the paper? It would need to be completed before closing time today."

Her planned afternoon dissolved. "If I can...what is the errand?" she offered, restraining a mounting sigh. Waiting for a reply, Lacy became conscious of Gardner's disturbed gaze. His countenance confused her. Was it something he and Maxine had been discussing? Yet Maxine's expression seemed cheerful enough. The office manager's next comment brought Lacy's attention back to the purposed errand. Maxine's face was alight with an eagerness to share.

"It's come to our attention that there are advance tickets on sale to the Morrison Spaghetti Benefit tomorrow night. Mr. Gardner has decided to purchase tickets for all *Gazette* employees as a symbol of community support. The drugstore is the closest available site. It shouldn't take long to purchase the tickets and return. I've phoned and asked them to set aside a certain number. If you stop by the front, I'll give you a money voucher." She looked out over the busy employees like a proud mother hen.

Lacy was outwardly relieved at the nature of the request. Unsure why she was reluctant to meet her editor's gaze, she countered her feelings with positive action. "That's a very nice gesture. The Morrisons and employees alike will reap a benefit." Her upbeat response didn't quell the uneasiness she'd experienced by the troubled soberness she'd seen in Gardner's earlier expression. She hurried to add, "It will be no problem at all. I was planning on doing some research over at the courthouse this afternoon after lunch."

"Really?" Maxine remarked, her voice filled with curiosity. It added to Lacy's belief that the little major general liked to keep her pulse on who was doing what—and why. When there was no response to her comment, Maxine looked briefly deflated.

"Well, then, I'll just go and prepare that voucher for you," she added wistfully. Her solid footfalls echoed away, leaving Lacy to stand alone with Jason Gardner. Glancing about, Lacy felt most anxious to leave his somber presence. Her nerves tightened in reaction to his mood. Had she simply imagined the subtle nuances?

She would have proceeded on to the copier if Jason Gardner's quiet words hadn't stopped her in place. "Be careful, Miss Cottrell. Accidents can happen in small towns as well as large cities. Cross with the light and keep an open eye. Isn't that what reporters are trained to do, keep an open eye? Try not to ruffle any more feathers."

"Yes, thank you. I promise to cross with the light. But when it comes to ruffled feathers, I can't promise anything." She forced an uneasy smile.

He was definitely acting strange. Was he talking about her encounters at the bank the day before? Everything within her urged her to complete her day's activities.

As she walked away with determination, though, Jason Gardner's parting admonition flashed again. There was an underlying ring of warning. *But a warning about what or whom?* Frustrated, Lacy told herself she was reading too much into his words and manner. *I'm jumping at imaginary shadows.* Crossing at the light was sound advice. It was a known fact that a good number of jaywalkers were struck down by cars in small towns every year. Then again, perhaps that was Gardner's attempt at humor. He was a complicated man, not easy to read.

Especially with those darn glasses, she thought tersely.

*

When the elevator opened to the file room in the basement, Lacy approached Nicholas. From her bag she withdrew a white sack and carefully extended it toward the grizzled, gray-haired man with the fixed frown. "They told me you liked the strudel from Mona's Bakery in town."

The gnarled, wrinkled hands took hold of the white sack without a word. His eyes rose to link with hers. "Is this a bribe, Miss Cottrell? It is Cottrell—Ellie Cottrell? I first saw you years ago at the burying of that little boy and his mother. You haven't changed much, you know. I could never forget those haunting blue eyes. I thought it was you yesterday when you breezed in here and headed for files dating back seventeen years. You're looking for something concerning the explosion, aren't you?"

From the instant she heard the name *Ellie,* Lacy's heart had increased its pace. She'd been wrong when she judged this man to miss little of what occurred in Gladden Hills. He missed nothing! "You remember me? You were at the cemetery, Nicholas?"

"Cooper, Ma'am, Nicholas Cooper." His marble-like eyes peered out at her from beneath heavy, haywire brows. Before Lacy could regroup and answer, he continued, "They've all looked, you know, and nobody's found nothing yet."

Lacy pursed her lips. "Yes, Nicholas, I am bribing you. It's not just your files I want to look into, it's your memory. And there's one thing about searching for something that's been searched for before and failed. All it takes is one overlooked item to bring out the truth."

He regarded her thoughtfully. "I believe those who don't want that truth to come out are still around, Miss Cottrell. Did you ever consider that?" His perpetual frown turned even more so.

Lacy nodded. "Yes, Nicholas, but my course is set. It means a great deal to me. And like the Good Book says, 'My times are in Your hands.' I have to trust in that."

“I suppose, ma’am, though I’ve never put a lot into that myself. I guess I’ve seen too much of life and what men can do. But I’ll try to help you the best I can, though my memory’s dimmed a great deal over the years.” He looked back down at the white bag. “I’ll just put this under the counter so I don’t forget it later.” She saw him take a peek inside.

Lacy smiled. “I’ll go on back and get started. There are files to go through before we get to the questioning stage. That should give you some time to recall incidents.” Noticing his scowl, she added, “Don’t worry about what you can’t remember. Often times, looking back is more illuminating than looking straight on in the heat of emotion and confusion.” Remembering her limited time, she moved toward the files.

Pausing, she turned and regarded the man that reminded her of a wary wire-haired terrier. “Nicholas, if you could concentrate on thinking back to that week of the bombing and perhaps a couple of weeks following, I would like to know who signed in to the file room during that period. If everyone has to sign in, wouldn’t there be records dating back? And if knowledge serves me correctly, wasn’t this basement in the courthouse the only storage area where files were kept at the time?”

The old man scratched his gray head. His hair curled slightly over the edge of his plaid flannel collar. His full bottom lip was partially hidden in his untidy one-inch beard. “That would have been before the new police department and legal office building was built across the way there. Yep, all the files were kept here beneath the old department. See that small elevator on the side wall. It’s not used anymore, but back then it would open into the hallway between the department and the old chief’s office.”

Lacy found herself gravitating back to his desk. “What’s up there now?”

“Offices for aides to some of the judges, I think.”

“But you’re sure that no one uses it anymore at all?” she asked, trying to work this knowledge in with what she knew and a lot of what she didn’t.

“Nope…at least not while I’m here, they don’t. And about remembering who came and went during that terrible time, I might not be able to call them by name, but I know no one who didn’t have authorization never came down here. That takes in a lot of people—the whole police department, the DA, judges, and anybody they signed a pass for.”

She exhaled at the thought of all that could entail. “Could I get a look at the old sign-in book? I know they keep them as part of their records. Things like that are never thrown out.”

Nicholas scratched his chin. “Oh, I expect we got them somewhere—but you’ll need…”

"Authorization—I know," she said dryly. "You round them up Nicholas, and I'll get authorization somehow."

"Miss Cottrell," he said softly, "I remember something that could be important."

Lacy whirled about, staring at him. "What's that, Nicholas?"

His lined features had contorted into a foreboding darkness. It brought an immediate chill to her body.

"I just remembered the last person who asked about that sign-in record book dating back to that terrible time. It was our former DA."

She wrinkled her nose, trying to register the former DA. "Would that have been Judge Shaw?"

"No, ma'am, more recent than that. Ralph Wagner, about seven or eight months ago before that Mr. Quinn Darling came to town. Before Ralph had his *unusual* accident." The word *unusual* was coated with an ominous tone that prickled the skin on the back of her neck.

"Mr. Wagner came asking about the sign-in records dating back seventeen years?" she asked hoarsely, working to get moisture back in her mouth.

"Yes, ma'am, how's your health?" he asked soberly.

"My health is just fine, Nicholas," she replied stiffly. Considering his troubled gaze in silence, she softened her attitude. Nicholas's warning was clear enough, and his expression told her he was afraid for her. Did he know who or what she needed to be careful of?

Trying to shake the new awareness of possible danger, she hefted the files over to the rough table. Pulling her hair back, she twisted it into a knot to keep it out of her face.

After a two-hour span, she admitted her time in the file basement had not been all that productive. Lacy was discovering that investigating was more tedious than doing research for a story. It was a long process of weeding out the unnecessary to find one helpful entry. She left the courthouse, her weariness embodying both mental and emotional stress.

*

Heavy clouds moving inland from Lake Michigan were bringing about an early nightfall. Aware that Kelly was having dinner with Jerome tonight and would probably be home late, Lacy slowly scanned the neighborhood for anything out of the normal. The reminder of the shadow man watching from across the street the previous night caused her to hurriedly close her car door and ascend the porch stairs to the dark house. Having her keys ready, she slipped inside the house, secured the lock behind her, and stood stock still in the entryway. Between the odd way her boss had acted in the morning and Nicholas's ominous remarks of the afternoon, she'd been jittery the whole day.

Lacy turned on as many house lights as possible on the way to the kitchen, where she pulled out enough leftovers to classify as a meal. Afterward, she migrated to Gran's parlor and soon had a nurturing fire ablaze in the fireplace. With a tall thermos mug filled with coffee, Lacy allowed her body to become one with the pliable sofa, where she soberly reviewed the day's events.

She'd learned nothing from the files this afternoon, but information about the former DA had definitely given her something to worry about. Ralph Wagner had obviously stumbled across something significant enough to warrant him pulling out the cold case file and initiating a secret investigation on his own. But someone found out, and now Ralph Wagner was dead.

So how should she proceed? Her plans to keep a low profile had failed. The Morrison article had spotlighted the town's attention upon her as brightly as the Morrisons themselves. *I have to find out the answers before the wrong person finds out why I am here.* She thought of her openness with Nicholas this afternoon. Had she been unwise? *If he talks with someone…?*

But Nicholas was not the type to speak of such things. It was something she knew within herself, a sensitivity she'd developed working at the Chicago paper. Slowly she sipped coffee and watched changing colors in the burning flames dance up between the glowing logs.

Even as the tension eased from her body, Lacy decided to wait up for her cousin. The memory of the prior night was still too vivid to rest easy in this large, old empty house alone. She bit her lip, feeling mixed emotions about going to the benefit for the Morrisons Saturday night. Would her night stalker be there too?

7

A Second Meeting

SATURDAY MORNING, LACY WAS UP CLEANING HOUSE by the time Kelly came in from the office. One glance gave her warning of her cousin's dour mood. Last night's stormy expression had not altered. If possible, it now appeared to be etched in stone, confirming Lacy's speculation that the dinner date with Jerome Collins had ended on a sour note. Her initial inquiry had been coldly ignored, warning Lacy to press no further.

But that was last night. Today she wanted answers. "I have to be straight with you, Kel. Being around you lately has been like crawling in a gorilla cage. What happened last night? You act like a plugged hose ready to burst. I don't know which way is safe to avoid the fallout."

Kelly faced her with a defiant look. "You tell me. *That man* can sell someone a house or talk a squeamish buyer into signing on the dotted line in a heartbeat, but can he open his mouth and tell a woman what she needs to know? Last night was a waste!" She dropped some lemon oil on a clean rag and started scrubbing the finish off the dining room table.

Lacy continued feather-dusting marble-like figurines on a shelf in the dining room. "Easy on that tabletop, or we'll have to have it refinished when you're done oiling. I gather *that man* is Jerry Collins?"

Kelly whirled about and glared at Lacy. "He talked nonstop business from the time he picked me up and entered the restaurant until he dropped me off."

"Really? He talked about all kinds of stuff here at the house. How is he at work?"

Kelly scrunched her face. "Fine, I guess. We talk easy all through the day, but people are coming and going all the time. I don't know what to think. Maybe he's just not interested in me? I must have misread the signals."

"After the way I saw him looking at you across the table in our kitchen last week—no way! And the way you two talked nonstop about everything under the sun. I finally gave up trying to join in the conversation. So tell me, what is different here? What does dinner at our house and your work area have in common?" She watched the slow revelation on Kelly's face.

"Last night we were alone! Well, alone as anyone can be in a restaurant with dozens of tables. Do you think that could be it? The fact we were alone?"

Lacy shrugged. "It might take more time if he is as woman-shy as you claim he is. And it stands to reason if he cares for you that he'd feel even more so when you're alone."

Kelly placed her hands on her lips as if she were thinking on the possibility of Lacy's words. "I guess time will tell."

"I bet the workplace was a little static today," Lacy commented, moving into their grandmother's parlor with the long-handled duster.

"You could have cut the tension with a knife. He kept asking if I was all right," Kelly called after her. "I could have choked him! Sometimes I don't think he has a clue," she muttered, attacking the rest of the table with her cloth.

Lacy tackled the bookshelves first. "Tonight should be interesting at the Morrison's banquet. Is Jerome going?" she countered.

"I really have no idea. I didn't ask him," said Kelly curtly, with a finality that encouraged Lacy to drop the subject.

"Yes…tonight should be very interesting indeed," she murmured.

*

When Lacy was forced to park her car about three lanes out from the Fairgrounds Community Center, Kelly's jaw dropped in shock. "Wow! Look at all these cars in the parking lot, and it's only 6:30 p.m.! Hope they have enough spaghetti."

"I think that's why they offered advanced tickets," said Lacy, opening the car door.

The two women walked into the bright room that rang with the laughter and happy voices of mingling groups. The center was crowded with friends and neighbors of the Morrisons, as well as those in the community who wished to be supportive. *And those who just wished to be thought supportive*, mused Lacy. She spotted Mr. and Mrs. Morrison, sitting at an out-of-the-way table off to the left.

The couple spoke with all the well-wishers who stopped by their table, but it was obvious they were dazed and somewhat uncomfortable with being the center attraction for the evening. Noticing Kelly was caught up in conversation with a group of people who'd entered the building behind them, Lacy lightly touched her cousin's arm and indicated to her she was going across to the Morrison table.

As she came near, the Morrisons stood to their feet and shook her hand so vigorously it tingled. A broad-shouldered, square-faced man with light, thinning hair and bright blue eyes stood with them. He was introduced as the Morrisons' pastor, Kurt Jaminson. His direct gaze held warmth and humor, and something extra Lacy couldn't readily determine. She liked him instantly.

While many moved through the long food line, the four of them sat talking at the table. Lacy learned their small congregation was moving their center of worship that next weekend from a local school into a vacant church. "The church is within our means to rent for six months. We feel the Lord will show us in that period what He has in store for our young congregation. If we continue to grow as we have this last year and a half, perhaps we will consider purchasing the church. We're renting with an option to buy." The pastor's face was alive with anticipation, the excitement of the coming venture.

Pastor Jaminson glanced over at the growing line. "I need to join my family, or I'll lose my place in line. I've had Mary Hanson's spaghetti's sauce, and I'm not about to miss it for anything," he said, chuckling. He nodded at Lacy. "It was good to meet you, Miss Cottrell. It was a fine article you wrote. If you're in the market for a church family, we'd love to have you visit us. With strong shoulders and God's grace we'll hold Sunday services in our new home a week from tomorrow."

"What church are you renting, Pastor?" she asked, toying with the idea of giving the young church a try.

"It's the old Free Methodist Church outside of Gladden Hills on County Rd. 10, past Madison Orchards. I believe there's a cemetery behind it. Do you know of it? If not, I'm sure someone can give you directions."

Lacy tensed but quickly regained her composure. "Yes, I know of it. I'm glad it's going to have the sounds of hymns and good preaching stirring the dust in its old rafters again. Those bats have long needed a good stirring."

"Bats?" he questioned. "They never told me about bats. I hate bats!" His face clouded with concern. "They're rats with wings! This is clearly going to be my thorn in the flesh."

The Morrisons joined Lacy in laughter as the pastor waved farewell. Seeing two of the kitchen staff approach with complimentary dinners for the Morrisons, Lacy politely excused herself and looked around to find Kelly. She spotted her cousin midway in line frantically waving to her. When she stepped neatly behind Kelly, she saw Eric Greer heading in their direction and groaned inwardly.

Nudging Kelly, Lacy whispered, "You talk to him. I don't feel very civil toward him right now."

Kelly looked mildly irritated.

Lacy searched the faces of the crowds for help and saw Jerome making his way from the doorway and threading his way through the crowd. Had he spotted her and Kelly as well?

As the line inched forward, Eric cut through the line to stand before the girls. "Evening, ladies," he said confidently. His smooth smile showed perfectly lined teeth. He was dressed in a suit jacket as if he'd just come from work, though the bank closed at noon on Saturday. The only effort he'd made toward casual attire was an open dress shirt and the noticeable absence of a tie.

Lacy pressed forward. "You're going to eat spaghetti in a tan silk suit—unbelievable!" She stared at him.

"I eat with a fork, Miss Cottrell, not my fingers," he replied, the lines around his mouth drawing tight. "I try to look my best wherever I go."

"It presents a better impression for the bank, I would assume," said Lacy wryly.

Kelly nudged her cousin hard in the side. "I'm glad you were able to make it," she said nervously.

At that moment Jerome arrived by Kelly's side. With a flick of her eyes his way, Kelly said with a heavy dose of sweet, "It's always good to see you, Eric. Would you like to sit with us at our table?" Turning to acknowledge Jerome's presence, Kelly smiled sweetly at him as well. "Jerome, you'll sit with us too, won't you?"

Both men looked briefly taken aback, but Eric responded immediately. "I, for one, would love to." He peered behind them in line, and the big, unshaven man glowered. Eric frowned in irritation. "I better stake out a place in line. You girls grab a table when you get through the line, and I'll find you." He appraised Jerome with a cool scan, then hurried away.

Jerome centered his gaze on Kelly, his expression obviously confused. He shifted to study the growing line. "You'll probably be finished eating by the time we're through the line."

"We'll eat slowly," Kelly promised.

"That went smoothly!" Lacy said in a cutting tone, watching Jerome's easy gait carry him across the room instead of to the end of the line. Had he decided it wasn't worth it to try, with Kelly's mixed reception? "What were you thinking?" seethed Lacy through clenched teeth. "That man is impossible! He invented the word *arrogant.* Dinner is going to be a blast. I claim Jerome. You can entertain Eric."

Kelly lowered her head. "I know. Give me a break. I don't know what came over me. When I saw Jerome coming across the room, my head raged with all those feelings from last night. Next thing I knew the words were coming out. You gotta help me out here." She sighed, looking pathetic.

"I can tell you what happened. You saw a chance to make Jerome jealous. Take it from me that approach rarely pays off the way you expect it."

Kelly slumped, appearing even more miserable.

"And in regard to Eric, I can't promise anything. You saw how that man affects me."

"Well, grit your teeth," Kelly hurled back. "We have to get through this somehow. It's only one meal."

Lacy continued to glower. Their place in line was nearing the food counter when she thought she saw Judge Shaw enter the building accompanied by two other men, all dressed in everyday slacks and casual sport shirts. The judge was wearing dark red plaid and a Western hat. Seeing that hat brought back the incident two nights earlier. The stalker had been wearing a hat similar to Judge Shaw's. She'd forgotten to mention that detail to the patrolman. Maybe because her view had been too distorted to be absolutely certain. Surely he hadn't been the one in the shadows.

When they finished passing through the food line, the two women turned to search out a place to sit down. All of the large tables were occupied by people in varying numbers. The women were deciding on a table when they caught sight of Jerome waving them toward a distant table in the corner nearest the outside door. They hurried to where he indicated five available places and quickly lowered their trays to stake their claim.

"Whew," said Lacy, purposely sitting on the left side of Jerome. "How did you get through the line ahead of us?" she asked as Kelly situated her table service on the right side of her boss.

Pushing his dark-rimmed glasses up on his nose, he grinned, a small, little-boy impish grin. "My aunt is one of the helpers in the kitchen, and she ushered me through."

"It pays to have contacts in high places." Lacy chuckled, amused to think of Eric still waiting in line.

"Small-town contacts always include family," added Kelly. Pressing her lips, she loaded her fork and glanced at Jerome. "Look, Jerome, sorry I've been a little testy today. I'd rather not explain, so if it's all the same..." She lowered her eyes.

Lacy wasn't able to hear Jerome's reply for subsequent comments as she silently blessed her meal. Looking up, she sighed. Every time those two got together, the rest of the world ceased to exist. But she was glad Kelly had cleared the air with Jerome. Her cousin's black mood was intolerable.

Testy didn't cover it, she thought, wadding a large forkful of comfort food into her waiting mouth. Noting a tight group of people in Western garb entering the building, she almost choked. "What's with the group of cowboys?" she asked hoarsely.

Jerome broke off his conversation with Kelly long enough to peer in the direction Lacy indicated. "Oh, that would be the Kerrigan spread. Harriet and Sam Kerrigan run an all-purpose working ranch, horse boarding and therapy included in a dude bed-and-breakfast. You name it, and they've got it covered. I recently sold them extra acreage to expand."

"I thought I saw Judge Shaw walk in with a Western hat a few minutes ago. Is there a connection?"

"Some townspeople board horses at the Kerrigans' ranch. There's also a registered riding club in the area. Rumor has it that the judge originally came from Wyoming, so I wouldn't be surprised if he was a member of the club." Jerome's interest returned to his plate.

Lacy thought back to the night of the stalker—how she had doubted there were people in Gladden Hills, Michigan, who wore cowboy hats. *Little did I know,* she mused, canvassing each of the Western-clad individuals. The Kerrigans were of small statue and easy to pick out. They looked like congenial people. Lacy hurriedly tried to memorize each face of the ranch hands standing with the Kerrigans. She'd hold their likeness in her mind for a season, in case she might need to compare them to a certain skulking face hiding in the shadows of her neighborhood. *It wouldn't be unheard of for one of them to be moonlighting—no pun intended.*

Jerome worked on his bowl of coleslaw, pausing to regard Lacy. "Well, have you found yourself caught up in feelings of déjà vu yet? Sadly, I've never gotten away from them." His brow wrinkled.

"The unanswered questions, you mean?" She leveled a probing look. Jerry Collins' attachment to Stevie had bordered on worship when they were children, and Lacy had the feeling his nature ran strong to the theory "loyal unto death"—maybe beyond. Thus far, Jerome still rated high on her list of prospects for her mystery contact.

"I'm a man who likes *I*'s dotted and *T*'s crossed and closure when it comes to questions." Jerome's hazel eyes were intense.

Although the Fairgrounds Center was a large room, the increased crowd intensified the temperature, causing Lacy to empty her glass wishing for more. She scanned for the drink table. "Save my spot, guys, I'm going for a refill. Don't let Eric take my chair." She charged Kelly with a look that told her she didn't want to come back and find him sitting next to her.

Their eyes connected. "Got it. Guard her chair, Jerome," Kelly ordered.

Jerome's sandy-hair fell across his forehead as a smirk creased his features. "Got it!"

Threading her way toward the drink table, Lacy slowed her steps upon seeing her boss, Jason Gardner, standing a few feet to the right side of the table conversing with Michael Quinn Darling, replacement DA. Hesitating to approach, she wondered what connection they might have, if any. Lately, she found herself questioning even the arrival of the mail carrier. Squaring her shoulders, she walked with confidence to pour a glass of iced tea.

As she approached, both men turned her way. To her surprise, Quinn Darling actually managed a smile. "Miss Cottrell, I was just sharing with Mr. Gardner that he should be proud of his editorial staff. You did a darn good job bolstering the efforts of the benefit for the Morrisons."

Her eyes canvassed Gardner's impassive face as he sipped a cup of coffee, then swung back to Quinn Darling. "Thank you, Mr. Darling. I only hope it's enough to save the 'family farm,' so to speak." She restrained a giggle, then rushed to explain. "Sorry, saving the old family farm sounded too much like the old 1920 movie where Simon Lagree was out to steal the family farm from a young, defenseless woman. Though, in this sense, Simon Lagree is the cold, impartial working of the bank's bureaucracy," she stated with conviction.

Darling chuckled. "Careful, Gardner, Miss Cottrell will be running for office on a platform against the evils of cold bureaucracy."

"Having passion for a good cause is not a bad trait, Mr. Darling. I'd vote for her," said Gardner.

Lacy blushed at her emotional display of fervency. Shooting her boss a grateful look, she lifted the cool tea to her heated lips.

"If you'll excuse me, Gardner, I'd like a private word with your reporter," said Darling, all signs of the light bantering instantly vanishing.

Jason Gardner lifted his coffee cup in a salute and moved off toward a group of *Gazette* employees a short distance away.

Darling touched Lacy's arm and drew her further from the table as people flocked there for drinks. "What is it, Mr. Darling?" Her body tensed.

Lowering his head, he spoke in low tones. "I was looking through a stack of police reports yesterday afternoon and discovered an answered call to your residence. "You reported a stalker watching your bedroom window from across the street?"

Lacy swallowed. "Yes. Everything I know should be in the report. I have no idea who it was or why they were there." She looked around to make sure they weren't being overheard.

He raised his eyes. "Perhaps your return to Gladden Hills has triggered a response…either that or you have a secret admirer, Miss Cottrell. I suggest you proceed with caution and call me if something suspicious is in the wind."

Her eyes narrowed. "Why you and not the chief of police?"

"Because I know what possible factors are involved. If I think the chief of police is needed, we'll both call him in…understood? I've noticed an underlying current in town that is disturbing."

"What current is that, sir?"

He pressed his lips into a thin line. "Always the reporter, Miss Cottrell?"

"Not really," she hurriedly replied. "I was just wondering if this current you've noticed might play into the whole picture."

"We'll see, Miss Cottrell. We'll see." He started to turn away.

"Mr. Darling, I did find out that your predecessor, Mr. Wagner, was looking through the old files in the timeframe of the bombing shortly before his *unfortunate* death." Her emphasis on *unfortunate* was rewarded with a stabbing look.

"You'd do well to keep that information to yourself," he whispered. "Be extra careful, Miss Cottrell. You're getting the idea of what is at stake."

"Call me Lacy, Mr. Darling. What do you know about purple feathers?" She chanced the comment for a reaction.

His face screwed up. "Purple feathers? What are they connected with? I've not heard of them." He stared at her with marked curiosity.

"Forget it, it's nothing," she mumbled, moving toward the drink table for a second refill. Her grilling session had increased her thirst. Balancing her full glass through the pressing crowd she nearly bumped into Jason Gardner carrying his loaded tray.

Gardner scanned the area, looking bewildered. "Lacy! Do you know where I might find an empty chair? This place is a zoo!"

Seeing Jason Gardner out of his element brought out her protective strain. She grinned and motioned with her hand. "Follow me. There was an extra place at my table, but I can't promise it's still there." She led the way to the far side of the room, increasingly amazed at the crowd who'd come out to support the Morrisons.

When they reached the table, she first noticed the addition of Eric Greer seated to the right of Kelly, whose pained expression told it all. Lacy felt a wave of relief that he hadn't taken the seat next to her. Amazingly it was still available. Jason Gardner set his tray down and nodded to Jerome, who nodded in return, his jaw lightly agape. "You brought a friend?" Jerome asked as Lacy took her seat.

"He followed me home," she said, grinning. A fast glance at Gardner caught his appreciative response. She watched him remove his dishes from the tray and arrange them in order, wasting no time before diving into the hefty plate of spaghetti with a gusto that gave her pause. Grabbing the salt and pepper set to her right, she passed them over. "I bet you skipped lunch today?"

Folding a piece of toasted garlic bread in two, he looked up at her. "No time. I had a lot to take care of." He took a huge bite of the bread. "Good," he commented around the mouthful.

She agreed. "The sauce is excellent. Do you know Jerome Collins, the guy on my right?" She pointed to Jerome, who was soberly watching Kelly and Eric converse.

"We were introduced at a Chamber of Commerce meeting a couple of months ago. He has a great vision for the community."

"Yes," Lacy said quietly. "He just has a little trouble narrowing his focus."

A small smile crept across Gardner's face. "Oh, I don't know. I'd say he is pretty focused right now." He kept his voice low.

Turning, Lacy could see Jerome's unhappy expression. With Eric commanding Kelly's attention, he no doubt felt like a fourth wheel on a tricycle.

Lacy edged close to Jerome. "Why don't you take pity and ask her to take a walk?"

"Me?" he asked, incredulously. "Now?"

"Yes, *you*, Jerome. I'm certainly not going to do it." She spied a paper dessert plate with some kind of yummy cream pie in front of her tray. "When did that arrive?" she asked, feeling prospects for the night improving.

"They brought pie around a few minutes before you returned, in case anyone missed it in line. When I told them you'd be back, they set it in front of your place. " Jerome wasn't taking his eyes off Kelly. "You really think she might take a walk with me?" His voice sounded unsure.

"You'll never know if you don't ask. Women aren't mind readers, Jerome. You have to tell them how you feel. They like to feel special. Talk to her."

He turned to Lacy. "Kelly invited him to sit at the table."

"She was being polite, Jerry. Plus she does stupid things sometimes—we all do. It's stuffy in here. See how flushed her cheeks are. A little air would do her good." She nudged him.

Jerome stood. Was he going to bolt? Instead, he announced, "I'm going outside to get some air. Would you like to join me, Kelly?"

Kelly swallowed her last piece of pie, her eyes wide with the shock of Jerome's invitation. "Ah, sure, I'd love to. It's quite warm inside." Turning to

Eric, she said softly, "You will excuse me, Eric. It was so good to see you here tonight. I'm sure the Morrisons appreciate it as well." Extracting her jacket from the back of her chair, she stood and faced Jerome in readiness to leave.

Eric sipped his drink. "I told you I'd be here the other day." Then, suddenly aware of what was occurring, he looked up. "Hold on there. Are you coming back inside soon?" He appeared perplexed, as if not understanding how someone would willingly leave his company.

"Certainly!" Kelly swiveled to give him a reassuring smile.

Lacy was lifting the dessert plate to position it in front of her when her fingers felt something attached beneath the paper plate. *Maybe it's a number for a door prize?* Seeing Eric rise from his chair, she swiftly intervened. Anything to distract him from preventing Kelly from leaving with Jerome.

She pointed her fork at the young banker. "I see you here, Eric, but thus far, I haven't seen your boss, Conrad Heywood. Is he also planning to make an appearance tonight in support of the community effort?" She adopted a wistful, innocent expression as she licked cream from her fingers…purposely detaining Eric to give Kelly and Jerome some time together.

Lowering himself to his seat, Eric stiffened his chin. "The bank felt that one representative from management was sufficient for a show of support tonight," he said curtly. He watched Kelly walk through the outside door with Jerome.

"Doesn't the bank management get tired of merely making a show of support, Eric?" she chided gently, knowing it would irk him further.

"Your remark was a shade snide, Miss Cottrell. You might give us the benefit of the doubt and assume we are sincere in our support, especially if any mention of it is made in your column." Eric peered past Lacy and zeroed his focus in on Jason Gardner. "I would hope as owner of the paper, Mr. Gardner, that you have some control over your reporters. I am here in good faith tonight, and I expect for it to be related that way."

Lacy forked a smooth bite of banana cream pie into her mouth while Gardner wiped the edges of his mouth free of tomato sauce. Pushing up his dark glasses, Jason eyed Greer. "Don't be a jackass, Greer! No one is planning on maligning you or the bank in the paper. If you'd been reading our publication, you might have noticed we don't make a practice of dealing in that type of press. Relax and enjoy your dinner. It's good stuff."

Lacy gulped down some tea and stole a glance at her quiet employer. She'd never have expected such a retort from him. A similar glance caught Eric with his mouth still open, and she felt a tad of sympathy. Clearly he'd not been anticipating such a comeback from Jason Gardner.

Pretending she was invisible, Lacy concentrated on the attached paper on the bottom of her plate and edged her forefinger beneath the plate and pried it loose. She drew it under her palm into her lap and slipped it from there into her purse. Secrecy was always more prudent when in doubt.

Greer threw down his napkin. "Look. I haven't been imagining your new reporter's overt manner of dealing with people, and she's shown her ability to sway public opinion. Just look around at the mass of people who've shown up tonight. Miss Cottrell's attitude toward me at our first meeting lacked in congeniality, to say the least, and I simply want it understood I don't want to be under the attack point of her pen."

Lifting a tall glass of tea, Gardner took a long drink. Flabbergasted at Greer's slanted comment, Lacy opened her mouth to retort Eric's negative review of their first meeting until Jason's hand rested on her arm, staying her.

Calmly, he lowered his glass. Angling his head toward Eric, Jason replied, "I heard all about that encounter between you and Miss Cottrell. If I'm not wrong, wasn't it in the center of the bank's main business area? Very indiscreet, Eric. General opinion favors Miss Cottrell. Admit it. What really bothered you was the fact she didn't cow to your impressive intimidation tactics like most do. You were not misused—just checkmated. Let it go and try your dessert. It's equally as good as the spaghetti. You came to a congenial social, Eric. Act accordingly."

Pushing away from the table, Greer stood and picked up his tray. "I don't believe I'll have any pie, thank you. I find the conversation not conducive to genteel dining. Tell Kelly good-bye for me. I'll call her and explain later."

The air was brittle as he went by. Gardner swiveled toward Lacy. "Eric might be a bore, but he could be a formidable enemy in the future. I backed you tonight but soft-pedal your dealings with him."

"I didn't note you making a lasting friendship, Mr. Gardner," she said with a touch of irony, seeing the very top of his brows rise at her comment.

"Like I said, I backed you. I always back my people if they're in the right. Try a little diplomacy in the future, Cottrell. I'm not so worried on my level. We're on too many committees together. Besides, Greer's basic need is to cater to people who might sway public opinion. Could be you may see a softening in the future. If that happens, watch your backside. If he thinks he can attack you and not be personally blamed for it, he'll take that chance."

Gardner's caustic remarks caused Lacy to consider her actions in light of his words. In an effort to protect Kelly from Eric's advances, she might have made an enemy she didn't need right now. Especially in lieu of what she was working on, especially in light of the night stalker's appearance two nights earlier. "I'll watch my step, boss. Thanks for the support," she said soberly.

"Accepted. Keep focused, Lacy. Your cousin doesn't need you playing Cupid. She and Collins will work it out." He stood. "Great meal! I'll go by and pay my respects to the Morrisons before leaving. See you on Monday morning. Call if you need me." He picked up his tray and walked away.

"Bye." She waved, musing on the fact this boss of hers didn't miss a thing. *Those darn glasses throw me every time. I'll have to be careful in the future to not underestimate him.* Gardner was a powerful man, and Lacy liked the way he'd stood up for her tonight. It reminded her of someone else who had been like that. It was hard to be in Gladden Hills and not think of Stevie in every situation. Her desire to learn the truth about his death was stronger than ever.

Lacy looked around at the vacancies on either side of her and sighed. She was stuck until Kelly and Jerome returned. Suddenly she was very tired and would have loved to go home to a hot bath. Then she remembered the attached paper on the bottom of her dessert plate that was now in her purse. As she opened the last fold, a small purple feather dropped into her lap.

Snatching it up, Lacy slid the tiny object into a small pocket within her purse, her heart beating faster. She remembered that particular feather. She had picked it because it was so small and cute. First scanning for any unwanted observers, she then read the paper: *Follow the money trail from the very beginning….* The words were printed from a computer unlike the fast scroll on the note in the cemetery. Yet this note had also been accompanied by a purple feather—one she'd dyed herself.

"More tea, Miss Cottrell?" a pleasant voice above her asked.

Lacy's head jerked upward. "Wendy? How nice to see you." She checked her glass. "No thanks, Wendy. I've drunk enough to be water logged. I see you volunteered your services tonight."

"Yes. It was a good cause, and I figured they could use some experienced help." Her gaze strayed a few tables over. "I see Mr. Darling is eating by himself as usual. Maybe I'll just go offer him some tea. See you later, Miss Lacy."

Lacy observed the pleased expression on Quinn Darling's face as Wendy approached his table. When the usually serious DA offered the pert waitress an opportunity to sit next to him in an empty seat, Wendy lowered her pitcher of tea and slid into the seat. The enrapt look on the young woman's face was a picture to remember. *So that's the way the wind blows….* They might have seemed an unlikely couple, if Lacy hadn't already discovered what a remarkable young woman Wendy truly was. And it appeared Quinn was discovering the same.

Lacy mused on all of the stories developing around her— mysteries, love stories, and human compassion. She'd never noticed all those happenings when she lived in Chicago. Surely they'd existed, but she'd been focused primarily on high-profile crime stories deemed worthy of print, week to week. It was her job. Was that really living? Resting her elbows on the table, she leaned her head on her hands. It amazed her that the lives of all these people were intertwined. This roomful had come out to encourage their neighbor.

Small-town living was giving her time to know people and see individual worth, even to care about them. In Lacy's situation, she wondered if that was good or bad. It might hinder her focus. Jason Gardner warned her about keeping focused, though he hadn't any idea what all she was involved in—or how high the stakes were.

Kelly and Jerome returned. "Where's Eric?" asked Kelly, staring at Lacy accusingly. "What did you say to him to make him leave?"

"It wasn't me," she fired back. "The man leads with his chin." She felt a small pang of guilt, remembering how she had prodded him on.

Sighing, Kelly asked, "Who, then?"

"My boss. I think he called it a checkmate. Not to worry. Eric promised to call and explain his hasty departure. You lucky girl." She forced a grin.

Kelly shot a distressed look at Jerome. "Lacy, are you ready to go?"

"Yeah, I just have one question. Who brought the pie to our table? Anyone notice?"

Kelly gave her a blank look. "I have no idea." She glanced at Jerome.

Jerome's hands rested in his pockets. "One of the women who was working in the kitchen. She was about five-foot-five, gray-haired, about sixty, and carried a large tray of pie slices around to tables. Why? Something wrong with your pie?"

"Pie was great!" Lacy said, distracted. How had her contact managed to get that message beneath her piece of pie? She stared hard at Jerome. He could easily have attached that folded paper to the bottom of her dish. If he did, why was he being so secretive? "Did anyone sit at my place or tamper with my pie plate?" she asked, drilling him for answers.

Jerome's curious gaze met her question without flinching. "You're asking if anyone tampered with your pie? No one touched your plate. What are you getting at, Lacy?"

His confused forthrightness took her aback. If Jerome Collins was lying, he was doing a bang-up job. His gaze never veered an iota.

She shrugged. "It's not important. Let's go."

Jerome exchanged a concerned glance with Kelly. None of the three spoke a word until they parted in the parking area. Following a simple good-bye, each headed for their respective cars. On the drive home, Kelly acted agitated. "You want to tell me why you got so weird back at the Center? What was all that gibberish about someone tampering with your pie? There's something going on with you, Lacy."

Lacy knew she was stuck. "It's nothing, really. I found a folded note on the bottom of my pie plate. I was simply trying to find out who might have put it there," she answered calmly.

Kelly laughed. "Somebody left you a love note, I bet. Two men approached me tonight and asked who you were and if you were married. I refused to introduce them or give them your phone number. Come on…tell me what the note said," she teased.

At last Lacy saw a way out of the situation. "Actually, I'd rather not. It's silly, and I don't bother with people who won't approach me personally," she lied, glad that Kelly had assumed an alternate reason for the note. Lacy was anxious to get home and have time to consider the real message: *Follow the money.*

What money, and how did it play in the bombing?

8

Unsettling Interactions

LACY WAS ON HER SECOND CUP OF COFFEE SUNDAY MORNING when Kelly wandered sleepy-eyed, clothed in pajamas and the same nondescript faded blue robe, into the kitchen. Squinting up at the kitchen clock, she asked Lacy, "How long have you been up...and why so early? I'd think you'd be hugging your pillow after the week you just put in." Yawning, she shuffled to the coffee pot and lowered a mug from the cupboard above.

Lacy sipped more coffee. "I have lots to think about." Watching her cousin circumvent the chairs to balance an overly full cup of coffee, she sighed. "When was the last time you bought a new robe, Kelly?"

Kelly eased into the closest chair and focused dreamily on the dark liquid in her steaming cup. "First, I suck the warmth through the cup to warm my hands, then I down it quick to heat up my insides and open my eyes—*amazing brew!*" Then her face sobered. "Grant bought this robe for me before he deployed to Afghanistan. He said it matched my eye color."

"You're due a new one. It no longer matches your eyes. I don't think Grant would mind," she added softly.

"Maybe next Saturday afternoon we can do a little shopping. I just never think to go. It's no fun alone, and most of my friends are busy with families on the weekend. My closest friends have all moved away." She lifted the mug with both hands and sipped slowly, looking increasingly depressed.

"Next Saturday it is. We'll go together," Lacy said brightly. "I've also been thinking of getting back to church. I met Pastor Jaminson last night. He's the Morrisons' pastor. Considering the kind of people they are, I thought I'd try the church. The congregation is moving into the vacant church outside of town. Wanna come with me next Sunday?"

Kelly rose from the table for more coffee and a breakfast roll. "Why not? I'm tired of feeling like a hypocrite whenever I say grace. You know, I think you coming back to Gladden Hills was ordered by God."

Lacy stared down at her empty cup. "I think the verdict may still be out on that subject." She only hoped the main reason she was in Gladden Hills was of God. If not, she might be in real trouble. Not overly thrilled she was searching the old files, the DA wanted to know every step she made in her investigation, and Nicholas, the file room attendant, more than hinted she might be in danger. *"How's your health, Miss Cottrell?"* She shivered, remembering his pointed question.

Then there was that subtle message Jason Gardner sent her yesterday. Whatever was that about? But what bothered her most was finding out about the death of the last district attorney. If it wasn't an accident, why were they keeping the fact a secret? Nicholas was the only one who inferred it was arranged. Lacy rubbed her head. She had nothing but shadows, which brought her back to the midnight stalker. She met her cousin's gaze. "Time will tell."

"That it will. At any rate, I'm glad you're back. While I study up on new real estate laws, what are you going to do today?"

"I've got some driving around and thinking to do. I'll put on a pot roast before I leave, and we'll eat later this afternoon."

"Sounds like a plan. Check in occasionally today, okay?"

Lacy grinned. "Worried about me, cousin, or just checking up?"

Kelly rolled her eyes. "I'd feel better if you checked in once in a while. Humor me. After all, if something happened to you, whatever would I tell Aunt Karen and Uncle Paul? 'Sorry, I mislaid your daughter. She went out for a drive and never returned,' " she teased.

"They couldn't keep me corralled; why should they expect you to?" Lacy laughed. "But if it will make you happy, I'll call in," she agreed, carrying her cup over to the dishwasher.

Kelly had always been keenly perceptive, but she'd become more suspicious of Lacy since the night of the stalker. Lacy hoped she'd soon be able to share some of what was going on, but for now it was better to keep things only between herself and whomever was sending the unsigned notes. There were too many unknowns in Gladden Hills.

Lacy thought about the new district attorney, Quinn Darling—the only other person in town who knew why she was here. In an odd way, it made her feel better to know he was around. Not that he might prevent something from happening, but if it did happen, he would know enough to continue searching. Finding the truth was the ultimate goal. She mused on the fact her contact had chosen to remain hidden. *What were they frightened of? Were they involved? If so, how did they know about the feathers?*

The temperate weather they'd enjoyed earlier in the week had taken a radical cold turn. Lacy donned a heavy hooded gray sweatshirt over a red turtleneck. Mid-March in northern Michigan took longer to catch up with spring than did the cities below Clare, "the gateway to the north." She shoved the heater gauge up in her Challenger before she eased out of the drive.

Her gaze sought the narrow lot situated between the two Victorian houses. It was there, betwixt the hanging branches of the two frontal trees, she had seen the long-legged stalker with the Western hat. The image of the Kerrigan Ranch Wranglers as they entered the Fair Civic Building the night before replayed, then was gone in an instant. *Was one of them the stalker? At least two of them fit the physical description.*

For some reason they seemed an unlikely crew from which she'd find her stalker, yet they couldn't be ruled out. Pulling away, Lacy had a definite direction in mind for her afternoon Sunday drive. She began with a slow pass down memory lane, cruising at a snail's pace past the home her family had lived in for the first eight years of her life. The new owners had taken out the three apple trees in the backyard where she and Stevie used to climb and had put in a three-car garage. *Priorities,* she mused. It was never wise to look back.

She sped up and turned two blocks over and down Stevie's former street, coasting slowly, trying to pinpoint where the Turner house had stood before the explosion. So much had changed she was forced to resort to using the Bradford family home as a landmark. Parking across from the houses, she shut off the engine and tried to picture the day before the explosion, when she and Stevie had played on the huge wooden lawn swing set his grandfather had erected in the backyard. Rolling down the window, she placed her folded arms on the sill and rested her head, allowing her thoughts to transport her back in time.

Seventeen years had blurred the events. She now wasn't sure why she and Stevie had been outside swinging. It was a windy, damp day, and she'd been bitterly cold—that much she remembered. What happened before and after they sat on that swing she couldn't picture. Was it possible her recall could have some bearing on the case?

The tree at the back of the old Turner place was still there. The yard swing had sat right in front of it, and sometimes they could touch some of the lower branches if they swung extra high....

Suddenly Lacy was aware of tears flowing down her cheeks. "I miss you, Stevie."

"What are you doing here? Are you spying on me, Miss Big City Reporter?" The voice dripped with disdain...or was it pure hate?

Lacy's temporary trance shattered. Her head banged the top of the car window, and she stared up in surprise at the irate blond in front of her. Cynthia Bradford's twisted features took away from her beauty, but there was no denying what a stunning woman she'd grown into.

"Not everything is about you, Cindy," Lacy retorted. "I honestly didn't even see you standing there." She focused beyond Cindy on the older couple standing outside the Bradford home. They looked in her direction, their expression puzzled. Cindy's sleek BMW was parked in the drive.

"I repeat, why are you parking across from my house? Not only are you upsetting my parents, your presence might qualify as harassment—even stalking."

Glancing again at the curious older couple, Lacy said, "They don't look upset to me. Being a lawyer suits you, Cindy. If you must know, I was reminiscing on the last time I was here, but that time has passed, and it's too chilly to talk over old times." She paused. "Unless you can think back on the day before the explosion."

"The day before...?" Cindy shot her a hard look. "What about it?"

"The police already established what happened the day of the bombing. I have questions about the day before...anything out of the ordinary. Did you see anyone visit, or a van pull up in the drive? You were always watching from between the hedgerow. I visited that afternoon with Stevie but can't remember much. I just wanted to fill in the blanks. It could help give closure."

When Lacy saw the secretive smirk appear at the corners of Cindy's mouth, she realized too late she'd exposed her jugular.

"Oooh, is little Ellie bothered by nasty nightmares? Well, I can't help you. He's dead, and remembering isn't going to help." She flipped her wavy blond hair and turned away. Whirling back, she added sharply, "And don't make a practice of parking on this street, or I will have charges drawn up!"

Bypassing her attitude, Lacy called softly, "Cindy, if the memories come, don't push them away. They might mean something. It's an unsolved case. How do you know whoever was responsible for the bombing ever left town? Try to remember, Cindy. It's important!"

"I was at dance class the entire afternoon of the bombing. There are no memories. Just leave, and take your nightmares with you. Stevie's gone!"

Lacy pulled away from the curb, wondering if Cindy had been honest. Putting *Cindy* and *honest* together had always been an oxymoron, yet people were often the most honest when they were unguarded. Did she have memories but didn't want to give Lacy the satisfaction? Or were her memories as vague as her own? *If Cynthia Bradford has dormant memories, my unexpected visit might jar something to the surface. But what will she do with them?* Lacy didn't hold any illusions about her old nemesis.

Driving up main street past the café and the newspaper office, she turned south down Broadway, about a quarter of a mile out of town, and pulled up at a large building connected to a warehouse, each boasting an impressive sign, reading *The Car Doctor, Master Mechanic, Charles Walden, prop. On call for emergencies—towing large and small.*

Lacy studied the layout of the buildings and parking area. It was an extensive operation, but she wasn't surprised. Chuck had always been aggressive in whatever he did, be it a game or a good fight. Never a great student, his passion was for active, physical, or mechanical work. In a strange way, she was proud of what he had accomplished. Though, after what she'd heard from Jerome about Chuck's rough exterior, she wondered how receptive he would be to questions about the past.

Staring up at the sign, she gnawed on her lip. *Receptive or not, you and I are going to have a little talk, Mr. Chuck Walden—and soon.*

Putting the car into reverse, Lacy backed around to head toward town. She noticed a nondescript gray sedan parked across the street in front of a lunch trailer. *It's Sunday. The lunch trailer is closed.* Her chest tightened as she entered traffic. On the short distance back to town, she peered often in the rearview mirror. The gray sedan was never totally out of view.

Sunday afternoons on Main Street were not exciting by any stretch. Most establishments were closed, and few cars were in evidence going through town. The gray sedan pulled out from behind the vehicle following her car. He'd caught the first traffic light, allowing Lacy a good lead. After a couple of quick turns, Lacy drove up the back side of the *Gladden Hills Gazette* parking structure and pulled into the area behind the large trash containers stored at the side of the lot.

Jumping out of her car, she hurried between the buildings through the alley. Keeping to the side she peered around the corner onto Main Street in time to see the gray sedan rush down the first turn Lacy had taken.

All she could make out was that the driver was tall. The tinted car windows blocked any chance to see his identity. Leaning against the rough, discolored brick, she tried to recall if she had ever seen that particular sedan before but came up dry. Lacy waited to see if the sedan came back through town, and after a reasonable time elapsed, she made her way back to her vehicle. Taking her time driving home, she drove an alternate route and came onto her street from the opposite direction. In so doing, she spotted the gray sedan parked at the far, opposite end of the street. The driver of the gray sedan knew where she lived and had waited for her to return home. Now her initial fear morphed into a galloping rage that superseded all emotions. Lacy was tired of being stalked. It was time to turn the tables.

Hitting the gas pedal, she sped up the street where the sedan was parked and slammed on her brakes. They were bumper to bumper head on. Before Lacy could roll down her window or push open her door, the sedan rocketed into reverse, spun about in a 180-degree spin, and sped away. Her heart pumping against her rib cage, she backed slowly around. Coasting down to the driveway, she pulled up and turned off the engine.

Whoever was following her had driven there to wait for her when they lost contact. Why did they wait?

She slowly opened the car door, wondering what would have happened if she'd not faced the car off at the end of street. *Friend or foe? If I could only have seen through those windows…*

*

Lacy leaned on the front desk across from a bleary-eyed Maxine on Monday morning. "It's not good when the office manager looks as if she stayed up all night with a crying baby," she teased, unable to avoid the temptation to tweak the major general.

The sallow-skinned, red-haired matron peered up at her under heavy, hooded lids. "No baby—my sister! She blows into town every two years and engages me in a nonstop talkathon. She says it's the only way to catch up for missed time. The woman needs only two or three hours of sleep and expects others to do the same. No wonder her first two husbands died. She wore them out." Maxine lifted a Kleenex to her nose and sneezed. "I was fighting a cold before she arrived and lost the battle this weekend." She sneezed again.

"I'm sorry," Lacy said tenderly, meaning every word. "Why don't you take the day off? I'm sure the boss won't mind. He's pretty understanding. He surely doesn't want you to work while you're sick," she encouraged.

Maxine eyed her. "Thanks for the concern, but the Chamber of Commerce is meeting in our conference room this morning, and I'm supposed to set up refreshments for 10:00 a.m. Mona's Bakery is bringing over a tray of mixed confections, and I've got the big coffee maker to set up. It's a lousy morning to feel so rotten! There's no way I can go home." She sneezed again.

"We've got a conference room?" Lacy scanned the area.

Maxine pointed to the partitioned area off to the right of Gardner's office.

"Really? I thought that was a large storage area. Listen, I'm no good with coffee, but if you set it up now and show me, I'll turn it on and serve everything at the appointed time. Chloe can clean up. If we share the work, you can go home. It's no problem."

"It might work. I'll walk it by Jason. Plan on meeting me in the conference room in ten minutes, and I'll show you what to do. I owe you one, Lacy Cottrell. Thanks." Walking away, she held her nose.

"No need to owe me. It's self-preservation." Lacy grinned. "I don't want half the office, including me, sick with your old cold."

Maxine regarded her with watery eyes. "I hope it's not too late. The germs are already in the air, I'm afraid." She waved her hand as if batting off germs, then moved in the direction of Gardner's office.

Lacy instinctively distanced herself. The last thing she needed was a head cold right now. Days were disappearing quicker than she was gaining strides toward knowing what occurred seventeen years ago. Seeing Chloe loitering in the area of Lacy's cubicle, she hastened her steps.

Before Lacy was able to take off her jacket, Chloe thrust two sheets of paper in her face. "I worked on it most of last night," she said, her cheeks bright with overt excitement.

"That was fast work, Chloe. I'll look it over before I leave for lunch today and get back to you. Right now I'd like to ask your help in covering for Maxine this morning."

After she told the girl what would be required of her, Chloe went back to her own work area. She'd been hired to help out wherever needed, running copies, working on the grunt operations that took up valuable time. A quick look at Chloe's cover page told Lacy that proofreading wasn't the girl's strong suit.

After connecting with Maxine in the conference room, Lacy sent the sick woman home with the assurance that the simple task of laying out refreshments for a few city leaders was not rocket science. Back at her work area, Lacy used the next hour to outline a couple of articles for the next publication. She was bent over her desk when she sensed the presence of someone looking over her shoulder. Glancing up, she was startled to encounter the eager face of Chloe Camry.

"What is it, Chloe?" she asked. "I haven't had time to review your article. I have other work. Remember, I told you before lunch." *Is she dimwitted or merely determined to get what she wants?*

The girl's countenance fell. "Oh. I was hoping you'd read it first off." She sighed with disappointment. Then, just as rapidly, her expression changed as if her brain had shifted gears. "I saw you, you know. Last Friday afternoon. I was on an errand for Maxine and I saw you go into the Courthouse." Her eyes grew secretive. "You were there a long time. Were you in the records area looking for material for a story? What are you working on? Will you show me how to do research like that? Maybe I could go with you when you go next time." The requests rolled from her tongue like an odometer on a race car.

In those few seconds, Lacy felt like she was being smothered. Something wasn't quite right with the girl. Chloe was becoming obsessed with shadowing Lacy at work and beyond. Lacy carefully chose the right words. "A reporter keeps what she's working on to herself. You have to understand that. And no, you can't go with me when or if I go the next time. I have a lot of work to do now, and I think it would be better if you went back to your work area."

Chloe clearly didn't take well to being told no. A shiver ran through Lacy. Behind Chloe's gushing schoolgirl manner lay a willful spirit. Suddenly Lacy was sorry she'd offered to work with her at all. She watched the round-shouldered young woman make her way from the cubicle. Yet it wasn't dejection she sensed from the girl's body language, but anger. Lacy debated talking to Maxine about it but decided to wait. She didn't want to cause the girl to lose her job. After all, she was the newcomer to the paper, not Chloe.

*

Lacy was in the throes of setting up the coffee area when Jason Gardner walked through the door carrying a stack of printed material. Glancing briefly in her direction, he pushed up his glasses. "I appreciate you stepping in to cover for Maxine this morning. I'd tried to talk her into leaving earlier, but she wouldn't hear of it. The woman oozes responsibility." He proceeded to the head of the table and laid down a gavel alongside the stack of papers.

"You in charge?" she asked, looking from the gavel to him.

He chuckled. "Only for today, Lacy. I'm stepping in for Dr. Harrbinger. He's the president this year. I'm still looked on as a newcomer."

Lacy considered his logic and dismissed it. "Yet it was you he called to take his place at the meeting—a newcomer?"

"Don't make too much of that, Lacy. Everyone else was busy." His features pinched in a frown as he reviewed one sheet of paper. "Looks like I need to go back to my office." He paused by Lacy's shoulder, reviewing the confections she had begun to arrange on the platter. She could smell his aftershave—a soft pine mixture that gave off a light woodsy smell. She liked it. It wasn't too strong, yet very appealing.

As Jason leaned in closer, she noticed for the first time how strong a profile he had. His high cheekbones were accentuated by the triangular shape of his face with a strong jaw line. Though quiet in his manner, the same pulsating energy was evident that she'd sensed before. It was as if it wrestled to burst out in some form—like a spirited thoroughbred held in check at the starting gate. This thought quickened her pulse and filled her with curiosity.

Ever so subtly, she was aware of wanting to know this man better. There had been little time for men in her life the last few years. Her career came first. What men she had spent time with had either been uninteresting or disappointing. Most lacked the convictions essential in a lasting relationship.

Lifting a delectable powder-sugared confection in his hand, Jason turned, standing very close. "Try this, Lacy Cottrell, and tell me what you think."

Her gaze focused on his dark glasses. Opening her mouth, she bit off the end of the crunchy confection and slowly savored its almond filling. "Yum," she purred. The sound flowed from her mouth like warm chocolate over ice cream. His crooked grin gave her such an odd feeling. *Am I attracted to this man? Is that what I'm sensing?* Confused, she blinked.

He backed away, encompassing the rest of the confection in one bite. "Make a note to order more of these for special occasions." His tone was matter of fact. Then his long legs stretched out, covering the distance to the open door.

Returning to finish her task, her thoughts lingered on Jason Gardner and the gentle way he lifted the confection to her mouth. *Don't get emotionally involved, Cottrell. Remember you're only here for a short while. Don't be an idiot and lay your feelings open to heartache,* she warned the vulnerable part of her that was even now hoping Jason would return quickly, giving them more time to talk before the others began to arrive.

But civic leaders arrived in groups of two or more. Lacy set the last box of goodies off to the side. She gave the entire refreshment area a last appraisal before acknowledging their presence. Almost immediately her eyes connected with the stern countenance of Judge Harold Shaw. He'd entered the room with two others, but when Lacy shifted away from the coffee bar she saw he was staring after her. His handsome features remained unsmiling. Without even a nod, he returned his concentration to his associates.

Jason reentered and raised his voice only loud enough to gain their attention. "Gentlemen, please avail yourselves of refreshments. I can testify to their fresh, most satisfying flavor," he announced, laughing. "Isn't that right, Miss Cottrell? And please thank Lacy for volunteering her busy time to make sure each of you had your mid-morning coffee."

"You're using your new ace reporter to set up coffee, Gardner? Kind of a waste of talent, isn't it?" asked Conrad Heywood, his broad shoulders squaring back as if to show his importance as Gladden Hill's youngest, newly appointed bank president.

"As I said, she volunteered. Maxine is home nursing a bad cold today. Glad you could make it, Connie. I've got some figures to run by you for that community project accepted last month. Could we do that before you leave today?"

"Always happy to help. Eric Greer is here with me, if I happen to prove to be a bit rusty on my codes."

"Doubt that will happen, Connie," returned Gardner. "I don't think anything much ever gets by you."

Heywood laughed.

At the mention of Eric's name, Lacy swung about to see him following Heywood up to the front of the room. His eyes never veered in her direction. *Just as well,* she thought. Even so, she recalled Gardner's admonition to counter her animosity toward the man. *Especially if I'm to figure out what* Follow the money *means in the note.* Still, the concept went against her grain. The man made her bristle simply being near him.

"Mr. Heywood," Lacy called, just loud enough to be heard over the din within the swelling room, "I want to thank both you and Mr. Greer for your helpfulness in clearing up the last of our grandparents' affairs. I speak for my cousin as well as myself. It's a great load off our shoulders."

Conrad Heywood looked slightly startled. "Why—why, that is most kind, Miss Cottrell. And truly that is our highest aim. Eric, here, is one of our up and coming executives. Glad to know he's treating our patrons so well." He nodded proudly at Eric before continuing his prior conversation.

Greer's head snapped around to view Lacy with suspicion, as if he was waiting for an acid follow-up. In contrast, she smiled sweetly at him. Catching the amusement on Jason's face, Lacy walked quietly from the room and returned to her desk to read through Chloe's first attempt at a news article.

Five minutes later she rested her head on her hands and groaned.

"Where to begin?" She mentally kicked herself for getting involved with the girl in the first place. She had written corrections off to the side, but the basic crux of the problem was neatly reviewed at the bottom of the page. Lacy intended to explain personally what she had written. It wasn't so long ago that she'd forgotten how difficult first critiques could be, no matter how well it was presented. Hopefully Chloe's zeal to learn would lend her to take suggestions and use them constructively. Looking at her watch, Lacy bit her lip. It was nearly lunch, and after lunch she was headed to the courthouse.

Lacy caught Chloe's eye and motioned the girl over. Chloe had stayed close, almost perched near Lacy's cubicle all morning. "Chloe, I've finished reading your article, but I'm short of time right now. When I return, we will go over your article together, and I'll explain any suggestions I've indicated on your material. That's how writers learn," she encouraged. Laying Chloe's article with other papers from her desk, she placed them all inside her top drawer, closed the drawer, and stood reaching for her purse. "I do have to leave now. I'm running late. Are you clear on what your duties are concerning the conference room when they break up their meeting?"

Chloe nodded like a bobble-head doll, her eyes fixed hungrily on the top drawer of Lacy's desk. "Yes, ma'am. I clean up the coffee area and refreshments. This afternoon when you get back we will go over my article, right?"

"Right."

"Are you going back to the courthouse today, ma'am?" she asked, her bright eyes demanding an answer.

Her tone put Lacy off. "My afternoon schedule is undetermined, Chloe. You may return to your desk now."

Chloe inclined her head, but not before Lacy caught the defiant flash in her eyes. Lacy resolved to distance herself as much as possible. There was something amiss in Chloe's whole makeup, like a picture slightly out of focus.

*

When she pushed the café door open, Lacy zeroed in on a booth midway up on the left hand side and slid far to the back. She wasn't in the mood for chatty conversation. Removing her spiral notebook from her purse, she laid it on the limited counter area and rested her head on her left hand. She needed quiet to look over the few pages of notes she'd managed to gather on the seventeen-year-old case. There wasn't much. Her pen lay quietly beside the opened notebook as her eyes perused the little she had to go on.

The strongest evidence was the fact someone was stalking her. There were people here who didn't want her back in town...why? Because of her connection with Stevie, or was there a chance they were afraid she might be nosing around? Reporters had bad reps for getting involved where they weren't wanted. So far, the only person who'd voiced an interest in what happened in the past, besides herself, was Jerome Collins...and just maybe that interim district attorney, Michael Quinn Darling. He knew what she was here for and seemed to be watching what she might stir up. Was he using her like a bird dog, waiting to see what flew out of the weeds? It wasn't comforting knowing hunters stood by with guns.

Pottery clinked nearby, and Lacy jumped.

"Hopefully, things aren't as bad as you look, Miss Lacy." Wendy poured a steaming cup of coffee into the heavy ceramic mug and dropped a plastic-covered menu on top of her notebook. "The special today is quite tasty."

Rolling her eyes toward the observant, pretty waitress, Lacy sighed. "It's hard to solve a puzzle when you don't have all the pieces, Wendy. How did your time go with our illustrious Mr. Quinn Darling at the benefit?"

A soft smile settled into place across her finely shaped lips. "He is every inch a gentleman, Miss Lacy. You don't see many of those any more. It surprised him to find out that I'm a student of history. Seems history is one of his passions, especially military. I'll have to read up more on military history. He caught my interest. Did you know he rides motorcycles?"

Lacy was surprised by the unexpected information. "Quinn Darling rides motorcycles...interesting. And you are a student of history? As someone once said, 'There are a million stories in the naked city.' "

Setting the coffee pot on the edge of the booth tabletop, Wendy cocked her head, her blond ponytails bobbing. "I hardly think Gladden Hills qualifies with the wild 'goings-on' as that grand metropolis of New York City. Still, there is much that goes on beneath its calm small-town manner that might cause a body to wonder."

Lacy scanned the sparsely populated café. Fifteen minutes from now there wouldn't be an available chair or booth. "Such as...?" Her tone was quiet but intense, and she could sense the easy manner of the waitress grow wary. While Wendy wasn't above passing on entertaining news bits, clearly she was aware that wasn't what Lacy was asking.

After glancing around the room, Wendy seemed to make up her mind about something. She lowered her head. "Such as late meetings in the office building of Morgan Streeter across the street, and the fancy cars that first turn off their lights before they drive into his back parking lot. I covered for Sam in the kitchen one night when his wife was sick. It was late, almost midnight, when I locked everything up. Because of the bushes and such, I was only able to make out one car of the assorted high-end vehicles that pulled into that parking lot behind his building, but there were as least four of them and the lights shining out the back windows of the building were bright and carefully shaded. It made me wonder some, but lawyers are always doing sneaky things, so I didn't pay much attention at the time."

"Was Cynthia Bradford at that meeting?" asked Lacy nonchalantly. Knowing Cindy as a girl, it wasn't difficult to assume she'd naturally be part of a clandestine appointment.

"No. But Eric Greer was." Her eyes were steady.

"Really! That's interesting. But how can you be so sure Miss Bradford wasn't there?" prodded Lacy.

"Because I'd seen Ms. Bradford earlier during the lunch crowd and overheard part of her conversation. She told someone in the booth that she was leaving for an out-of-town meeting as soon as she finished with lunch. What's more, she said she'd be gone until the weekend."

As the bell on the café door tinkled lightly, a cool breeze from the street wafted toward them.

"Speaking of the devil," murmured Wendy. Straightening, she flashed a sunshine smile. "Pick any seat you fancy, Mr. Streeter. I'll bring you hot coffee in a flash, and I'll put in an order for the usual," she called.

Too late Lacy turned her face away from his line of vision. His rich, baritone rang across the tile-floored building, "Lacy Cottrell! The darling of Gladden Hills. After the success of Saturday night's benefit, I do believe you could safely run for your office of choice next fall." His smooth glide made straight for her. Lacy was caught. She closed the cover of her notebook.

"I'll bring you the special. You'll love it." Wendy hastily moved away to check on her other customers.

Streeter eased himself down across from her and lowered his voice. "What an opportunity. Having lunch with the most sought-after lady in town. What's the chance of dinner at a nice restaurant in the near future—tomorrow maybe?" His teasing tone changed to a soft, intimate invitation. "You interest me, lady, as no one has in a long, long time." He ignored the menu that lay on the tabletop.

Lacy sucked in a breath. He was a dangerously handsome man, and she wasn't sure she had the experience to parry his skillful advances. His eyes, his voice, even his body language told her he was sincere in his attraction. That, paired with his amazing good looks, was a lethal combination. If he'd come on to Cindy Bradford like that, no wonder she'd acted so possessive of him in the bank when they'd met.

Lacy took her time responding, praying for heavenly wisdom. "And you, Mr. Streeter, are a force to be reckoned with! If I had the money, you could probably sell me a condo in the middle of a cow pasture in Iowa."

His brow wrinkled. "You doubt my attraction to you?"

"No, Morgan," she answered, "I just think our timing is all wrong. I'm here for a short time only, a leave of absence from the Windy City. I wanted to see what small-town news had to offer. When my family left, I carried this town in my heart for a long time, and I needed to get it out of my system." Everything she said was true...but not complete.

"There's no reason we can't take advantage of the time you're here. You might find a reason to stay." Morgan's expression was wistful, like a small boy at the circus.

"Perhaps, but right now I'm swamped. When I get caught up, who knows, maybe?" She left the hint of a promise, and she wasn't sure why. Was it personal, or did she feel she might use the connection between them at a needy time? Lacy's thoughts were too scrambled to rightly discern. *Morgan wasn't part of what happened seventeen years ago. There's nothing to indicate he had any part in the undercurrent evils of Gladden City. Just because he's a partner of Cynthia Bradford doesn't make him the enemy, does it?*

The instant recall of Wendy's late-night observation of clandestine meetings brought back the doubts. Still, the meetings could be perfectly innocent, like secret mergers of corporations. Morgan Streeter was a lawyer. Her eyes clouded when she remembered Eric Greer had also been present.

His hand reached across, his fingers barely touching the ends of hers. "I'll hold you to that maybe." His look was earnest. Glancing at his watch, he inhaled. "I'm running late. I'll have to pick up my order and head out to my next meeting. I'll take a rain check on lunch, Lacy Cottrell." He flung her a parting smile.

Morgan left as quickly as he'd arrived, and Lacy discovered she'd been holding her breath during most of their encounter. She turned, grateful to see Wendy approaching with a lunch platter.

Lowering the plate to the tabletop, Wendy followed Morgan's hurried departure. "Watch your step with that one, Miss Lacy. I'm thinking the path with him might be rocky."

Lacy nodded. Her own thoughts mirrored Wendy's, but there was no denying a certain attraction. She sensed a deep conflict within Mr. Morgan Streeter, sadness, plus an undercurrent of something wild warring against his nature. Was it the unknown excitement that drew her?

She quickly reminded herself she could do without outside distractions. For the past few years, she'd lived without the turmoil of emotional conflicts. Her goals had been focused on her career. But a short time in town and two powerful men had penetrated the long-established barricade around her heart. The longer she stayed in Gladden Hills, the more complicated her life became.

When Wendy handed back her change and receipt, the young waitress moistened her lips as if considering her next words. "Miss Lacy, I get the feeling Quinn is concerned about you—you know, in a protective way. He hasn't said anything, of course, but I saw the way his brow narrowed Saturday night when you walked away from our table. I'm not the brightest person in this town, but I get feelings about people and things sometimes. You be careful, Miss Lacy." Her blue eyes were darkened by her somber mood.

Thanking Wendy for her concern, she hurried out of the café. Shoes clicking loudly on the sidewalk, she made her way down two blocks to a crossing light, where she walked across Main Street to the impressive town square. Lacy mentally added up all of the warnings she'd received in the last couple of days. *Do I look like I'm wearing a bull's-eye mark on my back or something?* She shivered, trying to disregard the pending wariness.

*

The woman at the information desk identified Lacy on sight. "Nice day, Miss Cottrell." Her cheery voice resounded in the voluminous lobby. Lacy was sure all resident bats were alerted to her presence. She remembered seeing the sixtyish woman at the benefit on Saturday night talking briefly with the Morrisons. "Will you be going to the file room like before?" she asked, punctuating it with a short laugh.

The woman's personality was infused with laughter, her voice with volume. One of those who inserted a laugh in the course of every spoken sentence, whether or not from a nervous habit, Lacy had no idea. Wincing, she looked about to see who might be taking notice. Thankfully the room was empty with the exception of two men near the large doorway. They were in the process of exchanging a fistful of papers. The last thing she wanted was for it to be widely known she was searching the old records. The prior DA reportedly died soon after his search began.

Before the woman could utter another word, Lacy approached the desk. She held out her hand and lowered her voice to a whisper. "Miss…?"

"Ganson. Dede Ganson." The woman lowered her tone to match Lacy's.

Leaning in close like a fellow conspirator, Lacy whispered, "Dede, it's important for reporters to keep their actions secret. Would you help me out with this? I don't want the fact I'm looking through the old files known around…if you know what I mean?" She cast a glance about the near empty room to enforce her need for secrecy.

The pleasant-faced dark-haired woman with the sparkling hazel eyes nodded. "I understand, Miss Cottrell. I won't tell a soul." Her mouth worked into a hard grimness, as if she'd defend the knowledge even if it meant death.

"Just pretend I'm not here, okay?" asked Lacy.

"Got it!" Dede enforced with a stout nod, drawing her slight shoulders up to increase her height. She was a woman with a mission.

“Thank you, Dede,” she whispered and whirled about to head down the corridor toward the two elevators that serviced the big, old building. Lacy found the corridor unusually dark, giving evidence the fluorescent lighting was not currently working in this area. Reaching the elevator alcove, she was dismayed to find the first elevator taped off and a workman painting the inside walls, while the second elevator stood shut with an *Out of Order* sign taped to the outside. Frustrated, she pressed against the restraining ribbon in an attempt to converse with the painter on the ladder. “Why would they paint one elevator, when the other elevator is out of order?”

Without turning his head from his work, the heavyset painter mumbled, “Don’t think they knew the one was going to break down, Miss.”

“Is a repairman scheduled to work on it soon?”

“Think so. Not sure when, though. There’s only one elevator repairman in town, Harry Gunner. Might have to send for another repairman from the next town over. That could take time. ’Course, if Harry finishes up his first job might not have to send for another. ”

Lacy rolled her eyes and searched for the stairway door. It was three long flights down to the file department in the courthouse basement. Hopefully, the elevator would be fixed by the time she was done. She saw *Stairs* marked on the last door in the corridor and marched toward it with determination. Flinging open the door she rushed to the staircase and began her long deccent. This was not a good start to her afternoon. It would take precious time out of her research—time she couldn’t afford. Her mind kept returning to the latest note from her mysterious contact: *Follow the money.* What money?

Halfway down the first flight, Lacy heard a sound of undetermined origin. Jerking her head upward, she saw nothing. But the old, cracked marble staircase was suddenly ominous in appearance. The limited light was made dimmer by ancient fluorescent lighting, dulled more by painted walls darkened by age. The metal railing was loose in several areas but not yet to the point of being dangerous. Still, Lacy slowed her steps, listening at each footfall. Her nervousness increased with the eerie sensation someone was watching.

Hurrying her steps toward the second-floor landing leading to the ground floor and basement, she locked her eyes on the door opening. It was closed. Should she get out of the stairwell and take this exit on the storage floor? The fact there was no elevator service discounted that option. If she wanted to reach the basement, this was the only way.

Her heart quickened with the feeling of urgency. She raced down the steps to the second-floor landing, prepared to embark on the next flight. Each flight was a combination of two series of stairs with a small connecting landing between. As her foot touched the first step of the last flight, she felt as much as heard the swish of a door opening behind her.

Before she could whirl about to see who had entered, large gloved hands grabbed her shoulders on either side and propelled her toward the railing. Suddenly, the hands drew her back from the railing. She heard his brief hesitation, then his low voice hissed in her ear, "Leave town, Lacy Cottrell. Leave town and live."

As a faint familiar aroma reached her nostrils, a forceful push plummeted her downward. Her flesh was assaulted by blow after blow as it struck each stair on its descent. In the distance she heard screaming. Was it her own?

Then she knew nothing.

9

Unexpected Impact

THE BLURRED, GRIZZLED FACE OF THE OLD FILE KEEPER was the first face Lacy saw when she regained consciousness. "Nicho-las?"

"Now...don't you move, Miss Cottrell. The ambulance is on its way. Good thing I heard you screaming. What on earth were you doing taking those old stairs?"

Her eyes fluttered closed against her will. "The—the elevator was out of order."

"The elevator isn't out of order," Nicholas insisted. "One of them is being painted today. Dede told me this morning. Someone ordered it done today from the city offices. What made you think the elevator was broke down?"

"Yellow tape across the front and an *Out of Order* sign..."

"Well, it's gone now. Two security guards rushed downstairs on the elevator as soon as I called up to the desk for help. Dede called for an ambulance. I said I'd stay with you. The guards are waiting upstairs for the ambulance to arrive."

Lacy started to sit up, groaned, and clutched her side. Nicholas's gentle hands lowered her back down to the hard marble landing in the stairwell. "You go easy there. No doubt you got a few ribs either broken or badly bruised, and a sure enough goose egg on your head that would stop a horse. Those old steps are cracked and dangerous, easy to trip on." He nodded to punctuate his words.

"I didn't trip, Nicholas. I was pushed." She heard the old man's gasp.

"Dear me, Miss Cottrell, dear me! Maybe you shouldn't come to the file room anymore." His voice quivered with obvious distress. Lacy heard his fear.

Some of the initial shock was wearing off, and she could feel every one of the bruises afflicted upon her body. At first blush, the idea of backing off from the investigation sounded tempting—even reasonable, but she knew she wouldn't do that. "Don't you see, Nicholas, the very fact that someone tried to keep me from rummaging around the old files indicates they are afraid I'll find something. That shows there is something to find. "

"Might be—might not. Guilty people are always nervous, afraid of missing something, so they do things to warn people off. I worry about you, ma'am. I, for one, don't think it's a good idea for you to be here. I don't care what..."

Though her mind was dulled by the violent impact, his unfinished statement struck her as strange. "What were you going to say, Nicholas?"

He waved her off. "Just an old man's nonsense ramblings." His head tilted upward. "I think the ambulance people are coming. "You rest now—rest." He patted her arm.

Her hand reached for his. "Nicholas, find the sign-in book for that time...and locate the files for that week. I'll get authorization...and...and I'll be back." She gasped at the pain in her side.

As the stairwell door burst open and white uniformed people rushed toward her with a stretcher, Nicholas lowered his head. "Yes'm, rest and feel better now."

*

While Lacy waited alone in a separate ER room for her head and chest x-rays to be reviewed, she tried to breathe as shallowly as possible to avoid sharp pain. The hospital personnel had refused so much as an aspirin for pain until the results of the tests came back. Her hand went to the light bandage on her head. Two bruises on the left side of her face ached with a separate rhythm than that of the constant pounding in her head. All she wanted was to go home to two aspirins, hot chicken soup, and an ice pack. Rotating her head slowly, she saw the impressive form of Jason Gardner in the ER doorway.

Directing his eyes away from the bright lights of the hospital room, Gardner made his way to her side. "Received a call from the hospital that one of my reporters had been brought into emergency. I thought I'd better check it out." He smiled down at her, but the smile was not conveyed throughout the rest of his expression.

With the reflection of the bright lights, Lacy could see through his shaded glasses, noting a glint of steel in his dark eyes. "Want to tell me what happened, Lacy?"

"What would you say if I told you I was pushed down the staircase, boss?"

Jason looked around and drew up a stool next to her gurney. "I'd say you have my attention. I'd like to hear the whole story, Miss Cottrell." His serious tone reverted to her formal name.

She related the entire incident from the moment she'd walked through the doors to the old courthouse to the moment she'd regained consciousness, with Nicholas bent over her.

When she'd finished, Gardner commented. "You say one elevator was taped off with a sign reading *Out of Order?"*

"Yes, sir. But something wasn't right. It was all very strange. Nicholas told me the security guards used the elevator when he alerted them to my injury."

Gardner's brows pinched. "I can't remember the layout of the courthouse lobby. Can the operator at the information desk view the elevators from her position behind the desk?"

"I'd have to say no. At least, I wasn't able to view the information desk when I stood in front of the elevator, and it's a pretty large desk." She sighed, realizing Dede would be no help in discovering who or when the fake *Out of Order* sign and tape was put up. Finding the one responsible would not be an easy task.

"What was your reason in going to the file room in the old courthouse?"

"I'm working on a separate story, Mr. Gardner—one I'd rather not speak of yet."

He shrugged. "That doesn't leave me much leverage. I can do some probing to find out who was behind that fake *Out of Order* sign on the elevator, but I can't keep you safe. Are you sure you don't want to share what you're working on? Perhaps I can be of help?"

Refusing to meet his eyes, she shook her head gently so as not to increase her pain. "Not quite yet, Mr. Gardner. Not enough substance to make it worth your while."

"If someone is trying to kill you, I'd say there is some credence there is a story to uncover, but is it worth your life? I can't sanction risking your life for a story. But if you're determined to pursue this, I know enough to realize you will not drop this. I insist you keep close contact, Cottrell. I don't like this whole business, and I don't appreciate being kept in the dark by one of my reporters, confidentiality be…" His jaw stiffened even as he left off the last word, adding, "Do you read me?"

Lacy didn't like the hard look behind Jason's glasses. She nodded numbly. "I'll be careful." When he turned away, she asked, "Would you speak with the chief of police? Keep him in the loop but ask him to keep this in house so to speak, and that would include the paper also?" She looked up, seeking confirmation. The last thing she needed was to have this incident voiced all over town. It would automatically shut down any avenues of information.

His extended scrutinizing stare made her nervous. Raising his chin, Jason asked, "What story did you give the hospital?"

"That I fell down the courthouse stairs, that the lighting was very bad and I wasn't as careful as I should have been." She lifted her skinned palms to explain. "It was all true—in a way. I should have been more careful, the lighting was bad, and I did fall down the stairs." She braced against the increasing pain.

"I'll talk to the chief of police off the cuff. Be prepared. He may want to speak with you personally. You didn't get even a glimpse of the man who tried to kill you? You could have broken your neck on those stairs, you know."

"No. I couldn't see much. Everything happened so fast, and the man was strong—very strong, something I sensed. He could have been wearing a dark ski mask because I have a vision of seeing a black blur while I tried to twist away from him, but there are no useable recollections." Lacy reflected back to the first contact he had with her. "Boss, what would have happened if I'd have gone over the railing of the staircase?"

"We wouldn't be having this conversation. The ambulance would have brought you in a body bag. Had you been thrown over the railing, you'd have been dead instantly upon impact. The landing between the floors broke your fall. Why?"

A mask of confusion settled over her. "I'm not sure. I thought at first he was going to throw me over the railing. Had he tried, I wouldn't have been able to prevent him. I could feel his massive muscles beneath his clothes." She didn't voice all of the questions she had.

Gardner had distanced himself from the gurney. As he shifted to stare back at her, her heart skipped a beat at the unfamiliar softness around his mouth. His ruggedly handsome features were almost relaxed.

"Go home today, and don't come back to work until you're rested and healed. I'm truly glad you're all right, Lacy. I was very concerned when the call came in about you." He walked back to stand next to her…uncomfortably near. "If you need backup for anything, call! That's not just an invitation, it's an order! I don't want any Lone Ranger heroics. Are we straight?"

When she nodded agreeably, the brilliant smile he flashed held her momentarily mesmerized. Her vision blurred, and blinking only caused more pain to her head. Something about this man confused her emotionally. *What's wrong with me lately? Am I having belated surges of adolescent hormones?*

When Kelly entered the cold surgical room seconds after Jason Gardner exited, the lingering feel of his comforting hand upon her scratched, bruised arm was still warm. Her aching fingers covered the spot, wishing he'd stayed.

Kelly approached, her face flushed, her expression anxious. She pointed behind her. "The nurse told me you were in here." As her gaze roamed from the IV hookup to her cousin's battered features, she gasped. "Oh my! You look like you lost a fight with an alley cat and a Detroit Tiger batter. What happened? Are you all right? Why didn't you call me sooner? I had to hear from someone at the hospital who saw you come in."

Lacy couldn't help but chuckle at Kelly's end-on-end sentences. "I haven't had time to get out a call to you, and actually I wasn't hurt that badly."

Kelly leveled a hard look at her. "I heard you could have been killed! How many flights of stairs did you fall down?"

In trying to raise her head, Lacy winced. "It was one half of a double flight of stairs," she said, easing her head down. As Lacy listened vaguely to Kelly vent her emotions, a nagging thought broke through. It was something she'd forgotten to tell Jason. The would-be killer had spoken to her—warned her! *"Leave town, Lacy Cottrell. Leave town and live."*

*

Kelly drove Lacy home after the doctor's consultation. She had a slight concussion, at least two cracked ribs and a light bandage on her forehead with several Band-Aids in various places. All in all, she was one big walking bruise. While Kelly opened a can of chicken noodle soup, Lacy lowered herself into a bath laced with Epsom salt.

The conversation at the kitchen table was stunted. Kelly kept shooting covert glances her way. Finally, her cousin laid down her spoon. "However did you manage to tumble down a flight of stairs? You've always been nimble on your feet—I'm the family klutz! I'm having trouble believing you tripped over a cracked step. And no one knows anything about the out of order elevator on the main floor. I'm confused, dear cousin. I've got this weird feeling there is a separate world existing all around me, like those science fiction flicks. Ever since you moved back to Gladden Hills, there has been a rash of unexplained incidents." Kelly crossed her arms on the table, leaning in. "Can you shed any light on the situation because, frankly, I'm bewildered?"

Lacy broke another cracker into her soup before lifting her eyes to Kelly's troubled gaze. She drew in a deep breath and released it slowly, flinching at the sharp pain in her rib area. "Perhaps it would be wiser to bring you in on the said situation…such as it is. But absolute secrecy is required! Do I have your word, Kelly? You can't share what I tell you with anyone, my parents or Jerome. Can you agree to that?"

Kelly's face drained to a pale ash shade. "You're scaring me, Lacy. Stop it!" She gave a nervous half laugh. "You're not joking, are you? What in the world have you gotten yourself mixed up in, girl?"

Lacy laid her spoon to the side and carefully swung her long legs around in preparation to push up from the table, enduring the resulting pain. She winced. "Let's take our little talk into Grandmother's parlor."

*

Forty-five minutes later, both women stared into the tiny flames still active in the small fire glowing inside the charred grate. The worn, black fixture was situated deep within the discolored stone fireplace and reminded Lacy of less complicated visits to their grandparents' home. Kelly had spoken very little after hearing Lacy's story. From the instant she'd heard about the first note requesting Lacy to come to the graveyard in the darkness of night, Kelly had balled her slender fingers into tight fists within her lap. Now she sat pensive and distant.

"Then that man watching your upstairs bedroom last week was not just a random Peeping Tom?" Kelly's tense voice shattered the uneasy quiet.

Lacy was stretched out on the couch. "You now know as much as I know. The fact he was watching our house was suspect in itself. I forgot to tell the patrolman that I believe the man was wearing a Western-style hat. I watched to see who might be wearing a similar hat at the benefit dinner Saturday night and found out there is not only a working dude ranch in the vicinity, but a popular riding club with a large membership. So the Western-style hat doesn't exactly narrow our suspect field."

Kelly slumped back against the chair. "You think you were pushed down that flight of stairs today?"

Lacy shot her a hard look. "I know I was! The man warned me to leave town. I can't leave town, Kelly. I have to see this through." She touched her tender ribs. "Somebody must be worried, or they would not put out the effort to get rid of me. I just have to figure out what 'follow the money' means, and who in town lured me here to stir things up? Hopefully, they're a friend and might show up when I need them." Once again her thoughts returned to Jerome and his overt interest in the past.

Moving ever so slowly, she cleared her voice. "I think I will turn in early. Mr. Gardner told me to stay out until I heal up, but I can't afford not to get my columns completed before printing time. Somehow I need to get into work tomorrow." She gritted her teeth as she made the final effort to stand.

Kelly frowned. "You don't look able to make it into anywhere tomorrow. Why don't you work at home and send in your columns?"

"Some of my research material is still at the office. I was planning on returning there before coming home. That was before my new friend," she said tersely, "altered my plans."

"You're lucky to be alive, Lacy! This is not a laughing matter. I'm scared. I'm scared for you. I think you should turn whatever you have or think you have over to the chief of police and let him figure it out." Her hands trembled.

Lacy took hold of the edge of the couch to steady herself. "I don't have enough evidence for the chief of police to do anything. It's a seventeen-year-old cold case and random suspicious factors. That's not enough for him to reopen the case. The only real evidence is the fact my house was watched and I was pushed down a flight of stairs. There's no proof about that, other than my word. Telling them I think I was followed a couple of times will only raise eyebrows. There's nothing to tie those actions to the old case. This is why I didn't want to tell you. There's nothing you can do but worry. "

Kelly waved off her cousin's last remark. "What about the notes you received? They're real."

"A morbid prank by someone who remembered I was a close friend of Stevie's." She shook her head. "Anyone could have sent me those notes." But reality contradicted her words. She hadn't mentioned the purple feathers that only she and Stevie supposedly knew about. It would only confuse the issue more for her cousin.

"Listen, Kelly, you've got to keep what I've told you to yourself. Be my prayer partner, like that last summer at the Grans', and help me figure out what money the second note could be referring to. I'm going to see Quinn Darling before I go into work. I need his authorization to review the old sign-in logs for the file room. It takes time to check through records."

"Don't take the stairs anymore," Kelly said quietly.

"Sound advice." A wry smile tugged at the corners of Lacy's mouth.

Rising, Kelly walked over to the fireplace, stoked it one last time, and pulled the screen across. By the time Lacy had made her way to the bottom of the staircase leading up to her bedroom, Kelly followed her out. "That money the note referred to...was it money back then, seventeen years ago, or money now?" The lines across her brow indicated her troubled thoughts.

Having slowly stepped to the halfway point of the stairs, Lacy paused, holding to the railing. "That is a very good question. One I should ask my anonymous friend, if I could."

"How can you ask them when you don't know who they are?"

Lacy pursed her lips. "That's another question I'll have to think on." Lifting her foot to the higher step, she felt the sharpness of the rib pain.

Kelly frowned. "They say the second day following an accident is worse for pain."

"That's a happy thought to sleep on. See you tomorrow." She saw Kelly make her way to the front entrance and recheck the locks on the door before returning down the hall.

"Welcome to my world, dear cousin," she murmured. While it was comforting to have someone close watching her back, it distressed her to know a new element of fear had entered her Kelly's life, and Lacy was the one who'd brought it to her door.

10

Taking a Chance

LACY NERVOUSLY DRUMMED THE SIDE ARM of the chair sitting directly across from Vicky Subert, secretary to Michael Quinn Darling, specially assigned DA for Gladden Hills. She shifted uncomfortably, re-experiencing the inflicted pain from yesterday's fall down the courthouse back stairs. The cherub-faced secretary had eyed her bruised face several times, her eyes mirroring her sympathy.

There was no doubt that the story of her near deadly fall had traveled through the inner workings of Gladden Hills with the swiftness unrivaled by the internet. The grapevine of the courthouse and legal offices alone was unprecedented anywhere. No one had asked what had happened. But they'd all cast knowing glances as she passed by.

Finally, Lacy could stand it no longer. "Vicky, I thought you said it wouldn't be a big deal to get a slip of authorization from Mr. Quinn?" She shifted in the chair. Her back was feeling every ridge and bump in the upholstery, and she was anxious to get in to the office and pick up her resource material for this week's articles. Her soreness and lack of energy was taking its toll. Her hand went to her aching head.

"It's really not a big deal, Miss Cottrell. It's just that Mr. Darling wants—"

Her words were cut off by the abrupt opening of Quinn's office door.

Lacy turned and their eyes connected. Quinn's expression was stern. He raised two fingers and beckoned her into his office. Obviously he wasn't going to make this easy. Lacy stood slowly.

Once in his office, she took the most comfortable looking chair across from his cluttered desk. After indicating she should sit, Quinn hadn't given her a single glance. He rested his head on top of his propped left hand, his attention seemingly glued to the contents in a manila file. Closing the file that was stamped *Confidential,* he folded his hands and stared across at her.

"You, Lacy Cottrell, are getting to be a problem! You look terrible! But considering you could be laid out at McCormick's Mortuary this very minute..." He left the sentence unfinished. "After your boss talked with Chief of Police Brown, he called me on my private line. I just finished reading his report." Quinn indicated the file. "Told him I would talk with you, personally. Brown has promised to keep all information to himself. That means none of his deputies know what really happened to you and won't—I repeat, won't, which means they won't be watching out for you! So far everyone thinks it was no more than a bad accident that you were fortunate to survive."

"Good," she replied.

Quinn settled back in his swivel chair looking over his narrow, wire-rimmed glasses. At first glance he might be taken for a computer geek and little else. But judging by the hard, discerning glint in his eyes that even now held her in a vise, she would recommend not provoking this man. He was lean and tough. The ligaments and muscles in his hands and lower forearms were hardened like steel.

He launched himself upright. "Good? You think it is good that you are virtually unprotected as you walk around with a killer on the loose stalking you?" He stood and paced across his office.

Lacy prepared to defend why it was a wise decision to keep the truth from being known.

"Yet," he continued, "what else can we do? If we let it be known that someone deliberately attempted to kill you, we'll never discover what they are trying to hide. They'll go to ground." He whirled to face her. "I'm here to do a job." Abruptly he paused, causing Lacy to wonder what Quinn had first been ready to say. She leaned forward in her chair, eager to hear his next words.

"The governor sent me in to keep the legal system of Gladden Hills running smoothly until a new district attorney can be elected. I don't need a covert investigation by a rogue reporter to turn this town into a chaotic upheaval. You were supposed to keep me in the loop. I haven't heard a word."

"Outside of the fact I've been stalked in my own home and someone tried to kill me, I haven't found anything concrete," she retorted. Suddenly it struck her. "Quinn. I forgot to mention that the staircase assassin spoke to me before he shoved me down the stairs."

Quinn spun around from his pacing. "He spoke to you?"

Raising her fingers to her temple, she closed her eyes. "Something to the effect...*if you want to live, leave town, Lacy Cottrell."* She lifted her hands. "Why the big push to get rid of me? The only thing I've done is drive by the old homesteads and spend a few hours in the old file section of the courthouse. After seventeen years, you'd think anything incriminating would have been conveniently lost. You and I both know files could have been smuggled out long ago if they'd been considered a threat."

Pushing his doubled fists on the top of his desk, Quinn leaned over the stacks of folders. "Maybe not, Miss Cottrell. Consider this. If records come up missing, red flags go up, but perhaps they, these unknown people, are hoping the importance of certain items will be diminished and overlooked in the bulk of trivial information." He pointed at her. "You add that to the unknown quality of your memories from childhood. They don't know what coming back to Gladden Hills might stimulate in your forgotten memories. That in itself could be a threat, especially to a worried, paranoid mind."

Lacy held his forceful gaze, her thoughts flooded with the truth of his words. It occurred to her that this man was either brilliant or knew more than she first assumed. His last remark about forgotten memories coming to light struck a nerve. It was uncanny! Isn't that what she had tried to do on Sunday morning when she drove by the area where Stevie's home had once stood? She'd been trying to revive those images.

Instantly she was aware of a pounding heart. Lacy averted her eyes from Quinn's probing gaze. She needed time to cover her emotions, emotions that felt raw and exposed.

"Would you like a glass of water, Lacy?" Quinn asked softly, already pouring the liquid into a waiting glass.

She scrutinized this replacement DA as he walked around the large, messy desk and handed her the glass. Drinking it down near the bottom, she handed it back. "Your comments hold merit, Mr. Darling. I'll bear them in mind. Do I have your authorization to check all the files?"

Turning, Quinn backtracked to his desk and rummaged about in a pile on his right, pulling out a signed legal looking paper. "Here's your authorization, Miss Cottrell. I have one stern request." He fixed her with an intimidating stare. "Have a backup handy when you choose to do your investigating or go anywhere at night. It may mean the difference between life and death. You've stirred the pot just by returning to Gladden Hills. Do you have someone you can call to be backup for you—someone who might have offered?" His eyes demanded an answer. "Think, woman, this is your life!"

She jumped at his sharpness. One face immediately appeared in her thoughts, but she hated the idea of entering his name into the equation. "There *has* been someone who's offered if I should ever have a need, but he isn't someone I would want to take advantage of, nor put into danger." To Lacy, this was not an acceptable route.

"He?" he questioned, intensifying his stare.

She colored and quickly waved off his question. "His offer was merely polite, nothing more. He is much too busy and important for me to offhandedly call him to drop everything and come play babysitter to my prowling around archive records—or whatever!" Quinn's request was simply out of the question. She pushed herself up in preparation to leave.

"Sit down, Miss Cottrell!"

Lacy lowered herself back to the chair, staring at him in shock.

"I've been patient and given you a wide leeway, but all that stops now unless you enlist the help of that polite offer. In fact, two backups would not be too many. Surely there are one or two people you could trust to be good cover? It's this simple. No backup—no more leeway. Any more of what happened yesterday, and I'm clipping your wings. Do we have an understanding?"

She silently stared him down with no evidence of a backing down on his part. "I don't believe I have a choice if I want to operate in and around Gladden Hills."

When she rose again, Quinn added, "No more prowling around today. Go home. You look like..." He stopped, but she knew what he was about to say.

She rolled her eyes at his bluntness, anxious to be away from further demands. She had no idea how she was going to comply with the ones he'd just issued.

As Lacy exited the DA's office, Vicky said tenderly, "Be careful, Miss Cottrell."

Lacy gritted her teeth at the words, realizing the whole town now believed she was a klutz, tripping over her own feet down a full flight of stairs. As she limped past Vicky's desk, she endured one last look of sympathy before heading for the outside corridor and the waiting elevator that would give her the access fresh air. Quinn's orders stung. It didn't matter that she'd already decided to work at home after collecting her research from the paper; she didn't like being ordered about. And that business about securing Jason Gardner as her backup...

Lacy hurried from the building to her car in an agitated state. Normally it would have been a pleasant walk from Quinn's office to the paper. A good stretch of her legs. But nothing was normal when every moving part of her body cried out in pain. Easing into her car, she took special pains to shift with care. Lacy took time to watch the people walking the surrounding streets and the cars slowly passing as they navigated the crowded small town streets. Squinting through the car windows, something caught and held her interest.

That tan pickup truck across the street had been there when she first went into the building nearly an hour ago. There was nothing unusual about that, except that someone behind the wheel was supposedly reading a newspaper. *For over an hour? Unusual and highly unlikely.*

The windows were too tinted to make out whether the driver was a man or woman, but the fact that they sat in the truck with all the windows rolled up on such a beautiful spring day was most suspicious. Lacy bit her lip, wondering, *Am I paranoid?* Was she seeing "would be" assailants on every side—first the gray sedan, now a tan truck? Lacy pushed the start button and steered her car away from the curb.

Minutes later, she gingerly extracted herself from the confines of her automobile in front of the *Gladden Hills Gazette.* She parked in the limited parking space and inhaled gingerly, enduring the sharp pangs around the rib area. Placing one foot in front of another all the way into the main entry of the Gazette, she paused to catch her breath.

"Good heavens, Lacy, you look like a train wreck! What are you doing coming into work today?" A box of Kleenex sat near Maxine, evidence her head cold was ongoing.

Continuing on the path toward her desk, Lacy flung a greeting over her shoulder. "Good morning, Maxine. It doesn't sound as if either of us should be here. I'm staying only long enough to collect my info for this week's columns. I'll send in my finished write-ups electronically tomorrow before the paper goes to press." She paused again as her ribs stabbed her. "If you or the boss has a problem with anything, you can call…or whatever." She raised her hand in an offhanded manner and kept walking.

"Just for the record. I feel remarkably better today, regardless of how I sound. Thanks for your 'pinch-hitting' for me yesterday. I slept the entire day away. If you'd have called, we could have sent your material over to your house via a messenger. I'm sure Chloe would love to do something like that for you."

"Chloe!" The name came out like an oath as she stopped to line up her thoughts. Instantly she remembered her appointment with Chloe for the previous afternoon. Lacy had promised to go over the recommendations on the girl's practice write-up—a promise she wasn't able to keep. Resuming her steps, Lacy considered how she might handle the awkward situation. Their consultation would have to be postponed until Lacy was back at work, but she worried that Chloe might not understand. Chloe was not like anyone Lacy had met. Though not mentally disabled, the girl seemed to lack certain reasoning processes. "One problem at a time," she muttered to herself.

With her desk in view, Lacy centered on collecting her research material. Her pain level was rising, pushing her to hurry. She felt like a horse heading for the barn. All she wanted was to collect her stuff and head that shiny car home. Easing down to her swivel chair, she sighed and reached for the top, right-side drawer of her desk. Extracting a large manila envelope, she closed the drawer and tried to arrange her thoughts. *Is there anything else I might need to complete my columns—the list of confirmation contacts?* Her eyes scanned her desktop, alarmed at the disheveled mess she saw there.

Papers were scattered all across the top of her desk. *My desk was cleared when I left. I placed these papers in my top drawer. Did I forget to lock that drawer?* Someone had searched through her desk. In that instant Lacy sensed she was not alone.

Straightening in her chair she looked over to the left of her desk, where a stoic-faced Chloe stood, her long stringy bangs brushed haphazardly across her forehead. "Chloe." Lacy sent a prayer upward for restraint. She could feel anger surge through her system.

The unhealthy color of the girl's complexion had not improved in the short time Lacy had been at the paper. Her expression was smug. "If you're looking for my article, I took it from the top of your desk. Sorry you didn't like it."

Lacy kept her tone even. "No, Chloe. You went into my desk and rifled through my papers without my permission. That is a serious act. Did you know that? Our agreement was that we would go over your paper together so I might explain how you could improve your original work. That is not possible now. You knew I had been in an accident, correct?"

The girl glanced down briefly. When she looked up, her eyes were defiant. "I heard."

Lacy sighed, alarmed at the girl's lack of concern. Collecting the papers on top of her desk, she stuffed them in the manila envelope, visibly took her key from the top drawer, and locked the drawer, inserting the key inside her purse. "We'll talk of your actions at a later time," she said curtly. Pushing herself up from her chair, she collected her purse and envelope and turned to leave.

"What about my article, Miss Cottrell?' Chloe called in a shrill pleading.

Shifting with as little movement as possible, Lacy leveled a piercing stare on the young woman and struggled for control. "Consider our professional relationship terminated. As for whether I will report your actions, I haven't decided." Turning away, she walked in the direction of the exit. As she passed Jason Gardner's open office door, he looked up. Had he heard the confrontation? Lacy couldn't tell.

She would have passed by had he not called out to her. "Lacy? Didn't expect to see you today." His eyes took in her appearance and more. "I hope you're on your way home." It sounded like an order.

"I am. I needed information to complete my columns. I'll get them to you by tomorrow morning, the latest." She would have turned away but felt his intense gaze through those irritating dark glasses.

"We could have filled in for you this week, Miss Cottrell. We managed before you arrived, you know." He raised a brow. "It's common knowledge you took quite a tumble yesterday."

"Yes, I've noticed. But I don't like to miss a deadline. Besides, it will give me something to work at while I'm at home. Thanks for talking to the chief of police for me." She stepped inside his office and shut the door quietly behind her. "I got quite the lecture from the new DA this morning. He threatened to clip my wings, so to speak."

Gardner sat upright in his chair, his brow furrowing. "Clip your wings?"

She shrugged. "It's complicated." It was a perfect moment to tell Gardner what was going on, but she held her tongue. Silence enveloped the office, as if he waited for her to say something. "Look, I need to get home. I'm bushed."

"We'll talk later, then. Go home and be careful, Lacy Cottrell."

The softness in his tone was a caress to her bruised spirit. She nodded, feeling like a wounded bird searching for a safe place to heal. "Thanks, boss." She raised her hand in parting.

Pausing at the entry counter where Maxine was editing the classifieds for the next publication, Lacy lingered, scanning the multiple pages of listed submissions.

Maxine arched her neck to look up at her. "Why aren't you home in bed? Afraid of missing something around here?"

"Mmm, could be. There's lots of interesting happenings at the *Gazette,* not to mention the clientele." She patted the older woman's shoulder and exited the building. Pausing on the sidewalk, Lacy surveyed the street. A familiar tan pickup was parked across the way, almost hidden by a weeping willow. This time the window was rolled down. Although the face was obscured by the distance, she could make out the lines of something on his head—a Western-style hat. She moved closer to the curb to get a better look.

Instantly the tan pickup revved up its engine and tore away from the secluded parking place. She watched it go, her heart in her throat. Shifting, she stared at the door of the *Gazette,* thinking of Jason Gardner and Quinn's orders to enlist his help. Feeling a new twinge of pain, she sighed and headed toward her car.

*

Parting the front door curtain slightly to the side, Lacy scanned both sides of the quiet, residential neighborhood even as she slid the double bolt into place. No evidence of the tan pickup was a good sign. Kelly wouldn't be home for a few hours, and Lacy didn't relish the idea of any unwanted visitors while she rested. Confident all was as it should be, Lacy carried her computer and office bag up the stairs to work on later.

She plopped everything on the left side of the bed and downed a couple of aspirin before succumbing to the soft pillows and warm comforters. In seconds, she was asleep.

*

It was almost four when she awoke, head pounding. She phoned Kelly at work and asked her to pick up something for an easy supper and warned her that the deadbolt was in place. "Call before you leave so I can let you in." Laying the phone on the bed, Lacy propped up her pillows and went to work on her columns that would go to press the next day.

Most of the groundwork for her write-ups had been done, so the actual piecing together of the articles took little time. She was beginning a series of columns featuring little-known facts about historical places in and around Gladden Hills, coupled with pictures and modern-day personal twists profiling some of the hard-working residents. She always tried to throw in some humor or tear-producing statements with each article.

Having first run the basics by Maxine and Jason, she'd been given the go-ahead. Basically it was the backbone and heart of a small town that was rarely brought to light, something she'd always wanted to do. Replacing her material in the manila envelope, she laid it aside and spent considerable time musing on a challenging idea. One that could backfire on her.

She paused to reconsider her actions, then made a decision. Pulling out her personal address book, she picked up the phone and dialed a friend in Chicago she worked with at the paper. After a general catch-up, Lacy got to the point. "Nadine, I need a big favor. I want you to place an anonymous, classified ad in the *Gladden Hills Gazette* tomorrow morning at the latest. It goes to press tomorrow afternoon. I don't want it traced back to me, understand?...Thanks, Nadine. Now, listen closely while I tell you what I want the ad to read. "

When she clicked off the phone, she immediately wondered, *What in the world am I doing?* She knew she was taking a chance, but she had to make contact and this was the only way she knew of. Question was, would it work? A hand went to her head, touching the bruised place. She was playing a dangerous game. At some point she knew she was going to have to call Jason Gardner, but not until she knew if the classified worked.

When the phone rang next to her, Lacy jumped. Her nerves were raw from dealing with the pain from her fall. The headache had been manageable, but the fractured ribs were another matter. The doctor told her she was lucky. It could have been worse. A stiff Velcro brace when she was up and about and pain meds until they got better.

"I got it, Kel, one half hour. What are you picking up for supper?" She chuckled at her cousin's response. "All right, I'll wait and be surprised."

Lowering the phone to the bed beside her, Lacy carefully maneuvered her legs to the edge of the bed and pushed off. It was a short distance to the front windows overlooking the street below and the heavy thicketed area directly across the street where the stalker had watched her over a week ago. Much had happened since then. Whoever feared her presence in town had progressed to using violence to get their message across: Lacy Cottrell was no longer welcome in Gladden Hills.

Is my contact in town observing everything that happens to me? What was the purpose in luring me back to Gladden Hills? Was it, as stated, to bring the truth to light? Is this person to be trusted, or was the whole thing planned simply to bait the trap? Why haven't I heard more from them than a couple of notes? Lacy's doubts mounted.

Pulling the lace print sheer back from the window, she stiffened. A tan pickup sat at the end of the street with a good view of the house. Should she call the chief of police and report a stalker? Lacy groaned at the thought. There would be hours of reports to make out and she'd have to tell and retell when she first began to notice the tan pickup. And what could she answer when they asked why she thought the person in the tan truck might be a danger to her? She couldn't share that she'd been pushed down the stairs the previous day, but if she could speak to the chief personally, he might understand and send out a patrol car. If one car came up from one end and another blocked off the end where the truck was parked…?

Deciding it was worth a try, she crossed to the bed for the phone and returned to the window. A curt-sounding deputy answered. The chief was busy. She was welcome to leave a message. "Could I be patched through to him, officer?" Lacy asked.

"Is this an emergency, Miss? The chief is busy with an emergency."

"Thank you, deputy." She clicked off the phone. *Why didn't I think to set up a link to the chief or Quinn Darling earlier? You're going to have to think of these things, Cottrell. You can't blame everything on the headache.* She was still watching the truck when Kelly's car turned down the street. Even as the car neared the house, the tan truck backed out of the street and was gone.

Allowing the lace sheer to fall back into place, Lacy made her way down the stairs to unlock the door for Kelly.

*

Bags and containers were stacked across the kitchen table. Both women were devouring the food on their plates when Lacy broke the silence. "I didn't know there was a Chinese Restaurant in Gladden Hills. It's not bad."

"It's tucked in between a couple small businesses down a side street past the second street light in town. It's one of those places you have to stumble upon. So tell me when you first started to notice the tan truck was following you?" Kelly's eyes were lined with new worry.

"Today, when I came out of Quinn's office, then again outside of the paper, and finally at the end of the street. I wish I would have called you and asked you to pay special attention to who was behind the wheel," said Lacy, lifting a laden fork to her mouth.

Kelly's fork paused mid-air. "Actually, I did glance into the cab when I passed. I thought it was strange for a truck to be parked there. He was a big man with a big nose. His other features I couldn't see. With tinted windows and reflected sunlight, I don't know that I could recognize him on the street."

"That's all right. It's great that you saw anything."

"Well if that stupid cowboy hat hadn't been covering his face, I could have seen him better," retorted Kelly, forking in a large mouthful.

"You saw a cowboy hat on his head?"

"Yeah," Kelly mumbled around her food.

"I thought I saw a similar hat through the truck window the first time I spotted him across from the new county office building. And the night stalker was also wearing a Western hat. I don't believe that's a coincidence."

"Lacy, this is freaking me out. You really think all this business is because of what happened seventeen years ago? It doesn't make sense to me. And those weird notes you've been receiving...what's up with that?"

"Not much, unless I can stir things up." She gazed across the kitchen, wondering about the scenario she'd put into action.

Kelly heaved her shoulders as if trying to balance a heavy weight. "I caught myself a couple of times from telling Jerome about the whole situation. Maybe he could be of help if we told him what's going on. I hate this feeling of fighting against something and someone, or even a group of someones, that we can't see. It's eerie!"

"No, Kelly!" She'd reacted stronger than she'd meant to. Softening her tone, Lacy pleaded, "We have to keep this close. I know from experience that too many people knowing about something can be dangerous! You pestered me into telling you, but now you have to keep my confidence."

Kelly sighed. "I know. I'm sorry, kiddo, really. Now I wish I hadn't pressured you into telling me. No, I really don't mean that." She looked perplexed. "Honestly, I want to be here for you, and I will. I'm just not geared for this cloak-and-dagger type of living. I *like* being a small-town girl living a quiet life. Personally, I believe you could trust Jerome with your life."

"That's exactly what you would be trusting him with," Lacy said soberly. Somehow she needed an opportunity to get Jerome alone, to question and feel him out. Find out if there was a possibility he was her secret contact. If he was, it would also give him opportunity to make it known. Unfortunately, Jerome's connection to Kelly would complicate setting up such a time.

Kelly stood and started to consolidate the Chinese entrées. "By the way, Jerome's coming by later to work on some contracts. We have to finish them up by the end of this week. Don't worry about us bothering you. We'll sit out here at the table."

Lacy looked up at her cousin blank-faced. "Really? No bother. In fact, I'll try not to bother you when I come into the kitchen for coffee refills. I've completed my write-ups for this week's columns, so I might curl up on that comfy couch in the parlor with a nice fire tonight." She stood and stretched, wincing at the incurred pain. "Oooh," she groaned.

"Poor baby! I'll get the clean-up tonight. Go set up your nest in the parlor on the couch." As Kelly carried the cartons over to the kitchen counter, she turned toward Lacy. "Did you remember to reset the deadbolt on the front door after I came in?"

"I'll check." Clearly, fear wasn't far from either one of their thoughts.

*

Utilizing the soft light from the table lamp as well as reflected firelight, Lacy tried to center on the words of the book in front of her but finally laid it to her side. It was no use; her thoughts kept wandering. Puzzles were something Lacy could not leave alone, and she was living the most dangerous puzzle of all. Pushing herself upward on her pillows, she stared into the fire while vaguely listening to the exchanges between Kelly and Jerome in the kitchen. Occasionally she'd hear laughter, and it would make her smile. They were good together, and Kelly was due some happiness.

Stretching to the right, Lacy lifted her sweatshirt, undid the Velcro brace around her midriff, and refastened the stiff restrainer, leaving it looser than before. Tomorrow afternoon, this week's news would go to press and be ready for Thursday morning's distribution. What then? What kind of reaction would she receive from the classified?

A kitchen chair screeched against the floor. Her ears tuned to what might follow next. The connecting door between kitchen and hallway opened. Kelly was talking as she made her way down the hall into her bedroom.

"It will take a few minutes for me to locate that specific file I was telling you about, Jerome. I keep it in my personal file cabinet for reference for other contracts," Kelly called from somewhere within the confines of her room. "Pour us more coffee and eat some of those cookies on the counter. They're really good. Lacy can't leave them alone."

Lacy pushed away the restricting pillows propped around her and slowly unwound herself to a standing position. This was the opportunity she'd been waiting for. She carried her empty coffee cup for a convenient cover and walked the hall, passing through the connecting door to the kitchen to find Jerome diligently stacking cookies on a small plate.

Making her way gently over to the coffee pot, Lacy realized Jerome was so focused on his project he wasn't even aware she'd entered the kitchen. She purposely clinked her mug against the edge of the pot to announce her arrival.

His sandy-colored head jerked around in her direction. "Lacy. Didn't hear you come in." His eyes took in her bruised face and scratched forearms. "Sorry about your accident. It looks painful."

"It is. Thanks, Jerome." She noticed his observant gaze linger on her face. Her hand went naturally to the bandaged area on the side of her head.

"Strange, I don't remember you ever being clumsy as a child. You were always the surefooted one. You and Stevie would walk the rails on the monkey bars." His brows narrowed in thought.

Lacy laughed nervously. She didn't enjoy lying. "I appreciate that, Jerome, but I wasn't watching where I was going. Sometimes your thoughts get to wandering...and those steps are cracked and pretty irregular." *How can I get off the subject of myself and on to him?* After filling her cup, she asked, "Would you like me to pour you more coffee while I'm at it?"

"Ah, sure. That's my cup on the table. I could do with something to go with these cookies. Did either of you girls bake these? They're good."

Lacy could have laughed at the question. Reaching for his mug, she poured the coffee and placed it on the counter in front of his cookie plate. "Umm, no. We bought those, but they are good. We just can't seem to find the time to bake cookies lately."

She edged closer to the table and took a nearby seat. "Do you ever go out to the old cemetery? You know, where Stevie is buried?" She watched Jerome's face at the mention of the cemetery. There was not even an eyelash flicker—no twitch—no movement of any kind.

Crunching on a cookie, Jerome looked over his glasses at her. "I don't think I've been back to the cemetery since the day of the funeral. I'm not sure I could find my way to it without directions. Kids go where they're taken." His focus zeroed in on the cupboard above the sink. "I remember riding out of town and passing a few barns. Wasn't it out in the country?"

"Kind of," she said, dropping the subject. She had her answer. "Jerome, did Stevie ever tell you about any of our adventures? Like one time, we filled his dad's empty beer bottles up with vinegar and water and put them back in his refrigerator. Boy, did he catch flak for that one!" She chuckled at the memory. "Stevie was grounded for two days, but he never gave me up as his accomplice." She tried to shed the melancholy that came with the memory. "Anyway," she said brightly, "I was just wondering if he ever talked about some of those times when you two were together?"

Jerome brought his coffee mug to his lips and sipped before answering, his eyes never leaving her. "You and Stevie had a relationship Chuck and I envied. But answering your question, no, not normally. I don't recall Stevie sharing anything that the two of you did together. Though there was that one instance when we went fishing. He rambled on a bit then, but I didn't pay much attention. The very fact Stevie wouldn't tell his dad about you being involved in the beer caper should tell you something. You were always something special to Stevie. Chuck and I were his friends, but generally only if you couldn't spend time with him."

"I'm sorry. You must have resented me terribly."

"Nope. Envied, yes," Jerome admitted, "but Stevie was a good friend, and when we all played ball together or gathered for group things, everyone was equal. And…when it was just he and I, or even Chucky, he gave us his whole attention. You didn't enter into it…almost as if he refused to share you with us. I don't know if you ever knew what a special relationship the two of you had." The intense, somber expression on Jerome's face told it all. He, like she, still missed their unique friend.

Lacy worked to control her mounting emotions. "I did know." Lowering her eyes to her coffee, she stood. "I need to stretch out on that couch. I've got a lot of recuperating to do in a very short time. Sorry if I reopened old wounds," she apologized.

"It's good to remember, Lacy. It's when you try to suppress things that the wound festers and doesn't heal as it should."

Whipping her head about, Lacy stared at him. "Some things refuse to come to the surface even when you want to remember, no matter how hard you try."

"Being back in Gladden Hills should help that. Give yourself time. Kelly tells me you're a woman of faith. Ask God to help you...then wait."

"I'm afraid my faith isn't as strong as it should be and waiting has become a luxury I may not be able to afford. I need to remember, Jerome. I need to remember quickly." Her words conveyed an urgency that brought his astute eyes to stare in question. Lacy blanched, realizing she'd allowed her personal fears to enter into their conversation.

Kelly pushed through the connecting door, her blond hair mussed and her cheeks bright from exertion. "I finally found that file!" She looked from one to another with question. "Did I miss something?"

Jerome eyed Lacy. "Just reminiscing from our childhood days."

Anxiety flickered in Kelly's eyes. "Childhood days seem to be the main topic lately."

Lacy moved toward the door. "I'll leave you to your contracts."

Kelly touched her arm. "I checked outside, but I didn't see the truck."

Lacy stole a covert glance at Jerome, who'd frowned. Had he heard Kelly's comment? Lacy patted her cousin's arm in reassurance and left the kitchen. She paused on the other side of the door, wondering if Jerome would question Kelly but only heard the rustling of papers. She made her way back to the warm parlor. Poor Kelly. She'd been thrown into something totally foreign to her world.

Lowering her body to the welcoming arms of the overstuffed couch, she reflected on her short exchange with Jerome. He had mentioned one time Stevie talking more in depth with him, yet Lacy remained unsure. If Jerome was her mysterious contact, he'd chosen to keep it a secret. He was also great at covering his reactions. Still, he appeared to be a man of character, one she might be forced to call upon if push came to shove. Quinn said two backups were better than one, and as yet she had none. She wasn't ready to make that move—soon maybe? Not knowing whom she could trust with her situation, she felt it better to keep the inner circle of "people in the know" small.

As Lacy cultivated her nesting area on the couch, she thought back to the day of the "accident" on the courthouse stairs. Here, in the safe comfort of her home with people around her, she could finally review the whole terrifying ordeal. Remembering when she first became aware of hearing a noise on the descending first flight, she traveled those next few minutes in her mind. Her foot was on the top stair of the second flight toward the basement level when the exit door opened and a large, muscled man took hold of her shoulders in a vise grip. The part about him being cloaked in a ski mask was shadowy at best.

What happened next was clouded with confusion. The assailant had pushed her toward the railing. *Why did he stop and pull me back?* If the man had thrown her over the railing, she would now be dead. *Was he trying to frighten me, or did the assailant have a change of heart? No, it's more likely he took me to the edge to scare me and send me running for the city limits. "Leave town and live, Lacy Cottrell."* Even now those words brought fear to her heart as she stared into the dying embers.

*

Since there was no real need for Lacy to go into work on Wednesday and Thursday, she took the next two days to allow her body to heal and her energy to replenish. Maxine called to say her write-ups were acceptable the way they were received, and she could hardly wait to see them in print.

"Just wait until Gladden Hills finds out that the back of Mona's Bakery was once used to house out-of-town meetings for various members of the purple gang, that same notorious gang that ran illegal alcohol between Canada and Detroit during 1920 Prohibition era. Imagine, actual pictures and memorabilia found hidden between studs and old plasterboard when they refurbished a few years ago. The boss loved that," Maxine added.

Lacy basked in Maxine's last comment. It pleased her immensely that Jason Gardner liked her article. She hesitated before speaking her next words, unsure how they might be taken. "Maxine, would you look out for Chloe while I'm gone?" She left much of what she was fearful of out of her request.

The girl was making Lacy increasingly uneasy. Breaking into Lacy's desk was not acceptable behavior, yet she wasn't yet willing to get the girl fired. She'd give Chloe a second chance. Perhaps there was some way she could find to help her, though Lacy was at a loss to think of one at present.

The extended quietness on Maxine's end of the phone carried a current of electricity. Lacy had issued a simple statement of concern, yet the major general had seemingly picked up that there was more to know. Her reply sounded embodied with deep insight. "I will. I will look out for Chloe while you're gone. If you have further instructions, let me know."

"Thank you. I know I can count on you. I'll try to be back on Friday."

"Rest up. Don't come back too soon, Lacy. I'm concerned about you."

When Lacy hung up, she mused on Maxine's gentle tone. Was she speaking of her injuries, or did she sense impending danger? Lacy chided her new tendency to read double meaning into every statement.

*

On Thursday morning, Lacy ventured out to the expanded porch of the old house and picked up the newly delivered *Gladden Hills Gazette.* Peeling the thin plastic cover off, she held the rolled paper in her hands and walked back inside, heart pounding. She spread the paper across the kitchen table and flipped through the pages, bypassing her articles to get to the classifieds section. Her eyes traveled each column until she came to the one she'd asked Nadine to post from Chicago:

> Purple Feather: A question will be waiting for you—regular time and place. Await your answer. PF.

Lacy's brain whirled at the possible crisis situation she'd put into motion.

Now that the bait had been laid out, how could she manage to pull it off in her present condition? Between her physical injuries and those stalking her, she felt as if she were in an invisible prison. Slowly, a plan wormed its way in. She'd use one of the two feathers she'd received in her notes to insert inside her envelope and plant it at Stevie's grave. The trick would be to get out of town without the tan pickup or anyone following her. Her contact would be looking for the envelope at 11:30 p.m. tonight if they responded to her question. She was tempted to be there waiting for him, but it was too dangerous to consider.

Pushing the paper off to the side, Lacy grabbed a notepad from the phone area and sat at the table, her right hand drumming the pen top on the table. *Keep it simple.* She wrote out the words: *What money should I be following? Money back then or money now? I need some help here! Who are you? PF.*

Inserting the folded note inside a plain white envelope, she pulled out a sandwich-sized plastic baggie and placed all within the confines of her purse. *Tomorrow morning I'll drop off the note at the gravesite before work. Then we will see what develops.*

11

Backup

EARLY FRIDAY MORNING the antique, powder blue Volkswagen made its way out the west side of Gladden Hills and headed toward a predetermined destination. The engine of the old car was running rough, and Lacy was rusty at handling a stick transmission. Shifting into neutral, she turned off the engine and parked behind the old Free Methodist Church. The morning chill seeped through the many crevices of her cousin's car.

A new robe isn't all that Kelly needs to be shopping for, Lacy mused as she took a minute to clear her thoughts. Driving the relic out to the graveyard brought back earlier memories of Kelly driving up to college in the little car to spend the weekend with her after Grant was deployed to Afghanistan. She patted the steering wheel. "You ran a lot smoother in those days, old friend."

Climbing out of the compact car, Lacy scanned the area before making her way to the wrought-iron opening to the old graveyard. She noted the wire that secured the gate was still in place and undid it with care. In jeans, a heavy sweatshirt, and comfortable shoes, Lacy picked her way between the rough areas of sod and headstones. She maneuvered in and about the stretched finger shadows, mirroring the elongated, cracked tombstones, dotted here and there with monuments depicting angels or statues of the risen Lord scattered throughout the yard.

*

A muscled hand rolled down the window in his tan truck and dialed a frequently used number. "Listen, I lost her. I don't know where she is right now." The swearing that punctuated the other side of the conversation caused the first man to hold the phone away from his ear.

"Calm down! I didn't let her get away. She and her cousin switched cars this morning. They had it planned. I followed Cottrell's car to the Reality Company and got suspicious after a few minutes. When I looked in through the window, the only one who was inside was the Larson woman." He listened to the curt instructions that followed. "All right. I'll stake out the place she's most likely to return. I haven't decided yet about changing vehicles."

The broad-shouldered man in the Western hat shut down his phone and started up his truck, deciding that he'd have to step up his methods if they were to get the results the boss wanted. His foot jammed down on the accelerator with irritation. A whole morning wasted because he'd fallen for an old stunt like the one those two women played on him this morning. The trouble lay in the fact he hadn't expected it. Well, from now on...

*

Lacy tried to throw off the creepy feeling that accompanied her as she made her way through the cemetery. Day or night this place caused an inner turmoil. Someday she would lie beneath the ground in a place much like this. Just knowing Stevie's remains were here should have brought her comfort, but instead they brought back the day he was buried.

After she'd reached the back wall and extracted the lunchbox, she took pains to count the feathers, confirming that the feather in the note she'd received at the Morrisons' benefit had indeed been taken from the lunchbox. *My contact was at the benefit, had possibly walked to my place at the table, and I never spotted him.* Lacy walked toward the last two gravesites.

Bending in front of Stevie's grave, she paused to remember one of their special times together before carefully wedging the white envelope beneath a medium-sized rock. Just the right edge showed—enough for someone who was looking for it. Shifting, she stared beyond the ancient stone hedge down the partially overgrown path that led into the dense forest area. She knew it was a relatively small forest, bottoming out at a barrier of large boulders with the steep hill behind.

She and Stevie had sneaked off after church one Sunday, racing through the forest and up the hill, playing "King of the Mountain." She had ruined one of her better dresses, and neither Stevie's grandmother nor her mother had been too pleased. Shaking her head to clear her memories, she hurried back to the parking lot and Kelly's blue bug.

Lacy froze in place when she spotted a second car parked next to the Volkswagen. It was a Jeep Liberty, at least three to four years old. Slowly she shifted to scan the entire area. Had someone managed to see through the ploy she and Kelly had initiated and followed her here? But there was no one in evidence.

Striding toward her car, Lacy reached for the door handle, her pulse thrumming so loudly she never heard the footsteps come up behind her.

"May I help you?"

Whirling around, her heart pounding, she managed, "Pastor Jaminson?"

"Lacy Cottrell? What a surprise!" He looked first at his watch before scanning the extended area. "What brings you way out here at this time of day? Surely not a story?"

"Oh, no. I was visiting the grave of a friend of mine before work."

Kurt Jaminson looked at her incredulously. "You knew someone who was buried here? Why, you don't look old enough to know anyone in that old cemetery." He chuckled, the morning light shining through his thinning top hair onto his nearly bald head.

Lacy nodded. "Ah, my friend…he and his mother were the last to be buried in this cemetery. He was very young when he died."

"Oh, I'm sorry to hear that. I was told the cemetery was closed years ago." His sympathetic gaze told her that he saw the death had meant a great deal to her. He glanced back at the old church. "I'm getting ahead of the game and setting up some of my office area before the big move this weekend. I've got a coffee pot going right now if you'd like to come in and sit a spell. It would give me a good chance to take a break. I really don't know where to put the stuff I carted in, and I hate to go home a failure." His blue eyes twinkled.

"Sorry, I've got to get back. I've been out a few days from work on sick leave. It wouldn't do for me to play hooky today," she answered, wishing she could stay and unburden her heart to this kind man of God.

"I heard you had a bad accident. I'm glad to see you are healing. I'll pray for you, Lacy Cottrell."

"Good," she said softly. "I need your prayers, Pastor. I really do." Thinking of her situation, she hurriedly added, "I should go."

As Lacy lowered herself into the confines of the smaller car, Pastor Jaminson leaned over the edge of her door. "Well then, I'll pray a hedge of protection around you starting now." Somehow he had grasped the urgency of her need.

She nodded soberly as he closed her car door and backed away, watching her pull out. A mile down the road, the engine began missing more and more. Lacy pulled over to the side of the road and parked. Pulling her phone out of her purse, she tried to call Kelly but the signal faded twice. "Great!" she fumed and opened the door to climb out.

Standing on the edge of the road, she tried her cousin's number again, but the signal dropped. "Think Cottrell, what now?" She paced, thinking of her options. Physically she wasn't up to walking the distance. She stared up at the bright blue morning sky. "I don't understand. I'm trusting, but I don't understand." She opened the door to the Volkswagen and sat on the seat staring out at the little traveled two-lane road.

She'd watched three semis race by, their backdraft causing her to grab hold to the car door to steady her stance. Raising the hood to indicate a motorist in distress, she returned to sit in the front seat with the door open where she watched several fast-moving vehicles whiz pass. Once traffic was outside the city limits, they hit the accelerator to make up the time they'd lost going through town. Leaning her head back against the headrest, she closed her eyes and waited…for what she had no idea. A patrol car maybe?

Hearing a diesel engine slow down nearby, she opened her eyes in hope. A large tow truck had pulled to a stop across the highway, and a gigantic man with arms like a TV wrestler and a black ponytail hanging down his back swung down out of the cab. He was wearing a black T-shirt and a worn leather jacket with lumberjack hard-toed boots on feet that looked to be size thirteen. And, praise God, he was walking across the street in Lacy's direction.

The man looked like he had lived hard, his coarse features emphasized by a scar at the side of his chin. There was almost an Asian twist around his eyes. Lacy suddenly realized she'd seen eyes like that before. Her line of vision moved from the man to the writing on his tow truck door: *The Car Doctor, Charles Walden, Master Mechanic.*

Lacy stared in disbelief when the burly man walked up to her. "Looks like you could use some help, ma'am," he said, surveying the distressed little car. "Hey, I know this bug. Only one of them in Gladden Hills, and it belongs to Kelly Larson." His look of suspicion traveled to Lacy's face. "How do you come to be driving it, lady?"

Lacy was unable to hold back her amusement. "Because I happen to be Kelly's cousin, Chuck…Lacy Cottrell. How are you?"

"Ellie?" He gave her a thorough up and down once over. "Well, I'll be…I heard you were back. Didn't I read that you had a near fatal fall down the courthouse stairs? You've still got a shiner, I see. You grew up real pretty, Ellie," he said as a matter-of-fact appraisal more than a compliment. "Glad to have you back in town."

"Thanks, Chuck. I go by Lacy now. It's my real first name. Sure glad you stopped. I have no idea what's wrong with Kelly's car. I drive it for two hours, and already I broke it. She'd going to kill me," she said, frustrated.

Chuck maneuvered his body bulk inside the small car and started the engine. It only took a couple of minutes of listening and he turned it off. "Bad gas is my opinion. I'll siphon out what's left and replace it with a can I've got in the back of my truck. It might get you back to town. If you continue to have trouble, you might have to have the fuel filter replaced, but we'll try this first."

Lacy stood back and watched him work. A half hour later, she started the engine and heard the improvement while Chuck stood by and listened. He handed her a card. "Keep this on hand if you need me."

"What do I owe you, Chuck?" she asked, opening her purse.

"For Ellie Cottrell, it's on the house." He checked his watch. "I've got time to follow you back to town to make sure it doesn't fail on you again. Tell Kelly to avoid that new fly-by-gas station at the far edge of town. Some bargains are too expensive, if you know what I mean."

"I'll tell her, Chuck. I appreciate everything." Lacy ran her fingers through her mussed hair. "Listen, how about letting us treat you to a homemade meal one night next week? I'd really like to catch up with you. I've been away too long, Chuckie." Without meaning to, her words ended with an unexpected catch in her voice. Unaccountable emotion had been bubbling up at surprising times. *Nerves*, she told herself.

The huge man dropped his head without comment. Lacy waited. "We'll see," he said slowly. "I remember your mom was a good cook. It might be nice to talk around a table again. Remember when she asked Jerry and me to stay for dinner that time we were all playing in your backyard? I figured Stevie would stay, 'cause the two of you were so tight, but I was sure surprised when she invited us too. I use to wonder if maybe you and Stevie were related. None of the rest of us had a girl for a best friend. 'Course, you were all right…for a girl, I mean." He grinned.

Lacy chuckled. "I remember that night. Jerry was so nervous he turned his plate of spaghetti over on Mom's tablecloth. He waited for her to yell at him—we all did—but she just scraped up the spaghetti and gave it back to him."

"Yeah, I thought sure she was going to cuff him good. My old lady would have walloped me into next Tuesday. 'Course, we never had tablecloths at our house."

Lacy remembered. Chuck's family had a reputation of being a tough lot. There were four roughhouse boys in his big-boned, robust family. His dad was in construction, a known drinker in town, and his mom washed dishes at the bar around the corner to help support the family. Chuck was an outsider from the get-go of school opening, backward in most social graces and abrasive in his manner—but he was loyal to Stevie.

Stevie had a knack of drawing toward him kids who had trouble fitting in with the average crowd, like Jerry Collins, who was overly shy. Lacy had been the exception. Stevie claimed Ellie Cottrell the morning of day one in first grade. He walked up and placed a big candy bar on her desk and looked up at her with those special brown eyes of his—eyes that twinkled with reddish highlights. His infectious grin had dazzled her world, and when recess rolled around, he was right beside her like a shadow. By second grade they chose seats across from one another and their friendship bonded for life. *I just didn't know it would be so short.* Lacy sighed, recalling those few years. They had other friends, but always with them, the other came first. Stevie never gave up a friend.

Chuck lowered and fastened her car hood. "Well, get into that blue bug and see if it will track all the way to town. You've got my number on the card. You can leave a message on my box about that invitation thing. Just call and tell me when I can collect my meal." His grin slid slowly to the side of his mouth forming a frown. "There's just me and a no-account mutt that wandered in one day. My ex left me last year. Catching up may not be all that it's cracked up to be, Ellie Cottrell. Listen, you be careful walking down back stairs." His features tensed. "But should you need me beforehand, let me know. I mean it. Call if you need help. I worry about friends who fall down stairs."

Lacy eyed Chuck with speculation as he crossed back over to his truck. *I wonder to what extent Chuck meant, "Call if you need help?" Might his offer extend to agreeing to be needed backup? An aggressor would think twice before challenging Chuck Walden. Don't think crazy, Cottrell! The man helped with your car. Don't read more into it than what was offered.*

Climbing into Kelly's Volkswagen, she started up the little car. *Well, Lacy, you wanted to reconnect with Chuck Walden...*she reminded herself. *I just didn't see it happening this way.* Dinner with her and Kelly might give her the opportunity to feel out Chuck. Combining today's impression with past childhood recollections. Lacy wagered a shotgun assessment. *As loyal as Chuck is, it wouldn't be his style to leave mysterious messages in a graveyard. He had an upfront, straight-on personality. No.* She didn't think Chuck sent the notes. *Those notes were born of a calculating mind—a mind that could be devious and was used to dealing with covert affairs.*

At the first street light Lacy waved Chuck off. She drove first to the back parking lot of Collins' Realty and pulled in beside her black Challenger. Lifting a black floppy hat from the back seat, she pulled it down over her head and tucked her hair up inside before climbing out of the car and walking into the reality through the rear entrance. Following a quick survey of the large, sunny office, she made straight for Kelly's desk near the back of the room.

Lacy whipped off her hat and leaned across her cousin's desk, speaking low. "Your little powder-blue bug conked out on me on the highway—bad gas. Chuck Walden says not to get your gas at that new station from now on. Can I have my keys back? When you want to go new car hunting, let me know. See you at home tonight."

Startled, Kelly cocked her head at Lacy. Opening her desk, she handed Lacy's keys back to her. "Just for the record, a tan pickup was parked across the street earlier today, but I don't think it's there now. So…is my car okay to drive?"

Lacy took the keys. "Hopefully. I drove it back into town with no further trouble. But call if you need a ride."

Lacy left the same way she came in, nodding in passing to Jerome. Exiting the back entrance, she marched directly to her black car. Checking the street out in front, she drove carefully by the side roads into the rear parking lot of the Gazette building. Making her way to the back door, she rang the buzzer and waited until Maxine unlocked and opened the door.

"I got your note. Do you want to explain why you felt the need to be let in through the back door entrance?"

"I've been followed lately, but I wish you'd keep that information to yourself."

"Does the boss know?" The aging face wrinkled in concern.

"Not yet, but I plan to tell him soon. I can't explain right now, Maxine. Will you trust me?"

The woman nodded curtly and allowed her to pass by, following close behind. "It's been an interesting morning all around. Not only has comments of praise, all marked for your articles, been reaching our ears, but Mona sent over two free boxes of doughnuts. She says it's for all the free publicity you've given her. And she wanted me to tell you, she's taking your advice and having those historic papers mounted and framed to put on her wall."

"Good," Lacy murmured, her heels clicking on the corridor floor.

"Lacy?" Maxine touched her arm.

Hearing a change in the woman's tone, Lacy swiveled toward her in the narrow hall. She waited for the coming comment with some apprehension.

Maxine scanned the area before continuing. "We need to talk about a mutual colleague. I'm in charge of personnel, and I've been aware of a possible trouble area for some time now. Various personnel have come to me about problem situations."

Lacy stared at her. She'd been afraid that her casual comment would lead to possible censure of Chloe, yet how else could she handle the escalating situation? The young woman was behaving strangely, and her actions were definitely unethical. Still, if Lacy could put off her meeting with Maxine for a short time, Chloe's attitude might improve. Yet apparently others had previously approached the office manager. Lacy knew she wasn't ready to join them and admit defeat. There must be some way to help that young woman.

"Look, Lacy," Maxine said, clearly frustrated, "you're not the only one who has noticed something...let's say different...about our mutual friend? The boss wanted to give her a chance, but I was against it from the start. I can't put my finger on the root problem, but something isn't right with her. At any rate, I've probably allowed things to go for too long already. I'd definitely appreciate your input. You've been spending a lot of time with her lately. I'll set up a meeting to inform you." With that, the little major general marched back to her desk in the entry area leaving Lacy no opportunity to respond.

Lacy exhaled. It was nice of Jason Gardner to want to help Chloe. Not many employers took the time to reach out to people with a hand-up anymore. She frowned. Unfortunately, Chloe might prove to be more trouble than he anticipated. Chloe's personality was not mature enough to handle correction of any type in a positive way. If she was fired, it might crush her.

Not knowing how she could alter the situation, Lacy decided to think on it later. She advanced with the amount of swiftness her sore body would allow, motivated purely by the need to do research on the internet for next week's articles. The subjects of her purposed articles required it. Having made a list of potential material, she had yet to make final decisions.

Lacy worked through lunch, pausing to rest her eyes for a few minutes after most of the office left for lunch break. Chloe had skillfully skirted her when she'd slipped into work midmorning, which suited Lacy completely. She had no heart for dealing with the complex young woman today, having weightier issues to address. That tan truck was becoming a problem. What if she'd been followed out to the cemetery and the car had quit running with no one around? Quinn was right; she needed backup. Who could she actually trust? What did she know about the people in this town...especially those who were part of the local scene seventeen years ago?

Resting her head on the back of the chair, Lacy allowed her thoughts to wander. She'd found that some of her needed information was unobtainable though the internet, so she had to consider other avenues. While working in Chicago, she would automatically turn to Nadine for the difficult research. Therefore it was natural for her to think in that direction now. Nadine had a special magic that managed to conjure up unbelievable facts on people and places. Rocking forward, Lacy dialed Nadine. Finding the resource queen happy to accommodate her, Lacy checked off the places and people she required information about.

At the end of the list she tagged on a couple of names she'd been curious about ever since she returned to Gladden Hills. Lacy closed up her notebook and was planning to place it inside her top drawer until she remembered Chloe. Something told her a locked drawer would not be a sufficient deterrent. The girl obviously had no regard for personal privacy or simple rules of conduct. Lacy decided it might be safer to keep her notebook on her person or someplace at home.

Feeling the effects of her headache return, she lowered her head atop her folded arms on the desk, her eyelids heavy. It was in this position that Jason Gardner found her a few minutes later.

"Miss Cottrell," he said softly.

Her head shot up, and she stared bleary-eyed into the complex expression of her boss. The more she learned about the man, the more handsome he appeared. While he'd seemed stern on the onset, she observed that he took more than a professional interest in his employees. Though, perhaps in Chloe's case, it was erroneous. Lacy sat upright and pushed her hair away from her flushed face. "Mr. Gardner, it seems you literally caught me sleeping on the job," she said, yawning.

He sat easily on the edge of her desk. "Well, no one is more deserving. Excellent work this week in spite of your so-called *accident.* Do you have anything else you'd like to report about what happened on those back stairs of the courthouse—or why? I've tried to be patient, Lacy, but I don't like working in the dark with no intel. Attempted murder raised the stakes of whatever you're working on." She could feel the steel behind his words.

The sounds of workers returning from lunch drew her instant attention. People passed on their right and left. Lacy spoke hurriedly, her words hushed and impetuous. "Come to my house tonight about 7:00 p.m. to continue our conversation. I think it's time." Fear slashed through her like a hot knife. Was revealing too much to this man she hardly knew a mistake? It might not bode well for her position at the paper. But the die was cast and, as he'd stated, the stakes had risen.

Rolling off the edge of the desk, Jason bent his head. "Then we'll talk later."

Lacy took little notice as Chloe passed behind her cubicle on her way to her work station. Anxious to be at home, Lacy went back to arranging her notes on the computer, printing out a copy to for her folder. Locking her desk drawer, she closed out early and walked toward the outside doors. Home base was a beckoning beacon that couldn't come fast enough. The pressure of her Velcro bandage was crying for release.

Pausing outside, she took in the street. The tan truck was parked across the square at the end of a side street. On impulse she turned and walked up the street to Mona's Bakery for something to serve later with coffee. She'd taken Gardner's parting comment to indicate he would come to her place tonight—though he'd not actually spoken the words.

As she retracing her steps, one eye kept contact with the tan truck even as her thoughts went to the cemetery and her note for *Purple Feather.* Would her contact come before midnight to lift the note from beneath the rock? The thought excited her. She would check early tomorrow morning for an answer. Realizing Saturday was moving day for the church, she frowned. There would be too much activity in the area. This was her second week in Gladden Hills. Her sojourn at the paper was narrowing, and, as of yet, she had no answers. Monday she would return to the file room and, with God's help, find just one clue.

*

Kelly came out of the parlor and stood in the hallway regarding her cousin. "Watching outside that door isn't going to make him appear, Lacy. It's almost 9:00 p.m. and you told him 7:00 p.m. I'd take that to mean he's not coming, at least not tonight. Turn off that porch light and come in by the fire to relax. I know you think a lot of his integrity, but he's a busy person and, well, maybe he isn't sure he wants to get mixed up in whatever you've got going. Someone has already tried to kill you once." Seeing the tan truck outside her place of work had obviously unnerved Kelly today, more than was first apparent. Her comments during supper had alerted Lacy to her rising anxiety.

After turning off the porch light, Lacy studied the taut lines in her cousin's pretty face and was very concerned. Kelly's background had not prepared her for the type of mystery and danger now surrounding their lives and there was no way that Lacy could remove it from her—unless she gave up her search and left town. *But would that remove the danger?* She sensed that an evil energy had been released. The slumbering giant had been awakened, and somehow this whole scenario would be played out.

Lacy pared the curtain one last time before trudging down the hall. Leaning on the wall across the doorway to the parlor, she asked Kelly, "How about some hot chocolate and we'll tackle that box of cannoli from Mona's Bakery? She wouldn't hear of me paying for them after that article came out yesterday. I, for one, am certainly not going to let them get stale." Lacy laughed, trying to lighten the atmosphere.

Kelly nodded and followed Lacy into the kitchen. "I'll start some milk in a saucepan," she offered. Holding the pan in her hand, she stopped. "I wish your boss had showed up tonight. I wouldn't feel like we were so all alone in this. Everything is so under wraps and hush-hush that I don't know who, if anyone, is out there protecting us. You say the chief of police knows you were pushed but is standing aside, waiting for something more to happen…like what, you being murdered? Is he even trying to find out who pushed you down those stairs? Did you tell him about that tan pickup truck?" Her tone had an element of mounting panic, barely held in check.

Lacy turned from the counter where she was opening the fair-sized white bakery box. "It's not like that—it's complicated. I will inform the chief, Kelly, but I have to speak to him alone. I don't want any of his deputies to know yet. This is a small town…no telling who is involved. I can't take that chance. The chief can maneuver around all that. It's just a little awkward since I haven't discussed the situation with him personally. Quinn Darling has taken charge. He knows what I'm working on, that I was pushed on the stairs. It's that in-between thing with the chief of police and Quinn that leaves me hanging. But *I promise* I will report the tan pickup."

Kelly set the saucepan on the stovetop before turning back toward the refrigerator for the milk. Hearing a startling sound, the women froze, exchanging sharp glances. The light knocking on the back door continued. Lacy moved first. Taking hesitant steps toward the door with the blue-flowered valance, she saw the faint outline of a man's profile in reflected light and drew in a quick intake of air. Moving cautiously, she stared wide-eyed through the door window.

Jason Gardner stared back at her. *Jason Gardner without his sunglasses!* Lacy quickly fumbled with the locks and flung open the door. Sliding smoothly through the opening, as if he did covert work every night, Jason shifted away from the bright overhead lights and lifted his sunglasses into position before turning back. While he and Lacy regarded one another in stark silence, Kelly continued to hold tight to the open refrigerator.

Lacy spoke first. "I, ah, didn't think you were coming," she stated tersely, irritated at his tardiness.

His features tightened. "I was here all right, waiting for you to turn off that blasted porch light." Drawing over a kitchen chair, Jason sat down. "You had company across the street—in the shadows. If I didn't know better, I would think someone knew I was expected. They left when you turned off the light, so I walked up the street and slipped around back."

"Someone was across the street watching our house again?" repeated Kelly like a tense parrot, her fingers gripping the refrigerator door.

Lacy hurried to take the gallon milk jug from Kelly. Inching her cousin aside, she closed the refrigerator. "Actually, Kelly and I were just about to make some hot chocolate and lay out some cannoli, weren't we, Kelly? You're in time to join us."

Coming back to herself, Kelly moved toward the stove where Lacy set down the milk. "Yes. As soon as I locate the cocoa, we'll be in good shape. Make yourself comfortable, Mr. Gardner, and hot chocolate will be ready shortly."

"Jason, please, Ms. Larson. And if I may call you Kelly? Hopefully, we're all friends here." He glanced warmly at Kelly. "The fact someone was watching doesn't mean they meant to do anything more than that at this point. Though I would encourage you to keep your doors locked at night. They probably want information to find out what your cousin knows, which is the reason I am here tonight. Once I know what she is up against, then we can go from there. I have contacts; we can arrange for someone to watch out for you, if necessary. " His shaded focus remained on the back of the anxious young woman at the stove.

Lacy could have kissed him. Without knowing, he'd said the very words Kelly needed to hear—that they were no longer alone in this terror. Someone else was on their side. Lacy doubted how much protection Jason could arrange, given they had little tangible evidence to go on and no real targets. Law enforcement was funny that way, and small-town law was limited in their resources, but nevertheless, the offer had been made. She turned happily back to the box of cannoli.

There was no talking for the first few minutes as the treats were savored. "Man, these are so fresh they're melting in my mouth. I've been a lot of places, but Mona's cannoli are the best I've ever eaten," Jason mumbled between mouthfuls. "Any more hot chocolate, Kelly?"

The table scene implied a simple gathering of friends for friendly conversation. Lacy wished that was all it was. The atmosphere was filled with warmth, and she was surprised to find how pleasant it was having Jason sit across the table from her in this old family kitchen.

Responding to Jason's request for more hot chocolate, Kelly was up in a flash. Lacy watched in amazement. It was almost like the old Kelly—a natural-born hostess. As Kelly poured out the last from the saucepan, Jason focused on Lacy. "You want to start at the beginning? Is this a story you stumbled upon since you started work, or something you've been on the trail of for some time? I suspected an alternative motive for your applying for a position at the *Gazette.* The temporary situation tale seemed a little off-center."

Lacy nodded. "Actually that part is pretty much the truth—just not all of it." Since it was the third telling of her story, the words flowed quickly, though again she left out the part about the mysterious cemetery notes. "I was on the trail of this story well before I came, Jason. You are aware that I lived in Gladden Hills when I was a child?"

Kelly sat silently sober, listening to her cousin's story for a second time.

Jason stretched as she finished, folding his arms behind his head. "So when are you planning to review the old files again?"

"Monday, if it works out. I have authorization to view all the old files, including the sign-in registers. Oh, I forgot to report something to the patrolman who chased after our stalker that night. I believe the man was wearing a Western-style hat, a cowboy hat, if you will…and the driver of the tan pickup has been wearing a cowboy hat."

"Really?" He put his arms down. "Maybe I can get a hold of a list of all the members of the riding club. I think it's called Gladden Hills Horsemen's Association."

"What about that dude B & B outside of town?" Kelly queried. "They employ a few wranglers."

"The Kerrigan Place? Maybe, but unlikely. I can check them out and learn what connections they may have with the community. We might come up with something. Did the authorities ever make a suspicious connection between this Stevie Turner's mother…or father…to clubs, work, anything where a red flag popped up? "

"I know that Stevie's father was investigated thoroughly. There were a lot of speculations flying around, but he was eventually cleared. I've tried and tried to trace him so I could find out what, if anything he knew. I think he must have changed his name and probably moved a time or two. At any rate, I reached a dead end with him. And the only connection Terri Turner had was at work and a local woman's club that she hardly ever attended."

His eyebrows inched upward. "What does that tell you?"

Lacy made an effort to straighten up the table. "Only that either she happened upon a crime somewhere and had to be eliminated, or there was something undetected going down at that bank." She crumpled a napkin in her hand. "From what I've read there appeared to be a lot of foul-ups with evidence after the bombing—too many for my comfort. Apparently the chief of police and the DA took a lot of heat over it. Because of that, it took forever to track down the one who made the bomb. He lasted in jail only until a private detective named Jake Gibbons paid a visit to his cell. Both the arsonist, Clem Browning, and Jake Gibbons didn't live long after that visit."

"Both were killed?" Kelly's eyes widened in alarm.

Nodding, Lacy went on calmly, "Witnesses don't live long. Browning was safe until word got around that the detective had connections that planned to offer him a shortened sentence for his testimony. Then Browning became a liability. They couldn't afford to chance that he would keep quiet. It was obvious he'd been originally promised something for his silence. Now he had a chance to get out of jail, if not immediately, at least much sooner. That's when he became a liability. He wasn't to be trusted. The guilty tend to get nervous, as a wise man once told me." Lacy thought of Nicholas, the file room guardian.

Standing, she carried the dessert plates to the counter and returned, placing her hands on the back of her chair. "Getting back to Terri Turner...the only other reason I can think of for her planned death might have been a love affair. Perhaps she had a romance on the side that went bad?"

Jason's head jerked upward. He stared at her. "What have you read or heard on that angle?"

"Nothing really—only speculation. There was not one whiff of evidence Terri had a lover on the side. Considering this is a small town, a veritable hotbed of information, somebody would surely have seen or heard a whisper of gossip if she was unfaithful to her husband. And I have to assume that angle was looked into after the bombing. So...back to square one." Lacy blew out her breath in frustration.

"What do you need me to do, Lacy? I'll get that information about connections to the riding club, but what else can I help with?" Jason asked.

Lacy moved her hands squarely on her hips. "Backup. The DA wants...no, *he insists...*that I have backup when I'm out by myself. Oh, not going and coming to work per se, but when I'm traveling outside of town or nosing around for evidence. He wants me to ask a couple of people to be on hand if needed." She groaned. "I hate asking this of anyone! It's like I need a babysitter or something. Look, I understand if you don't feel you have the time. You're a busy man, and have only known me a short time. Already I'm more trouble than I'm worth." She turned away, despising being placed in such an awkward situation.

"Don't be silly," Jason said sternly. "It's not of your doing. But let's get this straight. You're asking me to be one of your protectors, right?"

Lacy faced him, nodding solemnly.

"Okay. That will work. Actually, I'm honored." He scratched the side of his head. "Did you have anyone else in mind?"

"What about Jerome?" offered Kelly. "I'm sure he'd volunteer if he knew the need."

Both Jason and Lacy turned toward her.

"I'm sure he would, but only if it's an emergency," Lacy said pensively. "We might need him to keep an eye on you and you know how busy he is. As it works out, I recently thought of someone else, but I haven't had time to discuss the situation with him yet."

"Anyone I know?" Jason fingered the sugar holder on the table.

Tilting her head, Lacy considered his question. "I don't know. This man used to be a good friend of Stevie's, and he came to my aid today when I had car trouble. Besides, he said something that has since made me wonder if he's heard something I should know. He offered his help as if he thought I might need it in the future. I sensed a warning in his choice of wording."

Lacy probed Jason with a look, wondering how he was adjusting to what she was saying. His face showed little expression. So she added, "At any rate, I plan to pursue that avenue and find out what he might know."

"What's his name?" both Jason and Kelly asked at once.

"Charles Walden! He owns the Car Doctor automotive service facility. He's a good mechanic and a big enough guy to scare anybody off. I offered him a free supper. We'll see what happens then."

"Dinner?" Kelly exploded. "You asked him to dinner? Lacy, Chuck Walden has a really tough reputation."

"I know, but he remembers Stevie and he offered his help. Look, my sixth sense tells me he's okay, Kelly. But if he's going to make you uncomfortable and you don't want to be around him, I'll do it on my own. It's all right, really. This has been awfully trying for you."

"Yeah right. Like I'm going to leave you here alone with Chuck Walden." Her shoulders slumped. "Should I ask Jerome to come too? That would be additional support."

"Ah," Lacy hedged, "I'm concerned about Chuck tensing up. I suppose Jerome could show up for dessert. But if Jerome and Chuck don't make a practice of spending time together, perhaps now is not the time to arrange a reunion. Chuck needs to feel at ease so he'll open up. What do you think, Jason?"

Jason had been watching the interaction between the two women from his centered chair. His mouth worked as if he was engaged in thoughtful consideration. “I think Lacy has a point. You say this Chuck went out of his way to help you today? In what way?”

“I was driving Kelly’s car, and it quit on me. Chuck not only got it running in short order, he wouldn’t issue me a bill,” she said with admiration.

Jason cocked his head. “Maybe chivalry isn’t dead. This Chuck must have some good qualities.” Pushing away from the table, he slowly stood to his feet, his eyes lingering on Lacy. “So when is the next opportunity you could possibly have need of backup? Are you driving out of town tomorrow?”

A vision of her purposed drive to the cemetery flashed, and her brain shot into overdrive. Lacy wanted to retrieve the note, but her situation was now complicated with the need for backup. She didn’t want to lie, but she wasn’t ready to discuss the notes with Jason. They were secret, between her and her mysterious contact.

She shrugged. “Undetermined. My plans aren’t set. Tomorrow is Saturday, daylight—what can happen? In truth, I was thinking of imposing on you basically at night, if I have to go somewhere…or if I know I could end up in a tight spot.” She studied his expression. Would Jason accept her conditions?

He looked thoughtful. “Is that what the DA had in mind when he told you to get backup? Think back a few days. Wasn’t the episode on the courthouse stairs orchestrated during daylight, in the middle of the afternoon?”

Lacy’s head swam. How was she to answer this man? He spoke the truth and had her boxed in, but somehow she had to get off by herself to retrieve the note from the cemetery alone. “How about I call you? This whole situation is difficult. You’re a busy man. I can’t expect you to drop everything and play guard dog.”

“Why don’t you let me be the judge of what can be worked out and what can’t? I think I can solve your indecision concerning tomorrow. I know it’s Saturday, but I need to have a special article written up by late afternoon tomorrow. I told my publishing friend in Ohio I’d ask my star reporter to put the piece together and email it before Monday. Don’t worry. I’ll pay double time for Saturday work. I, ah, didn’t know how to say no. Besides, it was right up your area of expertise. He needs an article with heart, and he’s short a writer this week. I was going to tell you tonight, but I haven’t had an opportunity.” He waited for her answer.

“Work tomorrow?” Her hopes of slipping away blew up in her face. “What about the research material? How will I ever have time to work everything up in one day?”

"My friend sent me the research material overnight delivery. Everything you'll need should be in the envelope. I'll be at the office with you as long as you're there. Maxine said she'd be in to help with whatever you need."

Lacy's hand went to her head. "Wow. Sounds as if you've got everything worked out! Sure, I'll do the article. I'll be in early to get a good start. What time will the office be open?"

"8:30 a.m. Now what's happening on Sunday? Are you going to be home?"

Lacy looked at Kelly. "We, Kelly and I, planned on attending Sunday services at that new Mission Bible Church. They're renting the old Free Methodist Church out of town. The one with the old cemetery behind it. You might not know of it."

He stared at her with question. "You're going to church? Well, the two of you together should be safe enough. Give me a call if you need me," he said, making his way to the door.

Frown wrinkles formed on Kelly's forehead. "Actually, Lacy, I've got to bail on you. Sorry. I was going to tell you tomorrow. Jerome booked a client who is flying in Sunday morning especially to see this house. It's a really big commission if it sells, and he wanted me there to answer any questions. This has been my listing from the start. There was no way I could get out of it. I truly am sorry. I'll go next week with you."

Jason stopped, turning back, even as it dawned on Lacy she'd be alone and completely free to retrieve the note in the cemetery after church Sunday morning. She brightened. "Don't worry, for goodness' sake. It's early Sunday morning. What killer gets up to go to church? There will be plenty of people around."

"What about going and coming? That's a long stretch of lonely road with little traffic on a Sunday morning." Kelly looked troubled.

Jason stared down at Lacy. "Can't you put your first Sunday off until Kelly can go with you? It would be the safer decision."

Lacy could tell Sunday wasn't a good day for Jason Gardner, either that or he wasn't keen on attending church—whichever, she hurried to reassure him. "I'll be fine, honestly. I practically promised Pastor Jaminson I'd be there, but there's no problem. I have a phone; I'll call if I have trouble." Even as the words left her mouth, she remembered that her signal faded out on that road. She held her tongue.

As Jason zipped up his sporty black jacket, his next words came definite and short. "What time do you need to leave to make services?"

Hearing the specific time, he nodded curtly and left by the back door as inconspicuous as he'd come.

The women exchanged looks. "I'd say the word *church* struck a nerve with him," Kelly commented.

"Yeah, it would seem. It was like day and night in his mood change the instant I mentioned church. Wonder what that is all about?"

Lacy stared at the closed door, puzzled at the type of man she was dealing with. Although church was obviously a sore point with Jason Gardner, he hadn't wavered in his willingness to accompany her, determined to be backup should she need him. "I might wish I'd gone alone," she mused, knowing his presence was going to make it difficult to retrieve the cemetery note.

"Let's lock up and go to bed. We've had enough excitement for one night," said Kelly softly.

12

The Note

MENTALLY, LACY DRAGGED HER FEET on the special writing assignment Jason had volunteered her for on Saturday. She took the first hour and a half to submerge herself in the reference material handed to her during their initial morning briefing. Jason was clearly in business mode, his attitude clipped and professional. Lacy found it hard to reconcile the Jason of last night, eating cannoli in her warm kitchen, with the Jason of this morning.

His distant attitude made her feel strangely rebuffed. Though the man had said nothing unkind, his manner had noticeably cooled. *Is it this business of going with me to church in the morning?* She wanted to tell him to forget about it completely, but there was no time for personal communication.

Maxine had been at the office before she arrived and assisted Lacy with anything she needed. She helped organize her resource material, made several telephone calls, and searched the internet on her behalf. When noon arrived, the major general had sandwiches sent over from the café, and they all ate in the conference room. Whenever she and Jason happened to make eye contact, Jason was quick to look away first.

Lacy was becoming more and more confused how their relationship stood. *Are we simply employee and employer, or friends, as he intimated last night?* Lacy had even dared to hope their friendship might, with time, ripen into something deeper. Had she only imagined that spark of attraction between them? Her emotions reeled from the whiplash effect.

Is he trying to show me our relationship is to remain strictly professional? She puzzled on the situation, creating more doubts. Even the fact he'd volunteered to be backup now made her wonder if perhaps it was merely to protect his reporter. Lowering the last half of her sandwich, she folded the wrapper to toss the rest away.

Maxine's sharp eyes narrowed. "Not hungry today? I would have thought all that hard work this morning might have given you a good appetite."

Lacy stared off to nowhere in particular. "Too much on my mind, I guess."

"From your expression, I might think you were weighted with heavy matters." The definite question in the woman's statement lingered in the air.

"At times it is, but such is the way of life, isn't it?" She tossed her hair and grinned, trying to lighten the somber effect she'd given without being aware.

"A beautiful young woman like yourself should be thinking of a sweetheart. Is there anyone on your horizon?" Maxine asked.

Jason's focus shifted to rest subtly on Lacy. His interest confused her all the more. Lacy lifted her soft drink to her lips. "After high school I was too busy with college, and then at work I was too busy. I dated some, but not seriously." Looking at Maxine, she chuckled. "But it seems my move back has cultivated some interest along that line. Morgan Streeter has been pushing me to go out with him…who knows?"

"Harrumph," Maxine spit out. "Morgan Streeter usually has the women asking him to go out. The grapevine has it that his lady partner has already staked out her claim. She won't like you moving in on her territory."

"Now that's almost enough incentive to coax me to go out with him." Lacy laughed playfully.

"You like to court danger, Miss Cottrell?" Jason asked, a smile playing on his lips. "Cynthia Bradford has the reputation of being quite the tiger in the courtroom."

Maxine frowned. "It's not always on the up and up from what I hear, but that's not for the record. That's small-town gossip. Those who've gotten their feathers singed when they've had dealings with her can't prove anything."

"Then nothing has changed much." Lacy downed the rest of her drink.

"Did you know her as a child?" asked Maxine with sudden interest.

"Oh, yeah!" she murmured. Realizing she'd already said too much and anxious to drop the subject, she stood and started collecting her lunch leavings, carrying them over to the trash. "I'm heading back to work. Maxine, I don't think there is anything more you can do to help me at this point. A couple more hours should hopefully do it—maybe even sooner. I'd hate to take up all of your Saturday with no real need." Looking at Jason with question, she asked, "What do you think, boss?"

She addressed him with a face void of expression. Lacy was trying to maintain an air of indifference to comply with Jason's detached attitude. His cool manner caused her to regret allowing herself to consider him as a protector or in any other way. It never paid to lead with your heart. She had cared too much about Stevie and still carried the scar.

His shaded eyes studied her before turning toward Maxine. "You're welcome to leave for the rest of the day, Maxine, with our blessing. You've done a great job." He finished a lukewarm cup of coffee and policed his area before standing. "Lacy, I'll be in my office when you're ready to run it by me." Throwing his trash away, he walked from the room.

Lacy chided herself for lowering her guard and allowing Jason's mood swings to affect her. She'd known the man less than two weeks. Perhaps it would be good to accept Morgan's dinner invitation and get her brooding about Jason out of her system. Thanking Maxine for all her helpful hard work, she plodded back to her desk and soon became engrossed in wrapping up her article.

Carrying a copy of her finished piece, she stepped into Gardner's office, alerting him to her presence. He looked up expectantly. Approaching the desk, she extended the article in her hand. "You wanted to review this before I leave?" Taking hold of the article, he immediately lost himself in the content, seemingly ignoring the fact she was still standing. Yet when she turned to leave the office, he put up a restraining hand and pointed to the office chairs. "Wait here."

Lacy sat down carefully. After several hours of sitting at her desk, her ribs were sore from the pressure of being condensed into a constant position and her back ached like blazes. She couldn't wait to get home. Her mind wandered, a natural respite from hours of total concentration on the one article. She was lost in her thoughts when Gardner spoke.

"I crossed out one sentence that I don't think was meant to be included for general public information." A flash of humor appeared briefly. "You were too thorough. Remove that sentence and forward it to my office file and it's a wrap, so to speak. Great work. Thanks. You'll see a more tangible 'thank you' in your next paycheck."

He handed the article back. With the papers in her hand, she nodded and left the office, unsure what else there was to say. Everything about today had been about business, and her footing was unsure where this unpredictable man was concerned. After forwarding the revised article to Jason's computer, she shut everything down, picked up her jacket, and purse to leave.

With her footsteps on automatic forward, Lacy made her way to the front of the building. She was totally absorbed on how she could retrieve the note in the cemetery, choosing to believe her contact would have read the classified ad and responded.

A glance at her watch caused her to speculate on her chances of driving to the cemetery and back before dark yet today, until she recalled Saturday was moving day for Pastor Jaminson's church. It would be too risky to try to retrieve the note with all those people milling about in the church parking lot.

It will have to be tomorrow, then—but how? If Jason Gardner was in earnest about accompanying her to and from church, how could she ever get free of him long enough to check Stevie's grave? *If I can't lose Jason while I'm at church, I'll have to return later to retrieve the note. There's no other recourse.* It hadn't seemed so complicated when she first asked Nadine, in Chicago, to place an ad in the classifieds.

As she neared the glass door opening at the front, a strong hand jerked her away and pushed her back against the wall. "Where do you think you're going?"

"Oof!" Her hand went up in protection of her injured ribs, and she uttered a small groan. She stared straight into the stern face of Jason Gardner. His hands had her pinned against the hard surface, his body leaning near.

Lacy rested her head against the wall, allowing her ridged muscles to relax. "Well, I was going to walk out through those doors and around to the parking lot where I would get in my car and simply drive home. Did you decide at the last minute you had more work for me to do?" Her sharp tone had an edge. "Or perhaps you were checking to see if my ribs had healed?" She fumed, irritated with his strong-arm tactics.

Dropping his arms to his sides, Jason released her, his face contrite. She was rubbing her midsection gingerly when he spoke. "Sorry. I didn't mean to push you so hard. My only intent was to stop you before you left." His head motioned toward the glass doors. "Weren't you even going to check if anyone was waiting for you out there?" He stepped away, giving her room to move.

Lacy rotated her neck from side to side. While she realized she had been distracted, she refused to admit the fact to him. "Excuse me. I've been walking outside that door every day for the past—"

Jason cut her words short. "That was before the stakes were raised. Lacy, you can't afford to get lax in your watchfulness. People are stalking your house. and someone tried to kill you a few days ago. The next time you get sloppy with safety measures could be the *wrong* time." Keeping her behind him, they edged along the wall to a place they could scan the area without being seen. "Do you notice anything that raises a red flag?"

Lacy searched the visible area beyond the building. "No. For once I can't even see that blasted tan truck!" she muttered. She felt Jason's hand on her arm; his touch, now considerably softened, gestured her away from the doors.

"Just to be safe, let's go out the rear entrance. I'll grab my jacket and keys from the office and we'll leave."

In the hall, waiting for Jason to gather his things and lock up, she tried to collect her thoughts, wondering if Jason Gardner planned on following her home. Such actions, Lacy thought, would be excessive. How far was he willing to carry this roll of protective backup?

Jason unlocked the rear door, rarely used by anyone at the paper, and held it open for her. The two slipped out of the building and walked briskly toward Lacy's car. Suddenly, their steps slowed to a stop. Almost as one, Lacy and Jason spotted the dark maroon SUV almost hidden behind the rusted dumpster at the far left side of the parking area.

Turning toward Jason, Lacy asked the question with her eyes. Jason shook his head, indicating he had no prior knowledge of the vehicle. His jaw tightened even as his hand moved swiftly, resting on the back of his belt under his jacket where a slight bulge existed. He stepped boldly in front of Lacy, placing himself between her and the ominous, dark-windowed SUV.

The SUV engine roared to life. Whoever was in the vehicle had obviously spotted Jason. They skidded their tires backing out and around into the back street behind the parking area and spun off down the street, barely missing a startled pedestrian.

Jason moved his hand away from the back of his belt. "As I said, you can't afford to get sloppy. What if you had rounded that corner of the building and approached your car alone in this empty parking lot?"

Lacy didn't feel the need to answer. In truth, she had no answer. The SUV had been waiting for her, not expecting Jason to walk out with her. She suddenly experienced a needle-like tingling down her arms. A fleeting question about the bulge at the back of Jason's jacket slipped away when he ordered her to move quickly.

"Climb inside your car and lock your door. Wait here for me until I pull around and follow you home. I'm parked out on the street." Jason hurried away only a few steps before whirling about. "Lock your doors!" he shouted before he resumed his course. Jason Gardner was clearly upset.

In contrast, Lacy waited inside her locked car feeling almost numb. Her mind was a filmy cobweb of interconnecting thoughts with no real beginning or end. This was the third vehicle that had followed or was spotted waiting for her, for whatever nefarious reason. Her time in Gladden Hills was narrowing. Not only had she managed to learn little, but she'd put not only her own life in danger but placed Kelly and now her boss in the line of fire as well.

What next? There was no chance of her retrieving the hoped-for note today.

Seeing Jason's gold-toned Durango roar into the lot from the side street entrance, she started up her engine and shifted into drive. *God, give me some hopeful insight to guide my next steps.* Driving much like a zombie through the quiet streets of Gladden Hills, she put her scattered thoughts on hold. The drive next to her grandparents' home was empty when she pulled in and parked. Climbing from behind the wheel, she watched Jason lock his car door and walk toward her.

He rolled up the collar of his jacket around his neck. The wind was whipping itself into the promised storm the news had spoken of on the radio earlier in the day. "What are your plans for the rest of the day, Lacy? Are you planning on going out again?" Before she could answer, he looked at the empty driveway ahead of Lacy's vehicle. "When do you think your cousin will be home?"

Lacy widened her eyes at his rapid-fire questions. "Wow! You would have made a fantastic DA." Her laugh was short, her expression sober. "I don't have definite plans for the rest of the day, but in lieu of our new friends in the maroon SUV, I suppose it would be prudent to stay close to home. I certainly can't keep you on a short leash in case I want to take a drive out in the country, now can I? If Kelly comes home early, we might decide to go out to the café for dinner." She glanced at him for acceptance. Suddenly, she felt like a teenager asking for curfew permission, and it angered her. "Forget it!"

As if reading her thoughts, he said, "I realize how confining all of this must seem. If you need me, please don't hesitate to call. I've some out-of-town friends staying with me tonight, otherwise...?" Jason left his statement open-ended, causing Lacy to wonder what he might have filled in the blank area. He looked frustrated as if he wanted to say more.

Lacy could identify with the frustrated part. "Look, about tomorrow morning, I can tell you are *not* anxious to attend church, and that's fine, really, I understand. The service is early on a Sunday morning, the quietest time of the week, and lots of people will be present at church. I honestly can't see any danger here. As soon as I return home from church, I promise to call and check in." She raised her hand in a Girl Scout hand signal and grinned.

Jason's brooding countenance did not lighten with her attempt at humor. "It was daylight and quiet in the parking lot where that SUV was waiting for you today. And the route out to the church has long, deserted stretches of road. Our arrangement stands! I'll be by to pick you up in the morning."

Not waiting for a reply, he pivoted and strode to the Durango.

Lacy stood stunned for a minute in the wake of his declaration, then swiveled abruptly and mounted the porch steps. The SUV in the parking lot seemed to cause Jason more concern than the tan pickup that had been following her around town. She wondered briefly why that was, before storing it with the other questions in her life.

*

It was almost 7:00 p.m. before Kelly and Lacy slid into a quiet booth in the café. Lifting her watch arm, Kelly scanned the interior of the busy restaurant. "Jerome promised to join us no later than a quarter after 7:00. He said to order and tell the waitress to give him his 'usual'…whatever that is. Honestly that man is such a creature of habit. One foot is always calculated ahead of the other. He's so different than me, Lacy!

"You know I'm inclined to be impulsive on occasion, as well as decisive." She stared at Lacy, who watched her with a cat-like knowing smile. "Unless it's dealing with dangerous people, as you well know," she quickly added in low tones. Kelly rambled on, as if trying to work something out in her mind. Pausing again, she punctuated her words like darts in a board. "Lacy, answer me. Do you think Jerome and I are suited for one another?" Her eyes looked hopeful, almost pleading for assurance.

Lacy patted Kelly's arm. "Perfectly—relax, will you? Admit it, Kelly, you feel safe around him. Jerome is sure-footed, but he's smart, too, and not afraid to allow you room to grow as a person. He didn't even get ruffled when Eric Greer showed up at our table at the Morrison benefit, and clearly, he wasn't intimated by the man's overbearing manner." Lacy allowed time for her words to sink in, doing some thinking of her own. *Kelly's feelings for Jerome are getting serious.* In that instant Lacy felt like an older sister.

Glancing around, Lacy noted the sassy waitress, Amy, was on duty again tonight. It'd been several days since Lacy had been in to chat with Wendy at the café. She missed their frequent interfacing. Their personalities had instantly connected. Wendy was an intelligent, insightful woman with a quick, inquiring mind eager to learn. Lacy related to the woman's inner drive to improve her situation.

Hadn't she, herself, pushed to reach for the highest rung on the ladder since grade school? In the beginning it had been hard to understand those who didn't do the same until she'd run into a couple of brick walls—losing Stevie was the first. She'd discovered on impact how life had a way of throwing curves into well-laid plans. She'd been taught ever since she was a child that God was in charge of those life curves, but ever since Stevie's death, her emotions had been in conflict, never quite able to accept God's decision. Every life curve since had thrown Lacy in the same turmoil. Her dad repeatedly told her to quit fighting God, to trust and accept. Now she was faced with trusting Him yet again in a new challenge. *Will I pass this test?*

Her thoughts returned to Wendy, sharing a table with District Attorney Michael Quinn Darling at the benefit a week ago. Mr. Darling clearly was also aware of Wendy's qualities. His eyes never strayed from her face as they conversed. Hopefully Quinn wouldn't break her heart when a new DA took office and his time in Gladden Hills came to an end. The idea troubled Lacy, as she'd come to think of Wendy as a good friend.

Kelly had opened and closed her menu half a dozen times as her eyes sought the café doorway. "He's here!" she announced, moving over to allow room for Jerome to sit next to her.

Lacy could hear the excited catch in her cousin's voice and felt a great longing. Would she ever have someone who made her feel that way? She hadn't allowed herself the luxury of thinking about Jason and the feelings she'd been suppressing in that area. Jason had made it clear today that she was strictly a reporter to him, someone to keep safe while she was in his employ.

Watching Jerome slide into the opposite side of the booth next to Kelly, she observed his silent movements, precise and in control. Everything about Jerome was calm until you focused on his eyes. A multitude of emotions raged there, and one very plainly had to do with Kelly.

"We haven't ordered yet. We waited for you." Kelly flashed him a brilliant smile.

Jerome leaned in closer. "I would have been here sooner, but I wouldn't have missed seeing our esteemed banking executive, Mr. Greer, strut out of the bank all duded up in his cream and tan Western suit with matching hat. It was a sight to behold." Jerome's eyes danced with humor. "You ladies surely missed a beautiful moment!"

Kelly lowered her head. "Eric is attending a big shindig the riding club is throwing over at the golf course club house tonight."

Jerome's light-colored brows knit into a frown. "And you learned this how?"

"Eric came by the office yesterday and invited me to go with him tonight. I declined, told him things were pretty hectic right now with my cousin staying with me. Our personal schedules kept colliding. He wasn't pleased." She shrugged. "He thinks Lacy is causing a headache for a lot of people."

Lacy grimaced. She could care less about Eric Greer's opinion. She was more interested in what Jerome had said. "Did you mention Eric wore a Western hat tonight?"

"Oh yes," answered Kelly, before Jerome could respond. "Eric holds one of the top offices in the riding club. He was elected last year. Mr. Heyworth sponsored him." Suddenly she sobered. "A Western hat?"

"Yes," Lacy said softly as their eyes locked. She could see Kelly was remembering the man who had hidden in the shadows across the street, as well as the driver of the tan pickup.

Jerome looked from one woman to another. "Western hat?"

Lacy interceded. "It seems everywhere I turn, I see someone wearing a cowboy hat," she replied, forcing a short laugh.

Jerome's sharp eyes took in Kelly's pinched expression. Turning to Lacy, he responded, "This area has become big on riding in recent years. We now have one of the largest registered clubs in the state. Probably why the Kerrigan Ranch continues to do a good business. They cater boarding and horse therapy to all the riding clubs. It doesn't hurt that the hills and acreage around this vicinity lend themselves to excellent riding…or so I am told. Personally, I prefer dogs." He gave Kelly a curious look and picked up his menu. "What's the special tonight? Maybe I'll order something different," he said, adjusting his glasses as the waitress arrived to take their order.

"Really?" Kelly cast him a bright look of approval. "I think I will too."

Their running conversation was lost on Lacy, who was distracted. The fact one more person she knew had access to a Western hat and both were bankers raised more questions. Could it be a coincidence that Terri Turner was working for the bank when her home was bombed? *Seventeen years is too long to make such a connection,* she reminded herself. Then she remembered that Jason Gardner would be grudgingly, out of a sense of duty, accompanying her to church in the morning. The scenario wasn't pleasant. The quick arrival of their food was a welcome relief from her troubled thoughts.

*

Sunday morning arrived too soon. Glancing across to the silent, stern-faced driver in the moving vehicle caused Lacy to groan internally. Yet what Jason Gardner lacked in congeniality, he made up for in appearance. The sky blue color of his dress shirt against the striped charcoal print of his suit was striking. Even his dark hair curling over his collar in back drew her admiring glance. One strand in particular caused her thoughts to slip back to her childhood, thinking how Stevie's hair would curl on a hot summer day. Lately, everything in Gladden Hills reminded her of Stevie. Returning to town was certainly jarring all her old memories.

She stared at the side of Jason's head behind his ear. She'd thought at first it was a shadow line running from the back of his ear down to his collar, but with the morning light, she identified it as a thin scar, jagged at the neck. It caused her to wonder the where and when of his injury, but his dark countenance told her now wasn't the time to ask.

Focusing on their present situation, she was uncertain how to engage Jason in easy conversation. The mood was uncomfortably tense—their conversation minimum. He'd said very little, but Lacy could almost feel his resistance to where they were headed. "You look *very* nice, but you needn't have worn a suit today. The dress code is more casual than it used to be."

"I wouldn't know." He handled the sharp turn with little effort. "Last time I attended church I was a child."

Lacy wondered what had happened to change him since that time. "So…is it church you don't like or God?" she asked softly.

Jason checked the rearview mirror of his Durango. "Does it matter?"

"Yes."

"Why don't we shelve that question for now? We may have company. It's possible that your house is being watched around the clock."

Lacy jerked her head to stare out the window to the mounted mirror. "I don't see anything."

"Behind that semi that followed us out of town. Wait until the van sways one side or another. He's behind the semi. I'm going to slow up…force the truck to pass at the widening in the road at the next junction. Then we'll see."

Instinctively, Lacy sat up straighter, her hands gripping the undersides of the car, preparing herself for what she didn't know. *Why does this have to happen on my first Sunday visiting a church?*

As the widening at the junction became a reality, the semi roared past them, causing the Durango to sway. Both Jason and Lacy looked to their mirrors where the form of a maroon SUV loomed large as life. Lacy glanced at Jason's taut expression. "Now what?" she asked in a small voice.

"Now we see what his next move is. Get your cell phone ready. I'll give you a number to dial if it becomes necessary."

Lacy's eyes watered from staring at the image in the mounted mirror. "He's falling back," she announced with a surge of relief.

"I see that. The church is just up at the next junction. I'll pull in in such a way that hopefully you'll be able to get a fix on the license plate. Get ready."

Instead of slowing for the coming turn into the parking lot of the old church, Lacy sucked in air as Jason increased his speed and turned abruptly, spinning in at a 180-degree turn. It was all she could do to keep the SUV in sight. Unfortunately the SUV had sped up at the same ratio they had and whirled by so fast, Lacy only got two numbers. Several in the parking area turned to stare. Lacy lowered her head, feeling very conspicuous.

"Nothing like making an entrance," Jason mumbled, turning off the ignition.

"We better go inside," said Lacy. "Do you think the SUV will return?"

Opening his side of the vehicle, Jason shot her a look. "I don't think so. Once they saw we were turning into the church, they probably lost interest. Besides, they'd been spotted. But expect to see them in the not-too-distant future."

Lacy could feel Jason tense as they filed into the church past a pleasant greeter who handed them a bulletin. They stopped inside the main sanctuary.

Lacy grabbed the back of the old oak pew to steady her emotions. "It hasn't changed." She took in the old rafters that she used to study when she and Stevie sat alongside his grandparents listening to the sermon.

Catching a glimpse of Jason, she wondered at his stone-like quietness. He gazed slowly around the white and cream-colored interior with the mahogany railings, his focus flitting from the stained-glass windows to the choir seats on both sides of the front and then to the organ and piano. "This church has seen a lot of Sundays come and go," he said, his tone measured and low.

"About 125 years of them to be exact," responded the mellow voice of Kurt Jaminson, who now stood directly behind them. "Good morning, Lacy. It's wonderful to see you." Turning toward Jason, he extended his hand. "Welcome. I'm Pastor Jaminson. I've seen you around town, but I've never had the pleasure, Mr....?" He smiled, waiting for Jason to fill in the blank.

"Jason Gardner, Pastor. I'm the new publisher of the *Gladden Hills Gazette.* I've heard good things about your church. I hope it does well in this old building."

Pastor Jaminson spread his arms. "It's a grand old building. But God has a plan, and we'll have to wait and see what comes in the days ahead."

"God's plan?" Jason regarded him from behind his dark glasses. "You believe the good and the bad are all God's plan?"

What was behind Jason's statement and his antagonism toward God? How would Pastor Jaminson answer that loaded question? Lacy was curious.

Tilting his head, Pastor Jaminson spoke slowly. "You've asked a worthy question. I wish I had the time to answer it the way it deserves, Mr. Gardner. One thing I can assure you. *Nothing* happens outside the realm of God's power. He is all-knowing, all-caring, and just. Perhaps we might have coffee soon so I can do your question justice. There is no quick, pat answer. I don't like to give coined responses to honest questions. "

Jason nodded, looking to Lacy. "I'm somewhat pressed right now, but perhaps something could be arranged when other matters are concluded."

"Fine! I'll wait to hear from you." Feeling the touch of a hand on his shoulder, the pastor turned to face a large man who seemed anxious to speak with him. The aisles now teemed with talking, laughing people, pressing in on all sides with several waiting to talk with their pastor.

Jason took hold of Lacy's arm, directing her to nearby seats on the far left end of a back pew where a window was propped open with a wrought-iron hinge. "Sit here on the inside. I want to keep checking out the window for the SUV."

The organ began to play a soft prelude as Lacy adjusted her position next to Jason on the seat. She felt nervous, wondering what might happen if Jason should spot the return of the SUV from his vantage window view. This man was transmitting noticeable energy this morning. Was he still uneasy about being here? His focus shifted from the window to his surroundings, viewing the incoming congregation, various couples young and old, children darting about out of reach of their parents. Several acquaintances greeted Jason, indicating they would talk with him after the service. Many seemed pleased, as well as surprised to see him. They nodded at Lacy in passing.

When the sound of the organ increased and the choir filed into their seats, Jason squared his shoulders and settled back. Lacy prayed silently for this unusual man beside her and for herself as well. It had been far too long since she had been in a place of worship. Strangely it felt like coming home.

Pastor Jaminson's message was sound in doctrine and concise in wording. There was no question he believed God's Word was true and that God could make a positive difference in every person's life. Many of the things he touched on struck home in Lacy's heart. Only once did she peek at Jason, noticing his tight jaw. He was not comfortable. *Is he steeling himself against any possible spiritual impact?* She knew all too well how futile that was.

Lacy recalled what her father had told her when she was still quite young. *"There is a special place in each of us that God has designed especially for himself. No one is complete until they allow God to reside in that spot."* She'd asked him what would happen if someone wouldn't allow God to live in that place. *"That person will walk around with an empty hole in their heart. Something will always be missing,"* he'd said.

"That's sad, Papa," she'd replied.

Even though she knew little about the handsome, granite-faced employer beside her now, something told her the words she recalled from her papa applied. Feeling as if she was intruding, she looked away.

As soon as the final chorus resounded with enthusiasm, the closing prayer was given and the congregation burst into animated movement.

Greetings and laughter erupted around them. Acquaintances of Jason clustered around him, all anxious to engage him in conversation. Lacy took the opportunity to slip away and accomplish her secondary objective for being here this morning.

Managing to catch Jason's eye for a split second, Lacy pointed downwards and mouthed the word *restroom.* He nodded, resuming his conversation with the man in front of him. She fairly sprinted toward the back of the church where stairs led off to the basement where the ladies' restroom was situated. If her childhood recollection was accurate, there was also a back entrance that led to the church parking lot and beyond that to the cemetery—and the note.

Moving swiftly across the cracked parking area, she cast a nervous glance to the church window adjacent to where she and Jason had sat earlier, fearful that he might catch a glimpse of her. Her heart pounded. There'd been no sight of the maroon SUV, nor the tan pickup. Lacy centered her focus on the cemetery, finding the answered note and returning before Jason missed her.

Experiencing the bite of the mid-March wind, she proceeded through the gate and beyond. A couple of people en route to their cars gazed curiously in her direction. Lacy lifted a hand and waved, hoping they'd get the idea she was visiting a grave of a loved one. Turning abruptly, she hastened down the main path toward the back of the cemetery.

The longish grass was still cold and wet. Twice Lacy stopped to shake off her shoes, hoping her sheer stockings wouldn't show water marks when they dried. Hating the squishy feel of her feet slopping around in her shoes, she continued to the back of the lot where she turned toward the parking area for a second look. No one followed her. Rushing to the end of the row, she knelt in the thick, wet grass without concern for her clothes. Had her contact read the ad in the classifieds and made the connection, or was this a wasted effort?

Her fingers pushed at the grass at the base of the headstone, thinking it was a good thing the graveyard caretaker was late in his ground-keeping rounds. Then she spotted the plastic-covered white envelope tucked at the left base of the headstone. Excitement tingled through her. Her contact had been here! She'd purposely placed the envelope on the opposite side of the stone.

Snatching the wet plastic bag, she stuffed it into the pocket of her off-white trench coat. Jumping to her feet, Lacy threaded her way back through the silent cemetery. There was nothing to fear in this quiet place—her danger lay among the living. Racing with an increasing fever, Lacy haphazardly secured the gate and dashed across the almost empty parking area. Only a few vehicles remained. By the time she reached the back door, she was worried what Jason would think with her gone so long.

Drawing in a deep dredge of air, she raced for the stairs leading up to the main sanctuary. Lacy stood briefly in the foyer of the church composing herself and her appearance. After running a comb through her smooth, dark hair, she marched into the sanctuary where Jason was closed in within the confines of a small group of men. He appeared to be heavily engrossed in conversation with a red-haired man in his forties. Jason's head tilted upward as she approached. His features revealed little, but he wasn't smiling.

How will I ever explain? She searched for a plausible excuse for her delayed return. Desperate, she wrinkled her face in discomfort. Her right hand lowered to her stomach area as if she'd experienced intestinal distress.

When Lacy grabbed hold of the doorway facing in a feigned attempt to briefly steady herself, Jason quickly disengaged himself from the talkative group and met her in the main aisle. "Are you ill?"

"It might have been something I ate last night," she said, wincing, even as the words flowed from her mouth. A wave of color rose upward from her collar. Here she stood, uttering a bold-faced lie while standing inside a worship sanctuary. A lie was wrong no matter where it was told, but somehow she felt even more of a sinner because she'd done it within the very walls where people met to worship God. She groaned in earnest, thinking of all she had to repent of when this day was over, with deceit headlining the list.

Jason ushered her out to the Durango with care, his face mirroring concern. Without a word, he helped her inside and hurried around to his door. As soon as the engine roared to life, he shifted into drive and headed for the highway. "Do you need for me to take you to the emergency room?"

Lacy drew herself upward in her seat, realizing at once she'd overplayed her part. There was no way she planned on spending the afternoon in a hospital emergency room. "I'm doing better. It was probably one of those attacks of gastritis that passes quickly. I should have known better than to order a burrito last night at the café." She smiled bravely, feeling like the hypocrite she was. "Spicy food and I never get along. What I wouldn't give for a bowl of homemade chicken noodle soup right now."

"Actually, there's a family restaurant on the edge of Wellington about ten miles from here. I've seen chicken soup listed on the menu. The restaurant itself is nothing fancy, but the food is great."

"I hate to hold up your entire Sunday," Lacy deferred politely but hoped he'd pursue the matter. "You've already stepped out of your comfort zone today just to be my backup. I can't ask more of you."

"In reality church wasn't all that bad after I got settled in. Concerning lunch, I have to eat somewhere. As I remember, this restaurant also serves an excellent meatloaf dinner, with homemade mashed potatoes and mushroom gravy, the *best* around. My grandmother never served better. Mmm." He smacked his lips as if savoring the meatloaf as he spoke.

"Meatloaf and mushroom gravy, huh?" She loved meatloaf. "It sounds great," she answered with little heart. Her first dinner out with Jason Gardner and she was restricted to soup—retribution for her lies. Anything else would send up red flags.

"It's too bad your stomach is upset. That meatloaf is wonderful." He aimed a sympathetic glance her direction.

She held her own sickly smile. *It's one meal,* she told herself. *Get over it!*

Spying a car pull out of an ideal parking place in front of the restaurant, Jason drove straight into the waiting spot with ease. "Our meal seems to be blessed, Miss Cottrell," he said with a touch of irony. Helping her out of the car, he stared down at her splotched black heels and frowned. "Somewhere you've managed to step in some water, it appears."

Lacy looked away. "Yes, I know. The grass is terribly long in our front yard, and I'm awful about watching where I walk." She ignored his questioning look and moved toward the restaurant door.

Jason hurried to get ahead of her. Lacy thought she briefly witnessed the semblance of humor but dissuaded herself against it by the time he'd positioned himself to open the door. *Is he playing me?* Had he seen through her stomachache ploy? There was no way to know for sure. This man was a puzzle. She was still musing on the matter as they took a table by the window. *How much of everything does he know?*

Lifting the menus from between the napkin holder, Jason shattered her suspicious train of thought. "Are you positive you're up to stopping for lunch? Say the word and I'll take you right home."

Lacy wished she'd never pretended to be ill. "Yes, I'm positive."

Shifting out of her coat, she faced Jason across the table. The light from the window splashed warm sunlight patterns across her face and the front of her lavender sweater. It had always been one of her best colors. She chided herself. It irritated her to admit she'd worn the blasted sweater simply because she expected to be in Jason's company today. This was turning out to be an ill-fated day all around.

Looking up, she caught something in Jason's expression, and her heart quickened. Then, as in everything of late, she doubted her first perception.

In truth, it both pleased and unnerved Lacy to sense admiration in his lingering gaze. Catching hold of her emotions, she took herself to task, remembering his cold, detached attitude of the previous day. Had she misread her initial perception then or today? Jason had made their relationship blatantly clear yesterday, yet today the lines were blurred again. It wearied her to think, and she rested her head on her propped hand, staring without interest at the menu where it listed soups.

After they'd ordered, Jason asked, "What have you scheduled for tomorrow? I'd like a rundown so I can plan my day's appointments."

Lacy shifted uncomfortably. This man not only owned the *Gazette* but ran its operation and was involved in several important city organizations. Now he'd agreed to play nursemaid to his new reporter, who had managed to line herself up in the sights of a dangerous stalker. How was he going to handle all of that? For the first time Lacy contemplated dropping her pursuit of the Turner bomber. Was the little she'd learned worth all of this hassle?

She pursed her lips. "Maybe I'm wasting my time and yours with all of this. You have more to do than become my daily watchdog. Besides, I don't think it's a job you particularly enjoy." She aggressively stirred the coffee the waitress had set in front of her.

Seconds passed before Jason responded. "Someone must think what you're doing merits enough muscle to have you watched. There's been at least one attempt to eliminate you. Concerning my time—or surmised lack of enjoyment—let me be the judge of that."

"But I've uncovered no facts so far, only more suspicions."

"Do you normally quit when you can't find the answers to a story?"

She shot him a scowl that would have withered a prison matron. "We're talking about people's lives, Jason. Two people have already died, and I've twisted my cousin's life into a knot. She looks over her shoulder every time she leaves the house. Kelly deserves a happy life with a good man."

"Like Jerome Collins?" He sipped his coffee.

Lacy stared off. "If that's who she chooses. So far he's proved himself a good contender. I've been impressed with the man he's become in the short time I've been back."

Jason sloshed the coffee around in his cup without comment. More seconds passed. "Does he know what's been going on with you?"

"Nooo," she answered slowly. She couldn't mention that she still believed Jerome might be her mysterious contact in Gladden Hills. "I've only told you because Quinn Darling ordered me to get backup. Either that or basically leave town. I was reluctant to even approach you, but after what happened at the courthouse, I felt I had to confide in someone. I was in shock, scared, and hurting like crazy when you arrived at the hospital, or I might not have said anything then."

"I'm glad I caught you at a vulnerable time then," said Jason, focusing on his coffee.

"Glad?" Lacy stared at him like he was crazy, rethinking her earlier assessment. *Is he enjoying this encounter with danger? Or does he really relish the opportunity to help me, no matter how hazardous?*

The waitress's arrival was timely.

Over their meal, Lacy laid out her itinerary for the next day. "When I return in the afternoon to the paper from the file room at the courthouse, I plan on driving out to the Novelties, Art & Antiques Store. According to Wendy, it's just outside of town. And then home, I guess, to fix dinner. It's my turn to cook. Poor Kelly," she said with little enthusiasm.

"Is the visit to the novelties shop essential?" Jason challenged. "You realize the fewer places you frequent, the better. It makes you less of a target."

"Maybe, but stopping at this shop is part of my work assignment. If you remember, you delegated the redecorating of your office to me not long after I started work."

Jason dropped his head, slowly moving it from side to side in disbelief. "Well, I'm tabling that assignment here and now. We'll deal with redecorating my office when you're no longer Gladden Hills's number one target."

*

After leaving Wellington, Lacy sat quietly observing Jason drive. There was no hesitation between mind and action with him. One eye was on the road ahead while the other constantly checked his rearview mirror for any sign they were being followed. His strong jaw was set, and her gaze gravitated to those solid dark glasses he was never without.

"Do my glasses trouble you, Lacy?" he asked as if reading her mind.

Startled by his directness, she stuttered, "Ah, no—I mean, well, yes, sometimes. I do wonder."

"I have a condition that has left my eyes overly sensitive to light. I'm much more comfortable with dark glasses in place most of the time."

"How long have you had this condition?"

"For several years."

Lacy could tell the subject was closed. Jason Gardner was not one to share much about himself. "Would you be offended if I asked about your negative feelings toward God? I sensed anger in the question you posed to Pastor Jaminson this morning. Did something happen in your life that caused your heart to grow hard in this area?"

His head jerked sharply to stare at her. "You think my heart is hard?"

Lacy took her time forming a reply. "Judging from your recent statements, attitude, and tone whenever God or church is mentioned, I'd have to say yes. Considering I suffered the same affliction, I can speak from experience. Bitterness can settle in like a low-grade infection. I allowed mine to separate me from God for a long time and lost the feeling of being loved and cared for by my heavenly Father. It's a lonely place to be," she said softly.

"A lot of people simply don't believe in God, Lacy," he stated.

"You didn't say you didn't believe in God, Mr. Gardner. In fact, your questions prove otherwise."

The silence inside the Durango swelled into electric tension. He looked as if he might've thrown back a quick retort but chose to clamp his mouth shut. Aware she'd gone too far, Lacy was instantly remorseful for her bluntness. After all, hadn't he spent half the day going to church with her and treating her to a bowl of soup? "Look, I'm sorry I pressed in a sensitive area. I..."

"Forget it. I intend to. Let's shelve that subject as well."

Lacy felt as if she should do something to try and repair the damage to their relationship. "I let my tongue get ahead of me at times. I guess being a reporter has taught me to lead with the hard questions."

A wry smile spread. "Tell me, is it totally an occupational effect of being a reporter, or part of your personality that's responsible for your directness, Miss Cottrell?"

Lacy's mouth parted at the perceptiveness of his statement. It was true. She'd always had a tendency to strike at the core of a matter on impulse. It had driven her parents to distraction and embarrassed them numerous times. On occasion, even Stevie had become angry with her. Though her approach had tempered with maturity, the trait served her well as a reporter.

"I would say a person is a totality of his or her personality, spiritual content, the environment they've been submerged in, and the choices they make in life," she said thoughtfully.

He chuckled. "Good comeback."

The Durango neared the city limits of Gladden Hills. Her fingers tightened on the note in her trench-coat pocket. In a few minutes she would read the message. The outcome of the investigation could rest on what she learned. Would her contact have a clue that might lead her to something substantial at last?

13

Leads of Folly?

WHEN THEY SAID GOOD-BYE, Jason's attitude was much the same as she had detected on Saturday, distant and cool. It caused Lacy to wonder if his thoughts were simply elsewhere, or worse. Had his earlier irritation with her settled in place? She was closing the car door with a heavy heart when his voice brought her back to his opened window.

Jason leveled a stern look at her. "Just so we're on the same page. You plan on staying put the rest of the day, correct?"

"If you are insinuating I might have plans of slipping out to do more sleuthing without you, no. I plan on a nap—my stomach, you know."

"Yes, I remember," he replied pleasantly. "Good. Get some rest, and I'll see you in the morning. I'll wait until you're safely inside before I leave."

Lacy saluted him with a half raised hand. "Thanks for lunch, boss, and for taking me to church. It meant a lot to me. I used to attend that church years ago," she added, her tone softening. Without waiting for his reaction, she whirled about, holding her injured ribs as she ascended the porch stairs and unlocked the door.

Once inside, she peered out the storm door. Sliding the gear into reverse, Jason backed out into the street in one fluid motion. The engine slipped easily into drive and moved up the street like a purring panther. Lacy shut the door slowly, feeling unsure about where she stood with her mysterious employer, even as he drove away from the house.

What did she really know about Jason Gardner? She pondered the question all the way up the stairs to her bedroom, her fingers clasping the note in readiness. Jason Gardner was new to the area, but where had he come from originally? The man had volunteered very little about himself. Did he have anything to hide? Lacy needed to know who her backup was.

She would put in a call to Nadine at her home tonight to do a little background research on the boy-wonder who had purchased the *Gladden Hills Gazette.* She paused to consider others that presented a question in her mind, resolving to make a list. Eric Greer sprang to her thoughts, especially now that she knew he owned a Western hat. Wendy said he'd only been in the area a few years. He was ambitious and had definite delusions of grandeur, but what else was there to know? Although too young to have any part in the Turner bombing, there was much about him that troubled her, such as late-night meetings with Morgan Streeter.

Once inside her bedroom, she turned the lock, in case Kelly came home early. Without bothering to change, she kicked off her water-splotched shoes and climbed on top of her bed, feeling her stomach rumble. She was still hungry—small wonder. The soup, though tasty, was not satisfying. But that was her own fault. When you told a lie, you lived with the consequences. She had inwardly asked for forgiveness many times over on the drive back. Somehow she had to try and avoid deceit from this point on. But could she manage it? Her life lately had been filled with secrets, and Lacy was learning that secrets often led to lying. One cover-up called for another.

The outside of the plastic bag was watermarked and still held dirt in the crevices. Emptying the contents of the bag on the bed coverlet next to her, Lacy observed the familiar purple feather drop out from between the folded paper. She picked up the note with stiff fingers and opened it. Bold printing declared:

Follow the money, then and now!...follow the players the same.

Her hand rose to her hairline, raking her glossy umber strands away from her face. Her head settled back against the propped pillows as a tired sigh slipped out. *What money? What players? I have to find a clue about the money and soon! Would it have killed him to tell me?* she thought, irritated. Once again she'd assumed her contact was a he. Why? Would he ever make himself known? What was keeping the unknown contact from doing so now? Was he afraid of someone?

Suddenly she recalled Chuck Walden, Stevie's rough-edged friend. Lacy wrote a reminder note to call tonight and confirm Tuesday for their dinner commitment. The thought made her somewhat nervous. As helpful as Chuck had appeared when Kelly's car broke down, she knew little about him except what she'd heard and the dubious looks that were sent when his name was mentioned. There was no denying the man's physique was large enough to be intimating. Coupled with that was his wild-appearing rough exterior, giving her pause to consider what she was initiating.

Were his actions prone to roughness as well? How might he respond to prying inquiries of any kind, and how would he take to the idea of being one of her backup protectors? The palms of her hands grew sticky at the thought of the coming encounter. She mused dryly on the fact that Chuck looked to her like he might be a meat and potato man.

At last Lacy allowed her disturbed mind to rest. There was nothing more she could do tonight. Tomorrow she would go back to the courthouse and search the files again. Now that she had authorization from Quinn, Nicholas would allow her to see the sign-in sheets dating back to the timeframe of the bombing. When she talked with Nadine tonight, she'd remember to warn the dear lady that more requests might be following her trip back to the file room. Nadine had told her upfront that she owed her big time for all the overtime, and Lacy concurred. *I'll work on that in my spare time.* She chuckled at the bizarre thought.

*

The next morning at the paper was harried. Jason was so busy Lacy saw him only in passing in the hall. Thankfully Chloe had thus far kept her distance. Lacy was in no mood to deal with the troubled young woman. Working diligently at her upcoming article, she pushed everything else out of her thoughts. In the short time she had been at the *Gazette,* Lacy sensed she had gained a certain amount of credence with Maxine. She dared to hope the woman might even have come to trust her at a beginning level, if nothing else. Working together on Saturday's special article hadn't hurt their relationship. Still it came as a surprise when the older woman stopped by and offered to help with some of her research for her article.

Puzzled, Lacy blinked at her. "Ah, that's very nice, Maxine. I appreciate the offer. "

"When I told Mr. Gardner I was light on work for the next few days, he suggested I might possibly be of help to you. He indicated you are balancing a few balls in the air at present." The red-haired office manager eyed her with a speculative look. Lacy knew the lady would love to know what all those balls were labeled. Maxine had a nose for news.

Lacy fumbled through a pile of mismatched papers until she came to a scribbled list. She shifted her roller chair to the left of her desk where she retrieved a printed form. Spinning the chair around center, she said dramatically, "You, Maxine, are an unexpected angel! Here is a list of people. I need their answers to these questions. Just tell them you are calling on my behalf. I have talked to each of them in length and they are expecting my call. I can't tell you how much help this will be."

Maxine scanned a few of the questions. "This will be much more interesting than what I was planning to do. I'll put Chloe in our stockroom inventory. I haven't noticed her around your desk this morning."

"No. Apparently, she's been busy elsewhere today," Lacy answered brightly.

"And you don't seem too broken up about it." Maxine's clear-cut statement told Lacy the matron was nearly as troubled about Chloe as Lacy was, but now wasn't the time or the place to discuss the matter. She shot her a knowing look and Maxine nodded, seemingly satisfied.

Turning away from the desk, Maxine paused to add, "I'll try to get these back to you as soon as possible."

Lowering her head, Lacy checked to see no one was within hearing distance. "Good. I'll be back later in the day. Now I have to scoot. Cover for me, will you? If anyone asks, you have no idea where. Mr. Gardner knows how to contact me should an emergency arise."

*

After a hurried lunch, Lacy left the restaurant. Aware of the café door closing behind her, Lacy scanned the area for unfriendlies, namely the maroon SUV or the tan pickup. *Bingo!* she mouthed, reaching for her cell phone. Dialing Jason's private cell number, she stared at the offending vehicle. "Jason, I'm outside the café, and I can see the tan pickup directly on the backside of the square trying not to be noticed under the big oak tree." She closed down her phone and walked to the light to cross over to the square and the courthouse.

Lacy briefly touched her hand to her sore rib area as she fast-paced her steps upward to the front door. Jason had promised to call someone about the tan pickup. Hopefully the driver of the truck wouldn't follow her inside.

Waving in Dede's direction, Lacy proceeded toward the elevators in the small hallway off to the side.

"Yahoo, Miss Cottrell, I sure hope you're feeling better. Such an awful accident that was." Dede's mournful face radiated honest concern.

Lacy pivoted toward the woman she would have quickly passed by. "Thank you, Dede. I appreciate your concern. I'm doing much better." Again, she laid her finger to her mouth as a reminder that her presence in the building was not open for public knowledge.

Dede nodded with recognition as Lacy moved toward the elevators. *A lot of good it will do for her to keep quiet. Obviously the bad guys know where and what I'm doing almost before I do.* Pushing the down button, she waited.

And why is that? She'd not paused to consider who knew she was coming to the file room the day of the accident. Either she had been followed to the courthouse or someone at the paper or café was sharing information.

Before the elevator door opened, she hurried back to sneak a glance at the lobby of the courthouse for anyone in the vicinity or any indication of someone interested in the direction she'd gone. The courthouse lobby remained empty except for Dede behind the main desk. Lacy raced back to step inside the gaping elevator, her mind shifting to various possibilities surrounding her attack. As she descended to the basement, all her thoughts enforced the fact her attack had been carefully preplanned.

Why have I not been working this angle? Of course! Her attacker knew she was coming! Had someone she knew betrayed her knowingly or by accident? She couldn't recall telling Kelly of her plans, but circumstances around that time were still foggy. She shivered. Neither of the possibilities was a pleasant thought. Her body tensed; even her skin felt clammy. When the door slid open, Lacy looked point-blank into the scrutinizing stare of old Nicholas Cooper. She gasped in shock and weaved backward.

His strong, wrinkled hands shot out to grab hold of her shoulders. "Whoa there, steady. You all right, Miss Cottrell?" he asked anxiously. "I didn't mean to scare you none. I saw the elevator lights and decided to check out who was coming. I've been jumpy as a cat ever since the day of your so-called accident."

"Nicholas," she said, concerned, "you haven't told anyone it wasn't an accident, have you?"

"Oh no, ma'am. I keep what I know to myself. I always found it's healthier in the long run." He chuckled softly.

"Good! I appreciate that, Nicholas. I was too out of it to pre-warn you the day of the accident." Fumbling in her purse, she produced the signed authorization from Quinn Darling for her to have access to the sign-in log from seventeen years earlier. "Has anyone else come asking for access?"

Nicholas looked pensive as if thinking back. "If you don't count our previous DA, nope. Not while I've been here and there's only two keys that I know of. I have one and the DA has the other."

"Has that always been the case?" Lacy inquired.

"Well now, when the previous DA had his fatal *accident*, Police Chief Brown held on to it until Mr. Darling arrived."

"I keep hearing about this accident. What kind of an accident was it?"

"His car was found in the pit at the bottom of the quarry outside of town on Townsend Road. He had an open bottle of alcohol on the seat next to him, but an autopsy didn't turn up enough alcohol in his system to warrant an accidental drive off the top edge of the quarry. Still, it was labeled *accidental,* and the case was marked closed by Judge Shaw. He said he was tired of all the indecision on the part of the police department." His shrewd eyes told her that he didn't hold with the decision.

"Does that happen often? That a judge steps in to take over an open case?"

Nicholas shrugged. "I just tend the file room. I've got them old log-in books you asked for, Miss Cottrell. I'll set them on the back table."

"Thanks. I'm going to pull a couple of the files and meet you back at the table." She rubbed her midsection and drew in a shallow breath.

"You all right?"

"Oh, I'm fine...or will be when these ribs finally heal." She headed toward the file area that was becoming familiar. Her finger followed down the line to the right time frame, then carried those files to the table.

Three hours of constant reading and cross checking later had rendered nothing noteworthy...until an arrest report for fraud raised a red flag. With a half-eaten sandwich in one hand, she reread the notation. The arrest was made the week after the Turner Bombing. Retrieving a notepad from her purse, she wrote down the date and information. The fraud had occurred at the same bank Terri Turner had worked. It was too late in the day to spend any more time on this angle. She'd think on the information later. Writing down all the names of those involved, she discovered one name stood out—someone still active in the bank.

Pulling over the log-in records for those weeks prior and after the bombing, she wrote down the familiar names of people who signed in during that period. Blinking tired eyes at her watch, she collected all of her notes in her large leather bag and replaced the files. Handing the log-in records into Nicholas's hands, Lacy said wearily, "Keep these in a safe place, Nicholas."

"Did you find anything interesting, Miss?"

"Interesting, yes...but nothing more. Though it does give me directions to pursue." Lacy eyed the old man with new curiosity. "I gather you've lived here all your life, Nicholas. You mentioned seeing me at the gravesite when I was a little girl. Do you have family here, or some connection to the Turner family?" She suddenly wondered why the custodian of the file room would have been present at the funeral.

His strong, wrinkled hand rubbed the short stubble on his face. "I had family here, Miss Cottrell. Most have died or moved away. Now me and a raw-boned cur dog occupy my sister's farm about ten miles out of town. Now and then someone comes to visit a spell, but usually it's just me and old Rupert."

"It was a terrible day in Gladden Hills when that bomb went off and killed one of the sweetest ladies I've ever met…and that beautiful little boy, so smart he was." Nicholas's grizzled face revealed his sadness. "Things like that don't happen in small towns without affecting everyone around. I believe the entire town came to the funeral."

Lacy's thoughts raced back to that rainy, dark day. There had been hundreds of faces everywhere she looked. People, sad people, who were taller than her. A small involuntary sob caught in her throat. "Yes, there were a lot of people that day. I couldn't get to the grave site because everyone was pushing us out. Then Mr. Turner parted the crowd and took me by the hand, leading me to the front row, where I sat with other family members. The poor man never stopped crying the whole time."

"I remember, ma'am. It's hard to forget something like that."

Instantly Lacy thought of the lateness of the hour. "I've got to get back to the paper. Like I said, hold on to those records. I may need to look at them again."

*

Maxine was on the phone when Lacy walked past her with a nod. She knew the lady would seek her out when she had accumulated the needed information. Jason Gardner's door was closed when she approached, causing Lacy to pause, wondering if she should tell him what she'd found in the records and get his take on any possibilities. She decided against it and proceeded to her desk and slid her purse underneath her desk. About the time she was engrossed on material for her next assignment, Maxine's ample form appeared beside her.

"Make a place for this coffee. You look like you could use a pick-me-up."

Lacy scrambled to find her drink coaster beneath scattered papers. Taking the steaming brew from the careful fingers of the matron of the paper, she looked with surprise at the outstretched pastry. "Whoa! Who sprung for these?" she said, laughing.

"Mona sent them down. Said she baked too many for the predicted number of customers. Personally, I think she is still trying to say thank you for that article you did. Word has it that people from outlining areas are flocking in to her shop now."

"I'm glad to know I did something right," she said with a defeatist air.

Maxine tilted her head toward Lacy. "What's with the depressed attitude?"

"Just tired, I guess." She sunk her teeth into the crisp, apple-filled delicacy.

"Well, finish your turnover and coffee, and I'll be back with the responses I was able to run down from my phone interviews. I'll finish up the rest tomorrow morning." Maxine clicked off down the hallway.

"Maxine, you're a jewel! I've been stretched to the max lately." Lacy reached for her coffee and took a gulp, blowing out as it burned all the way down her throat.

"Pastry and coffee are to be savored—like life. Don't rush through everything and miss the joy of the journey, Cottrell." His words spoken in clear tones sounded like a poetic "thought for the day."

She whipped her head around, looking into the passive face of her boss. "Mr. Gardner? You surprised me!"

He moved on her right side and bent down, pretending to study her computer screen. "I thought maybe you'd stop by on your way through." His words were guarded, but the meaning was clear. He wanted to know if she'd found anything.

"Uncertain of the outcome at this point. I need time to think on a few items before venturing an opinion," she said. From the corner of her eye she observed Chloe approaching quietly on her left. The young woman moved like a cat burglar in the direction of her desk.

Is she trying to listen to our conversation? Surely not, Lacy tried to reassure herself. *Am I so spooked I see stalkers at every turn?*

Twisting sharply to the left, she confronted her. "Can I do something for you, Chloe?"

Chloe stopped and tensed, her eyes darting from Lacy to Jason. "I-I was just wondering if there was something I could help Miss Cottrell with? I noticed Miss Maxine was helping and, well…" She licked her lips as if she was nervous.

Before Lacy could comment, Jason straightened and seemingly grew taller than his six-foot height. "Miss Camry, as you can see we are talking here. If Miss Cottrell is in need of your services, she'll contact you."

His stern demeanor stunned Lacy. *Whew! He doesn't soft-pedal a comment!*

The pale face seemed to grow whiter. "Yes, sir. Sorry I interrupted." She fled like a rabbit into the weeds.

Lacy searched Jason's face. Had he thought she was trying to listen, too?

He bent his head, speaking low, "I'll call you tonight. Don't go out alone. You're going straight home, right?"

"I plan to, but first I thought I'd stop in at the café to see Wendy. I foresee no problem there, unless you do." Again she wished she could see behind those glasses and read his true reactions.

"I might stop in for a cup of coffee and order one of Sam's famous chicken-salad sandwiches. I've heard they are awesome," he said with a slight hint of a smile.

She remembered Morgan Streeter mentioning Sam's sandwiches. She also knew Jason was only going to the café as protection for her. "I've heard the same about his chicken salad," she added with a grin.

With a final glance at her computer screen, he walked back toward his office, leaving Lacy to wonder about the worth of anything she'd found out at the courthouse or whether had her trip been a waste of time—something she was running out of. She scanned the area of the large room where Chloe's work area was situated against a back wall, but all she could see was the back of the girl's head, seemingly hard at work. She was still unsure what the girl's true motive had been in approaching her desk so secretively earlier.

It was a relief to hear the staccato of Maxine's heels coming toward her down the hallway. Tabling her thoughts on Chloe, she collected her papers to ready her desk for Maxine's research. She would leave other concerns for later. Next stop, the café and Wendy.

*

"You're kidding! That's wonderful!" Lacy exclaimed, careful to keep her voice low. She glanced around the café, confident no one was in position to listen in on their conversation. She did a slight double take when Jason sauntered in and slid into a booth on the opposite side of the horseshoe design—just close enough to keep an eye on her.

Wendy leaned across the table in the secluded booth in a confidential manner. She'd taken her late afternoon break when Lacy entered the café. "I wouldn't kid about something like that. Quinn was in the café last night and while he was eating dessert, he looked up and said in a serious voice, 'Wendy, would you accompany me to a concert this coming Friday night? I was given some excellent tickets and thought you might enjoy it, being the musician that you are.' So just like that, I'm going to a concert. I've been walking around in a fog ever since." She sighed softly.

"You're a musician?"

"My dad was a musician. I've been playing the violin since I was four and a half. Quinn plays the piano." Wendy worried her bottom lip. "Now I've got to go through my wardrobe and make sure I have a nice enough dress."

"Wear your hair down, nice and full around your face," Lacy encouraged.

"You really think so?"

Lacy nodded. "I know so. That blond hair of yours will wow him."

After rewarding Lacy with a beaming smile, Wendy eyed her critically. "How are you feeling, really? You're still favoring your left side. I'm not sure what is happening in Gladden Hills, but I do know something's not right. When I heard you'd fallen down the steps at the courthouse, it didn't set right. Is that what really happened, Lacy? Are you working on a dangerous case?"

Lacy pondered what to tell her friend. She didn't want to lie, but it might be dangerous if she revealed too much to too many people. "You can do something for me. Be alert for anything out of the ordinary, like those late-night meetings at Morgan Streeter's. I wish I knew if they happened on a regular basis."

Wendy straightened, a sober look replacing her earlier lighthearted one. "I'll keep my eyes and ears open, but you be careful, Lacy." Pushing her long torso out of the confined seat, she stood.

Lacy called out to the young waitress as she turned away. "Don't forget to call me on Saturday and let me know how Friday night's concert goes."

"Will do," Wendy called over her shoulder. Reaching for the pad in her apron pocket, she greeted the party of four who'd just entered the café.

Up-ending the dregs of her coffee cup, Lacy peered across the room at Jason, who sat sipping a cup of coffee with a carry-out sack situated on the table. She marveled at his dedication. He was prepared to follow her if necessary. Donning her sunglasses, she started toward the door, stopping abruptly at the last booth. "Chloe!"

The unkempt blond had her head slightly turned toward the back of the booth, her menu deflecting half of her face. It was an obvious ploy to avoid being seen. The head jerked around, and two startled eyes stared back at Lacy. "Oh, hello, Miss Cottrell. I decided to have an early dinner at the café. I-I forgot to go grocery shopping last night." Her laugh was unnatural.

"Really! Well, I hope you enjoy your meal." Lacy nodded curtly and hurried by, afraid she'd say something she'd regret if she lingered.

That young woman was getting on her nerves. This bizarre fixation of Chloe's had to stop. Was she sneaking around so Lacy wouldn't dismiss her? Whatever the reason, Lacy wasn't in a mood to deal with her yet—maybe never. She was still hot about Chloe going into her desk. It revealed a definite character flaw.

Lacy hit the café door harder than she'd intended, her disposition not on the upswing. With her eyes fixed on the brick sidewalk, she nearly collided with a large man in her path. "Sorry, excuse me," she murmured, her mind back on her encounter in the café with Chloe.

"I'm not sure I wish to do that, Lovely Lacy," a mellow male voice replied.

She jumped. This was truly the day for surprises. "Mr. Streeter! Shouldn't you be out suing someone or fixing a parking ticket or something?"

He laughed heartily. "Lacy, you are a breath of fresh air. Actually I'm between parking tickets right now." His gaze rested upon her features with admiration. "Why didn't you come into my life five years ago, sweet lady? Ah well, how about making that date you've been hedging on ever since you came back to town? Unfortunately my place in town is handy but small, not suitable for entertaining. Someday I plan on building…"

She could almost see the wheels turning in his brain. Grinning, he continued, "Uncle Heywood's ranch is just outside of town, and he recently hired this marvelous world-class chef to cook for him." He touched his fingers to his lips. "A much nicer arrangement than a stuffy old restaurant. There are plenty of chaperones around to guarantee your safety."

"From whom?" she asked, warily watching the handsome features of the rusty-haired man in front of her. She wasn't quite sure where Morgan was headed with all of his ramblings. Was this his idea of a date for them?

He chuckled at her comment. "So…how about coming out to Uncle Heywood's place this coming Friday night for a gourmet dinner? I promise a meal to end all meals. And don't worry. My uncle has other plans that night."

"Dinner at your uncle's ranch?" She regarded his expectant face. If what Wendy and Kelly said was true, Morgan was used to women falling all over him and few ever said no. "I'll think about it, Morgan, and call you with my decision tomorrow night, if that's all right. Right now, I'm too swamped to even think."

Morgan obviously hadn't counted on her not replying on the spot. His face showed disappointment and something she couldn't quite determine—surprise or anger? "You know how to keep a man on a string, Miss Cottrell. Tomorrow night it is. It's only one meal in a lifetime. How bad a night can it be? You might even enjoy yourself." His crooked smile slid into place.

Reaching into his inside coat pocket, Morgan withdrew one of his cards and wrote something on the back. He handed it to her. "My private number. If I don't answer, leave a sweet message and I'll get back to you. I can hardly wait, Miss Cottrell. A late-night call from a lovely lady?" He sent her a warm, intimate gaze in passing.

Lacy dropped her head. *Why didn't I simply say no?* What had held her back from refusing him? Sighing, she admitted that the tiny idea worming itself inside her thoughts begged for a chance to formulate clearly. The door of the café opened and closed behind her. Half turning, she saw Jason. Had he watched from the window and seen her encounter with Streeter?

He walked up to where she stood. "Met a friend?" His dark brows rose in question.

"I'm not sure. But he'd like to be, and he just invited me to have dinner," she said wearily. "I was too tired to think about it, so I put him off. I'm going home now and crash." Turning, Lacy started walking away, hardly aware Jason was keeping pace with her.

"When does Streeter expect an answer?" He kept his voice low.

"Not until tomorrow night. I'm supposed to call and give my answer."

"What are you planning on saying?"

"I don't know yet—haven't decided," she said lightly.

"Do you trust him?"

It was a good question. She frowned. "I'm not sure."

"Good answer. I'll follow you home. We'll say good-bye here like any normal evening, but I'll swing around the block and follow your departure at a distance." His voice level escalated. "Good night, Miss Cottrell. See you in the morning." Not waiting for a reply, Jason pulled away from her, his long legs making great strides. Rounding the corner of the Gazette building leading to the back parking area, Jason walked straight to his Durango.

*

At dinner that night, Lacy and Kelly worked out a menu for Tuesday night. "Are you sure about inviting Chuck Walden over to the house?" Kelly pressed. "When I took my car over for a tune up, he was talking and laughing with two tough motorcyclists who rode in while I was there. I'd bet my new sweater that Chuck's a biker too." She looked anxious.

Lacy laughed. "Talking with motorcyclists doesn't make him a criminal. Neither does riding a motorcycle. He's rough, that's obvious, but he was Stevie's friend, and I could use his help right now. I'll run in and pick up dessert from Mona's tomorrow after work and you can pick up the chicken." She stopped as she recalled her first impression of Chuck. "Make that a big beef roast and carrots. It's a sure-fire hit with a guy. I haven't entertained guests since last summer. I'm afraid I made little time for friends—too busy." She turned toward her cousin. "You know, Kelly, I think I've worked at being too busy most of my life."

"Why, Lacy? I often wondered why you avoided coming to visit. We were so close as children."

Lacy fingered the salt-and-pepper shakers. "I don't think I ever got over Stevie. Instead of crying my grief out, I simply shut down my emotions. Mom would try to talk to me about him, but I'd turn away. Guess I was mad at everyone—even God. All I know is, I pushed Him away like everyone else. But yesterday at church I felt the thrill of singing those wonderful old hymns for the first time in years. I'm praying and reading my Bible again. God didn't move. I did. When I did a U turn, He was there to welcome me with open arms! You said awhile back it was good that I came back to Gladden Hills. I agree. I had to face what I've been blocking out all these years."

Kelly nodded thoughtfully. "Hope you can still say the same when this horrid brouhaha is over and hopefully everyone is all right."

Lacy crossed the room and wrapped her arms around her cousin. She'd become her closest friend. "We'll weather this together! I didn't know my subtle investigation would kick up such a hornet's nest and place you square in the middle. Before I even had time to start looking around, the stalking began. It was as if just by being here, I was a threat. I find that curious."

"If that's true, then the one responsible for the bombing is still in Gladden Hills, like you said." Kelly shivered. "That's creepy, Lacy. You haven't told me if you found anything in the old files."

Flashes of the yellowed file pages registered in her mind, one entry in particular. "Do you remember ever hearing about the arrest of a Rob Corbin shortly after the bombing? I don't. Of course, I was merely a child. Corbin was a Union official who supposedly was caught embezzling Union funds in the range of twenty-five-thousand dollars. They discovered it at Gladden Hills National Bank, where Terri Turner worked."

Kelly stared at her. "Really! No, I don't recall. I wasn't much older than you. Considering the shock of the bombing, I don't think it was the big news that it might have been any other time. But then, everyone was so tore up over Mrs. Turner and little Stevie's terrible deaths, who would notice?"

"Exactly! It says Rob Corbin pleaded innocent. His statement reads, 'Mrs. Turner has my bank statements. She was going to call me back this week.' I find that interesting.' "

"And was she?"

"No way of knowing. She was killed first. Apparently the young accountant working with Terri had bank statements that disproved what Corbin claimed. There's more. A break-in was discovered at the bank before he was arrested, and they found Corbin's brand of cigarettes at the crime scene with his fingerprints on them. They assumed he was trying to change the records. They also located about five thousand cash in his apartment. Slam-dunk, everything neat and tidy. They found him guilty. I don't know if he's still in prison or not."

"You have to admit they had a lot of evidence against him," said Kelly.

"Maybe. Do you know who the young accountant was?"

Kelly's eyes remained on her face. "Well?"

"It's someone we both know—the prominent, newly appointed bank president of Gladden Hills National, Conrad Heyworth. I figure he had to be somewhere in his twenties at the time. He worked up from a teller, taking accounting classes at night. Wendy told me that today. She'd heard it from people who've worked at the bank for years."

"Mr. Heyworth? You think Mr. Heyworth had something to do with Stevie's death? That's pretty far out! I can't believe you get your information from Wendy...well, maybe I can. Everyone knows she deals in gossip. Personally, I credit the man for bettering himself by taking night classes. Be careful of casting shadows, or people will think you're on a witch hunt, Lacy." Kelly warned. "This is Gladden Hills you're talking about."

"Look," Lacy insisted, "I'm not saying anything yet, but it's a possible angle. Conrad Heyworth worked with Terri; that's a fact. She was mentoring him. If Rob Corbin was telling the truth—a big if, granted, then who better to switch bank documents, unless the manager himself, Drake Evans, who now has his own bank on the other side of the state? Then there's the bank president at that time, Robert Glock. I haven't checked his whereabouts yet."

"Like I said, be careful you don't get caught up in a witch hunt while looking for the real villain. A lot of people's reputations could be hurt. Conrad Heyworth was only a beginning accountant, basically a gopher for the bank seventeen years ago. What you're looking for is someone with enough clout to cover his tracks."

Lacy considered her cousin's wise words as she paced the floor. Her thoughts buzzed like a beehive, trying to make connections. "I checked the sign-in log for the week before and after the bombing when Judge Shaw, then the DA, signed in twice—actually, three times. One name was crossed out, but the ink has faded through the years and the name showing through is Harold Shaw. Why was an attempt made to cross out his name? As district attorney he had every right to be there, though I heard they usually send clerks for information."

"You're thinking Terri Turner had some connection to this Rob Corbin and was killed because of this? That's a stretch you'll need evidence to prove. Let me know if I can be of help. Bear in mind that Conrad Heyworth is a friend of the governor…are you understanding me?"

"Oh, yes," Lacy said, "loud and clear. Thanks for being my sounding board. You're right about evidence, and the fact it is a really long shot. But I have to start somewhere and explore each possibility to see where it leads me. Right now I've got some reading to catch up on upstairs." She added, "You're going to pick up the other items for supper tomorrow night, right?"

"I've got it covered. Should be interesting. Should I wear my leathers?" Kelly asked with a smirk.

Cocking her head in a saucy manner, Lacy replied, "Cute! Give him a chance, Kelly. Remember, he didn't even charge me for getting the car started last week. That should cut him some slack. "

Kelly turned with her coffee. "Mmm, you're right. I'm being a small-town snob. I promise to keep an open mind."

"Good enough. That's all I can ask. I'm upstairs if you need me. I'll check the front door on my way, though." Her brain felt heavy and muddled like warm peanut butter and marshmallows as she walked the long hall to the entryway. She slid the extra lock into place and would have turned, but her curiosity brought her back for a long look out the window. With only the soft haloed light of the street lamps in the moist spring air, she squinted down the street, reminding herself that the view was better from her bedroom window.

Is that a car parked near the end of the street? She squinted harder, frustrated at the limited visibility.

Turning on her heel, she dashed up the stairs down the short hall to her front bedroom, Careful not to turn on a light, she raced to the front windows and peered out. The street lamp shone on the front of the car that was sitting with its parking lights on. *Where are those old bird-watching binoculars we used as children?* Her tongue pushed against her bottom teeth as she hurried out of the room to the linen closet, rifling through the piles of extra towels. There they were, just as Gran had left them, packed up in the original box.

Carrying the box back to her bed, she removed the antique treasure from her childhood and hung them around her neck. Lacy took up the best vantage position and lifted the glasses to her eyes, adjusting them as she moved closer. The same swollen clouds that had obscured the sun most of the day picked this moment to release their burden. "Darn," she mumbled. "I can't catch a break."

Between the pelting drops on the parked car, the reflected lamp light glistened on the vehicle's hood. "Gray sedan?" Her memory flickered. Hadn't there been a gray sedan shadowing her movements that first Sunday when she'd made the rounds of the old familiar places in town? Why hadn't she seen it since? Did her stalker have access to several vehicles, or was there more than one stalker? She thought of the tan pickup and the maroon SUV. Nothing fit into place. Lacy was used to putting the pieces of a story together, like a puzzle. It had always brought her joy. But this time, if she couldn't compile the puzzle before long, it could cost her life. *They've already tried once.*

Lowering the glasses, she returned them to the box and closed the blinds before clicking on her table lamp. Lifting her briefcase upon the bed, Lacy removed her shoes and climbed on top. Maybe if she studied her notes, she would find something she might have missed the first time around. She still wondered at the attempt to cross out Judge Shaw's name. Had he changed his mind after first signing in? It probably meant nothing at all.

*

He'd watched the foreboding clouds all day, full, like Holstein cows ripe for afternoon milking. Having spent one of his summers on a dairy farm gave him enough visuals for a lifetime. Staring into the foggy night sky, he searched the shrubbery across from Lacy Cottrell's house. Had he seen movement, or was it only shifting shadows of windblown trees? An oncoming car from the opposite direction temporarily blinded his sight. Long seconds after the car had passed him, the strong-featured man blinked to clear his vision.

Shifting occasionally to keep his attention sharp, he suppressed a yawn. These extra hours at night were a bear added to his day job, but it was the only way to have any connection to his contact after dark. He blinked again. The shadow in the shrubbery was no longer visible. Perhaps it had been the wind in the trees after all. While he studied on the possibility, a running form sprinted from either Kelly's driveway or the driveway next door.

Shifting into gear, the gray sedan sped from 0 mph to 40 mph in just a few houses as the dark form disappeared into the trees and shrubs separating the houses across the street. Continuing down the street, his thumb clicked a number on his ready-dial pocket phone and lifted it to his ear even as he turned the corner with one hand, heading for the flipside of the block. Could he catch the intruder on the other side? Not for the first time he doubted his decision to keep his identity from Lacy. He knew he had to declare himself but was undecided as to the time. He didn't want to bring attention to himself and send the guilty to ground. As long as no one knew what he knew after all these years, it was safer for Lacy and himself.

*

Lacy's droopy eyes were almost to the point of dozing when police sirens shrilled in the street below, jerking her senses awake. Bounding from the bed, she rushed to the front windows and parted the blinds. Two police cars were directly in front of the house.

"Lacy!" yelled Kelly from the bottom of the stairs. "Hurry!"

Even as she dashed from the room in her sock feet, she heard the doorbell and loud pounding. The two cousins exchanged alarmed glances as they met at the front door. Kelly opened it, her eyes wide with apprehension.

When the immense-sized officer explained that a neighbor had called in a report to the police after spotting a dark-clad individual darting from the vicinity of their yard across the street into the vacant lot, Kelly's hand flew to her mouth. "Did you catch the person?" she asked hoarsely.

"Was the neighbor able to identify what the intruder was doing or where he was coming from? Could they tell how tall he was?" Lacy asked.

The stern-faced police officer stared at Lacy. "That's a lot of questions, Miss Cottrell. The neighbor refused to give their name, afraid of getting involved, but no, we were not able to apprehend the intruder. Did either of you see or hear anything to alert you that someone was on your premises?"

Both women shook their heads. Kelly clutched her old, faded, blue robe close to her chest.

"Can you tell me where the intruder was seen in regard to our premises?" Lacy pressed.

The officer squinted at the report. "He was spotted initially coming from somewhere out of your driveway. That's all the information I have, Miss."

Lacy nodded soberly. "Thanks, Officer."

The tall, large-boned man studied Lacy, giving her the impression that he thought she might know more about the situation than she was telling. She didn't, but hearing about the intruder made her uneasy. She knew Quinn Darling would receive a copy of the police report, and there was nothing else she could add. A sharp pang reminded her of the gray car that had been parked at the end of the street for who knows how long, but had she mentioned identifying the gray car, she would have to state when she'd noticed it following her two weeks earlier. Did the car have any connection to the stalker? None of it made sense.

She held her tongue and waited for the policeman to conclude their interview. She had nothing to add. It was one more stalker, more or less, only tonight this one had been on their property. It was becoming harder and harder to contain the growing anger within her. She was tired of being stalked and followed. It was time for her to take the initiative.

After reassuring Kelly about their safety, Lacy headed upstairs to turn the lights out. Going swiftly to the window, she peered out at the deserted street. Kelly was concerned about what the neighbors were thinking. The police had been to their house twice in a short period. It saddened her to think perhaps her cousin would be happier when she left town and everything returned to normal. *Whatever that is.* Lacy's life had been so altered in the short period she'd been back, she'd have to reassess her direction.

Everything looked just like it had when she stood in this spot as a child. Suddenly she was bone weary and wanted to go to bed and forget she was a target. Switching on her table lamp once again, she pulled her nightshirt out from behind her bed pillow and was starting for the bathroom when her cell phone rang. Springing for her night table, Lacy hurried to silence the ring before it could disturb Kelly. "Hello, yes, Nadine." She dropped the nightshirt on the bed.

Climbing up on the bed, she listened with interest as Nadine gave her a quick rundown on what she had obtained, little as it was. "Wait while I get my notebook." Lacy hurriedly grabbed her pen and pad that she always kept on the table. She wrote and listened for the next ten minutes. When they hung up, she laid her head back and thought over the information received on her boss, Jason Gardner. Nadine said she'd run into a snag after tracing his history from a newspaper in Ohio to Harvard. Nadine's records showed nothing earlier. Lacy was puzzled. She wished she knew more about him. Even when they were in Wellington for lunch their conversation revealed little to nothing about Jason's prior life. Mr. Gardner was still a mystery man.

Her head was spinning. The growing feelings she had about Jason were twisting her into knots. Lacy had been mentally kicking herself for allowing her emotions to go unchecked. She was here for a short time to do a job—most likely the most important assignment she would ever have. If she could only bring Stevie's murderer to justice, nothing else should matter. Grabbing up her nightshirt, she started back for the bathroom.

She'd given Nadine one more name to check out for her. When this was over, she owed the lady big time. Knowing the woman had a fondness for homemade quilts gave Lacy the perfect answer.

Her mind switched gears. The new information about Rob Corbin she'd gathered in the file room had strangely rekindled her memory back to the death of Clem Browning, the man who'd actually made the bomb killing the Turners. Browning was a known arsonist. The bombing and Rob Corbin's arrest occurred about the same time. Were they connected? The common denominator was Mrs. Turner…coincidence?

Following Browning's death, Lacy had seen that direction as a dead end. Recently, a new idea had sparked that she felt wouldn't hurt to play out. The thing was, she needed Quinn's help to execute it. Quinn would be delighted when all this was over just to have her out of his hair. Of course it wouldn't hurt his career if he had a part in solving a seventeen-year-old cold case during his time as a substitute DA.

Gradually the evening's excitement settled, and her heart rate quieted. In the shadowed light from the lamp she continued reading. Several passages in the book of Psalms caught her attention. One told how God knew the secrets of men, and she thought of Gladden Hills, whose undercurrent was fraught with secrets. Her heart still ached with the injustice of the Turners' death—death of the innocent. She knew God hated that from the Scriptures.

Lacy's gaze rested in Psalm 54: "For He has delivered me from all trouble. And my eye has looked with satisfaction upon my enemies."

"I hope so, Lord…I hope so." She also knew that God would mete out justice either in this world or the next. "Let any revenge be yours, Lord," she whispered as she turned out the light. In her sleepy state, her thoughts roamed often to Jason Gardner. Yet on the fringes lurked the handsome Morgan Streeter. She groaned and rolled over to block out both faces.

14

An Illuminating Meal

CLICKING THE TIMER ON TIME BAKE, Lacy grabbed for her briefcase and rushed for the door. She would be late for work, but there was no help for it. It took time to mix up the herbs and special sauce she liked to pour over her beef roast. With the potatoes and carrots cooked in with the meat, she hoped it would be as tasty as she remembered her mother's famous pot roast being. Lacy found cooking both creative and liberating. But she agreed with her cousin on one point: it was no fun cooking for only one person.

Lacy talked privately with Maxine, giving her the day's itinerary. It was understood in their look that no one else was to know. Lacy had not concentrated on the scary realization that someone knew she was at the courthouse the day she was attacked and the only people who knew she'd be at the courthouse were Wendy and a limited few at the paper. The fact someone could have overheard Chloe question her that morning was a possibility.

Lacy trusted Wendy. There was a basic honesty in the young woman's makeup. Quinn Darling knew Lacy was thinking of looking at the files. So where did that leave her? She was forced to trust Quinn for the present, but it troubled her that her safety required her to look at people with suspicion and her circle of trust was diminishing. When she abruptly turned away from Maxine's massive entry desk with its extended counter, she saw Chloe standing at the end of the hallway. Surprised to be caught watching her, Chloe dashed back to her area. Maxine and Lacy exchanged knowing glances.

"Mr. Gardner and I have grave concerns about that young woman," Maxine whispered. "She pleaded with him for a job to help support her family, or so she said, but she isn't proving to be a very good worker. Her concentration and work quality is erratic. And, ah, we have other concerns."

Shifting back, Lacy stared at the heavy features of the woman. There was a look of sadness on her face. "Why share this with me?" Lacy asked softly.

"Because of her unusual attachment to you. I believe she both respects you and despises you at the same time. She's jealous."

Maxine had hit the nail on the head. Hadn't Lacy herself seen the contradicting actions in the girl?

"She obviously needs more help than all of us first realized. Chloe is craving recognition. She wants to be a reporter so bad she can taste it, and though at first I agreed to help her, I haven't had the time, and frankly I've purposely been avoiding her lately." In her heart Lacy knew there were other ethical reasons. Chloe had broken into her desk.

Maxine glanced around her. "We'll hold off on a decision for a while, but we would like your input."

*

Later, when Lacy left the building, she was anxious about Maxine's words in regard to Chloe. She had no intention of saying anything that would result in her dismissal. It was clear the girl was troubled, but being fired would only plummet what little self-confidence she now possessed.

With a cursory glance around the square, Lacy directed her steps toward the library to complete her research. She'd assured Jason that she would stay in the company of people she could trust.

People she could trust in Gladden Hills—an oxymoron if ever she heard one. *Who are the people I can trust? Even Jason has a mysterious past.* She sighed, hurrying her steps. Her appointment with Quinn was right after lunch.

Vicky Subert's wide blue eyes lit with pleasure when Lacy walked through the DA's door. "Good afternoon, Miss Cottrell, Mr. Darling is waiting for you. I'll tell him you're here."

Lacy allowed herself to be shown in. They regarded one another across his expansive desk.

"Lacy, please sit, I've been reading last night's police report."

"Yes, about that. I...," she tried to explain.

"Never mind. It is pretty much self-explanatory. It's too bad they didn't grab the dirt bag, but I don't imagine that is why you asked for a meeting. Do you have something for me?"

"Coincidences. That's pretty much it at this point." She told him about the embezzling case and the young union official convicted for the crime, all in the time frame of the Turner bombing. "The fact it all happened simultaneously may be a coincidence; then again, the fact it went through the same bank as Terri Turner worked for may have a bearing. I'd like you to find out where this Rob Corbin is today and talk with him. Oh, and there's someone else I'd like you to arrange for me to get in to see." She drew in a deep breath, unsure of Quinn's reaction.

"Well, who is it?" Quinn asked, sounding impatient.

"Clem Browning's cellmate. You know, the last man who shared his cell when he was killed in prison." Quinn's shocked expression told her he wasn't expecting her request.

"You want to interview the cellmate of the arsonist who made the Turner bomb?"

"Yeah…I thought maybe I would. It's just a hunch."

Quinn leaned back in his chair, his fingers coming together in front of him. The DA's eyes were vague, giving the impression his mind had taken a holiday from his body. Lacy waited, secretly wishing she were privy to his thoughts.

In a fluid motion, as if a long rope was unwinding, Quinn sat forward and then stood. "All right. I can arrange the interview with Browning's ex-cellmate, and I will put Vicky onto finding Rob Corbin's location. It's been seventeen years, but we will see what we can do." His entire body pivoted in her direction. "And *you*, Lacy Cottrell, will report back to me what these interviews reveal *immediately—not when you get around to it.*"

She met his dark, penetrating gaze. "If you are referring to the fact I went to the file room on Monday, I'd say I've been more than prompt in relating what little I found, considering the nature of the information did not appear to be of an immediate importance."

"I'll get back to you when I have the information. Anything else?" he demanded.

Lacy thought of the log book from the time of the bombing, especially the frequent trips to the file room made by Judge Harold Shaw, District of Attorney at that time—unusual, but not illegal. "Nothing of importance."

He leveled a look at her. "Did you find backup like I requested?"

"I did, and I'm working on another possibility tonight," she said, smiling hopefully.

Quinn pursed his lips. "Anyone I know?"

Lacy's mouth twisted into a frown as she thought of Chuck Walden's rough lifestyle. "I hope not."

Quinn was quick to note her hesitation. "Why?"

She glanced up at him with a smirk. "Just remember you told me to find my own backup because the police department was stretched thin…or was it that you didn't want the entire force to know of my situation?" she questioned as the thought struck her. Her humor changed to suspicion.

Quinn avoided her eyes. "Bear in mind this is a small town, Miss Cottrell, and you wanted to operate *without hindrance*. Now if our business is concluded?" He gathered his desk papers.

Lacy nodded. "I'll wait for your call." Pushing up from her chair, she gave him one last probing look. This man knew more about the Turner bombing than she first surmised. Had he decided to get on board in this cold case because he thought it might help his career? The possibility weighed on her as she left the building and scanned for familiar vehicles. And what about that gray car she'd seen on two occasions, the most recent being last night when the intruder was seen in her driveway? Was there a connection between them?

Enjoying the relief of not seeing any of the vehicles in question, she drew her trench coat tighter around her against the sharp wind. Walking briskly down the street toward Mona's Bakery to pick up the specialty dessert she'd ordered earlier, Lacy wondered what this dubious dinner party might bring into play tonight. Kelly's apprehension hadn't helped her anxiousness. Praying for whatever decisions she might make, she quickened her steps. Her heart was made lighter by a sudden awareness of an increased faith…and the surety that God would be there tonight.

At some point, she'd begun to experience Christ's presence again. It was a fresh joy. Her faith was escalating at a rapid pace. Was it because of the intense threat of danger she was living beneath? *Nothing like a little life-and-death drama to increase a person's prayer life and highlight what's important.*

*

When the doorbell rang, Kelly and Lacy stopped dinner preparations to exchange looks of apprehension. Lacy's eyes rose to the wall clock: 6:30 p.m. "He's prompt," she said huskily.

"You answer it, Wonder Woman," Kelly prodded, smirking.

"Wonder Woman? You haven't called me that since we were kids."

"Lacy, you always were Wonder Woman. The one who scampered up the neighbors' tree to unhook my tangled kite. The one who crawled though that buggy culvert to get that rangy-looking stray cat when the storm hit and the cat freaked out and sought cover. You brought it in and dried it on Gram's best bath towel, then rocked it in the kitchen rocker, and Gran and Papa never said a word. They just shook their heads."

The doorbell rang with renewed zeal as Lacy laid aside the colorful kitchen smock and raced toward the front door and whatever the evening held in store. Opening the door, her eyes traveled up to Charles Walden's six-foot-four stature. She swallowed hard. Somehow he seemed even larger in the door frame of their front door than he did in the open countryside.

Pushing the door wide behind her, she stepped back. "Please, Chuck, enter and be comfortable. We'll be eating in the kitchen where we can relax and enjoy." She held her hand out to take his oversized black leather jacket. He was wearing a brand-new dark green and white plaid lumberjack shirt with a pair of neat black jeans. Her gaze rested briefly on his shiny, coal black pony tail, tied back at the nape of his neck.

Lacy led the way through to the warm, bright kitchen that was filled with the aroma of savory beef and cinnamon apples, one of Kelly's special side dishes. Kelly turned from the warm stove with flushed cheeks. Lacy speculated if it was the stove heat or heightened tension in her cousin's countenance. Kelly stared up at Chuck's dark complexioned, rugged features with hesitant awe. Between his coloring and black eyes, the man could have passed for a Native American and Asian blend.

"You too have met before, right?" Lacy asked as Chuck and Kelly stood silently regarding one another.

"Uh, not really," said Kelly, laughing. "I've heard of Mr. Walden's competent auto service...which reminds me, I truly want to thank you for coming to Lacy's rescue when my temperamental vehicle left her stranded by the side of the road. When I brought it in, you weren't around for me to thank you properly."

"I get busy and miss people sometimes. Sorry. I hope my guys treated you right. If not, you just let me know and I'll find out why." Chuck's dark massive brows rose and merged together like a brooding broom. He looked every inch an Indian chief ready for war.

Kelly appeared to be quite taken aback. "No. Really! Everyone was great. They treated me fine and fixed my car in nothing flat. Why don't you sit at the table, Mr. Walden? Dinner is ready to serve."

"Chuck...or Charles, Mrs. Larson, please. Ellie and me go way back. Why, we threw mud balls at each other in Stevie's backyard after that big rain—remember Ellie, I mean, Lacy?"

Lacy skimmed back over the years. "Yes." She laughed. "I'd forgotten until you mentioned it right now. It was a couple of weeks before..."

"Yeah," Chuck replied huskily as he fumbled to lower his huge frame into the sturdy wooden kitchen chairs. "It was about that same time."

Kelly breached the awkward moment. "I'd like you to call me Kelly, Chuck. Mrs. Larson is someone I used to know a long time ago." She looked at

Lacy. "If you'll bring out the salad from the refrigerator, I'll dish up the gravy, and we can sit down." She turned back to finish taking up the roast and vegetables.

Seeing the back of her cousin's shoulders rise and fall, Lacy relaxed. Kelly was a trouper. She could tell how nervous she was around Chuck. He had always been a big, awkward kid, but now his size and appearance was quite intimidating. But remembering him as a child and the man she'd met again alongside a lonely road, Lacy found it hard to believe him dangerous. Then again, circumstances could change a situation in a heartbeat.

When they all were seated at the table, the girls exchanged looks and Lacy took the initiative. "Will you join us in a brief moment of giving thanks for our food?"

Lacy saw the slight color rise on the big man's neck and face. "Sure. No problem." He dropped his head like it had a boat anchor at the end, his eyes lifting to see what would happen next. Lacy prayed briefly, also thanking the Lord for Chuck's presence at their table.

Chuck looked up following the pronounced amen and fixed his eyes on the impressive beef roast in the center of the table. Lacy stood and carved while Kelly began passing him a continuous line of steaming dishes, including her own mouth-watering cinnamon apples. Not a sound escaped their lips in the next five minutes, except for Chuck. After the first few mouthfuls, he heaved a sigh. "This is out of the ballpark, ladies! I can't tell you how long it has been since I've eaten a meal like this. Not even my wife could make food taste like this."

Kelly's countenance beamed with satisfaction. She glanced at Lacy, her expression showing a new warming toward their guest. Lacy hoped the rest of the evening would go as well.

Laying down his dessert fork, Chuck inhaled deeply and slowly released a contented sigh. "There is nothing like good chow to relax a man. You've more than repaid me for everything, ladies." He cocked his head toward Lacy. "That is, unless you mean to ask something more of me?" He grinned slyly. "You always were a cagy one, Ell…excuse me, Lacy. I have to tell you it's hard to hang a new tag on you."

Kelly looked to her cousin anxiously and spoke before Lacy could form her words. "Yes, Chuck, we do mean to ask something more of you. We *desperately* need your help. Lacy does. She needs protection, someone to be her backup. In simple language, a body guard. Her life is being threatened. She was almost killed more than a week ago, pushed down the courthouse stairs. The police are too short on manpower to help, or so we've been told."

Lacy stared at Kelly, awed by her passion. She felt humbled by her plea on her behalf. "I won't require twenty-four-hour protection—just backup, as Kelly said."

Chuck heaved his considerable upper portion across the table, his face tight. "I wondered when I heard about that business at the courthouse. Falling down stairs is not an everyday happening, and I remember you scaling a back fence before I was halfway up. I was embarrassed that a girl would put me to shame."

Lacy patted his arm. "That's all right, Chuck. I used to envy your powerful swing. When you hit a ball, it was still on its way to Indiana by the time you rounded the bases and blasted home plate. I remember you as the terror of the playground at school. No one messed with you—or us, when you were around. It came in handy sometimes."

His mouth curved up at the ends, but his eyes were like flint. "Who's after you and why? Is it because of some story you're working on?"

"It's an old story I'm working on. I'm after the truth of who was behind the bombing that killed Stevie and his mom. I believe that somehow the people who instrumented their death and paid for that bombing seventeen years ago are aware of why I'm here—either that, or simply my presence is making them nervous." She proceeded to fill him in on specific incidents that had transpired since she'd arrived in town. "Maybe they think I know more than I know, or maybe they're afraid, I'll remember something."

She paused. *Is there something I need to remember?*

"Something bothering you, Lacy?" Kelly stared at her.

"No. Just addle-brained." Shaking her head, Lacy threw off strange feelings of the past and faced Chuck, waiting for his response.

His lips set in a firm line. "I always wondered why they never found the guilty ones. Didn't I hear awhile back about them finding the dude who made the bomb? Whatever came of that, and why they didn't get the lowdown out of that—" He stopped abruptly, as if he meant to say something unacceptable and looked around sheepishly before finishing his thought. "Why didn't they make that guy tell who it was that paid for the job?"

"The man's name was Clem Browning. He was serving time for arson on another offense when the connection was made between him and the Turner bombing. Almost as soon as the news hit the air, someone in prison got to him, and Browning became an instant dead man. The authorities didn't have a chance to question him. The only one who talked to him at length was the detective who'd traced the bomb back to Browning. Unfortunately, he was killed in a hit-and-run the very next day."

Chuck nodded in a knowing way. "Whoever issued the order to kill must have had connections in prison, or knew someone who did," he mused out loud, glancing from Kelly to Lacy. "I got something to say. Your telling me about those in town who are trying to harm Lacy isn't totally a surprise."

Both women stared at him in shock.

He rubbed his shadowed jaw. "What I mean is, I've heard second-hand comments when your name is mentioned concerning an article. There're those who are nervous about you—a dangerous sort I've never seen around here before. I noticed some talking taking place in dark corners, and money exchanged. At first, I thought maybe that whoever they are, these people were nervous because you are a big city reporter. Maybe they were afraid you knew some deep, dark secrets about people in the town, things you'd blast for all to read on the front page. People are funny about guilty pasts."

He looked at her apologetically. "Lacy, most people didn't play ball with you in Stevie's backyard. They know you only as an outsider who is here looking for big stories. I figured maybe these people were just suspicious and needed time to get to know you. That big benefit you set in motion for the Morrisons was a good thing, and most of the town saw you in a new light. He—ck," he said, catching himself. "Now you're a town hero!"

Kelly and Lacy exchanged tense glances. "And the ones who were making negative comments…has their attitude changed?" Kelly asked anxiously.

"Most murmurings have stopped or gone underground, but there is *one* woman who is in Floyd's Bar and Grille off and on. And when she's soused, I've heard her swear and use your name in the same breath. I think the guy she is with is feeding her drugs along with the booze she's swigging down. The police have hauled him off twice that I've heard of, but he always gets off. Rumor has it he knows someone who knows someone."

"Who is this woman? Do you know?" asked Lacy, wondering what this woman had against her.

"Naw, I don't know, but I'll find out." He peered at Lacy shyly. "I don't want you to think I'm in the bar *every night,* but I'm in there enough to get a line on her." When Lacy smiled indulgently, he added, "It gets lonely sitting home every night."

"Yeah…I know, Chuck." She thought of all the nights she'd brought work home just to keep from dwelling on how alone she really felt. "I appreciate your input, especially your giving me a heads-up about this woman. Would you keep an eye open for anything else that might be helpful?"

"You got it, Lacy. Listen, I've got a couple of friends…they're good boys, and they have friends. Now some of them work for me, but I believe I can speak for them all in that they would be willing to help. They're not the type who like people who gang up on a woman. We all belong to a club. If you're going somewhere and need me to be backup, let me know. Of course the more notice I get, the better I can prepare. Sometimes I'm out on a job."

He leaned forward and pointed at his chest. "I'm with you 100 percent. There is nobody who would like to see the scum bags who killed Stevie and his mom get what's coming to them more than me." Pulling out another one of his cards, Chuck wrote a number on the back. Pausing, he hurriedly wrote an additional number at the bottom.

Extending his hand, he said, "The top number is my private number, but just in case you can't get me and you're in a real fix, dial this number at the bottom and say the word *Geronimo*. The person on the other end will ask you your name and what you need. You tell them I gave you the number."

Looking over at Kelly, he added, "That includes you, Miss Kelly. These people might not be too particular who they hurt to get what they want." His eyes were black and deadly serious.

Lacy gulped. For some reason she restrained herself from asking about the connection to the code name *Geronimo.*

"How about more coffee?" Kelly offered, her voice sounding strangely thin. "I think there's more cheesecake if anyone is interested."

*

After Kelly and Lacy said good night to Chuck and closed the door, they exchanged glances, neither needing to speak. While Chuck had assured his help, their interaction with the physically powerful man had left them slightly unnerved. His exterior appearance and connections to the rougher element of town had been somewhat unsettling at first. Though Lacy had more experience in this area because of her work, Kelly had trouble adjusting.

Yet Chuck's committed loyalty to Stevie's memory had quickly been transferred to Lacy's safety, offsetting any uneasiness, leaving no doubt about Chuck's worth. Underneath his exterior persona, Chuck was pure gold. Out of habit, Lacy pulled the door curtain aside and checked both sides of the street. Shifting back, she sighed. "All clear, for now. What an interesting night."

Kelly's return laugh had a hollow sound. "Yes, and now it's time to clean up the kitchen. If anything happened, we wouldn't want to leave a messy house," she quipped.

Lacy held her silence as they walked the darkened hall back to the brightly lit hub of the house. They mechanically went through the motions of clean-up, exchanging few comments.

Minutes passed before Lacy paused from the work. "Kelly, I've been thinking…I'm not sure what lies ahead in the next few days, or weeks, for that matter. Should I hear back from Quinn about information I'm waiting for, I might need to be out of town for a couple of days. If that happens, you'll need to keep yourself surrounded by people you can trust. If you feel it is necessary, alert Jerome. I'll leave the decision of how much to tell him to you. Copy these phone numbers that Chuck gave us and keep them near."

"Lacy, if you're expecting trouble…?"

"I don't know what to expect, but I want to know you're safe."

Kelly walked across from the table where she was collecting the dirty dishes and drew her cousin into a strong embrace. "What about you?"

"I'm learning that God's Word is true. My times are in His hand, but I'm also trusting in His promise that He will give His angels charge over me."

The sharp intrusive ring of the phone on the end of the counter halted whatever Kelly might have replied. Lacy slowly approached the phone as if it bore sharp fangs. A glance at Kelly told her that she wasn't expecting a call. Lacy forced volume into her apprehensive voice.

"Hello?" The response on the other end of the line drew her up sharp. "Morgan? Yes, yes. I remember that I was supposed to get back to you tonight." She gave her head a shake and rolled her eyes.

Kelly walked over to stand beside her.

Lacy cleared her throat. "I'm sorry, but the evening has been quite busy. Our dinner company just left." She listened, realizing she hadn't given one thought to his invitation since they'd last spoken.

"No Morgan. I'm glad you called. I hope I didn't interfere with your evening?" Biting her lip, she nodded as the telephone voice continued. "Do I have an answer for you about dinner Friday night?" She held up her unrestricted hand and looked to Kelly.

Just then, an idea struck her. It would take considerable planning and might even be dangerous to pull off, but if there was a chance…. "I'd love to accept your dinner invitation. You'll have to give me directions. No. No. I'd rather drive out myself, but thank you. 7:30 p.m. would be fine." Her pulse was rapid when she hung up, more from fear than romantic nervousness.

Kelly shocked her out of her internal thoughts. "You're going to have dinner with Morgan Streeter on Friday night? Are you crazy? Do you have a death wish? I thought you wanted to stay out of Cynthia Bradford's gun sights? She considers Morgan her private property. I've heard her brag that she and Morgan are a twosome at the country club every Friday night when they have a dance band. You know her better than I do. What do you think she'd do if she learned you were out with him on Friday night? "

Actually, Lacy hadn't remembered Cindy Bradford. She'd been too busy. Drawing up a chair, she sat on it backwards and rested her head on her arms, thinking about her cousin's admonition and the situation. Glancing up, she saw Kelly staring at her. "It's just possible, if I get in a tight place, that could work for us. Do you by chance have Cynthia's cell phone number?"

Kelly frowned. "Yes, at the office. She gave it to me if I found just the right property for the fancy new house plans she had drawn up. Why?"

"Get the number and put it in your phone in case we need it. I need to think on a few ideas." A small plan was developing. It was awkward at best, but if she got into a desperate situation, she'd use any method available. "Well, I can't solve everything tonight. Let's finish up and go to bed." Her eyes lingered on the large container of cinnamon apples, as an avenue of opportunity opened.

Looking to Kelly, she asked, "Didn't I hear Eric Greer mention at the Morrisons' benefit that cinnamon apples was one of his favorite dishes?"

Kelly's head whipped around. "So?"

"So, you told me that Eric came by the office today and invited you out to lunch."

"Yes...and I also said that Jerome told him I was already having lunch with him. He said we had work to catch up on." She smiled.

Lacy nodded. "Good. Because when you come by the bank tomorrow about 10:30 a.m., break time, Eric will be so delighted to share those cinnamon apples with you that he won't even notice me waiting alone in his office."

"I'm going to do what? Just where will Eric and I be eating these cinnamon apples while you're waiting alone in his office?" Kelly dried her hands and walked toward Lacy.

"Remember that sweet little employee break area outside Eric's French door in his office? I spotted it the last time we were there. If you bring plastic dishes and spoons with napkins, it will be an easy clean-up. Who knows? Eric may even quit pestering you to go out if you do something so thoughtful." Lacy beamed her best winning smile.

"Oh, right. Like that will happen! It will be more like an engraved invitation. And don't give me that cherub grin you used to work on Grandpa when you wanted him to buy you something after Gran already told you no."

Lacy felt frustrated. "Look, if there was any other way...I don't need a long time in his office, just a few minutes to scan his files. If..."

Kelly held up her hand. "Hold it! You are planning on looking inside Eric's bank files?" She waved her hands. "No-ooo, I don't think so."

Lacy rubbed her forehead. "Listen. I'm not looking for anyone's bank statements, except maybe Eric's. I need to get a feel for possible illegal money being transferred. Not that I'll have enough time to do a thorough job, but I might stumble on something useful. If I tag along with you, Eric will be happy to get rid of me and won't care if I pick up one of those magazines in his office. I'll act like I'm interested in an article while you share break time with him on the patio. I'll even spring for the coffee. Everything will go like clockwork—you'll see. I noticed the layout of his office. If you could get his back to the French doors."

"It's March, Lacy. It's still cold to eat outside."

"The news predicted it would be almost 70 degrees tomorrow. You could wear your heavier jacket…a spring picnic will be romantic," she wheedled.

Kelly grimaced, ignoring her sarcasm. "What do you hope to find?"

Lacy shrugged. "I don't know exactly. I was told to follow the money. I know it sounds like a bad spy movie, yet I figured the best place to start was the bank. Everyone knows they have all the money."

"What—what did you say about money?" asked Kelly.

"It was a clue to the Turner case. I was told to follow the money. Remember what I found in the courthouse files? The entries about that Union official accused of embezzling funds interested me. It was the first direction toward any money. The timing of all that going down doesn't track. Coincidences like that are rare."

Kelly's expression was blank. "Eric wasn't even around back then. How could he play into any of that? If Jerome hears about this, he isn't going to like it."

"You hope." Lacy grinned. Sobering, she added, "I wish I had an opportunity to get in to see Conrad Heywood's office. He was around at the time of the bombing. Have you noticed how cozy he is with Eric? I'll have to watch out he doesn't walk in to Eric's office the way he did that day when we were there. If Heywood catches me going through Eric's files…I know it's chancy, but I'm willing to risk it. What I'm sorry about is having to ask you to help. Eric Greer is such a jerk, but I'm desperate."

"Eric's not a jerk, Lacy. I know you don't like him, but he is a handsome man who holds a high position of respect in this town—it's just that I prefer Jerome."

A glimmer of hope sprang in Lacy's heart. "Then you'd be willing to share your cinnamon apples for a good cause?"

Kelly heaved a sigh and nodded. "I suppose it wouldn't hurt to push Jerome along some. And you won't have to worry about Conrad Heywood walking in on you if you get into the files. Eric mentioned that Heywood was going to be gone most of the day at a big banker's meeting in Lansing."

"Really? How interesting." Lacy grabbed a dishrag to help finish up the dessert dishes.

15

Dangerous Plan

LACY FINALIZED HER WEEKLY COLUMN at her desk. This story featured the Collins' Dairy farm and the now defunct Collins' Creamery building, located near the main entrance of a winding drive at the outskirts of town. It was reported the business had at one time been one of Gladden Hills' major industries. Personal interviews and pictures of the present Collins generation provided an interesting tidbit. The famous recipes of Collins' celebrated ice creams were still in the family. Though now rarely used in comparison to past years, they were still revered. The recipe was tasted at every Collins' family reunion and occasionally catered for special events around town.

Maxine stopped by the desk with a final interview printout from a neighbor who lived nearby the Collins family and often catered their ice cream. "I can't tell you when I've had so much fun, Lacy Cottrell. I've got all the highlights in this printout. I think most people have forgotten about Collins' ice cream. I tasted it just once, and it was the best of anything I'd ever experienced in the way of homemade ice cream. I'm anxious to see the final column. The Collins family can hardly wait."

"My thanks to you, Maxine. Your telephone interviews helped immensely. And those old photos are marvelous! I think I can finish everything up with this last interview."

The waif-like form of Chloe caught Lacy's eye as she passed like a specter behind Maxine's back, darting to her work station. Lacy frowned, experiencing a wave of guilt on the girl's behalf. Surely there was something she could do to help that poor girl.

Maxine's head jerked in time to catch the back of the young woman moving away from them. Placing her hands on Lacy's desk, she leaned down, her soft-spoken words surprisingly stern. "That is the third time she has come into work late with that hung-over appearance. We can no longer allow her actions to go unchecked."

Lacy nodded in agreement as Maxine turned away. She had an idea Chloe would not long have her job. Her feelings were mixed on the subject. The girl's behavior was not acceptable, yet there was something so lost about her. *Is there anything I can do?*

Deliberately seeking out Chloe at the coffee nook, Lacy came up behind and took the girl unaware. "Morning, Chloe, I was wondering if you might have been ill lately?" she asked with measured concern, giving her an opening to explain some of her unusual behavior.

The startled woman turned wide-eyed toward Lacy. "Why would you say that?" she snapped with defiance, even as she drew her disheveled form up to her full medium height. "I'm fine."

Lacy's appraising gaze took in the girl's unhealthy pallor. It had deteriorated in a week's time. Her eyes were now encased in dark circles beneath her short lashes. Lacy thought it best to change the subject. "I was wondering if you were still interested in discussing your article? I'll have time tomorrow morning after the paper goes to press."

Chloe's eyes lowered, taking on a convert appearance. "What's wrong with today? Are you busy or something?"

Lacy fought against the stab of irritation at being pinned down by this demanding girl. Chloe didn't make it easy to be nice to her. "As a matter of fact, I am. I have a column to finish this afternoon."

"What about this morning?"

Lacy kept her expression placid. "I'm busy this morning." She stirred her coffee and started to turn away before she said something she'd be sorry for.

"You going back to the courthouse file room?"

Whirling back, Lacy stared the girl down. "What do you know about the courthouse file room?" Was this girl the informant? Her pathetic look dismissed the idea.

Chloe averted her eyes. "I heard people talking, that's all. Isn't that where you tripped on the stairs and had your accident?"

Wanting to scream out that the courthouse stairs wasn't an accident, she held her tongue. "Sometimes it's better not to repeat rumors, Chloe," she said soberly. "If you truly want to be a reporter, you will learn to silence your tongue. You will also learn that rumors don't always have all the facts, now do they?"

For an instant Lacy thought she saw a flicker of fear in the girl's darting gaze, but it was so quick she couldn't be sure. *What is Chloe afraid of—or whom?* Lacy admitted to herself she knew nothing about the girl's life after work. Did she live with her family or alone? Lacy sensed the waif-like woman had few friends. Finishing her coffee, she glanced at the hall clock and knew she had no time to waste. It was almost time to meet Kelly at the bank.

*

Pausing at Maxine's desk in the lobby, she checked to see if Jason Gardner had called in and left any messages for her. "Nope," Maxine said, "and he didn't say where he was going to be or when he would be in."

"Thanks," murmured Lacy, feeling disappointed. Her eyes lifted behind Maxine to the hallway leading back to the offices. She scanned the shadows, searching to see if anyone was watching her departure to see where she was going. Chloe had twice tried to pin her down on where she would be and when. Lacy was unsure if it was because the girl simply had no manners, and knew not to ask direct questions, or if there was more to Lacy's earlier suspicion.

She had trouble connecting Chloe to the people behind the attacks. It was more likely as Maxine had observed, Chloe wanted to mimic Lacy's actions for success. Hadn't Maxine said the girl idolized her, yet despised her at the same time? *That would explain Chloe acting so hateful at times. Could she have one of those bipolar disorders?* Weird stuff.

Maxine stared at Lacy as she stared fixedly on the empty hallway behind her. "Lacy, is something wrong?"

Coming to herself, Lacy said sheepishly, "Just trying to organize my thoughts before leaving. There are some mornings I'm more distracted than usual," she said in her defense and turned hurriedly toward the outside doors.

Her thoughts were heavy as she reached the sidewalk. She tried not to worry about what might happen at the bank in a few minutes. She'd prayed about it; now it was in God's hands. *What will be, will be,* she told herself. Actually, she was distracted by other important matters. Lacy had wanted to talk with Jason this morning and catch him up on what was happening. Finding he hadn't come into the office and had left no message for her was disconcerting. Mentally, she chastised herself for not making more of an effort to talk with him last night.

Why hadn't she? She reviewed the events. It was late when Chuck finally said good-bye to her and Kelly. Then came that stressful call from Morgan Streeter that turned into a fencing match. It left her in no mood to talk with Jason or anyone else. A pang of conscience struck her. Truthfully, she hadn't felt up to telling Jason that she'd accepted a dinner invitation from Morgan for Friday night. Why the situation made her feel awkward, she couldn't say, but it did. It wasn't as if Jason had ever made any romantic overtures, yet she hesitated to tell him about Morgan. Of course, there was no way of knowing how he would react to such news. *How do I want him to react?* she asked herself, perplexed about the nature of her thoughts.

Would he be angry that she was putting herself in unnecessary situations that could open her to danger? But surely Morgan would be her protection if she was with him? Besides she had a secondary reason for accepting...if it played out as she hoped. *Should I tell Jason about my plan? Would he think it's too risky and nix the whole idea? But if I don't take risks, how will I ever learn the truth?*

I'm getting as bad as Kelly about Jerome, Lacy fumed, angry with herself. *Jason Gardner doesn't see me beyond the fact I'm a reporter he feels responsible for.* Why did that fact trouble her so?

Thinking of risks, Lacy stared up the street to the Gladden Hills Bank where Kelly would be waiting for her in the parking lot as prearranged. Her muscles tightened. There was no turning back. Hadn't she determined that it was time to quit being the stalked victim and start pursuing the truth?

Stopping midstride, she remembered the coffee she'd promised to bring and backtracked to the little doughnut shop a couple shops back. At that moment her eyes locked on the tan pickup truck partly hidden on the back side of the square. She sighed. *Back again, are we?* Her jaw clenched in new determination to see this muddled fiasco through—wherever it led.

*

As Lacy walked alongside Kelly from the parking lot, she could see her cousin's tight expression and regretted what she'd asked her to do. Noticing the wrapped loaf in Kelly's opposite hand, she queried, "What's that?"

"Cranberry bread. I stayed at home this morning and baked. I thought it might round out the coffee break nicely." Kelly faced forward, her face unflinching.

"You didn't want to explain to Jerome where you were going this morning, right?"

Kelly shot her a look that confirmed her suspicions.

"Don't worry, I'll set the stage when we connect with Eric," Lacy offered.

Kelly nodded as they walked through the door. A fluttery assistant ushered them inside Eric Greer's private office. Lacy's eyes went to the little employee patio outside his French door—one of several offered to bank employees. He had an impressive office for a bank manager. Eric's enthusiastic greeting brought her focus forward, "Welcome, welcome. What brings you to my world?"

Lacy stepped forward. "Actually, we'd planned to do a little shopping this morning, but Kelly wanted to stop by here first," she lied so Kelly wouldn't have to. So much for her desire not to do any more lying. She was faced constantly with her own imperfection.

On cue, Kelly flashed her prettiest smile and stepped up alongside Lacy. "Eric, I realize I've had to refuse your many generous offers. I was hoping this few minutes of sharing your morning coffee break will put me back in good standing? I've brought some cinnamon apples and cranberry loaf. The sun is so warm today. Is it possible we could have a spring picnic outside?" Her gaze went beyond the French door.

Eric followed her line of sight. "Outside? Today?"

"Oh, yes. That spring air is marvelous! I've brought plates and everything. Lacy brought the coffee."

Both sets of eyes went to Lacy, who had picked up a thick magazine from his bookcase. She looked up at them. "What? The coffee is on the desk. Leave mine. I'd just as soon stay inside and finish this article. It's still too cool for me." She looked back to the article.

Eric seemed pleased at the possibility of spending time alone with Kelly. He grinned. "What a creative idea. It will be fun. How did you ever think of it?"

Kelly went slightly pale. "Lucky I guess." Clutching her bag, she motioned toward the French door and Eric picked up their coffee containers and followed her, talking nonstop.

Holding the magazine, Lacy's head shifted slightly to follow their movements as Kelly maneuvered Eric to sit with his back toward the window. Slowly, she took the magazine with her to the window and carefully pulled the drapes to the center where they would shield her being watched. Turning, she went immediately to his file cabinet in his desk drawer. Seeing nothing out of the norm, she went to the tall case at the back of the office, her deft fingers exploring file after file. She found nothing that even hinted of Rob Corbin's embezzling case, not that she'd expected to find anything dealing with such an old file. It was more a cursory search.

Lacy stared at the connecting door leading to Conrad Heywood's office, and her pulse raced. She had told Kelly to take her time. Glancing back to the outside patio through the French doors, she watched Eric energetically express himself to Kelly.

Kelly nodded in response and ever so slowly laid out their small picnic.

Lacy's hands itched to explore Heywood's files. She moved stealthily to the inner door and listened. It was quiet. Turning the knob ever so carefully, she pushed, finding the heavy oak door glide fluidly across the plush carpet. She scanned for any mounted surveillance cameras, but saw none. Heywood obviously wanted his privacy. The office was neat to an extreme…and silent. Lacy drew the door lightly closed behind her before tiptoeing straight to Heywood's desk.

Hurriedly she opened drawer after drawer until she came to a large one that wouldn't open. Returning to the center drawer, she carefully searched under assorted items for a loose key. Finding one, she tried it on the locked drawer and was almost surprised when it opened. It was filled with thick files for various trust funds. None of the names meant anything to Lacy, but she had to wonder why they were locked when nothing else in the room was locked. She concentrated on statements Heywood had made in the past. Hadn't he told her that Eric was in charge of trust funds? Maybe she'd misunderstood.

Relocking the drawer she slid the key back inside the center drawer. She was closing the drawer when she heard the door opening from Heywood's secretary's office. Lacy dropped down, scrunching inside the center hole of the massive teakwood desk. She quickly pulled the chair in as far as it would go to shield her from detection and prayed the secretary wouldn't drop anything on the floor. The seconds ticked by like hours as the secretary opened file cabinets. When the phone rang, Lacy almost jumped out of her skin. The woman's footsteps walked to the desk.

After a click, the secretary fumbled for pad and pen, telling the caller she was taking a message. Hearing the woman say good-bye, Lacy waited, hoping Kelly was keeping Eric busy until she could get back inside his office. It wouldn't do to be found inside Heywood's private office. *Will this woman ever leave?* her brain screamed.

Once the inner connecting door closed, Lacy scurried out from beneath the desk and hurriedly scanned the room before rushing for Eric's office. Peeking inside the office to check if it was safe to return, she was alarmed to see both Kelly and Eric rise from the patio chairs. He was rubbing his arms with a vengeance. Lacy had forgotten about the possibility of him getting cold and rushing break time to an end.

She slipped through the opening, slowly opened the drapes and rushed to the desk where the magazine lay waiting. Starting for the small couch, she remembered her coffee and raced back to grab the container. She was seated on the couch when the French door opened and Eric's voice cut the air.

"It may be spring, Kelly, but that wind is still sharp. We can finish up inside."

Spotting Lacy, Kelly looked relieved. "I'd really love to, Eric, but I think Lacy and I should be leaving. It's a good thing we were almost finished. My coffee is stone cold—that wind, I guess. "

Eric stared at Lacy as if he'd forgotten she was there at all. "Yes, I suppose I should get back to work as well." Shifting to concentrate on Kelly, he added softly, "It was an awesome plan for you to come with this wonderful surprise. Maybe we could do it again when the weather warms up?" He glanced over at Lacy as if she were a wart he'd like to eradicate from the equation.

Lacy smiled up at him, keeping her eyes innocent.

By the time Kelly and Lacy reached the bank parking lot, Lacy felt exhilarated in the fact they had gotten in and out in a clean sweep.

Kelly, on the other hand, looked exhausted. "I am so cold. I wore my heavier jacket, but it wasn't enough, and Eric was almost blue. I felt so bad for him."

It was on the tip of Lacy's tongue to retort a sarcasm toward Eric. Pressing her lips, she handed her cousin her unopened container of coffee. "Here. It's still hot. The lid was never removed. I was too busy."

Kelly took the coffee container, lifted the lid and smelled the dark brew. "Thanks. I need this. Did you find anything?"

"Not really...but Heywood has a locked drawer filled with trust fund files."

Kelly frowned. "If it was locked, how do you know what was inside?"

Grinning, Lacy replied, "He kept the key in the center drawer. A lot of people do that just because they don't want to be bothered hunting it up when they need it, and they assume that no one will look there. It's too obvious. There's definitely a reason that drawer was locked. I just wish I knew."

Kelly's features grew stern. "Lacy, if this little episode makes Eric come on strong..."

Lacy felt uncomfortable. "I hope not. If he does, then you'll just have to refuse and keep on refusing. Now if Jerome were to ask you to marry him, that would solve your problem."

"Lacy!" Kelly glared at her. "This is not funny." She glanced at her watch. "I'm going to work now and try to explain why it was necessary that I went with you to the bank. Hopefully Jerome won't push for details. But if this should get back to him?"

"If it's really necessary, I'll explain to Jerome that you were helping me on a big story. Which is the truth." Lacy looked with longing at the bag in Kelly's car. "Do you have any of that cranberry bread left? It sure would go good with coffee after I get back to work."

*

It was almost lunch when Lacy returned to the paper. Carrying a steaming new coffee container with her, she sat at her desk and unwrapped the remainder of the cranberry loaf. Heaving her shoulders, Lacy gently rotated her head in a semi-circle and back trying to relax her tense muscles. She was in this rotation movement when Maxine approached her desk.

"Looks as if you are settling in during the lunch period. Do you want me to bring you back a sandwich?"

By now most of the paper's employees had vacated the building for lunch. Lacy looked at the matronly office manager. "Sounds good, Maxine. I was tied up this morning and now need to finish the column. I appreciate the offer. Something with layers and plenty of mayo would be great. I'm starved." When she started digging in her purse for her wallet, Maxine waved her off.

"I'll get you when I bring back the sandwich."

As the little major general walked away, Lacy mused on her changing feelings for the woman. Not exactly sure when the shift in their relationship began, Lacy was thankful for her in more ways than one. Taking a gulp of hot coffee, she wolfed down a luscious slice of cranberry bread. Kelly sure could bake. The bread took some of the heat out of her inflamed throat.

"That cranberry bread looks good," spoke a voice from a short distance away even as Lacy bit into another slice.

Her head lifted in the direction of the rich, deep voice she was beginning to know well. "It is. Would you like a piece?"

"I wouldn't mind at all. I didn't bother with lunch before I headed back to the office."

"You were away all morning." Her voice had an edge of rebuke, revealing she had looked for him.

From Jason's vantage point in the shadowed part of the hallway, he scanned the entire working area. "I hear you were out as well. Why don't you bring that bread and come into my office?" He turned and strode down the hall.

Glancing at her computer screen with longing, Lacy swallowed the mouthful she was working on and wrapped up the rest of the bread. Carefully carrying her coffee container, she entered the boss's office and lowered the bread to his desk. She closed the door and pulled an office chair close to his desk. "If you've got a cup, I'll share my coffee with you if you don't mind cream and sugar."

He chuckled. Reaching across the desk, he took a wet wipe from a canister and gave a cup a cursory swipe. "Actually I do mind…but right now I think I'd drink it with prune juice. I need the caffeine." He held up his lemony smelling cup for her to pour the creamy liquid into.

"Whatever." She wrinkled her nose, then filled his cup. Lowering her body wearily into the chair, she replaced her container lid and sipped on the remainder of her coffee, watching Jason devour a huge piece of cranberry bread and down half of the coffee in his cup.

"You're hungry?"

"I had a meeting. It went longer than I figured." He stared across at her. "So, talk to me, Lacy. Maxine said you were asking after me before leaving this morning?" His statement sounded more like a question and his eyes confirmed it. He wanted to know where she went.

"I—ah— went to the bank with my cousin."

"For an hour?" He raised his brows above his sunglasses.

"Would you turn me in if I confessed to searching Greer's files?" she said in a small voice.

He almost knocked his cup over. "You did what? Lacy? Where was Greer?"

She lowered her head, peeking up at him. "Out on the patio with Kelly, having cinnamon apples, cranberry bread, and coffee."

"Outside, leaving you inside doing what?"

"Eric was happy to be rid of me. As far as he knew he left me engrossed in a magazine article with coffee. I'm sure he didn't give me another thought," she said, grinning.

"You used your cousin to get into Greer's files?" Jason leaned back in his chair and began rocking nervously. His right hand raked his thick hair.

"She was sitting on the patio wearing a winter coat. I didn't sell her to gypsies!" she defended. "And it wasn't just his files. I also got a look-see at Heywood's files." She figured she might as well be hung for two offenses instead of one.

His muscles visibly tensed. "And?"

"And…I nearly got caught. Praise God for big desks. I opened a locked drawer full of trust funds. I keep wondering why they were locked up."

"But you found the key?"

"He was careless. It comes from being overconfident."

Lifting his cup to his lips, Jason rocked back and forth in his office chair. "Trust funds, huh? Were you planning on telling me what you were going to do? Is there anything else I need to hear?"

"Two questions in one…wow! I don't know—I'm debating…"

"Quit being coy, Lacy. How can I protect you if I don't know where you are?"

"Where were *you* this morning? Trust is a two-way street." Her voice had a hurtful tone, a little like a demanding wife, and that made her mad. "All right. I might not have a need to know, but you were inaccessible to me and I was going into a potentially dangerous situation. I could have needed, if not the backup, at least the moral support."

"Moral support for breaking and entering?" He chuckled. "I'll remember that."

Lacy stood to leave the office. "I have an article to finish, and it wasn't breaking in. The door was open."

"Anything else you need to tell me?" His levity was gone.

She froze, biting her bottom lip. "I…I—ah, sort of got backed into a dinner date with Morgan Streeter this coming Friday night." Half turned toward the door, she managed a sidelong glance in time to see his jaw tighten. "What, you don't think I should have accepted? I figured if I was with Morgan, he could protect me; an opportunity for you to take the night off." She held her breath waiting for his response.

He asked her one question. "Where are you going for dinner?"

"Morgan's uncle's house. He bragged that Heywood has the best chef in the state. Apparently Heywood has plans elsewhere that night, leaving the house to us."

By the look on Jason's face, that comment did not go over well. "Why did you agree to go out there? His ranch is in the country. Is Morgan picking you up?" His questions were like missiles, fast and deadly.

Feeling like she was being interrogated, she swallowed her pride. "I didn't have much time to consider the idea. He called right after Chuck, our dinner guest, left last night, and I honestly forgot he'd asked me the day before. I had to come up with an answer fast…and when I heard it was to be at Conrad Heywood's house, I…ah, had another thought about a possible opportunity. The next thing I heard was me telling Morgan that I accepted his invitation. No. He is not picking me up. I am driving out there—once I find out where he lives."

Partly lowering his sunglasses, Jason leveled a stern look at her. "Tell me you are not planning to try and search Heywood's home office while you are there having dinner with Morgan?"

"The thought occurred to me," she admitted sheepishly. "It seemed like a good idea at the moment…if I can get away from Morgan on a legitimate excuse. I only wish I knew the layout of the house ahead of time and how to arrange a diversion to get Morgan outside for a few minutes on some pretext. That would give me an ideal opportunity." She peeked at Jason, not knowing what to expect.

"Lacy, you are playing with fire!" He thumped the table loudly and paced the small area, his hand raking his thick hair.

Minutes passed.

At last he turned. "Go ahead and have dinner. I'll be nearby in my car. If you need me, hit the speed-dial on your phone. Depending on what you need, I could either call and give you an excuse to leave or drive in with reinforcements. But watch him. He considers himself a ladies' man."

"No kidding!" Her dry tone caused Jason to eye her sharply. "Oh, keep the rest of that bread," she encouraged, reaching for the doorknob.

His clouded expression followed her from the room. "Nothing else, Lacy Cottrell?"

She whirled, remembering Chuck. Rushing inside the office, she whispered to Jason, "Good news. I now have a second backup. Chuck Walden came on board last night. Do you know him?"

Jason studied the cranberry bread, his hand reaching for a second piece. "I might have seen him around town. Big fella, right?"

"Big fella…and tough! I'll get his number to you."

"It's good to have him on board. He might come in handy."

By the time Lacy returned to her desk, she was rushed to finish her column and purposely ignored the presence of Chloe whenever the girl hovered near her desk. It was almost as if she was checking up to see if Lacy was as busy as she said. Truthfully, Lacy was getting tired of feeling the girl's eyes follow her everywhere she went within the confines of the building. She was glad when the workday came to an end.

*

Driving up behind Kelly's Volkswagen, Lacy noticed the car parked directly across the street, trying to remember where she'd seen the car before. Carefully locking her car and ascending the stairs to the porch, she approached the front door with trepidation, unsure who or what she would find inside. Should she dial Jason? *It's too early to push the panic button,* she told herself. *I'm starting to jump at shadows.*

With her hand on her pepper spray she entered the house and closed the door. "Kelly?"

"In the kitchen," came the reply. "Come on back. I've fresh coffee waiting."

Releasing her hold on the pepper spray, Lacy scanned the rooms as she walked the long hall, still sensing an irregularity of some kind, but unable to pinpoint what it was, except the sound of Kelly's strained voice. Standing in the threshold of the kitchen, she stared first at her cousin, standing by the coffee pot, and then at Jerome, who sat at the table. He regarded Lacy with an indiscernible expression.

Lacy looked over at Kelly with question. Her cousin was nervous as an ice cube on a hot burner. "Is there something I should know about?"

Jerome spoke up. "You tell me! I think that should have been my line a few weeks ago." There was no wavering in his hard gaze.

Kelly walked toward her as if trying to head off an unpleasant encounter. "I had to tell him, Lacy. He knew I was with Eric on the patio this morning. Remember Alma, who works at the office? Her sister is a teller at the bank and saw us on break time. She immediately called Alma with the newsflash. I couldn't allow Jerome to think...well, you know."

"Small towns!" muttered Lacy with disdain. It was one of the foremost faults of small communities she could remember.

"Yeah, as hard as it is to believe, the word of mouth in a small town is even faster than the clicking of the presses of a small-town newspaper," said Jerome sarcastically.

"You told him *everything?"* Lacy looked to Kelly.

When Kelly shook her head, Jerome stared from one to the other. "There's more?"

"Not important," said Lacy curtly. "I'd say you already know enough to make it dangerous for yourself if you should become involved...and be a danger to us, if you should tell anyone else. I don't remember you involving yourself much as a child, Jerome. You always watched from the sidelines."

Her eyes demanded an answer to the unasked question: *Where do you stand?* Part of her was hoping that Jerome would declare himself now, if by chance he was her mysterious contact in Gladden Hills. There was no better time.

Jerome lowered his head, as if pondering.

The two women exchanged glances.

Raising his eyes to meet Lacy's cold stare, he said simply, "I'm no longer a child, Lacy, and I'm more afraid of the danger directed toward Kelly and you than for myself. I wish you had trusted me sooner. I might have some helpful insight you don't know about. And from the sound of things, you could use someone else to watch your back. Kelly said Gardner and Chuck Walden are in. Tell me what you want me to do."

As Kelly's eyes pleaded with Lacy to let him help, Lacy inhaled deeply. She had to wonder what possible insights Jerome might have. "Oh, all right! I'll not turn down the help, but you *have* to keep your silence." She refrained from looking at Kelly, knowing her cousin already felt bad enough that she'd spoken to Jerome without permission. Lacy gazed longingly toward the fresh pot of coffee.

"I'll bring you a cup. I've cut the second loaf of cranberry bread. It's on the table. Go sit down, Lacy." When Kelly slid the colorful mug in front of Lacy at the table, she motioned toward Jerome. "He asked if you have anything for him to do," she said softly, reminding Lacy that an offer of help deserved to be addressed. She was quick to follow it up with a question. "Are you still planning on going to Heywood's home for dinner with Morgan on Friday?"

Lacy's jaw dropped. She felt like her life was an internet video. Soon everyone would know of her dinner plans. Pouring milk in her coffee until it became the creamy color of dry sand, she stirred in a packet of low-cal sugar and stirred some more. When the warm cup was firmly between her hands, she looked at Jerome's patient face. "You don't happen to have house plans for Heywood's ranch house, do you?"

Jerome's features twisted in consternation. "As a matter of fact, I might. I sold him that house five years ago when Conrad was ready for an upgrade to fit his new image in Gladden Hills society." His tone revealed no love lost in that direction.

The startled look on Lacy's face brought a chuckle from Kelly, who slid into a chair next to Jerome and stared up at him with admiration. "What do you think about *that coincidence*, Lacy?" she said, her voice ringing with delight, as if Jerome had single-handedly pulled a rabbit out of a hat.

Suddenly Lacy felt humbled. "Frankly, I discount coincidences, Kelly. I believe God's timing is always perfect." She laughed softly. "Yet I'm constantly surprised whenever it happens." She looked up at Jerome, amazed at the jewel he'd just dropped in her lap. "How soon can you get those plans to me, Jerome? I need to do a little homework before Friday night."

Now if I could only lay my hands on a convenient diversion right after dinner. She sipped her coffee and stared at the cranberry bread, visualizing Jason wolfing down the bread to make up for his lack of lunch. He'd been absolutely relaxed and natural in her presence. Such times were rare, and she treasured them.

Lacy couldn't help but wonder where her boss was planning on stashing his car to wait out his stakeout near Heywood's ranch. How many editors would put themselves out to that degree for someone in their employ? She wanted to think Jason's feelings for her went deeper but was afraid to build herself up for a huge disappointment. Nothing in his words or actions had given her any romantic encouragement—only a growing hope.

Then her thoughts flashed to Morgan Streeter. *Now there's a dangerous man. He plays on his physical attraction to women, as Jason was careful to point out to me.* Hopefully, Morgan would be respectful enough not to make a serious play for her on their first evening together. Her attraction for him wouldn't help the situation. Morgan's eyes had played havoc with her emotions the last time they'd met—deliberately so, she thought.

The man was fully aware of his allure to women and used it when he wanted something. What she didn't know was what he wanted in regard to her. Was it attraction as he pretended? It irritated Lacy that she was lumped into the large equation of being like most women and finding herself emotionally responsive. Her ego warred against such weakness.

Thankfully she was a nondrinker. She had to make sure Morgan took no for an answer. It was essential her thoughts remain clear, focused on the goal. Friday night was not a social date; it was an opportunity to search for evidence. *Bear that in mind, Cottrell,* Lacy reminded herself. Her contact had written: *Follow the money!* She mustn't fall into the trap of getting caught up in the evening. Her emotions of late had been very vulnerable. She tried to tell herself it was the effect of coming back to Gladden Hills. Lacy refocused on the sounds and people around her.

The upbeat conversation of Jerome and Kelly was well peppered with laughter, yet strangely it pained her to hear their secret joy. She was in the same room, yet no part of what they shared. She hated the fact that she envied the close relationship the couple was developing. In truth, Lacy did want her cousin to have a new chance for love, but being in their presence made her heart ache for such happiness for herself. Though she'd successfully acquired what she'd worked hard for, the continuous pushing to achieve had waned in its luster. Lacy was ready for a meaningful relationship—someone she could love and come alongside, be a helpmate to, as God designed her to be.

It would do no good to entertain such thoughts when she was around Morgan. He would sense her vulnerability, literally, like a wolf to the jugular. Although she believed he was attracted to her, she guessed his desire for commitment was nonexistent. Rumor had it Cynthia believed she would be the exception and was determined to make it happen, yet here was Morgan planning a secluded dinner with Lacy.

Perhaps Cynthia's obsession for Morgan could prove useful in the long run. The thought had come to her earlier and now again. She would do well to prepare in case this ploy was needed. Cynthia was a force to be reckoned with. The question was: Could that force be controlled?

Pleading a headache, Lacy left Kelly and Jerome in the kitchen and took a refill of coffee along with a piece of cranberry bread up to her room. It had been late when she'd devoured the huge sandwich Maxine had brought back for her.

Out of habit, she drew the drapes back and peered across the street to the dark and brooding foliage that so quickly swallowed up her stalker whenever he sought refuge in its tangled branches and shrubs. She shivered and scanned the head of the street where a few nights ago the tan truck was parked, and last night the gray sedan.

Who are all these people watching me? What do they want? Then she thought of the stairs in the courthouse and the strong hands that had first held her back from the railing and then pushed her down the stairs. *Do all of these people want me dead, like the man on the stairs? The street was clear tonight.* She allowed the drapes to fall back in place.

Lacy was reading in bed when her phone rang. It was Nadine from Chicago with information about Conrad Heywood. It had taken her friend several days to run Conrad's background to ground and it verified Wendy's grapevine information. Settling back, Lacy listened to what Nadine had managed to gather. Apparently when Conrad Heywood was fairly young, he and his mother moved into an old rambling house within driving distance of town. His mother obtained a job at the Gladden Hills Bank to support them, and Conrad went on to get his accounting degree. A couple years after they moved in, Conrad's uncle joined them, following his release from prison.

"Heywood's uncle did time—what for?" interrupted Lacy.

Nadine replied curtly, "Hold your horses, I have it right here. He was an uncle on his mother's side. Franko Ulrich was quite the guy!"

Lacy listened intently to Nadine's fact findings, then said, "No kidding! That is interesting. You say this Franko stayed with them the rest of his life because of poor health? Then he would have had a hand in raising Conrad."

"Do you want the info on Judge Harold Shaw now?" asked Nadine.

Lacy listened. Nadine didn't have much. "Shaw, like Heywood, moved to Gladden Hills from somewhere else. He had been a cop in Indiana before going to law school and following his graduation he applied for the position of district attorney in Gladden Hills after working in the DA's office in Indiana.

He was married while he was a cop to a Constance Gomer, but they divorced after a year. That's pretty much it," said Nadine.

"What about Eric Greer?" murmured Lacy, allowing her muscles to relax. She listened to a rustle of papers at the opposite end of the phone.

"I don't have a whole lot. He came into town in his mid-twenties and began work at the bank. Wait a minute. I almost missed this connection. He had an aunt working for the bank when he first arrived. Apparently, it pays to have connections in a small town. First Heywood and now Greer," said Nadine. "Carol Cummings was bank manager when he applied, which explains how Greer got the job. Carol started work in the accounting department years earlier, along with Conrad Heywood. She was there when Terri Turner was in charge. That's quite the coincidence—all of them in accounting together—kind of cozy."

"Greer's aunt worked with Terri Turner and Heywood? Yes, that's quite the coincidence! Thanks Nadine." She rubbed her head. *How does this information play into the equation? Up until now I never knew* Carol *Cummings existed.* She pondered the connection between her, Conrad Heywood, and Terri Turner. "What happened to Eric's Aunt Carol?"

"Died of a heart attack. It happened at work of all places, about two years after Eric Greer started at the bank."

After Lacy clicked off her phone, she did some heavy thinking. Now more than ever she knew she had to get into Heywood's private files. She would try anything short of breaking into his safe.

16

The Mad Hatter's Dinner Party

LACY MADE IT A POINT TO GET WITH CHLOE first thing in the morning to keep her promise. She went over paragraph by paragraph, sharing the meaning of each of her notations on the side of the article. Once finished, she followed her writing lesson with an offer. "If you would care to address these areas and do a rewrite, I'll be more than happy to review it again. You'll be surprised how your subject will jump to life," she encouraged Chloe.

The girl's focus darted here and there like an irritated bee. Her chin went up. "My boyfriend thought it was great the way it was. He says you're jealous of my talent."

Sucking in a deep gulp of air, Lacy slowly released it, telling herself she had just wasted forty-five minutes of time she didn't have to waste. She tersely handed her back the critiqued article. "Then retype it as it is and give it to Mr. Gardner for his consideration." Standing from the chair adjacent to Chloe's desk, she shifted back to add, "Be sure you let me know how it works out for you. I think this concludes our working time together, Chloe. Good luck." She kept her voice cheerful.

Even as Lacy stepped away from the irrational woman, she recalled a situation in the Bible when Jesus had instructed His disciples on what to do whenever they left a village that would not listen to the truth, "*Shake the dust from your shoes when you leave.*" These words were somehow comforting and removed all vestige of guilt. Lacy had done what she could, and now it was time to move on. Calmly bypassing the stunned Chloe, she walked toward her desk, surprisingly content.

"You're not going to read any more of my articles?" whined Chloe.

"That's right. Ask your boyfriend." Lacy kept walking, ignoring the muted snickers from various workers eavesdropping on their conversation.

At her desk were several messages, and she systematically went through each of them. A few told her how much they enjoyed her column on the Collins' Dairy, but others wanted the Collins' number so they could order some of their specialty ice cream. Lacy chuckled. She might not win the

Pulitzer Prize, but the economy of Gladden Hills had improved since she came back to town.

Knocking lightly on Jason's door, she opened it to find Maxine and Jason in a meeting. "Sorry. I just wanted to say I'd be gone for a short time." Looking around her for anyone listening, she stepped inside. "I'm going back over to the courthouse. I'll be back after lunch."

As she turned to leave, Jason spoke softly and clearly. "I'll wait here until late this afternoon." Lacy nodded as their eyes connected.

Maxine shot Jason a puzzled look and glanced after Lacy with concern.

Lacy's heels clicked rhythmically across the entryway floor as she headed for the door. Striding away from the building, she paused, finding it had become second-nature for her to scan the area for possible stalkers. Just as seeing the tan pickup parked across the square had almost become commonplace, though seeing it now sparked a reminder of something she'd meant to do the night before. Extracting her cell phone from her purse, Lacy brought up Quinn Darling's office number and pressed the button.

After Vicky connected her to Quinn, she began immediately, "Listen, before you yell at me for not calling in sooner, I've two additional people for backup. One more or less fell into place accidentally." After relating their names and situations, she added a rushed tidbit. "Remember that tan pickup I told you about? It's parked on the backside of the square. If you hurry and send someone to the square now, you might be able to get a license number that you could run a check on," she directed with authority.

The chuckle on the other end of the phone angered her.

"You think this is funny? My heart stops every time I come out and see that truck lurking across the square—just watching and waiting."

"I'm sorry, Lacy. It's just that you sounded like a cop." Quinn's tone was contrite. "I really should have told you earlier, but I've been swamped and simply forgot. That tan pickup is one of my boys. I asked him to keep an eye on you while you're at work and elsewhere if needed. I wish now that I'd told him to follow you from building to building. If I had, we might have caught the man at the courthouse. I honestly didn't expect them to go so far so fast."

Lacy stopped directly in front of the café and steadied herself against the white siding next to the entrance. She tried to reconcile Quinn's revelation with all her unnecessary fear about the skulking tan truck. A middle-aged man exiting the café turned to give her a curious look in passing. Lacy waited until he was out of earshot.

"You forgot!" It was the loudest whisper she could manage. Her fingers were balled into fists.

"Yes, and I'm truly sorry, for what it's worth at this point. It wasn't my intention to put you under more pressure or fear. It just slipped my mind."

"What about the maroon SUV?" she demanded.

"That's not one of mine. Call me the next time he shows up." The DA's coolness was back. "Where are you now? Did you let Gardner or someone know where you are going to be? You've got to be careful of that, otherwise we can't protect you." She heard him sigh.

"I let Jason know. Have you found out anything about Clem Browning's last cellmate? What happened to him after Clem was killed in prison?"

"Working on it. I'll get back to you when I have something. Keep my number handy."

Shutting her phone, Lacy stared across the square to the tan pickup hidden partly by tree limbs. The rim of the large Western hat was barely visible, but Lacy knew it sat on the driver's head. She frowned. The driver of the maroon SUV also wore a Western hat. *How am I supposed to keep them straight?* In early Western movies, the good guys would wear white hats and the bad guys would wear the black. *If it were only that easy.*

A second later she yanked the café door open, expending excess frustration. She searched out Wendy, finding her busily serving a customer. Lacy made her way to her friend's section and slid into a booth separated from others on both sides and waited for her to notice she was there. Only a few minutes passed before Wendy arrived with water and steaming coffee.

"I thought I would start you out with this. Just like you like it." Wendy's smile warmed Lacy's whole being. The young woman's blue eyes sparkled with such joy that Lacy doubted it would waver even in the heaviest of storms. Wendy's pen was poised. "Are you ready to order?"

Lacy lifted her hands in indecision. "You decide. My brain is fried!"

Wendy whisked a chicken-salad sandwich in front of her a couple minutes later. "Lacy Cottrell, you're in for a treat! Isn't this the first time you've tried the café specialty?"

"Yes, first time, though I've heard others rave about it." She wondered briefly who had told her it was so good. No matter. Lacy concentrated on the extra sparkle in her friend's appearance. Could it be love? "Are you all ready for your super date with the illustrious DA of Gladden Hills? If I recall, it's this coming Friday night, right?"

"Actually, it's been moved to Saturday night," Wendy informed her. "Good thing Quinn could exchange the tickets. I hated to cancel on him for Friday, but I couldn't turn down the big bucks I'll make waitressing on Friday night at the country club."

"Whoa! Back up. Since when have you started 'moonlighting' at the country club?" asked Lacy, pushing aside the sandwich while they talked.

She shrugged. "Since their head waitress broke her leg, and they needed a sub in a hurry. Somebody recommended me. I've got the job until their other waitress mends if I want it. I told them I'd do it this once and let them know afterward. I don't know how to turn it down when I need the money for classes and books. Quinn was so understanding."

Lacy tried to conjure up a picture of an understanding Quinn Darling. He'd been anything but with her, though she had to admit he was probably more understanding than most DAs she'd encountered.

The wheels in her head rolled like an express train. With Wendy on site at the country club on Friday night, Lacy's standby plan would work out much more smoothly than any arrangement that might involve Kelly making some pretext phone call to Cynthia Bradford. It was another golden opportunity dropped in her lap. Could God be answering her prayers for help?

She asked Wendy to sit and talk for a minute.

Giving the café a sweeping scan, Wendy nodded. "I've only got a minute. Talk fast—what's up?"

"You're going to be working at the country club on Friday night, right?"

Wendy bobbed her head.

Lacy continued, "May I ask a really big favor of you?"

Wendy's large blue eyes widened as she listened.

*

Leaving the café, Lacy hurried to the courthouse. The tan pickup parked a block and a half away no longer threatened her. She fought the urge to lift her hand and wave, but what of the gray sedan and maroon SUV?

As soon as Dede Ganson spotted her in the lobby, a hearty laugh erupted. "Lacy, it's so good to see you! Your articles are bringing life to this community. I swear, we didn't have a clue what a rich heritage we had in this old berg until your newsy column brought it to light. I remember eating Collins Cherry Vanilla ice cream at a social one summer, and it made my tongue hum."

"Thank you, Dede. Your comments are very kind, and I have to admit writing them has been lots of fun. You'd be surprised how much a reporter learns while researching a story."

The rounded chin nodded. "I s'pose. You headed back to the file room? Beats me what kind of research you could be doing down in those dusty old archives."

Lacy moved covertly close to the information counter and slowly surveyed the voluminous space. They were the only people in the open, large-tiled area. Dede leaned in close to listen.

"The truth is, I'm crushing on Nicolas Cooper, and I think I'm wearing him down. By next week, tops, we should be a steady new item around town." She chuckled at her own attempt at humor.

Dede cuffed her arm lightly. "You are a stinker, Lacy Cottrell! Imagine, you and old Coop. Now that would be a picture for sure!" She laughed at the absurdity of Lacy and old Nicholas Cooper being a romantic twosome.

"Old Coop?" Lacy questioned.

"Coop is what all the old-timers in Gladden Hills have called Nicolas for as long as I can remember, and I'm no spring chicken!" She bobbed her head.

"Thanks again, Dede." Lacy waved as she walked toward the hallway where the elevators were housed.

Nicholas greeted her as soon as the elevator door opened. "I was waiting to make sure you were all right. Don't want a repeat of what happened." He exhaled and headed back to his counter and small cubicle corner.

"I appreciate your concern, Nicholas…or should I say, Coop," she teased.

"One thing you can't escape in Gladden Hills is the wagging tongue, I see." He shook his head in disgust. "I don't mind being called Coop. Been called that since I was a teenager. What bothers me is the way people talk in this town, though I doubt it's different than any small town. Sooner or later everything will surface." He stared down at a pile of papers on his messy desk area. "You here to go through those old files again?"

"Yeah. Something is nibbling at me that I can't put a name to. I was flipping pages and writing notes so fast that I might have missed something. I'll go on back." She followed the most direct path to the area where she knew the files to be kept.

"I'll come with you and turn on a fan. It gets pretty stuffy in that corner," said Nicholas, shuffling behind her.

The old man was a comfort. More insightful than most people realized. Hefting the file books over to the long pine table, she laid them out. Because of something that had spiked her curiosity when she'd last been here, Lacy planned to zero in on a specific time frame on this search—the two days prior and the day following Terri and Steven Turner's death. She pulled a yellow legal pad out of her large leather bag and placed it next to the files, settling in for concentrated study. Then she sent a prayer heavenward for blind eyes to be made seeing.

When she glanced up, Nicholas was watching her with a moody gaze.

"Nicholas?"

The old man slid his hands into his pants pocket. "Lacy, with gossip in Gladden Hills being what it is, I figure I should be up front with you on something. Wouldn't want you to hear it from someone else and think maybe I was deliberately keeping information from you and all."

Lacy inclined her head. "Yes..." She had no idea what to expect.

"Remember when I said I saw you at the graveside service for the Turners?" He didn't wait for her to reply. "I was at that service because I was family...well, sort of family if you can count great uncle as family. Terri was my great niece. Can't say our families were all that close. Terri's mama, Edna, was the youngest in a family of ten children from two different marriages. My daddy remarried and had himself a whole second family, of which Edna was the youngest." His eyes narrowed, as if checking to see if Lacy was keeping up.

Lacy blinked, visualizing a maze of interfamily connections. Nodding slowly, she tried to reassure the old man. "I think I understand. It's all right, Nicholas. In small towns, half the population is related in some manner or form." She thought back on her conversation with Nadine. Her focus returned to the files as Nicholas lumbered back to the front.

"Just didn't want you to think I was hiding something, Lacy Cottrell."

She honed in on the file for details, anything she might have glazed over in her first hurried search. Flipping pages back a week before the bombing, she carefully read day by day, entry by entry, stopping at the short notation of a late-night break-in at the bank. Several offices had been ransacked, but nothing was reported stolen. The investigation was dropped when the Turner bombing took priority.

Lacy arched her neck, stretching to relieve muscle strain, and turned back to her methodical search. Her finger followed every police entry down the line, including phone calls logged in. Two days before the Turner bombing, something caught her eye. On the bottom line of the page a call came in to the police chief's office late in the afternoon about 3:30 p.m. It was recorded; the call was redirected to the district attorney's office, which at that time was in the same building.

Knowing all calls came through the same major circuit board, Lacy turned the page looking for an obvious entry after noting the transferred call to the DA's office. There was none. Had someone changed their mind and hung up? There was no indication who had called. The paper was rough textured in that area, as if something had been erased. Her neck felt tight again. Erasures made her nervous.

Stranger yet was the fact there were no incoming calls noted on the following page logged in until after noon the next day. The entire morning was a blacked-out time frame. It simply was not there. Where were the log-ins for morning calls ringing in to either the chief of police or the DA's office? It wasn't a holiday, and as far as she knew the chief of police's office was never closed. Pushing the pages apart she looked closer, down to the binding, running her forefinger from the top to the bottom of the page. There was a ragged edge—a page had been ripped out.

Rising from the pine table, Lacy walked to Nicholas's area. "I need the old log-in book for the file room again, *Coop,*" she said with a hint of humor.

He grinned back at her, his wrinkled face folding into craggy furrows. "Ma'am, you can have any file you want with your authorization permit and those big blue eyes of yours. I've been keeping them handy." He reached underneath his counter and pulled out the faded log-in book, quite similar to what Lacy used every time she entered.

There at the counter, Lacy went back to the date that the phone records were missing to see who signed in to see the files that day. There was a page missing for that day as well. *Big surprise!* She scanned the pages before and the pages following that date. Not many had signed in and the only name she recognized was the DA from fourteen years earlier, Harold Shaw. Lacy had noted his name in the file log-in before, wondering why he'd come in person to look through files that any office flunky could do for him. What had he been looking for? Was it possible he didn't feel he could trust certain people?

Had his search reached a dead-end similar to hers? Harold Shaw, DA, was now Judge Shaw, with his intimidating stare that made Lacy think he knew everything running through a person's mind. That brief encounter in the café, when their eyes had connected, she'd known he knew who she was. She shivered. *That man must be a caution in the courtroom!* Whatever he knew or didn't know, Lacy had gone out of her way to avoid him.

She had put off interviewing Harold Shaw. None of her columns had warranted a personal meeting with the town's prominent judge. *Maybe it's time to arrange one,* she mused, not liking the idea. With a shrewd, sophisticated man like the judge, it would be awkward to interview him about that difficult time fourteen years earlier. It had been the low point of his career. The gangland-type bombing had blindsided the young DA. He'd come to the smaller town to gain confidence and low-key experience and got blasted with a high-profile, ugly case in which a mother and young son were brutally murdered for no apparent reason. Lacy had read some very uncomplimentary write-ups about the young DA, but Shaw had weathered the storm to rise above those sad obstacles all the way to the position of Gladden City's illustrious judge. He had a very remarkable story. Perhaps she should do a profile before she left town.

But Lacy knew Judge Shaw was sharp enough to see through a staged interview. How could she bring up that period fourteen years earlier and expect to get any answers? There were some who were suspicious of his bungling of certain evidence. Even Lacy had wondered about it after reading case write-ups. Shaw had taken a lot of flak, but an informal board of inquiry had cleared him of any implication. They apparently figured his youth and inexperience had been the major problem and gave him another chance. It was said his remorseful attitude had gained him big points. Of course, it hadn't hurt that his uncle was the mayor of Gladden Hills at the time. The deeper she dug, the more family connections she ran into.

Viewing the now proud and arrogant Judge Shaw as someone who'd displayed an attitude of remorse was next to impossible for Lacy, and she'd always considered herself a person gifted with a good amount of imagination. Closing the old log-in book left her with great heaviness.

"Thanks, Nicholas. I think that's all for today." Her shoulders sagged as she walked the long room back to the table, her senses dulled. How could she put pieces of a cold case together when many of the pieces had long ago been spirited away? Where were those pieces now?

"Miss Lacy," he called after her, causing her to turn, "something's bothering you. Did you find something in the files?"

She stared at the man's grizzled face. It reflected curious concern. "It's what I didn't find, Nicholas."

"Ma'am?"

She walked back to face him. "Did Ralph Wagner, the previous DA, indicate a discrepancy in the old files and ask to see the old log-in register for the file room?" Her heart rate increased.

The old man inclined his head. "Yes, ma'am, Mr. Wagner was quite upset after looking into the old files and wanted to see the log-in book for that same time period. He checked it and wasn't too happy about that either."

"How long was that before he had his fatal accident?"

"Not long. He was mad when he left here. I could tell he meant to shake some trees to see what might fall out." Nicholas stared at the log-in book. "That's why I was none too pleased when you came wanting to see them, too."

"Why didn't you tell me, Nicholas?"

"I guess I figured I was protecting you. What are you going to do now?"

"There's not much I can do. It's a vicious circle. I know someone has tampered with the files because of the missing pages—but without the missing pages, I can't prove who might be behind the tampering." She let her arms fall to her sides in frustration.

"I'll help you put the files away. You look tired, Lacy." He said the words with such tenderness it might have been her father speaking.

She nodded, feeling moisture gather in the corners of her eyes. "I—ah—appreciate that, Nicholas."

"I don't mind you calling me Coop, Miss Lacy, really I don't. It's the man, not the name that's important."

She patted his arm. "I know, but you'll always be Nicholas to me. I think it's a splendid name."

His faded eyes sparkled. "I think so too." His footsteps quickened, as if lighter. Together they lifted the file books back into place on the shelves and Lacy signed out of the file room.

Descending the courthouse steps, Lacy withdrew her phone. Once Vicky patched her through to Quinn Darling, she spoke quietly into the phone, telling him what she'd found out. "There's not much we can do about the missing pages, but it's one more puzzle piece."

Hanging up, she glanced up at the laden sky. It would be raining by the time she left the office for home. It was her turn to cook. Tomorrow night was the big dinner date with Morgan Streeter. He'd called earlier to give her directions. She'd fumbled over her words, fearful of driving out to the ranch where he would be waiting and they'd be alone.

Morgan Streeter was an intriguing man and not for the faint of heart, she reminded herself. *Brace up, Wonder Woman.* Grandma often quoted, "Fools rush in where angels fear to tread." Lacy's chuckle sounded hollow in her ears, hanging heavy in the damp, spring air.

She thought of Jason's promise to be staked out nearby if she should need his assistance. *What if there isn't time to call for help?* A sharp chill penetrated her trench coat down to her bare arms.

*

Once safely escorted home by Jason, Lacy mounted the stairs in time to view her cousin pull into the drive. She waited for her, noting Kelly's flushed expression as she rushed the steps.

Pausing, Kelly pivoted to point to Jerome's car backing around in their drive. "I *can't believe* the way he has hovered around me ever since I told him what was going on. I think he really might care, Lacy." Her eyes danced with delight.

Lacy rolled her eyes as they entered the house. "Duh! Of course he cares. I don't know how much of a backup he will prove to be on my behalf, but at least I'll feel better about your safety." She started down the hall. "Hurry and change and meet me back in the kitchen. You can help me figure out what we can do with 1½ pounds of ground beef," she called over her shoulder.

"What's wrong with hamburgers?" returned Kelly. "Let's keep it simple."

When supper was over and the kitchen cleaned, Lacy secluded herself in her room with the house layout for Heywood's ranch. True to his word, Jerome had sent the plans home with Kelly. Assembling her notebook, she added what she'd learned in the file room to the other entries. She still didn't have any idea what money her mysterious contact in Gladden Hills was talking about. The only money she'd run across was the missing money from the Union embezzlement case that coincided with the timing of the bombing.

Rob Corbin had served time for that crime. Where he was now, she hoped to learn. Just as she hoped to learn more tomorrow night at Heywood's ranch. Lacy could only speculate if the man would keep important records accessible. If they were hidden in a locked safe, her trip would be for nothing except an exceptional meal, as Morgan had promised on two different occasions. Unfortunately, she was almost certain the handsome young lawyer had more planned for the evening than she had in mind.

After turning out the lights in her room, she stood at the window and stared across at the vacant lot. Satisfied it held only shrubbery, her focus then moved up to the end of the quiet street. Under the street light sat the gray sedan. She exhaled. *Would it never end?*

*

The next day at the paper flew by. Friday was the day when all the mop-ups took place. Everything that had been set aside during the hectic week was cleared away on Friday. Tensions were lighter once the paper was out. They all took a breather before the push began anew on Monday.

When Lacy had stopped by Jason's office to say hello, he held her gaze. "Everything still on for tonight?" His calmness caused her to wonder if he was truly as placid as his exterior led her to believe. It was impossible to tell with his glasses in place and it irritated her that her own emotions were churning. What did she want him to express—jealousy? His initial reaction had been one of surprised anger, but that had seemed to dissipate quickly—too quickly.

"Yes, everything is lined up perfectly," she heard herself reply. "I have my directions leading to the lion's den, so what more should I need?" Her voice had an edge. She shifted toward the door.

His face twisted slightly. "You could still call it off."

She turned to stare at him. Did he care that she was having dinner alone with the notorious Morgan Streeter? For a second the publisher of *Gladden Hills Gazette,* Jason Gardner, appeared openly vulnerable and concerned.

She drew her sagging courage back to herself to project a false bravado. "A reporter will never find anything out by backing out of a fashionable dinner invitation that might provide valuable information, now will she?"

"There's more to you than being a star reporter and getting a top story, Lacy Cottrell. There's always another story." His voice was a little sharp. "Besides, a story isn't worth more than the person themselves. At least that's the policy of this paper." He looked down at his desk, once again the impersonal publisher.

"But this isn't just another story, if you recall. It's personal! I'll stay on schedule. Are—are you still planning on being on stakeout?" She tried to keep the wistful tone out of her voice.

His eyes remained glued to whatever lay on his desk. "I'll be there."

She closed the door when she left his office.

*

Maxine made it her mission to whisk Lacy out early from the paper, announcing in a conspiratorial voice she'd heard Lacy had a dinner date.

"Who told you?" whispered Lacy.

"I ran into your cousin at the bakery this morning. She told me you didn't have time to bake this weekend because of your big dinner date. Who is it?"

Lacy winced, picturing Kelly's neck in her hands. "Ah, yeah…well, I wouldn't say it was anything special—just a date, and we're only friends. I can use the extra time though this afternoon, thanks." She waved and moved away before Maxine could press her to tell who she was having dinner with.

Once at the house, Lacy laid out several outfits and tried to select the right one. Nothing backless or scooped neckline; they were out. She settled on a long-sleeved, high-necked periwinkle blue dress with a silver strand necklace. The blue of her eyes leapt to a startling shade that almost made her change her selection, and the flattering line of the dress that followed her slender form caused her additional concern.

I could always wear burlap and put a sack over my head.

Morgan didn't need any stimuli to start his engine. She sensed the man wouldn't think twice about making a move on a woman of his choice. While she believed it was only a game with him, chalking up conquests, yet she had also sensed a yearning in him for a deeper relationship. Could be Cynthia Bradford had sensed it also.

Lacy stepped back from her dressing table mirror. *What am I doing?* Feeling dismay at the covert actions she'd planned for the evening, she realized the truth of her glib remark about entering the lion's den.

It was 6:45 p.m. when Lacy peered through the rain-pelted windshield traveling the paved snake-like lane leading far back into the estate. If Heywood had sought a prestigious atmosphere, his money had accomplished his goal. An entrance gate embossed with the emblem *Heywood Hills* barred her way until a knobby-faced man stepped out and asked her name before pressing a button that released the gates to swing wide. *How could Jason ever get to me if I needed him?* But she drove her black Challenger through the entrance, continuing on the long extension up to the rambling ranch.

Following the wide circular drive around, Lacy spotted a large barn set back to the right of the ranch. Lacy slowed her speed to a snail's pace to allow her the time she needed to observe as much as possible. Several workers were standing in a group under the overhang of the barn out of the rain. One stood apart from the others, a large, bulky man wearing a Western hat. Her pulse sped up. His size resembled both the driver of the tan pickup and the maroon SUV, but the distance and the rain made it impossible to distinguish. Remembering what Quinn had told her about the tan pickup, she dismissed any chance of that man being on Heywood's property, leaving only the possibility of the driver to the maroon SUV. Then she remembered all the ranch hands that worked for the Kerrigan Ranch.

As the drive swung further around, she spied a separate house-like structure situated between the barn and the ranch. She speculated on the chances of it being a guest house. Trees blocked her view from future speculation as the impressive face of the ranch caught her attention. It screamed that someone important lived inside its perimeters. Half-circle brick steps led to the plant-lined spacious porch. Golden lights gleamed from sparkling windows.

Mounting the steps to the porch, Lacy's head felt too light. Pausing, she allowed oxygen to fill her lungs and brain before she rang the bell. A tall Hispanic man answered the door and indicated she was to follow him inside a spacious entryway. From there, he led her to the edge of a gigantic living center that appeared to be constructed on two different levels. The Spanish, Western motif was so splendid to the eye, it was difficult for Lacy to focus on one area. Gradually her eyes were drawn to a stone fireplace on the second level, clean as the day it had been constructed. She wondered briefly if it had ever been used.

Seeing Morgan walk toward her from the long hallway on the left, she braced her shoulders, as if a huge curtain had been drawn on act one. "This is a fascinating house!" she said, scanning the beamed ceilings. "It's actually a compound, isn't it? I believe I noticed a good-sized guest house tucked in behind the big house. Is this a working farm or a ranch?" She swallowed hard, realizing her voice was a shade too high pitched, and she was running all her sentences together. *Relax, Cottrell!* Lacy chided herself.

"Yes, it's quite the place," said Morgan, his focus on her. He led her back through the entryway to look out a large front window. "Uncle Conrad actually has two guest houses: the one you saw coming in, and the other, a small cabin tucked away back in his wooded section on a tiny pond."

He motioned beyond the barn area. "Uncle Conrad gets in these moods where he goes off by himself. He's basically a loner, but enough about him." Taking her hand, Morgan led her to the edge of the top level, where comfortable chairs were placed artistically.

Releasing her hand, Morgan stepped down two stairs into the lower level and gazed up at her in wonder. "He-llo, Beautiful," he said, as if she just appeared in a cloud. His compliment vibrated from the softly lit area.

Lacy blinked to keep from thinking she'd stepped onto the cover of a romance novel. Gentle mood music played in a surround system that added to the feeling she was at the theater.

Lacy rubbed her arms as she stepped down into the plush sunken area by the fireplace. There was no messy fire ablaze on this damp, spring night, but a clean gas burner distributing small amounts of heat into the immense space. Lacy was glad she'd brought her bulky purple cardigan.

She gazed around to the enormous walls and ceilings. Much like Heywood's office, with not a book or decoration out of place. Lacy was curious to know if the man's character and personal life were as orderly as his office and home...and what of the nephew?

The lavish surroundings, the music...the stage was completely set by her host. Was it for now or perhaps later after a leisurely meal, after she'd been plied with red wine? Lacy felt her spine stiffen. She was not here to be one more of Morgan's conquests. She cast a sidelong glance in the area of the front door where her car waited in the pouring rain. All she'd have to do was ask for her coat and leave. Her pulse raced.

Almost as if he'd read her mind, Morgan inched closer to her, his fingertips touching her arm. She edged away.

"Relax Lacy, come sit by the fire and warm up."

His smile hadn't altered since she'd entered the house. Morgan was dressed in an elegant, long-sleeved, light gray silk shirt, complemented by a pair of charcoal-toned pants—a striking combination. His constant staring contributed to her unease. To her it seemed as if his eyes devoured her like she was on a banquet table of hors d'oeuvres. Resisting the urge to back away, she stood her ground when his hand extended toward her. He indicated a plush chair in front of the soft glow from the gas heater.

"This is the best seat in the house on a cold night. Now...what may I get you to drink that will help take the chill off this wretched weather?"

She shivered. "A hot cup of tea would be delightful," she said, sending him her most engaging smile.

"Tea?"

"Oh, please, that would be fantastic. I've plodded through the wetness all day and haven't slowed up for a cup of tea to relax." She heaved a sigh and rubbed her sweater-covered arms.

He chuckled. "Your wish to half my kingdom, my lady," he said, bowing with extended arm. "How would you like it?"

"A teaspoon of honey would be great." She moved to a sofa closest to the gas burner flame, hoping for greater heat.

"Alcohol would warm you faster," said Morgan, moving in next to her. "Relaxation is a given." His expression became inviting, like a little boy who wanted you to come out and play in the rain.

"Not for me. Alcohol puts my brain to sleep. I heard something once that struck with me. Purpose never to put anything into your mouth that will steal your brain. I like to know when I'm having a good time, thank you very much." She cocked her head, giving a curt nod.

Morgan's mouth turned upward into a quirky grin. "For real? You are an interesting woman, Lacy Cottrell."

When he left to see about her tea, Lacy glanced at her watch. Morgan had told her they would eat at 7:30 p.m. Hopefully that schedule would hold. Allowing a leisurely meal, she predicted dinner would take forty-five minutes, an hour max. That was the time frame she'd told Jason. Where was Jason? Hearing thunder, she raised her head to see lightning flash in the skylight overhead. What a nasty night to be on a stakeout!

With the mug of hot tea and honey nestled between her cupped hands, Lacy strolled about the elaborately decorated room. Original Western art was displayed on prominent walls in the extended room, but one particular section of the wall near the fireplace interested her more than the rest. The two watercolor landscapes were quite good. She read the signature, *C. Heywood. So Heywood dabbled in art…interesting.* She moved to the next grouping. These looked to be family photos. She moved in close to see the faces clearly. One photo was recent—Heywood and Morgan on horses. "Who took this?" she asked.

"Ah, a friend who was visiting at the time, if I remember correctly."

Noting the slight hesitation before Morgan replied, Lacy wondered if that friend was Cynthia Bradford. Continuing to the next, she saw Cynthia and Morgan standing next to an outside sign announcing their law office. "That's the day Cynthia and I opened our law office practice."

The photo following that was also of Cynthia and Morgan standing in a restaurant dining area holding what looked like wine glasses. There was a cake on a table behind and a few people talking in the background. Morgan slid an arm around Lacy. "That's a dinner party celebrating the opening of our law offices," he said with a hint of pride.

Pointing at the two men talking in the background, she inquired," Is that your Uncle Heywood?"

"Yes. Uncle Conrad paid my way through college with the agreement I would come to Gladden Hills to practice after graduation. He introduced me to Cynthia, who had returned with the same idea. Naturally, we talked about a combined office—better business."

"I'm sure it is better to work together than compete for business in a small community." Even as Lacy spoke, she was looking at the second man in the background photo talking with Conrad Heywood. It appeared to be Judge Shaw. Though it was a side profile of the two men in shadowed light, the likeness was unmistakable. *Curious. Is there a closer connection between Shaw and Heywood than I first thought?* Lacy turned to the next cluster of photos. These were obviously from an earlier vintage.

The first was a faded color photo of a young Conrad Heywood. He looked to be in his late teens with thick dark hair, his small, black eyes intense even then. He stood next to what appeared to be his mother. The family resemblance was remarkable. They were together in a shabby kitchen. The picture next to it was in the same kitchen, but in this picture the woman stood next to a man seated at the table. The man's face was deeply lined, his eyes hollowed and dark. He wore loose-fitting slacks and a sleeveless undershirt, and in his hand was a bottle of beer raised in mock salute.

When she glanced at Morgan with a questioning look, he shrugged. "Conrad's family. That woman is my Aunt Edna, Conrad's mother and the older man is her brother, Conrad's uncle."

Confused, Lacy swiveled toward him. "How can that woman be your aunt? If she's Conrad's mother, wouldn't that make her your grandmother?"

Morgan chuckled. "I'm going to share a family secret with you." His voice lowered, as if it was something to be kept in close confidence. "Conrad's not my true uncle. I've called him Uncle since I was quite young—a respect thing, you know. Besides, my mother insisted. Actually we're cousins. He took a liking to me when I was a kid and has been mentoring ever since. My family was poor and Conrad had money, so I figured he must be smart and could help me on my way."

Lacy was truly surprised at the revelation. "Considering he isn't a true uncle, I'd say that he has been very generous with you."

Morgan stared out the side windows at the raging storm. "Y-es, hasn't he? Conrad always admired my ability to get things done. He told me I showed promise and could go far if I had the right kind of education."

At that moment dinner was announced by the tall, stoic Santos. He was there in the doorway and then he was gone, disappeared into the shadows. Lacy sighed with relief and checked her watch while lightly taking hold of Morgan's arm to be led to the dining room. *Right on schedule…7:30 p.m.* Instead of a long, formal type table, leaves had been removed to convert the table into an intimate area for two. Low candlelight and gleaming silverware. Briefly, Lacy lamented that it wasn't a normal night, and she wasn't on a normal date.

The food was as tantalizing as Morgan promised, if only her stomach wasn't so nervous. Lacy nibbled on a flaky roll to calm the turbulent motion inside. They talked on many subjects and the time went as Lacy had predicted. As soon as the dessert plates had been cleared, Morgan guided her back to the fireplace area to a loveseat close to the heat.

"Now, we have the rest of the night just to ourselves—a time to get to know each other." His arm slid around her shoulders like a warm sweater. He was dangerously near with those penetrating eyes that sent a message of banked passion. His breath was warm, and Lacy found it hard to think as his lips moved in the direction of her neck.

Grabbing her abdomen, she uttered a small groan, causing Morgan to pull back. "Are you all right?"

Lacy's face was flushed. She could feel perspiration rising on her forehead. "I'm not sure. Help me up." She tried to push herself up from the loveseat but faltered.

Morgan helped her to her feet, her hand still clutching her stomach. She swayed to the right. Morgan caught her. "Steady there."

Lacy let go of Morgan's arm, her left hand rising to her damp forehead. "Whew!" she groaned again. "My stomach was queasy earlier today, but I thought it had passed. Kelly had the flu several nights ago," she lied, her face twisting in obvious discomfort. "Do you by chance have a restroom with an available chair? I might need to rest for a few minutes while I'm near a bathroom. I'm terribly sorry for the inconvenience. Hopefully this will pass as quickly as it came on."

"Certainly." Morgan looked to the hallway on the left as if making a decision. "We've two restrooms in this section. I think the one down that hall should fit the bill. It has a small couch in an adjoining room if you should have a need to lie down." His brow wrinkled. "Do you need help getting there?"

"I'll-I'll be okay. A little cool water and a few minutes to settle my stomach. Dinner was marvelous, but that duck was terribly rich, and my stomach is protesting. I might take your suggestion to lie down. As you said, we have the whole night." She sent him a weak smile of promise.

Morgan walked with her a short distance down the hall before turning back. "I'll order you a cup of organic tea for when you get back. I'll be waiting for you by the fire. Call if you need me."

"Thanks. The tea sounds wonderful," she threw back as she made her way to the restroom. Once inside, she went immediately to the wash basin and turned on the faucet, allowing it to run. Now was her time. This would be her only opportunity to get inside Heywood's private office. Lacy remembered the house plans Jerome had loaned her to study. Dashing back to the hallway, she turned the opposite direction from the fireplace area and took a short hallway jag to a dark, closed door. Her heart was beating like a frightened bird as her fingers fumbled with the small leather packet from her purse.

Lacy had never picked a lock under duress before. It had been a game that she practiced for many weeks. Back in Chicago, Mick Galloway, the rogue investigative reporter, had taught her all the moves of picking several types of locks. "Never know when you might need the skill. Learn it well, Lacy." She had never thought she'd need to use it.

Now it pained her conscience to invade someone's privacy, and her resolve faded. She considered abandoning her risky plans. Then a vision of Steve flashed, and she continued working the lock until she heard the solid click of the door opening.

Moving through the shadowed darkness, she made her way to the desk, not surprised to find it almost clean of papers. The man was a neat freak. She searched the top center drawer, recalling how she'd found the key to his files in the center drawer. Apparently Heywood was not a creature of habit because she found no key. Carefully removing the drawer, she balanced it against the desk, praying it wouldn't fall. With her free hand, Lacy felt underneath the drawer for a hidden key but came up empty. Everything was taking so long that Lacy feared Morgan would come looking for her. Even as she debated the merits of replacing everything and rushing back to the bathroom, she heard police sirens outside the house.

Quietly laying the drawer on top of the desk, she rushed to Heywood's office door and listened. Her heart leaped to her throat when she heard Morgan yell from the front that he was going outside to investigate what was happening. *A diversion right when I needed one.* It was a weird coincidence she didn't have time to figure out. Racing back, Lacy felt around inside the hole that the drawer had come out of, discovering a key taped on the inside.

Almost identical to his office at the bank, Lacy found the key fit a large bottom drawer. With her small flashlight she fingered the different file names, finding them oddly familiar. The names were the same as the files at the bank office. *Are these identical files?* Taking out a trust fund file, she lay it open and took pictures of several pages. Tipping the small camera, she shot a photo of the names in the drawer. Careful to replace everything as it was, beginning with the taped key, she silently tiptoed out and down the hall to the restroom.

First she pinched her cheeks to keep them looking flushed. Next, Lacy dabbed some water around her face and messed her hair up. Smearing a little mascara under her eyes, she rumpled her clothes some as if she'd been lying down. Holding her stomach, she made her way down the hall toward the front, reaching the entrance area just as the door burst open and Morgan and Heywood entered, both excited and talking at once.

"I was in an important meeting when the security company called to tell me the silent alarm had gone off at my ranch," Heywood fumed. "What do I find after rushing home? It was a security malfunction! The president of the company is going to hear from me in the morning. I can't understand why *someone* didn't call the home number first. My car is filthy after running down muddy roads to get here in time."

Before Morgan answered, he spotted Lacy standing in the entryway still holding her abdomen. "Lacy, I hope you feel better than you appear."

"I'm afraid not." She raised her eyes from Morgan's concerned gaze to Heywood's shocked stare.

"Miss Cottrell? You're here? In my house?" There was no welcome in his startled black gaze. Clearly, the man didn't react well to surprises. He looked accusingly back at Morgan. "When you said you were having a lady friend to dinner, I just assumed..."

Lacy realized in that instant Heywood was referring to Cynthia. She could feel the man's silent irritation to find her here instead of Cindy. Suddenly she was unsure what to say or do. More than anything she wondered why the bank president didn't want her in his house. Because she was a reporter? Was he aware she was investigating the Turner bombing? If so, he might feel she was accusing him just by investigating. Up until now, she'd been doing a broad stroke investigation. Had she struck a nerve somewhere? She looked to Morgan to handle the situation, alarmed at the strangeness in his manner.

Morgan seemed almost gleeful at his uncle's surprised discomfort. "What can I say? I had an opportunity to share some quality time with this lovely lady. Unfortunately she developed a bad stomachache soon after we ate dinner."

Heywood squinted suspiciously. "I hope she's not claiming there was something wrong with the food." He seemed almost indignant that anyone would dare get sick after eating at his house.

Lacy raised a hand to stay his concern. "Oh no, Mr. Heywood, relax. The food was marvelous! I'm afraid I may have a touch of some unpleasant bug. My stomach was a little queasy this afternoon, but I'd hoped it had passed."

Heywood grunted, pursing his lips as if he restrained the urge to say more.

Flashing headlights on the entryway windows drew everyone's attention. The men exchanged puzzled glances and stared at the front door, waiting to see who had pulled up in their drive. After a sharp rap, the door flew open and Cynthia Bradford marched inside, eyes ablaze.

With one sweeping scan, the wild-haired blond took in each person standing in front of her. Still in shock, Lacy stared in wonder, her mouth agape. The atmosphere suddenly felt cold, charged with tension. Cynthia shook the water from her coat and stepped aggressively closer. Her smoldering, hostile glare lingered briefly on Lacy's face before moving to Morgan Streeter's mildly amused expression.

"Cynthia? What a surprise!"

After dismissing Lacy with obvious disdain, Cindy aimed a steely stare at Morgan. "Even when I heard it at the country club, I didn't want to believe it. Honestly, Morgan, bringing her here…what were you thinking? I thought we had an understanding…I thought…"

Before Morgan could reply, Lacy said in disgust, "I think this is my exit music, people. What can I say…the warmth of your hospitality is overwhelming! Morgan, would you get my coat, please?"

"Lacy, please wait. Santos has your tea ready. It will soothe your stomach." He looked around at the hostile faces. "What do you say we all have a friendly drink?" he offered, ignoring Cynthia's accusations. "There is no reason for you to go, Lacy. You're here as my guest." He rested his hand on her arm as his gaze challenged both Conrad and Cindy. He turned Lacy to look at him. "Stay, please!"

She trembled. Morgan's entreating words were in earnest and almost swayed her, until she glanced at the glowering faces of Conrad and Cindy. "I don't believe that is in the best interest of all concerned," she said sadly to Morgan. "It's better for me to leave now. Thank you for a lovely meal."

Turning to face Heywood, she bowed slightly, her eyes piercing his stoic façade. "Mr. Heywood." His features clouded with new uncertainty, as if he was second-guessing his initial reaction to her presence.

Morgan went immediately to the front closet. Helping her slip into her off-white trench coat, he whispered, "We'll have to reschedule our special time. Feel better, Lacy Cottrell."

Lacy smiled warmly at Morgan and walked out the front door through the rain to her waiting car, knowing it would be cold, but no colder than feeling unwanted, even hated, inside that house. A question flashed: *When Conrad Heywood first noticed I was there, was it surprised fear I saw, before the anger set in?* She was so confused. *I just want to go home.*

Lightning flashed close by Heywood's barn as Lacy fumbled to start the car. Feeling the powerful engine roar to life, she shifted into drive and spun away from the front of the unfriendly house, following the circle drive around to the entrance leading to the guarded gate. Muted reflections bounced off the gate from the headlight beams as the gate opened and she pushed her foot to the gas, anxious to leave.

Rounding the first curve, she peered in her rearview mirror, squinting between the pounding pelts on the back windshield. Were those reflections behind her on the pavement from headlights? Was she being followed? Though she couldn't believe either Heywood or Morgan would follow her, yet it didn't stop the wave of panicked fear that encompassed her. It was ten miles to town, mostly rural subdivisions and farmland between. Lacy felt like a little girl in the dark, sensing monsters all around her bedroom. Where was Jason? It was ridiculous to think the man would remain at a stakeout in such weather. She prayed to gain control over her unreasonable fear. She needed to think. Chances were, the lights were nothing but her imagination.

Now that Lacy was on the straight-away, her eyes stayed glued to her rearview mirror. The breath she'd been holding in expelled in a rush when the strong flash of headlights became visible behind her. *Get hold of yourself! Heywood owns a hundred head of beef cattle and employs workers from the outside. It could be one of the workers going home.*

But Lacy didn't believe that was the case. Someone else was following her—on whose orders? What was their purpose? Were they trying to scare her? If so, it was working. *How much further is it to the main road?*

The headlights were gaining. Now was the time to give that Hemi engine a workout. She pressed the accelerator to the floor and held on as the Challenger took flight. *Fairly flying on a strange road in a rainstorm on a dark night…where is the sense I was born with?* she berated herself. But she saw in the mirror that she'd accomplished her goal, leaving the car far behind. Groping for her purse, Lacy found her phone, clicked it on, and pressed Jason's number. As it rang, she spied the main road no more than a half mile away, where passing headlights looked like angels landing on her runway.

Jason fairly shouted into the phone. "Lacy, is that you coming toward the highway out of Heywood's lane?"

"Yes, where are you? There's someone hot on my trail. I was able to put some distance between us, but they're still coming."

"Hang up, Lacy, I've got you covered." The phone went dead, and Lacy dropped it inside her purse, grabbing the wheel with both hands. It would take everything in her to keep from spinning out when she intersected with the highway. Praying no car would be in her way, she eased her foot off the gas pedal and steered with all her might as her car sped onto the main road heading toward Gladden Hills. She allowed herself a second to check on the headlights coming on fast from the private road.

From the corner of her eye, Lacy spotted a second set of headlights peeling out from a drive across the main road. The car cut off the vehicle from the private drive and sped up behind her. Her phone rang. She grabbed it up.

"Lacy, I'm in behind you. Head for home."

Her hands were shaking on the wheel as she eased off the gas. She allowed the car to hum along on low speed, needing the space to unwind. Vaguely she became aware of water drops coursing down her cheeks and swiped them away. "Don't go to pieces now, Cottrell," she told herself.

Jason had waited all that time in this terrible storm. More tears followed the first. The car that followed from the Heywood complex probably meant only to scare her. She might never know if it was an independent act or someone from the house had ordered it done. Just knowing Jason was following her home felt like a warm blanket on a winter night.

*

They sat around the table. "So whatever happened to that car that was following me?" asked Lacy, as she sat with Jason and Kelly back at her house.

Kelly held to her coffee cup fiercely, her lips tight. The woman's facial features had been tense ever since Lacy and Jason had roared up into the drive. Something told Lacy that her cousin had been worried the entire time she'd been gone. Kelly was watching out the front window when they arrived.

Jason slowly sipped the freshly brewed coffee and glanced at Lacy, who was towel drying her wet hair. "The last I saw, the car turned off on the first side road and disappeared. Any idea who it was? Did the car drive out of the complex or pull in behind after you went through the gate?"

Lacy shook her head with a vengeance. "I don't know. I didn't see anyone run from the house, unless it happened after my view was blocked. And I couldn't tell exactly when the headlights first appeared."

"It was a large, blocky vehicle, I can tell you that much," offered Jason.

Lacy frowned. "Was it shaped like the maroon SUV?"

"Couldn't tell. Too much rain. So tell me about your date with Morgan." Jason leaned back in the large oak chair.

"The only time it felt like a date was one instant when I saw the lit candles and crystal dishes." Glancing at Jason's nonexpressive features, she gave a highlighted view of the few hours she'd spent at Heywood's domain, which in recall appeared more like a night at the circus. "Something of interest was the small lineup of family photos…"

Lacy went blow by blow, as if unwinding old slides from a vacation. She saw Jason stiffen when she briefly touched on her entry into Heywood's private office and hurried on to the next segment. Finishing up, she laid the pocket camera on the table. "I'll run off some copies as soon as I transfer the pictures to my computer. What was most curious was seeing file folders with the same identical names on them inside Heywood's locked office file the other day at the bank."

He chuckled. "You missed your calling, Lacy. I think you should've taken out a private investigator's license. Your information wasn't acquired legally for a court of law, but it should give Quinn something to go on. You better give him a call tonight." As Jason sipped more coffee, his face clouded. "I wonder how Cynthia Bradford found out about your intimate dinner date with Morgan. He's a pretty secretive guy about his private social life apart from her—at least, from what I've heard." A slight smile emerged.

Anger shot through her at any inference that she was only one more woman on Morgan's hit list of playmates, but she filed it away to address later. More important was how much she should relate about her own involvement. Then she remembered how she'd felt when Jason had been there for her in the rain. Lining up the major points of interest, she spoke haltingly.

"I-I was a little nervous about how the night might progress and wanted some insurance. After I found out Wendy George, from the café, was subbing for a waitress at the country club tonight, I asked her to *innocently* drop the information that I would be with Morgan at Heywood's estate tonight. I didn't figure Cindy would get suspicious about information coming from Wendy."

Kelly's jaw dropped. "Talk about throwing gasoline on a fire!"

Lacy smirked. "Knowing Cindy was insanely jealous of Morgan made it easy. Remembering her nasty temper, I bet on the chance she would freak and do something crazy like showing up. I hoped it would give me an excuse to make an exit. What I didn't count on was Heywood showing up and all those bells and whistles with the cops arriving. It's hard to believe they would have a security glitch at the exact time I was sneaking inside Heywood's office." She stared at Jason with new suspicion. "Did you have something to do with that happening?" she accused.

Jason shifted toward Kelly, whose whitened fingers still clutched her cup. "Could I trouble you for more coffee?" he asked. "Mrs. Larson—Kelly?"

Kelly seemed to come to herself. "Certainly." She rose to refill Jason's cup.

Lacy watched her unnatural movements with concern.

"Kelly, I was near Lacy all night. If she had come into any danger, help could have reached her quickly," he said, obviously picking up on the woman's stress.

Kelly turned and nodded. "Thank you, Mr. Gardner—Jason. I'm just not used to all this dangerous business and secrets. I-I think sometimes Lacy thrives on it. She was always a daredevil." She inhaled, as if in need of oxygen.

Jason shot Lacy an indiscernible look, which Lacy chose to ignore, concentrating instead on her cousin. "Would you feel better not knowing these things, Kelly? I wanted to include you, but..."

The tense honey blond whirled toward them. "No! I want to know. I have to know! It would drive me crazy not knowing. Just give me some time to adjust and take all this in. And don't worry about me. I was married to a soldier, remember?"

"I remember, Kelly. You're doing great," Lacy soothed. "This has been a lot to throw your way after what you've been through."

Kelly gave her an appreciative glance and carried Jason's coffee to the table. She lowered her body wearily to the chair. Then her eyes met Lacy's and Jason's with determination. "Well, let's get on with the briefing."

Jason chuckled. "Good girl." When his gaze returned to Lacy, the edges of his eyes were crinkled in amusement. "You asked about the security glitch? You can thank Quinn Darling for that. I filled him in on your purposed evening and a need for a distraction around 8:30 p.m. He did the rest."

"But how?" Lacy pressed.

Jason shrugged. "It's better we don't know too much. He knew someone who was connected."

Lacy pressed her lips to keep from asking more, but her puzzlement continued. Michael Quinn Darling, a substitute district attorney, was also a man with many surprises and amazing contacts.

Lacy wondered what the days ahead would bring. Hopefully the information she'd asked Quinn to line up for her would be available soon. She knew she would have to move as secretively as possible. Chancing a look in Jason's direction, she wondered what part he should play. Had she reached a point where she could trust him with her next plans?

Outside the rain pelted the house with no mercy. Her gaze lifted to the wall calendar. Her time in Gladden Hills was dwindling very quickly.

Feeling Jason's gaze upon her, she lifted her head to meet his shaded eyes. Strangely she wished she knew what exact color they were.

She moistened her lips. It was time to call Quinn.

17

Intel

IT WAS A SLOW SATURDAY. Both Lacy and Kelly rose later than usual. Jerome had given Kelly a half-day pass after she called him, keeping him in the loop, as promised. Lacy had been up late placing her own call to Wendy George shortly after she and Quinn finished their conversation.

She'd thanked the waitress profusely for her timely comment to Cynthia Bradford at the country club and invited her to a special lunch date, yet to be determined. After making Wendy promise to tell all about her date with Quinn, Lacy had said good night, falling asleep almost immediately.

By midmorning, Lacy was up cleaning house. In the afternoon Kelly went in to work for a few hours at the office, leaving Lacy the space she needed. She half expected a call from Nadine in Chicago. There were still a few outstanding questions in the wind. If anyone could run them to ground, Nadine could. Lacy hated to bother Quinn with any more than necessary.

Pausing in front of her grandmother's gilded hall mirror, Lacy fluffed up her dark hair, causing it to swing into her cheek line. Her long bangs emphasized her moody eyes. Staring vaguely at her reflection, her thoughts replayed the final minutes of the previous night when Jason had stood with her at the front door.

With only the hall light behind them, Lacy had hoped he might say something personal, but instead his attention had been centered on her situation. "Watch yourself, Lacy," he'd murmured. "From what you've told me, Heywood acted suspicious of you being at his house. And who knows what game Morgan Streeter's playing?"

"He enjoyed riling Cynthia Bradford tonight, I know that." Lacy remembering his unveiled amusement. "Whether it's a weird game between the two of them is unknown." Lacy also recalled Cindy's penchant for getting even and shivered, fleetingly thankful that the woman seemed more irritated with Morgan than she was with her.

"Cynthia won't look with kindness on you, either," said Jason, as if reading her mind. His arm had slowly moved around her back in a protective manner, resting against the entry wall. Leaning forward, his nearness caused her to catch her breath. "Don't go on any tangents without checking in. And make sure you have backup. Got it?"

"Got it." Her eyes roamed the walls of the entryway, trying to steer her gaze from the powerful line of his jaw, but the rapid beat of her heart stole from her confidence, even as she forced her mind on work. "You think I'm getting close to something don't you?" she asked, aware that her own sense of danger had intensified in the last several days.

His expression never altered. "Unfortunately, I do, which is why you must take extra care. Your cousin is worried for you, Lacy. Is your passion so great for the truth in this Turner incident that you would risk probable danger? I'm worried for you, too. No story is worth that."

"I thought you understood that this is not about a story, Jason. I-I can't stop now. But I understand if you want to step aside. You've done over and above what I'd expected of you. I don't think I could bear it if I was the cause of something bad happening to you." She'd come close to crying at that moment. She'd suppressed an audible sob from surfacing. Her emotions were hyped to the max.

"Don't worry about me, Lacy Cottrell. I can take care of myself." He gave her arm a squeeze and turned toward the door.

"Jason, about Sunday. Kelly said Jerome plans on attending church with us. That lets you off the hook, so to speak. I know you were uncomfortable last week and..." She dropped the sentence that was going nowhere. "Anyway, I-I just thought I'd let you know that we're covered on Sunday morning."

His lingered look on her face warmed her to her toes. Then he turned abruptly without comment and was gone. What was it about Jason Gardner that affected her? She had sense enough to realize that Morgan's appeal came from his masculinity, his charisma. Realizing she had been too long without the feel of a man's arms around her, Lacy recognized her vulnerability. But with Jason, it was different.

Leaning against the window, Lacy had watched him rush through the rain to his car. When he motored up the quiet street, she flicked off the porch light and walked back to the kitchen. It had been a night of tossing and turning.

A stab of sunlight jerked Lacy's thoughts back to the present and the mirror in front of her. She wiped her eyes and blinked at her blurry image. Part of her wished Jerome hadn't promised to go to church tomorrow. Then Jason would be forced to go with them. She moved toward the parlor and the warm fire she'd kept going all day.

A book was waiting, and she planned to sink deep within the cushions until Kelly returned later. After a light supper, she envisioned a hot bath and early bed. When her cousin was late in returning, Lacy fell into a spiraling sleep, awaking more restless than when she'd fallen asleep—restless and apprehensive.

After Kelly finally arrived home, it was nearly 7:30 p.m. by the time the women cleared the table. "Go ahead, I'll finish up what's left," called Kelly. "You've done nothing but talk about soaking in a hot tub and going to bed early tonight—so go!"

Rounding the end of the staircase, Lacy was two steps up when the phone rang on the table below. She whirled around and reached to pick it up.

"Hello," she said cheerfully. "Chuck! I can hardly hear you. Is that country music in the background?" She stuck her finger in her free ear but found it was still difficult to understand. Why was Chuck calling on a Saturday night? She strained to hear his words. "Where are you?" she called loudly to be heard. "You're where? Chuck, are you sure? All right, give me the directions."

*

Two days of constant rain was ridiculous. Lacy took consolation in the fact the lightning and thunder had passed. She gave the wheel a sharp turn to the right, her wipers beating a constant rhythm as she peered between the pelting sheets. Chuck's instructions were simple. Keep coming down River Road until she reached the intersection of River and Sturgeon. Then hang another right and pull in behind Floyd's Bar and Grill and park. "Flash your lights twice." Chuck said he would come out and escort her inside.

Kelly was still protesting when she left the house, threatening to call Jason Gardner. Lacy had tried to explain that Chuck would be her backup for the night and there was no reason to bother Jason. In truth, she didn't know exactly what she was getting herself into. What did Jason say about wild tangents, but what else could she do? Seventeen years had not changed the dynamics of Gladden Hills. River Road was still the rough section of town. Chuck had made her promise to keep her phone open and his number handy. It was too noisy to hear what he was trying to tell her, but he was insistent that she should park in behind Floyd's place near the rear exit.

The parking lights behind the bar were haloed with fog. Even as Lacy checked her door locks, she noticed two men weaving their way to a dented pickup truck. She ducked down so they wouldn't notice her and waited.

When the truck backed out in a half circle and sped off, she drove up to take their parking spot, placing her directly in line with the back door of the bar. Overflowing garbage cans staggered across the back of the building, obstructing her view.

Lacy stared down at her phone and debated about calling Jason. Resisting the urge, she determined to trust that Chuck wouldn't bring her into danger. Flashing her headlights twice as ordered, she waited nervously, her blood pulsing through her veins. "Come on, Chuck. I've got a hot bath with my name on it tonight," she mumbled, her eyes fixed on the door.

The immense form of Chuck Walden filled the backdoor of the bar backlit by a red cast light. She flashed her headlights again and watched as he headed for her car. Lacy remembered the Bible words she'd read only this morning: "Greater is He that is in you than he who is in the world." Just as she committed her mission to God afresh, a flicker of doubt made her question. Her tongue ran over her dry lips as she unlocked her car door to greet Stevie's childhood friend.

Chuck gave her a solemn nod and ushered her to the side of the back entrance. Pulling his collar higher, he looked up at the rain. "She's in there, Lacy. The woman who has been bad-mouthin' you. I hadn't seen her in days; then she showed up tonight. Her and her 'friend with the magic pills.' I don't know his name. I first noticed him right *after you came back to town.*" Chuck emphasized the last words as if he thought there might be a connection.

"When I point him out, you'll see the woman next to him. He's a brute. No one knows anything about him. He keeps a low profile. But the woman is a different matter. Rumor has it she lives nearby but comes from a large farm family. I personally don't think she's quite right in the head. 'Course it's hard to tell because she's always juiced."

Lacy shivered, pulling her dark, hooded sweatshirt around her. She'd purposely left her trench coat at home. She felt like a spy on a covert mission. "Let's go in, Chuck. Find us a place across the room and keep me to the side so that I can observe her without her seeing me. Is that possible?"

It was like every bar Lacy had ever stepped inside, dim lighting, the mood somber and downright depressing. It almost appeared as if those who sought comfort inside were sad or ashamed and couldn't bear the light. The red cast to the overall interior gave the room an eerie glow and the music assaulted her ears upon entering. In the shadow of Chuck's huge mass, Lacy moved across the table-cluttered room to an intimate booth with dark curtains. Sliding over to the far corner on the opposite side of the booth, she sat across from Chuck, careful to keep her hood around her face.

A waitress attired in jeans and a plaid shirt approached their booth and Chuck ordered two beers. Lacy shot him a questioning look, but he shook his head in the negative, so Lacy let it go. She had hoped for a coffee to warm her.

Chuck rested his forearms on the table and said quietly, "If you don't want to create attention, you best pretend to be a drinker. Just let the bottle sit, and I'll get to it later." He grinned.

Lacy kept her focus on Chuck. When he tilted his head toward the long bar across the room, Lacy pivoted forward to get a good view. Her eyes traveled systematically from right to left, stool by stool. While some had their backs to her, others were half profile. Near the end of the bar on the left was a large framed man, who looked to be almost as big as Chuck. His back was full toward Lacy, blocking the last few bar stools and anyone seated there. Lacy was frustrated. If the man would only turn or lean forward…

She blinked to keep her eyes focused, should the large man shift his position. When it finally happened, Lacy almost missed it. She'd turned to say something to Chuck when the corner of her eye caught movement. Her head jerked back, staring at the scraggy-haired blond sitting next to him. It was Chloe! She was upending a beer and, from the way she was acting, it wasn't her first. Her shrill, slurred voice rose above the din of the music.

The girl hit the muscled arm of the man beside her. "Pay attention to me! Don't treat me like that uppity, big-shot reporter who thinks she knows everything…but she don't know nothing, does she, Jimmy?" She laughed again.

The brute grabbed her arm. Lacy saw Chloe's face twist in pain.

"Don't do that, Jimmy. I didn't say nothing. I just said, Miss Snooty Cottrell doesn't know what good writing is. You should have seen the way she crossed out all my words like they weren't good enough—not like hers. You were right; she's a jealous, hateful witch." Chloe wobbled and grabbed hold of the bar counter, almost tipping off the stool.

The man quickly propped her up and leaned in close. Whatever he said to Chloe shut her up in a hurry.

Lacy had had enough. She slid out of the booth and marched to the middle of the room before Chuck could stop her. As her hood fell from her head, her eyes centered fully on Chloe, not sure what she intended to do, yet something told her she had to do something.

Chloe teetered precariously on her stool, rotating to the right. When she saw Lacy, her jaw dropped in shock. She tilted her head to the side like she thought she was hallucinating and squinted, trying to bring Lacy's image in focus. "Miss Cottrell?" her whiny voice squeaked in disbelief.

"Yes. We need to talk, Chloe." Lacy walked toward her, her eyes never leaving the girl's cowering expression.

The huge bruiser to Chloe's left turned sharply to the right and back, almost jumping off the stool. His ham-sized hand grabbed his hat and shielded his face while pushing his way through the tables toward the back door. Seeing the cowboy hat in the hand of the large man caused Lacy to gasp.

Too late she made the connection from the hat to the driver of the maroon SUV, and most probably the stalker in the shadows. "Chuck!" she yelled, pointing at the man sprinting for the rare exit.

Chuck's bulk moved with the action of a linebacker. He covered the room in a matter of seconds. Grabbing the man's shoulder to spin him around, Chuck was met with a powerful fist to his solar plexus, sending him to the floor gasping for air. Meanwhile the man with the Western hat was out the door into the night.

Darting across to where Chuck had fallen, she knelt beside him. "Are you all right? Should I call for help?"

"Give me a minute," he gasped out, his words running together. Soon there was a grouping around him, obviously confused about what had transpired. A well-built guy, in a gray leather jacket covered with emblems, got behind him and helped him to his feet over to a nearby chair.

Inclining his head, the tall, muscular man spoke softly, "Take it easy, Chuck, I'll get a line on that dude." Straightening with a determined look, he strode out the back.

Staring after the departing man with question, Lacy returned her attention to Chuck and his labored breathing. She observed him with concern, having momentarily forgotten about Chloe. When Chuck raised his head, she saw a rage in his eyes she hadn't anticipated. It frightened her. This man had a lot of anger smoldering inside. She had no doubt he was capable of violence if the situation was right. Keeping her voice low, she asked, "Did you get a good look at him?"

"Oh yeah! I got a *great* look at him. And next time we meet..." His dark look finished his sentence, and Lacy didn't push for an explanation.

Lifting her gaze to the bar, Lacy refocused on Chloe. The drowsy-eyed woman sat open-mouthed, holding to the counter at the bar for support.

Lacy covered the distance in a flash and climbed on a stool to her left. "Tell me who your friend is, Chloe."

Wetting her lips, Chloe blinked at her. "You talking about Jimmy?"

"Jimmy who...what's his last name?" Lacy's voice rang with authority. She was in no mood for nonsense.

Chloe's clouded gaze took on a sly look. She laughed. "Who knows? He's just Jimmy." She slipped off the stool and had to grab hold of the counter to keep from falling.

The bartender frowned and took away her last beer.

Lacy could see there was no point in talking to her further. Chloe was too wacked out to talk lucidly about important matters. Besides, she didn't seem favorable to dealing with Lacy at all. Sighing, she asked, "Did you drive here?"

Chloe looked as if she had to think about the answer. "No. Jimmy picked me up. Jimmy always picks me up. He treats me right." She waved her finger at Lacy. "He don't like you at all, Miss Lacy Cottrell." She stared blindly at Lacy. "Neither do I."

Lacy glanced over at Chuck, indicating for him to join her. The two talked quietly. Lacy glanced up at the bartender. "We'll take her home."

The bald-headed bartender nodded, seemingly pleased he wouldn't have to deal with her. With Chuck's help, Lacy walked Chloe out the back door to her car, where Chuck put the limp woman in the back seat.

Lacy set Chloe's purse on the seat beside her and closed the door.

"I'll follow you to your house. Think about what you are doing here." Chuck's look conveyed disapproval. "You heard her. That woman doesn't like you."

"I can't question her here. Look at her; she's in no shape to tell us anything, or do me any harm for that matter."

Chuck's massive frame loomed dark and hovering against the night sky. "Stevie said you were a scraper—like a terrier with a bone." He strode toward his truck.

What else did Stevie tell you, Chuck? Did he tell you about our purple feathers? Her mind raced with the idea. Chuck was the last person she would have considered, but it was possible he could be her contact in Gladden Hills.

On the tense drive home, Lacy's focus was divided between the road and the backseat. With no idea what all the girl had in her, Lacy didn't have a clue what to expect. If Chuck was right and Chloe was downing drugs along with her alcohol, she could have violent reactions. The continuing rain pounded the windshield, adding to Lacy's stress.

Every mile Lacy drove, she fought doubts about her course of action. They were taking a big chance. Perhaps they should have driven her to a hospital or rehab center. Then again, it was possible that if they got her to bed, Chloe would be able to sleep it off. Biting her bottom lip, Lacy steered with white knuckles all the way home.

*

Kelly's drop-jaw frown told her reaction in a heartbeat. Lacy winced and avoided looking directly at her cousin. "Give us a hand, Kelly. Chloe will be staying the night with us. How about we put her in the room you used to stay in when we were kids. Are the sheets clean?"

Kelly stared at the unconscious woman. "Do you think she'll care?" Her tone was laced with sarcasm. "Yes, the sheets are clean."

Lacy and Chuck exchanged nervous glances. Chuck lifted the feather-light body of Chloe with no effort. "Will one of you tell me where to take her?" he demanded.

"Upstairs," Kelly and Lacy replied in unison. "First door on the left," Lacy added.

Gently touching Kelly's arm, she turned to her cousin. "I'll explain everything later…trust me." She dashed up the stairs behind Chuck, rushing to fold down the bed.

Kelly stood at the base of the stairs calling up. "I don't know why your parents aren't totally gray, Lacy Cottrell."

Lacy paused to look back at her cousin. "I *never* tell them about the *unimportant* aspects of my job." Turning back, she dashed up the remaining stairs.

After lowering Chloe to the crisp sheets, Lacy stopped Chuck as he turned to go. "Thanks, Chuck. I'll let you know what happens with her. Maybe I can find out who that guy was who struck you in his rush to get out the door. He seemed more afraid of being identified than confronting you, and that says something. Not many people would go up against you without considerable thought. He was definitely not anxious to answer any questions."

Pausing, she eyed Chuck with interest. "Who was that man who helped you to the chair, the one who went after that guy?"

Chuck's sober features lit up. "Johnny Fey, a friend." He jammed a thumb toward Chloe. "You watch her. She's trouble. She's got a hatred inside her because you're everything she would like to be. You know. One of those love-hate things."

Lacy grinned. "When did you get so smart?"

"I picked up a minor in psychology when I cruised through school." His leather coat and black pony tail belied his last remark, and Lacy once again marveled at the incongruity of the man before her.

"You are a caution, Chuck Walden." Getting to know the grown-up version of little Chuckie, terror of the playground, was a special privilege. He was definitely a jewel in the rough. "I guess Stevie was the only one who saw the real you."

Their eyes connected. The intensity of his gaze held her mesmerized for long seconds. "He was my *only friend* for a very long time," he said slowly. "About that terror of the playground handle…I had to grow up tough or else. If I ever came home with a black eye, my old man would have whipped the hide off me."

"I heard rumors, Chuck. I'm sorry," she said softly.

Color flooded Chuck's face. He looked uncomfortable. "Yeah, well, I gotta go. Let me know if you need me."

Lacy laid Chloe's purse on the nightstand. Leaving the light low, she quietly closed the door and followed Chuck down the stairs. Locating her phone, she hit the dial for Quinn Darling. "He's going to love this," she mused, walking into the parlor. While waiting for an answering click, she lowered her weary body to the sofa with too many cushions, grateful for the low fire Kelly had kept alive while waiting for her. Her cousin was a rare treasure she'd never fully appreciated until these last weeks.

Her attention came alert at the sound of Quinn's voice. When their conversation was concluded, she'd felt like she'd been in the witness box, wrung out from all Quinn's probing questions. They'd agreed on the theory that Chloe was most probably the link to whoever had pushed Lacy down the courthouse stairs. From what she'd told him about the physical appearance of the man with Chloe at the bar, he also thought it could be the driver of the maroon SUV who'd been stalking her. Quinn told her to wait until he arrived in the morning to question Chloe, but he seemed reluctant to bring in the police cief at this time.

"Let's keep things between ourselves for the present and see where our questions with the young woman lead," said Quinn, with no hint of changing his mind.

Lacy felt somewhat dazed. If nothing else, Quinn was a man of decision. When their call ended, she found herself scrolling down her address list to Jason's number, anxious to get his input on her night's activities, hoping he wouldn't think she had been reckless in her actions. It had been a long time since Lacy had cared what others thought. Getting her story had always been primary. Now she found herself second-guessing her decisions.

I'm getting soft, she told herself. That's what J.T. Goff would say if he knew the situation. She sighed. The last time she'd stood in the Chicago editor's office seemed a century ago. Lacy knew her senses toward Jason were heightened. For some reason she wanted him to think well of her.

It was almost midnight before Lacy was able to sleep. Even after she'd said good night to Jason, she'd lain awake and stared out the window, too wound up to relax. Like Chuck, Jason had concerns about Chloe staying in the same house. The last time Lacy had checked in on her, Chloe seemed almost unconscious. Surely the inebriated woman would be in a solid sleep for several hours. Lacy played soft music and read Scripture for almost an hour before her eyes became drowsy, allowing her to drift into an uneasy sleep....

Her eyes popped open, staring into pitch blackness. It took her a moment to remember where she was. What had awakened her? Lacy glanced at the night table clock: 1:45 a.m. The constant rain had stolen the moon and stars, burying them in the heavy folds of murky, angry clouds. She listened to the old house, making sure no one was in the room with her. She'd known the sounds of the house since childhood.

Suddenly, she picked up the barest semblance of a foreign sound. Someone was prowling around upstairs. *Chloe!*

Lacy was out of bed in a flash, reaching for her housecoat. She heard Chloe's high-pitched slurred laughter, then the crashing of something solid. Shuffling into her slippers, she threw open her door and dashed down the hall, her heart pounding. Laughter split the air a second time, but it wasn't coming from Chloe's room; it was behind her. Stopping, Lacy whirled, noticing for the first time that the bathroom light beyond her bedroom was spilling out into the hall. Again, the slurred laughter erupted. *The bathroom!*

"Lacy?" Kelly stood at the top of the stairs. "What's happening? Is it that woman?"

Raising her hand to stay her cousin, Lacy ran toward the bathroom. For some reason she dreaded what she might find. Holding to the door facing, she looked down on a deathly pale Chloe. The pathetic woman was half on the floor hanging over the toilet, her eyes glazed and terrified. "He-eelp me," she cried, falling on her back, her mouth spewing white liquid.

Confused, Lacy scanned the bathroom counter. The contents of Chloe's purse were sprawled across the counter as if they'd been searched in haste. An empty prescription bottle lay turned on its side next to a half glass of water. Grabbing up the bottle, Lacy scanned the bottle for the name of the drug, but there was no label.

"Oh, dear God!" she cried. Turning, she looked with horror into Kelly's face, now standing behind her. "Call an ambulance, hurry! I don't know what she took, but she's in a bad way."

Kelly spun about without a word and fairly flew to the hall phone at the foot of the stairs.

Lacy grabbed a clean cloth and ran cold water over it. Squeezing out excess water, she dropped to her knees and began washing Chloe's white face. She saw her eyes roll backward into unconsciousness. Hurriedly sponging off the woman's face, she prayed Chloe would be reached in time. *Why didn't I think to search her purse?* A wave of guilt flowed over her and gripped her stomach. *Please, God, let her live.*

"Chloe!" she yelled. "Wake up, Chloe!"

The sounds of voices and pounding feet caught Lacy's attention, but not before she saw Chloe's eyes flicker. The woman was fighting for her life. "Good girl, Chloe, wake up!" Lacy cried one last time before the paramedics took over the scene.

While Lacy and Kelly watched the medical personal work swiftly and efficiently on Chloe, Lacy broke away and ran back to her room for her cell phone, dialing Quinn's number. This would definitely alter their plans for the morning. It would be a miracle if Chloe was alive by morning. Quinn told her he would take it from there. He planned to arrange for someone to guard Chloe while she was in the hospital.

"Go back to bed, Lacy. Either this woman overdosed on her own, or she had help. It's not your fault," he told her.

Then why do I feel so guilty? she asked herself as she and Kelly watched the paramedics lift Chloe's listless body into the ambulance and drive away. Lacy shivered from shock and cold as she and Kelly stood on the front porch. "Maybe if I'd taken her straight to the hospital, this wouldn't have happened." Her words were almost a cry for help—for her and for Chloe.

Kelly turned abruptly, staring at her. "Lacy, cut it out. The last we knew Chloe was sleeping off a drunk. She took the drugs on her own while you were asleep. Both the man who gave them to her, and she, herself, are to blame, not you."

Kelly's anger-tinged voice got Lacy's attention. It was rare that her cousin was moved to such a strong declaration. Moving closer, Lacy enclosed her arm around Kelly's shoulders. "No girl could have a better sister. Thanks."

Together they walked inside and locked the door, ignoring the curious stares from their neighbors, people who would, no doubt, be glad to see Lacy return to Chicago.

It was almost 2:30 a.m. It took everything in her to tread the stairs to her room. She would pick up the mess in the bathroom come morning. The paramedics took all of Chloe's purse belongings with them.

Lacy wasn't looking forward to morning. She'd promised to go to church with Kelly and Jerome, but going without Jason left her feeling flat.

She'd tried to call Jason to tell him about Chloe but was forced to leave a message. It was short and cryptic but enough to let him know what had occurred. Yawning, she crawled under the covers and was lost in sleep almost as soon as she rolled over. Her last thought was a prayer for Chloe.

*

The two women sat across from each other at the breakfast table, not having said more than a dozen words since Kelly had shaken her awake. Lacy stared at her coffee and up at the wall clock. She had half an hour to dress and put on what makeup she could muster. It wouldn't be long before her leave from the paper would be up. More importantly, her time in Gladden Hills would come to an end. Could she leave the way things were? She couldn't think on it now.

"Lacy, I'm dressed and have time to clean up the kitchen while you run upstairs and finish." Standing, Kelly refilled Lacy's cup. "Take that with you. You look like you need it."

Nodding without eye contact, Lacy pushed up from the table. There had been no word of Chloe. When she'd tried to contact the hospital about the woman's condition, she'd been told that the hospital could not give out information without authorization. Lacy felt like she carried weights on her shoulders and chains on her heart.

As she walked from the kitchen, Kelly called after her, "Trust God, Lacy. You reminded me of that the other day, now it's my turn. Whatever happens, He's still in charge. Don't try and take the responsibility out of His hands. It's very freeing to realize you don't have to fix everything."

The moisture forming in Lacy's eyes rolled down her cheeks. "After a few short weeks in Gladden Hills, I'm getting to be a real sissy."

"Being a sissy doesn't have anything to do with feeling things, Lacy Cottrell. It was pretty obvious to everyone around you that, after Stevie died, you changed. You developed a crust, an outer shell that was hard to penetrate. Maybe it was to keep from feeling that kind of pain again, don't know. What I'm trying to say is, the special caring nature you were born with was buried for a season. It's nice having that part of you back, so don't go apologizing for a blessing. Hurry!" she added. "Jerome will be here in a few minutes."

Lacy heard spirited talking when she stepped from her bedroom and headed for the stairs a short time later. She straightened her white, long-sleeved, silk blouse into her black slacks as she slung her shoulder bag in place and descended the stairs to join the small group at the bottom. Pausing on the last stair, she locked her eyes on the shaded lenses of Jason Gardner.

All the talking around them ceased. Kelly and Jerome watched with interest.

The corners of Jason's mouth curved up. "You didn't ask, but I thought I'd tag along anyway. Is there a problem?" he asked softly.

Stepping down on the floor, Lacy continued to stare. Her head tilted. "No problem. I'm just surprised to see you. Did you get my message?"

Jason nodded. "We'll talk in the car. I have news as well."

Looks were exchanged, and everyone gathered their things to leave the house. "Who's driving?" asked Lacy.

Kelly spoke up. "That's just what we were trying to decide."

"We'll take my Durango," said Jason. The matter seemed to be settled and the small group moved as one outside and down the porch toward the shiny Durango parked on the street.

Kelly and Jerome settled into the back and immediately were engrossed in conversation while Lacy pulled her seat belt in place. Jason chanced a glance up at the overcast sky while revving up the engine. Waiting for him to pull out and merge into traffic, Lacy tapped her fingers anxiously on the window ledge of the car.

"Are those nails filed, Cottrell, or will I have to have my upholstery replaced?" said Jason, grinning.

"Sorry. What's your news?"

"I talked with Quinn this morning after I listened to your message. Chloe's alive…but barely. They pumped her stomach and discovered what she'd taken. Quinn didn't say. Whatever it was, it was a lethal dose. You reached her just in time. If you hadn't found her when you did, she'd be dead. It's a good thing you're a light sleeper." He tilted his head to emphasize how close the situation had been.

Arching her neck, she leveled a look at him. "But I'm not a light sleeper. I had the feeling someone woke me. I was surprised it was still dark. I heard nothing at first. Then sounds that made me get up. God wanted Chloe to live—it's that simple," she said, her tone matter of fact.

He shot her a scowl. "Really! Lacy, you've confided to me how you've felt about your little friend's death. Not only the child, but his mother was deliberately bombed. Am I to assume that God didn't want them to live?" The subdued anger in his voice was unmistakable.

Lacy felt as if she'd been splashed in the face with cold water. "Whoa, Mr. Gardner. Theology before church? Actually, it's a question I struggled with for years." As she fought the mounting emotion, she was vaguely aware that suddenly the back seat was silent. Were they waiting for her reply as well? Clearing her voice, she kept her focus on the highway ahead. It was the only way she could speak her heart without losing control.

"As a matter of fact, Jason, I've blamed God for years for Stevie's death. Not once did I doubt He could have somehow stopped that bombing. He could have easily gotten them out in time or done whatever it took. But God didn't promise He would remove all of our painful experiences. He's there to support us through them. Our days are numbered, many or few...and only God knows."

Lacy centered her thoughts. "Jesus promised His believers He was preparing a wonderful place for them. Some translations read *mansions.* I've struggled a long time, and it's only recently that I've asked God to forgive my anger against Him, as well as my lack of trust. Finally I've been able to accept the peace that's been waiting for me all these years."

Casting a glance in Jason's direction, she saw his side profile, jaw tight. The man was definitely an enigma. She sensed he was fighting his own private war with God. *Wonder what it is?* Feeling Kelly's fingers on her shoulder, Lacy shifted to see the soft radiance on her cousin's face. Jerome inclined his head toward her, his eyes shining with admiration.

The rest of the morning went well, although Jason's mood was decidedly subdued. Periodically through the service, he'd look out the window. She assumed he was checking to see if they were observed.

On the way back, the four of them stopped in Wellington for lunch before returning to Gladden Hills. Once they were on the road again, the hum of the wheels almost lulled Lacy asleep. At some point during the service, the sun had broken through the clouds and now streamed through the car windows. Lacy's eyelids grew heavy, her body crying out for the missed sleep from the previous night.

"Lacy." Jason's voice was low, meant only for her ears.

Her head lifted, not sure he had actually called her name.

"Quinn wants to talk to you tomorrow morning. Something you and he discussed a few days ago?" Jason eyed her.

Her brain whirled with questions. "I'll call him in the morning."

"He wants to see you in person. Go over before you come to the office."

"Okay," she said slowly, her pulse quickening with speculation.

When Jason dropped the women and Jerome off at the house, he nodded at Lacy. "See you when you're finished at Quinn's office. Now go in and get some sleep. You look dead on your feet."

"Thanks. I took up the biggest part of your weekend. Sorry about that."

"Not at all. I had ample time on Saturday to get my Durango washed." He flashed her a smile before rolling back out of the drive.

Lacy quietly passed Kelly, who was still saying good-bye to Jerome by his car. She mounted the porch stairs to the house. Hearing Jerome call her name, she turned.

"Listen, Lacy, Kelly and I've been talking. It sounds as if things are heating up. I'll stand ready for a call. Get word to me…and be careful."

"Thanks for being willing to take us to church this morning. Honestly, I didn't expect my boss to show up and offer to go."

"No problem! It was my pleasure. It's been a while since I've been to church. Pastor Jaminson said some things today that I've never heard before. The truth is, he caught my interest. I might even attend Bible study on Wednesday night." He looked over at Kelly, who was grinning from ear to ear. "Both of us, actually."

It took everything in Lacy not to show overt surprise. That was the last thing in the world she'd expected to hear. "Ah, that's great!" Amazing things kept happening around her, and she was having trouble keeping up. Jerome was right: things were heating up on every front.

Lacy jerked her head around, feeling uneasy. She'd seen movement. Stepping forward, she squinted at the house across the street. In the window at the right of the door, a face was peering out at them, watching. She sighed. Even the neighbors were wondering what would happen next. She grimaced and went into the house.

*

Later that night, Lacy picked up the phone to hear the seductive tones of Morgan Streeter inquiring about her health. Lacy sat upright, remembering she had pleaded a stomachache on Friday night. Playing sick had never been her strong point, even as a child.

"Much better. How did your little talk with Cynthia go after I left? Is she planning on murdering me in my sleep…or you?"

Morgan laughed. "Well, it wouldn't hurt to lock our doors for a while. Oh, I've been instructed to relate something from my Uncle Conrad. He wishes to extend his apologies to you for his 'uncalled-for rudeness' last evening." Morgan's voice filled with mockery. "Conrad claims his disposition was soured by the security blunder that dragged him from an important meeting and alerted every police car in a thirty-mile radius. He feels he unwittingly took his anger out on you."

"Unwittingly? Well, you can tell your uncle that most sincere apologies are delivered in person." She heard more laughter.

"I would be most delighted to share your remark, Miss Cottrell. Now, let's talk about something more pleasant. How about a second chance on our evening out? One night next week? We'll drive to Lansing, where our chances of having unwanted company will be limited. It's a nice long drive, plenty of time to get better acquainted." She heard his confidence.

"Look, Morgan, I got the impression last night from Cynthia that your relationship with her is closer than you have given me to understand. I feel like a pawn between you two. Perhaps it would be better to straighten that out first. I don't want to be in a triangle relationship."

"I don't have to answer to anyone—not her, not Conrad, not anyone," he said curtly.

The anger in his quick retort took her aback. It made her wonder if Cynthia's possessiveness and Conrad's domineering ways were having a negative effect, but she didn't want to be the catalyst that ignited an explosion.

"That may be Morgan," she said softly, "but I didn't appreciate the response I received from either your uncle or Cindy Bradford last night. Let's give it some time. I think your relationships are too complicated for me right now. Simplify your life; then call me, okay?"

"I'll call again, Lacy Cottrell. Good night."

Their conversation left Lacy troubled. There was a haunting quality to Morgan's voice, a wistfulness, as if he were an animal caught in a trap. If Morgan could free himself…? Lacy refused to allow her thoughts to go there.

*

Vicky rose from her desk as soon as Lacy walked in the office on Monday morning. "This way, Miss Cottrell. Mr. Darling has been waiting for you."

Quinn was in shirt sleeves and a loosened tie at 8:30 a.m. A cup of coffee sat on a stack of papers to his right. He looked up at Lacy when she entered and indicated she should sit. Nodding to his secretary, he said, "Thanks, Vicky. Hold my calls."

When the door clicked shut, Quinn's hands came together in front of him. "I've been waiting for those pictures you took at Heywood's office Friday night. Don't wait on sending them over, Lacy. There's much work to do." His dark eyes were as serious as Lacy had ever seen.

"I thought you didn't approve of how I got those pictures?" She couldn't resist the little taunt, remembering how he'd blustered when she'd told him how she had obtained the pictures. "But you came through when I needed you. I have to thank you for that timely distraction that enabled me to accomplish my task."

"I didn't realize you planned on picking his lock. Nevertheless, I'm glad it was timely. We can't have you getting caught inside Heywood's office. Gardner said you might be in a bind and were doing a little snooping. I didn't particularly want to know the particulars."

"Deniability?"

"Something like that." He refocused his concentration on his papers.

Lacy watched with fascination as Quinn mentally switched gears. The man was a marvel. She sat silently as he stared at a sheet of paper as if mesmerized by whatever was written. Grunting, he looked up at her, his hand holding a pen like a bird's bill, thumping it on the paper below. His eyes drilled her, almost as if he were trying to decide a course of action.

"All right. This is the way we'll play this." He scratched the side of his nose and laid down his pen. "I've got the info you requested about the late arsonist Clem Browning's last cellmate, a guy by the name of Haden Parker, now finishing out a five-year term. After Clem Browning's stabbing in jail, Parker requested a transfer to a different facility, but somebody got to him before his transfer came through. Two inmates beat him up badly before a guard intervened. The prison transferred him immediately, admitting him directly to the new prison hospital and kept him there until he recovered."

Lacy leaned forward with interest. "Somebody must have been worried about Parker knowing something." She hoped this was a good indication that Parker had useful information…if he wasn't too afraid to tell her.

"Sorry to put a damper on that wishful thought," Quinn explained, "but they would have beat him up on the general principle that he even knew Browning. Apparently the word was out that Browning had spilled his guts to a P.I. He was marked as a stool pigeon. So…on the wild premise that Clem Browning told his cellmate even the time of day, they left Parker with a reminder of what happens to cons who open their mouths."

"But how did they know he had talked—" Lacy tried to interject, but she was stopped by Darling's uplifted hand.

He leveled a look at her. "Who knows? A guard on the take might have bugged the room. An ongoing investigation is still working on it. About his cellmate, unfortunately there wasn't much chance of Browning saying good morning to Parker, or anything else. Browning was a surly dude. He had the reputation of being a loner, particularly nasty when riled. His previous cellmate of three years said Browning never spoke more than two dozen words to him in all the time they occupied the same cell. He was questioned at length after Browning's murder, but they came up with nothing."

Quinn's chair creaked as he settled back into it. "This brings us back to the last cellmate, Haden Parker, a little guy who was much too cowed by Browning's brute size to even approach him about which bunk to take. Besides, Parker had only been in Browning's cell for less than three weeks before everything hit the fan. I personally think it's a waste of your time, not to mention the hassle involved." Quinn watched her like a sheep dog on duty.

Lacy felt as though she'd been squeezed flat of any remaining air. Nothing Quinn had said had led her to believe she'd learn a thing from the man who had already borne a beating as a warning deterrent from speaking out of turn. However, she faced the stern DA with determination. "I'd still like to talk with Parker. It's a loose end I'd like to tie up. Can you arrange it?" Her reporter stubbornness wouldn't allow her to leave any stone unturned.

He dropped his head, obviously not pleased. "I had a feeling you wouldn't take no for an answer. It's already set up as if you're doing an article for a ladies' magazine about what's it's like in a modern prison. Not even the warden knows you are going to question Parker about Clem Browning, so watch what you say. Someone will be watching out for you once you are outside of the prison—repeat, *outside of the prison*—but you are on your own *inside those walls.* Remember that."

Lacy read his meaning loudly and clearly.

"As added protection, I've made secret arrangements to scan the room for bugs where you'll be conducting your interview. Listen up. When you come out of the prison, look around for my guy. He'll escort you safely from the area. I expect you to contact me *immediately* when you're at a safe distance."

Lacy made notes on a pad she'd taken from her purse. "Fine! Now, I also asked about Rob Corbin, the Union official convicted for embezzlement seventeen years ago. Do you know anything about him?"

"It was a white-collar crime. Corbin only ended up doing a year of actual prison time when it was finally pushed through the system, but he had years of probation. We're still trying to get an up-to-date address on him. It takes longer to get information when you're trying not to make waves that will bring unwanted attention to your investigation. But I'll get that information to you as soon as it comes in."

Lacy exhaled, venting her tension. Things were falling into place. "When is my appointment set up with Haden Parker?"

Quinn's hand began drumming that annoying pen on the paper again. "If anything happens to you, Wendy will *never* forgive me," he said gruffly.

Lacy almost laughed outright at this bizarre comment from the stern DA. "Quinn! You just told me someone would be waiting outside the prison to protect me."

"I know." He paused, his eyes avoiding hers. "Just watch yourself, Cottrell. No grandstanding. Get in and get out. Is that clear?"

"Clear."

"Tomorrow at 10:00 a.m. present this at the gate and this to the officer in charge. You've got my cell phone. Keep it handy." He handed her two official-looking papers across the desk.

Lacy stood, meeting him halfway, and took time to scan the papers. *This is it then. I'm committed.* She felt a sense of foreboding. Was it merely nerves or the thought of going inside prison walls? She'd never liked to hear the slam of the heavy metal doors behind her, locking her inside. It was freaky! Lacy assumed it was how the prisoners felt on their first experience inside…the difference being she would be allowed to leave…if all went well.

Why did her mind tack on the phrase *if all went well?* Maybe because all too often things didn't go well. There was always a slip-up, a miscommunication. *What if they didn't have time or opportunity to check for a bug in the room where their interview would be held? Snap out of it, Cottrell. Trust God and quit borrowing trouble.*

When she reached the door, Quinn caught her attention. "Send me those pictures!"

Nodding, she was turning to leave when a nagging question made her pivot back toward him. "Quinn, remember when I told you about finding the ragged edge in the old police record book? The one listing all recorded calls to the department day by day. What call was such a threat that someone didn't want anyone to see it? I've been racking my brain. Any ideas?"

Quinn took his time in answering. "I've done some thinking myself. The timing indicates the torn page would have contained incoming calls 48 to 72 hours before the Turner bombing. If Terri Turner called in a report about the missing funds at the bank, that would be significant."

Lacy frowned in confusion. "The last incoming call on the page prior to the torn out page was transferred from the chief's office to the district attorney's office. But without the next page to verify, I couldn't tell if the call came through, who made it, or what it was concerning."

Quinn's face turned flintlike. "Exactly!"

She sighed heavily. The implications were left to Lacy's own thoughts, and she had more pressing matters. Nodding at Quinn, she left quickly, mentally laying out her plans to leave town for a least one day, maybe two.

It looks like I'm driving to Indiana today. I'll need a full gas tank and a motel close by the prison, she reminded herself, thinking of other items to cross off her list before leaving town. She had just enough time to run over to the paper and let Jason know what was happening. He'd have to cover for her column in this week's paper, unless she returned in time to complete the workup she'd already begun, and time wasn't on her side.

Lacy's mind was fragmented, so much so she didn't check before crossing the street on the light. She was about two feet into the street when someone yelled, "Watch out, lady!"

Jumping back to the curb, she saw the blur of a dark SUV speed away.

"What a jerk! That guy wasn't even looking. Probably talking on the phone. They should be outlawed for drivers," said a middle-aged black man. "I got his license plate number if you want it, lady."

Lacy was jarred out of her stunned daze. "You got a license number? Yes. I want it!" She stared at the man as if he might dissolve into space any minute.

He ripped off a piece of notepad paper and placed it in her hand. "Sure glad I saw that irresponsible…" He swore. His rough-shaved jaw moved from side to side, like he might be thinking about how close Lacy came to being struck down by the reckless driver.

"Not as glad as I am. What's your name, sir?" She regarded him with admiration.

"Joe Walters. I work at the water plant outside of town."

"Thanks again, Joe Walters. I'm Lacy Cottrell. I work at the *Gazette.*" She extended her hand.

"I thought I recognized your face. You organized that benefit for the Morrisons. Nice people."

"Yes, they are, and I only got the ball rolling." She pulled a pen out of her purse and wrote Joe's name on the same paper as the license number and waved good-bye.

Her legs were still a little wobbly when she entered the paper and approached Maxine at the entryway desk. "Is the boss in? I need to see him."

"He told me to keep an eye out for you. He's in his office."

Lacy would have passed, but Maxine touched her sleeve. "Have you heard from Chloe? She hasn't come in, and I haven't heard a word from her. I get no answer when I phone."

The fact Jason hadn't informed Maxine about Chloe caused Lacy to hold her tongue. "I guess you better consult the boss if she isn't in by this afternoon," said Lacy, striding away. *Why didn't I remember to question*

Quinn about Chloe when I was in this morning?

It bothered Lacy that she might have to wait until she returned to town to learn how Chloe was doing. Hopefully the girl would tell what she knew about the mystery cowboy who'd slugged Chuck and run from the bar.

One thing at a time, Cottrell, she reminded herself. She fixed her eyes on Jason's office door.

*

Lacy hurried away from Jason's office perplexed and deflated. She'd been prepared for a grilling about her plans, when all he wanted to know was when she was leaving. He hadn't even been concerned about her weekly article. "Don't worry. If need be, I'll run something in its place that I've been holding back for a rainy day. If you get back in time, fine. If not, don't sweat it. Drive carefully." Then he'd waved her off to get back to his paperwork.

"Whatever!" she'd murmured, whirling about to exit. *He doesn't seem the least bit concerned about my safety. One minute he's waiting hours in the rain to protect me, the next he could care less.* As soon as she reached the hall, Lacy remembered the ripped piece of paper handed to her by Joe Walters, hero of the day. As much as she hated re-entering Jason's office, she spun about, approaching his desk in a rush.

"Here is the license number of the maroon SUV. A passerby happened to note it while I was jumping to safety. The driver tried to run me down on my way from Quinn's office. The name at the bottom is the guy who warned me in the nick of time." She dropped the ragged paper on top of his paperwork, then left without any further explanation.

Out of her peripheral vision she saw Jason pick up the paper and then stare after her.

18

Interview

THE AUTHORIZATION PAPERS QUINN HAD GIVEN HER were creased from Lacy folding and unfolding them. She had memorized the names of the people who had authorized her visit, as well as the number of the room she was scheduled to have her interview with Hayden Parker. She intended to make sure everything went as prearranged. She wanted no surprises. Her chest was tight with tension. Walking away from her car, she scanned the gray fortress sprawled before her.

She'd played down her appearance, pulling her hair back tight in a professional style. Attired in a classic skirt and styled blouse with matching accessories, Lacy carried only her briefcase as she walked the extended cement path to the entrance gate. It limited the concerns in case of an emergency. Lifting her chin, she gave her name and handed over her first paper.

Once inside the facilities, having passed through security screening, she was met by a large, unsmiling, black guard about forty. A thin, long scar ran the length of the side of his face. His eyes, well hidden by dark glasses, revealed nothing as he took her second paper and studied it silently. "This way," he said, turning to the right down an empty hallway that rang with the click of Lacy's moderate, sensible-styled heels.

It was hard for Lacy to keep up with the man's long strides, but the guard took no notice. They'd gone the length of half a football field when they came to a set of imposing doors. As soon as the guard pressed in a code, she heard a release sound, and the two of them went through to a short extension void of heat before re-entering a second set of doors in the same manner.

Lacy's feet were feeling the effect of hiking long distance in heels when the broad-shouldered guard stopped abruptly in the darkened hall at a blind-drawn door and took out a set of keys. "The prisoner will be brought to you in this room in a few minutes," he said in a monotone. Pushing the door wide, he gestured for her to enter, pointing to a table and uncomfortable metal chairs.

Lacy peered at the number over the door. It was a different number than indicated on the paper she'd received from Quinn. Her heart raced.

She looked up at the unfriendly face of the guard and forced a bravado. "I'm sorry. This is *not* the right room. I need to speak with the warden as soon as possible. My boss was specific about the room number. It was supposed to be set up especially for the interview." She grabbed the paper out of the guard's hand and stabbed at the number printed. "See this. The interview is to be here. Please take me to the warden's office."

The guard's face twisted in irritation. "I was told to bring you here."

"I'll relate that information to the warden and let him straighten out who's responsible for messing up. My boss and the warden are friends and set this up together," she lied, hoping he wouldn't see through her bluff. She stared him down. For all she knew Quinn might be friends with the warden. He seemingly had contacts everywhere else.

Lacy noted the first hint of uncertainty in the guard's granite-like features. Staring down the hall they'd just come, he spit out, "Follow me."

As they headed back the way they'd come, she stiffened her resolve even as her feet groaned. Back through both sets of doors, they walked past the entrance and traveled approximately the same distance in the opposite direction. This area was amazingly more open and lighter in content, possibly because of the windows on the outside corridor.

The door the guard stopped at was on the inside corridor. Glancing quickly at the number above the door, she confirmed they'd finally arrived at the correct room. The guard opened the door to reveal a much nicer area for conducting an interview. Though free of windows, it had bright lighting and comfortable chairs—a marked improvement over the last.

"Wait in here," he said, standing in place until she entered.

The door closed, and she heard the dreaded click, locking her in. She sighed at the sound, making her way to the white molded table and padded chairs. Pacing the silent room, Lacy tried to work off her anxiety from the mix-up over the interview room.

Was it a mix-up? She wasn't altogether sure. Gazing at the institutional styled pictures on the wall, she didn't want to think on the ramifications of that being true. It might mean her activities were known prior to her arrival, or the fact Haden Parker had a personal interview with a magazine writer was threatening to someone.

Is it possible something was planned to happen in that room? Or it had been fitted with a listening device? Neither possibility was pleasant.

Lacy spun around at the sound of the heavy door opening across the room. The guard filled the doorway, having returned in no better disposition than when she'd last seen him. He moved aside and a small man in handcuffs and prison garb was nudged inside by a second beefy guard who stood behind him. The wiry prisoner stretched to the far side, scanning the room and lastly resting on Lacy's person. He eyed her with suspicion.

"Thirty minutes is all you got," the guard called out as if announcing her life sentence. The door closed behind Haden Parker's lightweight form, leaving him to stand in place, his face stoic and closed.

Lacy patted the chair beside the table. "Please, hurry, our time is short."

Parker eyed the room again. "Is this place bugged?"

"No. I was promised it would be clean of any device. Now please, sit. We have to hurry." Her eyes pleaded.

Haden Parker walked over and sat down, his eyes roaming the contours of the chairs beneath the table.

"Mr. Parker. I've actually come about Clem Browning, a former cellmate of yours. I have to know if he ever said anything to you that would lead us to his killer. My life is in danger because of this investigation," she added hurriedly when he looked bored. She chided herself, wondering why she'd mentioned the fact that she had a personal interest. This man didn't know her from a cement post outside the building and probably cared less.

"Anyway," she continued, "we think the same person who ordered his death has committed other murders. This person is increasingly fearful of being found out, which might indicate a possibility he'd come after you."

Her last statement claimed Haden's wandering eyes, gaining his instant, full attention. "Say what? Are you putting me in danger? I was told this was some freakin' magazine story about prison life. I never had my picture in no magazine before and I thought, *What the hey?* Now I find out I've been set up, so you can pump me for information. You really think they're coming after me?"

"Not if we can catch this guy," she said, her tone quiet but intense. "Now, I realize you were only in Browning's cell little more than two or three weeks, but it was during this time that the P.I. came and offered Browning a special deal. They wanted to learn who had hired him to make the bomb used in the Turner bombing, killing a woman and her child."

"He bombed a woman and child?" asked Parker, showing honest surprise. His disgust was evident.

"You didn't know?" she asked.

"I never asked. He never said." He stared down at his shoes.

Lacy's hopes of Clem Browning having confided anything to Parker shot down in a dull crash. It didn't sound as if they'd spoken at all. "Then he never told you anything before he was killed?"

The man's face puckered into a frown, his lower lip protruding. "Yeah. He told me plenty the day he was stabbed with that shiv. He'd noticed a group of guys in the cafeteria looking at him funny…the kind of funny you don't ignore. He figured his time was up."

"What did he tell you, Haden?" Lacy asked, her voice so low she could hardly hear herself.

"You really think you can get this guy?" he asked, suddenly nervous.

"With what you tell me, it will make it easier. We've been closing in on him."

"Are you a cop or somebody with justice?" His eyes narrowed.

"No. I'm a reporter. The child who was killed was my friend. But I'm connected with a district attorney."

"Yeah, well, I don't have much of a chance. News will get around about this so-called magazine interview."

"If we hurry with the information, I can also get enough facts to do a magazine story for a good cover. I know someone who can get it published."

He chuckled. "Wouldn't that be something?"

"Haden. What did Browning tell you?"

At the end of the thirty minutes the door clanged open right to the second. The forceful entry of the guard told her there would be no extended time allowed. She closed her notebook and stood, looking down at Haden Parker. Her heart beat faster as she remembered the fate of Jake Gibbons, the P.I. who had offered Browning a deal. A short time later he was found dead. *Would she or Haden be safe after this interview?*

She heard her voice speak with hollow confidence. "My magazine will let you know when the story will be run. You'll receive a complimentary copy. Thanks for your time, Mr. Hayden," she said in passing.

The guard stood like a mountain beside her and escorted her out. "Thank you," she said in her most businesslike tone as they waited for the release of the locks.

Then she pushed through the doors, glad for the cold rush of spring air in her face—and safety. Maintaining as much dignity as possible, she hurried toward the final gate to the freedom on the other side. Smiling briefly at the guard at the gate, she scurried in the direction of her car, her thoughts on everything she'd heard from Haden Parker.

If an arrest came because of what he'd shared today, Lacy meant to ask Quinn if he could arrange a special deal for Parker. Although the man had his own interests at heart when he'd chosen to speak up, Lacy thought it deserved some merit. Mentally, she railed at any pre-victory celebrations before she had actual, credible evidence in hand. Walking across the extended parking area with the sun at her back was therapeutic to mind and body.

Just then a full-figured male shadow appeared on the blacktop alongside her moving up fast. Lacy whirled around to face whoever was following her. Her drop-jawed position froze. Jason Gardner strode formidably to the place she stood and took her by the arm, turning her quickly forward. "You," she gasped. "You're Quinn's man?" she asked, remembering the protection Quinn had promised her only yesterday.

She was being marched along at a fast pace. "Keep walking until we reach your car. Unlock it before we get there. I'll explain once we are inside."

With the comfort of her upholstered seats beneath them and the locks of her vehicle secured, she stared at him, her very manner demanding an explanation. Jason's strong jawline was stiff and no-nonsense as he checked out every window and mirror. "I want you to start up the car and drive to the very back of the lot toward the outlet entrance to the road. My car is parked there. I'll follow you to the Old Clock Café about a mile down the road. We'll have coffee and talk there." Realizing she was seemingly frozen in place, Jason said softly, "Lacy, start the car."

She did as she was told, like a robot, holding her breath lest someone jump out in front of her. Her short-lived feeling of well-being was totally shattered. *What did all of this mean? Are Jason's abrupt actions orchestrated to maintain my safety, or is there real danger nearby? And why is he here? I thought Quinn was going to send a trained lawman to protect me, like maybe the cowboy who's been watching me from the tan truck.*

A reminder whispered that Jason had done a good job of protecting her on many occasions so far. *But why him?*

It was a short punt to the end of the lot by the entrance and no time to ask questions. She stopped, allowing Jason to exit the car, and waited while he started the Durango. He motioned her to drive out and turn to the right.

Ten minutes later they were sitting in the café with coffee in front of them. "Do you want anything to eat?" Jason inquired, looking over the menu.

"Not hungry. My stomach is tied into knots." She frowned. "I don't understand, Jason. Why are you here? Quinn didn't tell me..."

The tight lines she'd seen in Jason's face in the parking area of the prison softened. "Quinn was short a man and in a bind. He had his best man guarding Chloe. When he asked if I could help, I said I would. It's that simple."

Lacy tilted her head, still wondering why Quinn would allow a civilian like Jason to tackle a potentially dangerous assignment. Jason owned a newspaper for crying out loud; he wasn't law enforcement. She set aside the question she'd planned to ask and asked another instead. "Who's putting out the paper this week?"

"Maxine. She can manage that paper without me. She was running the paper when I bought it. She's a very capable woman."

"I'm learning that." Lacy peered over her cup of coffee before taking a long dreg of the comforting liquid. She enjoyed the opportunity to sit across from this quiet, handsome man and allow her mind to wonder what it might be like if he were truly interested in her, and this was a special date…and no one was trying to kill her.

It was Jason who broke the peaceful respite and tore aside her fanciful thoughts. "All right, Lacy. Tell me everything Parker said and did." He took out a small pad and pen.

Typical newspaper man with ink in his veins, she noted, strangely sad for the loss of her dreams. In an eye flicker, everything was back to business. "It might be better if I began when I first entered the prison." She offered her cup up for refill to the waitress who'd just walked up. Lacy intended to make the most of this time, knowing what would follow.

*

Everything was happening too fast for Lacy. She eyed her granite-faced editor from the passenger seat of his Durango as he pulled away from the café and left her car behind. Jason turned a sharp left down the road that would lead to the Latino section of town. There was a city map lying between them.

He shot Lacy a glance. "Tell me again how this woman was related to Clem Browning?"

"The way Haden Parker told me, this Latoya Montez was a stepsister of sorts to Browning. The girl's mother lived with Browning's father for years and brought Latoya with her into the relationship. Clem started looking out for her when she was just a tyke and their closeness continued. Latoya married a guy with a big house, and they began renting out rooms to bring in extra money. After her husband died, Latoya continued the business, and Clem would occasionally stay with her when he needed a place to lay low."

"And supposedly she has a book from Clem with his client list?" He lifted a querulous brow. "Sounds too good to be true. Why didn't Parker speak up before now? He could have gotten a deal."

"No," Lacy said swiftly. "Quinn found out Haden was severely beaten right after Clem Browning's death. Haden was afraid to open his mouth. He told me that the prison walls had ears and long fingers to an outside network."

"I believe that," murmured Jason, stopping at a light. The GPS fixed on top his dash kept telling him to work his way over to the right lane. "It has to be somewhere in the next few blocks. Do you want me to talk to her?" He shot Lacy a serious look.

"No. I want to talk woman to woman. I'll motion to you with my hand, if I think I need help, but I'm betting that she will open up better with me."

Jason made a final turn, pulling up in the wide driveway of a three-story house. Climbing out of his car, she glanced upward, thinking she saw a face appear in one of the second-story windows. But it was there and gone before she could identify any specific features. One thing she'd noticed. It looked like a woman with coal black hair.

Focusing on the porch stairs, Lacy whispered a silent prayer before mounting one at a time. What they found here today might solve a seventeen-year-old mystery and allow Lacy to fulfill a promise she'd made to Stevie after the funeral, the day Lacy's family moved away from Gladden Hills.

Leaning on the bell a second time, Lacy waited. Now that she was this close, she wasn't about to leave. She willed the woman to be home and answer her door.

The door slid open slowly, no more than eight inches, with a hand on the door edge. From a dark background part of a face emerged, a woman with heavy lids and coal black hair—the woman from the window.

"Are you Latoya Montez?" asked Lacy in a friendly manner.

The olive-skinned woman eyed her with mistrust. "Who wants to know? All my rooms are filled—no vacancies!" she said, beginning to close the door.

"I'm here about your brother…not a room, Latoya," Lacy pleaded.

"My brother is *dead*." The door closed further.

"I'm trying to find his killer and stop him from killing again. Help me, Latoya!" Lacy cried, injecting her hand on the face of the door to keep the woman from closing it all the way.

The door slowly opened again. "How can I help? I know nothing! What do you want?" The black-eyed Latino studied Lacy. The woman looked to be in her late thirties and had at one time been quite pretty, but time had not been kind.

"May I come inside? Maybe sit down at your table while we talk?" Lacy inquired hopefully.

Reluctantly, Latoya stepped aside for her to enter. Lacy noticed dark-haired children scampering up the stairs and peering down at her from the second-floor railing. Smiling up at them, she followed Latoya down a hallway carpeted with a faded Mexican rug. The ground floor was clean, if it was an indication of the rest of the house. It smelled of spicy cooking and aged wood. The kitchen was long and brightly colored with yellow and red accessories, accented with chicken decorations. Latoya pointed to one of six chrome chairs at the oblong table.

Sitting down at the closest, Lacy placed her briefcase on the floor and would have clasped her hands on the vinyl tablecloth, but for Latoya's staying hand. The agitated woman hurriedly brushed crumbs away from her place while spewing a rapid string of Spanish words. Their intensity rattled Lacy.

"My daughter was told to clean this kitchen, and look at it! There are dishes still standing in the sink." Latoya's eyes flashed fire, making Lacy glad she was not her daughter. She obviously ran a tight ship.

"It's all right, really. I'm more interested in talking with you about Clem," Lacy assured the woman. At that moment she could see both unresolved grief and fear in Latoya's eyes.

The woman sat stiffly in the chair opposite her. "I'll tell you what I know."

*

Lacy had no idea how long she was inside the house, though it hadn't taken Latoya very long to relate her last connection with her brother and his final request. Leaving the house, Lacy heard the door close with a definite finality. Latoya lived with a fear and now that she had shared her knowledge, she wanted no further dealings with Lacy. Even when Lacy promised to let her know when her brother's killer was caught, the woman looked distraught and disagreed venomously. Clem's death had severed all her ties with the shadowy world he had moved within during his life.

"I have kids to raise and keep safe," she had stated. "Don't come back. I've done what I can. It is done!"

Climbing inside Jason's Durango, Lacy settled herself within the confines of the seatbelt before addressing his watchful eyes. She knew he would see all her disappointment in one look at her face. It had always been difficult for her to hide her feelings.

"So?" His voice was tense.

Lacy looked through the windshield to the scudding clouds overhead and felt instantly drained of every viable emotion—hope being the strongest.

"The book is gone! I've got Browning's letter to Latoya, telling her about the book and asking her to keep it for him. Clem smuggled the book and Latoya's letter out in an addressed envelope through Haden Parker the day before he was killed. Haden's girlfriend brought it to Latoya in person after his death. Browning figured no one would ever make the connection between him and Latoya because they were not legal kin."

"What happened to the book? Where is it now?" Jason demanded with a passion that took Lacy aback.

"A big man came at night, Latoya said. He wore a cowboy hat and stood in the shadows of her porch. All she could see was his teeth, and he frightened her." Lacy related the words Latoya had spoken: 'His teeth smiled, but they were not friendly. I was afraid, because he had a darkness of soul. *This one is connected with death,* I said to myself! *He is wounded and will wound others.* I've seen his kind before. I was afraid for me and my children. When he asked for the book, I went and got it, but I did not tell him about the letter.' " Lacy waited for Jason to digest what she had said.

He frowned. "Again, the cowboy hat. Read me the letter word for word."

When Lacy had finished reading, she laid the paper in her lap. "Can't the letter be of some help? Browning stated the book was a list of his arson clients as well as those who ordered bombs assembled to explode at specific times. He also said that he was afraid of one client in particular who lived in Gladden Hills, the client who'd ordered the Turner bombing. He specifically wanted heavy explosives on a delayed timer. Browning called him a paranoid killer."

"Only as substantiating evidence. Without that book, we'll never get him. We can't tie the mastermind to the bomb if he isn't identified. That book is back in Gladden Hills, I'd bet anything." Jason sighed, causing Lacy to feel as if somehow she had failed and all his efforts on her behalf had been a waste of time. Then surprisingly he added, "Well, we'll just have to work harder from our end," almost like he'd taken an instant energy booster.

His recalibrated enthusiasm was lost on Lacy. She felt increased pressure. This trip to Indiana had cost her a full day, shortening her remaining time in Gladden Hills. She doubted her chances of finding the necessary evidence before her leave of absence was up in Chicago, and she'd be forced to leave. Jason had given her a month of evaluation, the exact amount of time she'd taken on leave from Chicago. Would Jason now think her a quitter? When she cast a furtive look his direction, her spirits sagged even lower.

What had made her think she could pull off a miracle? That was God's job. She'd never considered these difficulties when she stormed into town, armed only with her burning goal to solve the cold case, and a desire to honor a memory that held her emotions in bondage.

She tried to shake off her depression at the thought of leaving Gladden Hills. She'd known this was a short-term plan with high expectations. The case had remained unsolved for seventeen years for lack of evidence. Her secret contact who had sent the purple feathers had proved disappointing as well. She'd expected more support and direction from whoever had lured her here. The depression weighed like a heavy mantle on her shoulders.

Lacy reminded herself that she had another life in Chicago, a high-paying job she had set her sights to achieve. She could never have afforded her new Challenger on what she earned at the *Gladden Hills Gazette.* Everyone she knew thought the job in Chicago was an ideal position with unlimited potential. It was ridiculous to even consider staying on in Gladden Hills.

So then why did she feel like such a failure? Why was she so depressed?

Even as she removed her hair clips, allowing her thick dark hair free to fall about her face, her heart labored under a burden. At some point during her short stay in Gladden Hills, the thrill of her Chicago job had left her, replaced by a new appreciation for the richness of small-town living, creating close ties with friends and neighbors. It was everything she'd avoided in Chicago. There had been something missing in her exciting treadmill existence. Had she found the missing element here?

Lacy was musing on these thoughts until reality broke through, and her throat constricted with a stark realization. *Will the attempts on my life simply stop if I leave town, or will they follow to finish the job? The attacker on the stairs told me to leave…did the offer still hold? Even if I left under these conditions, I'd know that at any time a paranoid killer could appear.*

Her thoughts were as thick and moody as the accumulating clouds overhead, each heading for a violent storm. Lacy had felt the increased humidity when she departed the Montez home. She drew on her renewed faith and resolve. *I have to go back and finish the job before he strikes again.*

She turned toward the ridged features of her employer-protector. "You're right, Jason, we have to find concrete evidence." Lacy knew too much had occurred for the killer to allow her to leave town at this point. He couldn't let her live.

It took a second to realize Jason was talking to her. "Sorry. Did you say something?"

"Yes, I did. After we pick up your car, I'll follow you back to Michigan. It's going to be late getting home. Are you up to it?"

"Yes. Maybe the time in the car will help clear up some of my foggy thoughts."

He tilted his head. "What are your foggy thoughts about, Lacy?"

"Take your pick. The facts I've learned, which aren't as many as the suspicions I've gathered. But there are other things from long ago troubling me. I've often had the feeling there are gaps from that time that I've suppressed, but the harder I try to make them surface, the further they go from me." *Why did I share that?* She censured her readiness to share something of that nature with Jason Gardner. It wasn't like her. He was still her boss.

Her head snapped in his direction with suspicion. "Jason, why are you really here? I mean, why did you volunteer to drive all the way to Indiana to act as bodyguard? You have a business to run."

She honestly couldn't comprehend his actions. It wasn't as if he was interested in her personally. He'd not given her any indication of such feelings. All the attraction between them seemed to be on her part. Whenever she thought there might be something, a feeling, a look, it was snatched away in the context of business.

After a space of silence, she wondered if he was choosing to ignore her question. Jason had showed himself to be a man of action. He obviously wasn't in a hurry to explain his actions or his decision to volunteer. She could see it in his hard-pressed mouth.

"Look," he finally said, "I bought the paper initially as a business challenge. Hearing your reason for coming back to Gladden Hills sparked a similar interest in me to reveal truth—to right a wrong, so to speak. Besides, I agreed to be your backup." He paused. "Seeing justice done for such a despicable crime became important to me, especially when my reporter was caught up to her pretty neck in the heart of danger." He shot her a sly grin. "I also have a yen for adventure. Another reason I bought the paper."

His mischievous grin softened his usually hard features. Lacy had a feeling that Jason hid a depth of humor never fully tapped, and she realized, to her own surprise, that she enjoyed discovering new and interesting things about this complex man.

They rode in silence back to the place they'd left Lacy's car, both accepting it would be a long drive back to Gladden Hills, Michigan.

19

Fallout

LACY'S EYES FLEW OPEN, starkly awake and aware of potential danger. Coming fully alert, she fumbled in her purse for her phone. The dark, never-ending highway had nearly lulled her to sleep. The ringing phone was timely. Her pride hadn't allowed her to admit to Jason she'd been too tired to drive straight home, especially after all the time they'd lost in pursuit of the stolen client list. She clicked her phone on.

"Hello?" she said, groggily.

"I was expecting a report a lot sooner than this, Cottrell! Do you know what time it is? Why am I calling you? I thought we had an agreement—full disclosure?" said Quinn Darling, shooting a warning shot over her bow. "Where are you anyway?" he demanded before she had a chance to answer.

"About two hours away from Gladden Hills, and I'd rather talk with you in the morning. I need all my concentration to stay awake and drive. It fell through, Quinn. Someone got to our source before we did. I don't know how."

"You mean Haden Parker?" Quinn asked, sounding confused.

"No. There was another source, someone we didn't know about. We'll talk tomorrow. There's one other thing we'll talk about. I need to follow up with an actual published interview from that prison visit. Can you arrange that with one of the major magazines?"

"I'm sure I can work out something. Call me early. I have news as well."

Lacy wasn't too foggy to catch the edge to Quinn's voice. Something was wrong on his end. Jason was right behind her in the Durango. She speed-dialed his number. "Let's get off the road and get some coffee."

When she told Jason about her short, cryptic conversation with Quinn, his face remained passive, offering no comments. They sipped their coffee quietly. The quick supper they'd grabbed at a mom and pop restaurant off the interstate was past history, and although food was the last thing on her mind, she yielded to Jason's urging to get a plain doughnut. They'd been made fresh for the truck drivers coming through, and Lacy had to admit they hit the spot. She shook her slightly mussed hair and heaved a sigh.

"I have to tell you, Jason, this afternoon I actually considered packing my bags and heading my shiny new car back to the Windy City." She looked up in time to see the skin around his eyes crinkle. "You think that's funny? It's true. Listen, I gotta know. Do you take your sunglasses off when you drive at night? How about when you sleep?" she asked, regarding him with half closed eyes.

"That information lies somewhere in the same jurisdiction as the question of whether Santa Claus sleeps with his beard above or under the covers—classified. There's a small motel down the street, cheap but clean, and we're going to check in for a couple hours of sleep. You're too tired to keep driving. We got too late a start heading back. Finish your coffee and let's go. You need some sleep."

"Then why did you let me drink that coffee?" She peered up at him with a quizzical, troubled gaze.

Helping her up from the booth, Jason guided her out of the way of a tired-looking trucker entering the door. "You looked thirsty. Besides, I hadn't made up my mind yet. Once I saw you couldn't walk a straight line...."

And then they were outside in the cold night air. He stood behind her, placing his hands on her shoulders. His nearness caused a shivery sensation to tingle up her spine.

Jason's lips touched the back of her ear. "Somewhere this afternoon, we picked up a tail," he whispered. "Don't turn around. Just look out of the corner of your eye to the far right...an old white-paneled van—see it?" He patted her arm in an affectionate manner, keeping his voice low. "I'll walk you to your car. Lock the doors immediately. I'll swing around in the parking lot, and we'll drive down to the motel. It's across the street to the left."

Jason paid for two rooms on the first floor near the lobby. Lacy carried in her night bag, and Jason asked for toothpaste and a brush at the desk. He gave a final glance out the front door of the building before they went to their rooms. They said good night at her door.

"I'll knock on your door about 6:30 a.m. We—ah—have connecting doors, in case you need me. Make sure the bolt is on this door." He turned abruptly, moving the short distance to the room on the left.

Lacy walked inside, locked the door, and inserted the safety chain. She was asleep in ten minutes, her clothes thrown on the nearest chair.

It was pitch black when she heard the corridor door open and bang against the safety chain. She clutched the covers, trying to remember where she was. Bolting upright, she looked to the nightstand. It was 3:00 a.m. They had driven until 1:30 a.m. and Lacy had immediately pitched to the deepest level of unconsciousness.

Now, stumbling to the door, she peered through the hole, seeing the top half of a dark-complexioned face she'd never seen before. *He looks Hispanic.*

"Who's there?" she called as once again the door banged against the chain. She had no illusions of it holding against another attempt. Someone was forcing their way inside. Dashing to the connecting door, she pounded and screamed, "Jason! Jason!"

The door flew open, and Jason stared at her through the shadowed threshold, barely illuminated by the threads of light piercing the blinds from the outside street lights. He was in boxer shorts and a T-shirt, his dark hair tousled with wayward curls. "What?"

She pointed at her door. "Someone's trying to get in!"

Jason bolted for her door, unlatched it, and threw it wide open. The hall was empty. He squinted down both directions. Stepping back inside, he checked the door, staring at the damaged chain. Closing the door, he said angrily, "He's gone now" and rushed back to his room.

Lacy stood in place, trembling.

In seconds, Jason re-entered through the connecting door, his dark glasses back in place and wearing long pants and shoes. "Stay here," he ordered, exiting through her corridor door and closing it behind him.

Lacy reopened the door and watched him walk to the lobby a short distance away. Running back to grab her terry robe, she followed Jason to the lobby and stood at the corner where she could keep her door in view.

Jason loomed over the check-in counter. "What did the man look like who was just in here?" His tone left no doubt that he believed the person on the desk had seen someone.

When the scrawny-necked, young desk clerk on duty stuttered a response, Jason growled, "Someone tried to break into my friend's room a minute ago, and there is only one way inside after 11:00 p.m. Do we need to call the police?"

"Ah, ah, the guy said he was a relative of the lady's, and she'd forgotten something at his place."

"So you gave him a room key without calling the room first?" Jason tilted his head. He was dog-tired and clearly in no mood to be toyed with.

The kid looked cornered; his eyes darted to the side and back. What he'd done was unethical and against policy. It was almost certain a bribe had been accepted, and he was fearful of the consequences. The uncomfortable clerk lowered his voice so only Jason could hear.

Having pulled out a small pad and pen, Jason wrote down a few items and asked the kid's name. Afterward, he scowled and stalked away from the counter, his strides marked with the rage that obviously propelled him.

Lacy hurried to keep up with him. When they reached her room, he halted. "I don't think we'd be bothered further tonight if you want to stay. Once caught in the act, the perp generally aborts his plan. Do you want to try for more sleep?"

Lacy shook her head. "I've never been so awake in my life."

Jason smiled at her. "Get dressed and we'll leave." He looked back up the hall toward the lobby. "I'll get our refund," he said, his features hardening.

Seeing the set of his jaw, Lacy had no doubt he'd do just that. "I'll wait in my room. Knock when you're ready."

Two hours of concentrated driving brought them to Lacy's house about 5:15 a.m. Lacy quietly exited her car and walked back to the Durango parked behind her. Jason rolled down his window to speak with her. "I'll see you at the office this afternoon. Tell Quinn about last night at the motel. I'll call him later with the description I got from the night clerk."

"Right. I have to brief Quinn at 8:00 a.m." She winced. "It's going to be a long day." She leaned on the window ledge. "Did I only imagine you had your glasses off last night or was it fact? I was so panicked, the details are unclear."

He regarded her, his poker-face firmly in place. "You snooze, you lose, Cottrell. See you later." His foot eased off the brake to roll backward.

Her head bobbed forward. "Hey, boss, thanks from the bottom of my sleepy heart."

His gaze held her motionless, and butterflies fluttered in her stomach.

Jason's chin lifted. "Later, then. Get some sleep." The vehicle rolled back into the street and was gone, leaving Lacy watching its form diminish as it neared the end of the street.

*

Lacy was brushing her teeth in the upstairs bathroom when Quinn called and asked her to meet him at the café in the back booth. He was talking with Wendy George when Lacy entered the café. Wendy motioned her on the left to the booth. As Lacy neared she noticed the tall blond was looking particularly flushed of face for so early in the morning. Wendy inclined her head in passing. "I'll bring you coffee and keep the booths close by empty. Most of the breakfast crowd has passed. Just the retirees come in at this time."

At the minute Lacy would have slipped into the booth opposite Quinn she heard the shrill voice of Gladys Pruitt, her former piano teacher. "Ellie Cottrell, I want to speak with you."

Lacy raised her eyes in a plea toward Wendy, who'd whirled in place when the old woman called across the café. Wendy waved Lacy to go ahead and marched toward Mrs. Pruitt. Taking her gently by the arm in the direction of her usual booth on the right, Wendy talked directly in the old woman's ear.

"It must be nice to have a following," said Quinn wryly.

Lacy shot him a scornful look. "You better hope Wendy can keep her occupied while we talk. Have you spoken with Jason yet this morning?"

"He called me at 7:30 a.m. so I know what happened at the motel last night. We'll keep an eye out for the guy around town. Now fill me in on your interviews."

After Lacy related everything she could remember, plus her own impressions, she settled back in the booth and sipped on the coffee Wendy had eased on the table while she finished up her summary. The wink the waitress gave her let her know that Mrs. Pruitt was on hold for the time being. Quinn's distraction over Wendy's presence at the table was evident to Lacy, bringing a smirk to her lips. When she and Quinn were alone once again, Quinn leaned his elbows far on the table.

"And now for my news. Chloe's gone! One of her brothers arrived at the hospital yesterday morning, the very morning she became lucid enough to question. He had a court order signed by Judge Shaw for her to be released to the family. With no reason to keep her in custody, we were powerless to hold her at the hospital. There must have been a lookout on the staff. We were coming in to question her at 10:00 a.m. The doctor had only alerted me about 8:30 a.m. Her brother arrived at 9:30 a.m. and was pushing her out the door when we pulled up." His hands balled into fists.

"Did you send anyone out to the house to question her?" countered Lacy, equally as upset as Quinn. Every time they got close to getting information, they were blocked.

"Her brother wasn't the least bit receptive to our visiting her as he was loading his sister into the front seat," Quinn stated bluntly.

"Did Chloe say anything?"

"She wasn't all that alert and kept mumbling, something about Jimmy."

"Quinn, Jimmy was that dude with her at the bar who knocked Chuck to the floor on his dash to the door. I wonder why she was asking her brother about Jimmy?" Perplexed, she stared at the intense DA.

He looked like a studious man with a perpetual tan, a cultural oxymoron. Few book nerds were sun worshipers. Whatever the man was, he certainly made Wendy's eyes light up.

Lacy's fingertips taped the tabletop. "Quinn, I'm going out to her house and talk with her. I work with her and have a clear reason to visit. I'll pick up some flowers on the way." She stood, anxious to be doing something to counteract the blindsiding they'd been dealt.

Quinn's head shot up. "Wait a minute. Don't run out there half-cocked. Her place is about ten miles out of town. A lot could happen on ten miles of country road."

Tilting her head in a sassy angle, she retorted, "Send the tan truck as backup."

She was turning away when Quinn added, "Check in with Jason before you head out there, and keep in touch with him. That's an order!" The hard edge to his tone told her he meant every word.

Lacy noticed Mrs. Pruitt in her booth happily focused on her coffee and pastry. Someday she would sit down with that dear old woman and share a cup of tea, but it wouldn't be this morning.

Rushing through the entrance at the paper, she slowed her steps, seeing Maxine walk in her direction.

"Good to see you, Lacy. Boss said you'd be in late." The woman's gaze kept flickering back to Lacy even as she leafed through a stack of papers.

"About this week's column, Maxine, I—I'm going to need for you to cover for me. I've only the beginnings of the article worked up, and the way things are going, the chances of my making deadline are almost nil. Is that going to be…?" She fumbled for words, feeling guilty about her awkward position.

Maxine's hand came up. "Boss already talked to me. I'll handle it. I, ah, heard that Chloe spent the weekend at the hospital."

Lacy knew the woman's shrewd eyes knew more than she was letting on. Inhaling, Lacy nodded. "Yes, I'd heard that too. It's too bad. Actually I was thinking of visiting her this afternoon. Apparently she was released yesterday when I was out of town. Listen, I gotta run and check in with Jason."

"You be careful, Lacy Cottrell. Rumor has it, this town is filled with an unhealthy tension. I ran into someone who said you were almost struck down by a crazy driver the first of the week. Do you need someone to ride with you out to see Chloe? I've got a little time."

Lacy was overwhelmed by Maxine's offer and curious what all lay beneath her invitation. "That's very kind, but I'm not sure of my schedule yet. Thank you for the offer, though." She backed away.

"You let me know," said Maxine, her hair looking brighter red than usual.

Jason was standing in the doorway of his office when she walked up. He gestured her inside and secured the door behind her. "Take Maxine with you, Lacy. Someone will think twice about making a move on you in broad daylight with Maxine by your side."

Lowering herself into the nearest chair, Lacy stared up at him. "You heard?"

He balanced on the edge of his desk, his tone deliberately low. "I heard, but I already had a heads-up from Quinn on the matter. I guess he didn't trust you to fill me in. I'm stuck here, otherwise I'd go, but Maxine will be good company and a formidable ally if necessary."

"What if someone decides they don't mind including Maxine on a fatal accident? I'm not keen about involving her in anything potentially dangerous."

"You have a cell phone and can call me if anything is suspicious. Maxine is no piker. Don't sell her short." He rubbed his jaw. The effects of lack of sleep gave him a haggard look.

"I'm going to go buy some flowers for Chloe and charge them to the paper. Just thought I'd tell you," she said, rising from her chair. The room between Jason and the space to the door was tight. Glancing up, she noted his slight smirk as she attempted to squeeze by. "You could make this easier, you know."

The indiscernible quick softness that emerged on Jason's features puzzled Lacy. Her heart leapt at his look, destroying all attempts to hold her emotions in check. She stood, unsure if she should say something or move further away.

Before she could decide, Jason turned away and moved quickly behind his desk, his stoic mask back in place. "Call me later," he said.

With her hand on the door facing, she added too quickly, "Will do."

Striding from the office, her eyes searched for Maxine, who was absent from her area.

"Lacy," Maxine called from the mail area. She held something in her outstretched hand. "You haven't checked your mail for two days now and things are piling up.

Lacy walked over to take the mail. The return address on the manila envelope was from Nadine in Chicago. She said she was going to send her some research material on names Lacy had asked her to check up on. She tucked it under her arm, reaching for the white legal envelope Maxine handed her next. Seeing the handwriting, Lacy wanted to tear into the envelope immediately, but the timing wasn't good. Instead, she slipped it into the front pocket of her purse and looked at Maxine. "You still want to go with me?"

A small smile slid across the older woman's face. "I already ordered a bouquet of bright flowers. Pour yourself a cup of coffee and relax at your desk for a minute. The flowers should arrive shortly. I'll get my coat. Where are you parked?"

"Across the street in front of the café. Is the coffee fresh?"

The major general nodded. "We'll pick up some sandwiches at the deli on the edge of town and eat on the way. I've got her parents' address in my book, looked it up on the internet. Jason learned from the hospital that the brother was taking her home to her folks' place. When Chloe started work, she gave us an address for an apartment somewhere down near the river."

As Lacy regarded her with pure admiration, Maxine stalked confidently off to the cloak room and came back with her coat. By that time a fresh-faced teen rushed through the entryway of the paper with his fist full of stemmed, wrapped spring flowers.

Downing the last gulp of strong coffee, Lacy drew her coat around her and grabbed her purse. Together the women met the flower delivery boy at the front desk and proceeded out the door. While Maxine settled herself in the seat, Lacy pressed the starter button. With her foot on the brake, she paused and turned to the woman in the passenger seat.

"Maxine, I can't in all honesty start out without telling you that you're traveling with a woman who has an invisible bull's-eye on her back. I've had more than one attempt on my life. The 'accident' at the courthouse was not an accident. I was brutally attacked. If you would rather not be in a closed car with me, please speak up. I will not hold it against you."

Maxine's jaw clamped shut in a disgusted expression. Her sharp gaze leveled a withering look upon Lacy. "You think I don't have an inkling of what's afoot? I might not know all there is to know, but I put two and two together about that courthouse fantasy the boss printed up in the paper. One of my best friends is Dede Ganson at the courthouse. Dede told me that no one knew a thing about the elevator that was supposedly out of order, not even the painters who were working on the next elevator. It was in perfect working order when the paramedics came through. She thought it was a strange mix-up, but I have a more suspicious mind, working for a paper like I do. And you and the boss have had an awful lot of secret meetings." Her eyes darted to Lacy's stunned expression.

"Whew! Remind me not to underestimate you again." Lacy shifted into gear and pulled out of the parking spot. From the corner of her eye, she spotted the tan pickup pull out across the square and experienced a new comfort from its presence.

"Consider yourself reminded, Miss Cottrell," said Maxine stiffly in an affected air of having being offended.

Lacy chuckled at the dear woman's humorous manner, while lifting her eyes to the rearview mirror to observe the tan truck pull in behind them.

Lacy consciously worked at relaxing and focused on what she would say to Chloe when she saw her. Would the girl remember anything about that night, the scene in the bar when the man she called Jimmy knocked the wind out of Chuck Walden in his wild attempt to escape being recognized, or later at Lacy and Kelly's home when she overdosed? She had no clue what she could expect, or what type of reception she would get, now that she knew Chloe's true feelings about her. She glanced over at the bright flowers and hoped they would run interference for her. Her teeth bit down on her lip in consternation.

Two miles out of town on the south road, Lacy saw a cloud of dust off to the right coming like Mario Andretti. *What idiot would drive that fast on a dusty hillside road?* At the speed he was coming, he would intersect the highway somewhere behind her. Hopefully the tan pickup would speed up and close up the gap, keeping the speeding dust car in the back. Why was the pickup laying back so far? Didn't he notice the oncoming car on the far hill?

Both Lacy and Maxine watched the mirrors, keeping the fast-traveling vehicle in their sights. Lacy's Challenger was approximately a quarter mile ahead when the dusty vehicle emerged full blown on the highway. Lacy snapped her mouth shut at the sight of the maroon SUV. He was coming to complete the job he'd failed on Monday. "Maxine, call Jason and tell him the maroon SUV just pulled in between us and the tan pickup."

Maxine cast her a flickering look of question even as she pulled out her Droid. She repeated verbatim what Lacy had said, her gaze fixed on the side mirror. Closing her phone, she faced Lacy's tense profile. "He's going to alert the chief of police. He said to use your head and let the guy in the tan pickup do his job."

"He did, did he? Well, he doesn't have that SUV nipping on his heels." She shifted her Hemi engine and left the SUV practically standing still, gaining the length of a football field. She could hear Maxine's rapid breathing, but she had to give it to the little major general, she didn't break under pressure. Maxine's eyes stayed glued to the side mirror.

There were two sharp noises behind them, causing a sickening feeling in Lacy's stomach. She was afraid to tear her eyes from the road at the speed she was traveling. "What happened back there?" she exclaimed anxiously.

"That tan pickup truck gained on the SUV and rammed him from the back." Maxine turned away from the mirror, her eyes wide. "There's a passenger in the SUV with a gun. He just leaned out his window and fired at the guy in the tan pickup." Her voice squeaked as she spoke, as if she was running out of air.

Lacy spotted a driveway a short distance ahead that led to a visible farm house, flanked on three sides by barns and outbuildings. She slowly applied the brakes, aware that the SUV was gaining on her. She wondered anxiously about the man in the tan pickup. With both hands on the steering wheel and a prayer on her lips, she jerked the wheel sharply to the right and held it tight, steering the car in a wide arch into the drive, its back wheels shifting dangerously to the left. She managed to steer the front straight once again and down the drive up to the farm house. As if on cue, both women jumped out and ran up to the door, pounding to be heard. Seconds later, a large woman cautiously opened the door, her eyes questioning their frantic actions.

"Please! We need protection! Someone is following us with a gun. He's driving an SUV. We've called the chief of police from the road, but we need your help now!"

A barrel-chested man came up alongside the woman. His expression indicated he'd heard their loud petition. "Get inside to the front room with my wife," he ordered. Turning abruptly, he headed to another part of the rambling house and came back shortly with a large shotgun. Lacy watched him from the hall and heard him cock it. She ran to peer out the front room window, searching for any sign of the maroon SUV.

Will he have the gall to come up in these people's drive after me? she wondered.

The large woman looked from Maxine to Lacy and back. She was clearly curious and waited to hear if either of the women offered an explanation. They didn't. They stayed at the window.

Long minutes later, the tan pickup chugged halfway up the drive and sputtered to a stop. A brawny looking man in a black shirt and Western hat stumbled up to the back door of the farm house. He was clutching his arm tight against his chest.

Lacy dashed back to the kitchen where she knew the farmer waited with a shotgun. "Don't shoot this guy. He works for the DA of Gladden Hills. I think he's wounded." Lacy's lungs felt as if they weren't getting enough air.

The farmer stood stalwart by the door, his weathered face stern in his determination to defend those within his care. He lowered the barrel of the gun slightly, keeping it by his side and handy.

The brawny guy in black looked winded, his good hand braced against the door facing. Staring through the screen door at the farmer, he noted the ready shotgun. "Are the women all right?" he asked.

"The women are fine, but it looks like you're not. Come in and sit." The farmer turned toward the front room where the women stood watching. "Barb, get some hot water and bandages. This fella's been hurt."

The woman named Barb moved swiftly without question, and Lacy and Maxine hurried into the kitchen where Mr. Black Shirt was stepping up into the house.

Lacy noted that he weaved slightly. "Should we phone for an ambulance?"

His shadowed eyes beneath his hat stared at her. "No. I just need to sit down. I'm not hit bad, but my truck took a direct hit to the radiator. I need to call in and get you backup."

"I don't think he'll try again today. You probably scared him off," she said, believing her words. She remembered what Jason had said about the man who'd tried to break into her motel room.

"Scared him off? I think it was more the other way around. I wasn't anticipating the second man in the car. I couldn't drive and shoot too. He had someone riding shotgun, so to speak. You should probably wait here until Mr. Darling sends help."

"Mr. Gardner at the *Gazette* was going to call the chief of police. Someone should be here in a few minutes. If they use the sirens, that bad dude will be scared off for sure." Even as Lacy finished talking, the wail of distant police cars could be heard.

Lacy glanced at Maxine. "I think we should leave the clean-up to our friend here and go on to Chloe's house." She shot the man in the black shirt a questioning glance, observing Barb roll up his sleeve to sponge off his bleeding arm. When the woman wrapped a towel tightly around Black Shirt's arm, Lacy saw him wince in pain. She wondered if she should stay. Their eyes met.

"Go ahead." Black Shirt indicated with his head toward the door. "Get ahold of Darling and fill him in. Tell them I'll report in later."

Lacy nodded. She and Maxine thanked the farmer and his wife, Barb, and left the house, hurrying to their car. Starting the engine, Lacy told Maxine, "He knows we'd be hung up here for hours answering questions. It's better this way. I have no idea what he is going to tell the cops. I'm sure Quinn Darling will take care of everything."

Maxine's face was filled with questions, but she didn't voice them. She simply belted up and faced forward. "And to think, I thought you would prove to be a boring big city reporter. How wrong could I be?"

Lacy grimaced. "You don't know the half of it, Maxine."

It was only a few miles further down the road to the Camry farm. If the GPS had failed, the stench would have led them straight there. The pungent aroma alerted them long before the farm became visual to the eye.

"They raise hogs," stated Maxine, evidently observing Lacy's wrinkled nose. "Chloe was ashamed of them. She tried to duck questions about her family in her interview. She said she was still washing the stink out of her clothes."

"There's no disgrace in raising hogs. Everyone loves pork chops and bacon...well, not everyone." Lacy grinned, hitting the inside air button on the dash of her car. It might be the last fresh air they'd breathe for a while.

A small sign at the end of the drive said *Camry Hog Farm.* They turned down the dusty lane. Lacy wondered how the girl would receive their visit, let alone answer her questions.

*

"I don't understand, Mrs. Camry. Chloe's brother said he would be bringing her back to the farm to rest up from her hospital stay."

The woman's painfully thin arm and hand reached to her hairline in obvious dismayed confusion. She was an older, worn version of Chloe herself. "My Chloe was in the hospital? What was wrong with her? No one called us. She's not here, Miss Cottrell. In fact, we haven't heard from her in weeks. She hasn't returned my calls."

"Her brother?" pressed Lacy, ignoring the distressed woman's questions about her daughter. It was not her place to inform her that Chloe had almost died of an overdose of drugs.

The woman's chin came up. "Chloe's younger brother is out working with the hogs alongside his father. Her two older brothers are in the Marines overseas. Half the time I don't know where they are."

Maxine and Lacy exchanged troubled glances. "Thank you, Mrs. Camry. I'm sorry we alarmed you. If we find Chloe or hear from her, we will let you know."

"You do that, Miss Cottrell. Our girl has been a trial since she reached her teens. We couldn't do a thing with her." Mrs. Camry wiped her face with a handkerchief. "But we do love her, and I have to know what happened to her. Please let us know." The poor woman was distraught, and Lacy couldn't think how to make her feel better.

They said a quiet good-bye and hurried back to Lacy's dust-covered car. Once they were belted in, Lacy turned to Maxine. "Do you have Lacy's apartment address?"

"It's in the system," answered Maxine, pulling out her Droid and scaling down to the needed information. "I'll put it into the GPS. I think it's somewhere along River Road." She sent Lacy a dubious glance. "The area is..."

"I know the area, Maxine." She recalled the night at the bar down on River Road.

The tired buildings and unkempt streets looked worse, if possible, by daylight than at night. Lacy pulled in behind the small apartment building and turned off the engine. "Perhaps it might be better if I went in alone, Maxine," she said, eyeing the lot and the alley beyond.

"Not on your life!" shot back the older woman. "I'm not letting you go in that building by yourself. The boss would skin me alive."

Squaring her shoulders with more confidence than she felt, Lacy climbed out of the car, Maxine close behind. Feeling unsure about entering the back entrance, the women walked around to the front. It was shabby with litter lying about in the small entrance. Noting Chloe's name on a front panel, they took the stairs up to the third floor on the back side.

Neither woman had said a word until Maxine broke the uneasy quietness. "Chloe didn't make much at the paper. It was more or less a gopher's job, made up of odds and ends we could find for her. Jason took pity because the girl had such unrealistic dreams."

"There is no such thing as unrealistic dreams with God's power beneath your sails and determination in your heart," said Lacy softly.

"What happened between you and her anyway? If you don't mind me asking?"

Lacy shrugged as they neared the top of the third set of stairs. "Chloe wants everything too fast. She hasn't learned to work and listen to sound advice in order to achieve her goal. She took offense at my suggestions. From what I heard the other night, she was deliberately being manipulated by someone on the side."

"Too bad. She could have learned from you," replied Maxine, her voice lowering as they walked the dank hallway toward the end.

Lacy was pleased that the crusty old newspaper woman would hand out such a compliment. They stopped at number 366 but received no answer to their persistent knocking. Laying her hand on the door knob, she hoped for the impossible. The knob wouldn't turn. So she reached into her purse and drew out her small black case, clutching it firmly in her hand.

Pausing, she spoke in a conspiratorial tone. "Ah, Maxine, I'm going to try the knob again. Why don't you check the end of the hall for any unwelcome visitors?"

The sharp eyes of the matron fixed on the black case in Lacy's hand. "Right, I'll check the end of the hall. It's not good to have witnesses."

Lacy was startled at the woman's shrewdness. "You're a game ol' Dame, my lady, and I appreciate the support." She heard Maxine chuckle as her heavy short heels clicked down the warped wooden hallway.

The lock was old and gave easily to Lacy's sharp pick. Pushing the door open, Lacy stood on the threshold and scanned the room. It was surprisingly neat, and it pleased Lacy to see the pride Chloe had taken in this apartment. It was her first attempt of independence. The girl had tried to pretty up the shabby furniture with bright pillows, garish as they appeared. It made Lacy's heart ache. This girl was lost and stumbling in the dark against odds she couldn't win. Unsavory people had taken advantage of her. Lacy gritted her teeth as anger fired inside.

There was no need to call out. Chloe wasn't in these silent rooms. The bad guys had her. They had posed as her family and spirited her away to keep her quiet, but where?

Maxine was back at Lacy's side. "We might as well look around now that we're here. No sense wasting a good sick person visit," said Maxine, pushing ahead of her into the room.

"Don't touch anything without gloves. A Kleenex or something similar to it will work," said Lacy, hoping the girl would surface soon and it wouldn't come to a full-scale police investigation. But, just in case, they moved carefully throughout the apartment, trying not to disturb anything.

Lacy took out her pen and moved items collected on the small table. There was a stack of unopened bills and advertisements. Using the edge of a napkin, she checked drawers and found a pile of paperback romance novels. Moving across the small room to the pictures on top of the TV, she saw one that looked like Chloe's whole family on a special occasion and another with Chloe standing next to a white-haired older person, probably a grandparent. But none were what she'd hoped for—a picture of the man called Jimmy.

Ambling into the tiny bedroom where Maxine pried though Chloe's clothing drawers, Lacy pulled out the nightstand drawer to find several pair of earrings and personal mementos. Extending the drawer further, she discovered a small, inexpensive camera. Lifting it out, she held it in her hand. There was a small chance, but it was worth a try. She pocketed the camera. "I think we've pretty well covered everything, Maxine. Let's head back to the office. I need to talk with Jason and Quinn."

Maxine closed the last drawer and followed Lacy from the room. Before pulling the door shut, Lacy locked it from the inside. They walked silently down the stairs, encountering no one until they reached the main floor, where a roughly dressed man eyed them with suspicion. They passed him quickly, left the building, and rounded the distressed apartment structure, hurrying to Lacy's car.

"Where do you suppose that girl has gone?" Maxine asked with strained concern.

"I don't think it was up to her," answered Lacy, maneuvering the sleek car through the narrow streets to the other side of town.

Maxine's eyes widened with the inference in Lacy's words. "You believe she is being held against her will?"

"I do. Someone picked her up at the hospital. She knew too much."

Maxine was instantly taken aback, but her curiosity seemed to take the upper hand. She peered shrewdly at Lacy, as if dying to know what information Chloe held that was so important, but Lacy volunteered no further insight. Her head was buzzing with more questions. When she parked in the lot behind the Gazette building, Maxine directed her through the back entrance.

When they would have parted at Jason's closed office door, Lacy touched her sleeve. "Like the old cowboy stories, I consider you, Maxine Flanders, someone to ride the river with. You were good backup today. I know you'll keep what happened to yourself." Lacy took the bouquet she'd carried all day and placed them in Maxine's arms. "Enjoy! You earned them."

The stern mouth pursed against the rising emotions that Lacy observed on the face of the office manager. Then Maxine said, "I'm available whenever you need me, but I'm hoping that whatever nastiness is happening in this town is done happening soon. If you hear anything about Chloe, let me know immediately." She patted Lacy's arm and headed toward the coffee station, her flowers bouncing in her arms.

Knocking lightly on Jason's door, Lacy heard his mellow voice say, "Enter." She stood in front of his desk, noting his tousled hair looked much like it did in that motel doorway the night they stopped on the road. "Sit, Cottrell, we got the report from Frank. What did you find at the Camry farm?"

Dropping her purse on his desk, she stared at him. "Nothing good." Lowering herself to the chair opposite his desk, she closed her eyes, feeling tired from the top of her head to her feet. A subtle knock at the door caught their attention. The door opened without waiting for an answer. Maxine stepped through the opening and handed Lacy a steaming cup.

"It's fresh. The other had grown dark roots from being on the burner so long. Thought you could use it. How about you, Boss?"

"I'm good, Maxine, thanks," Jason replied.

Lacy smiled up at her gratefully.

After the robust woman left the room, Lacy slowly sipped her coffee and allowed her tense muscles to relax. She looked at Jason's taut features and related her findings, knowing it left them even further in the dark. Raising her eyes, she asked, "I don't understand why the judge's office didn't check to see if that guy who impersonated Chloe's brother was actually her family?"

"This is a small town and things are handled more casually. There are a lot of farm families in the area and it's logical they would take his word that he was Chloe's brother."

"What about the hospital? Chloe was barely conscious."

"A release from Judge Shaw's office carries a lot of weight. I doubt anyone at the hospital would question a formal release bearing his signature." Jason's jaw was tight. "We'll find them, Lacy."

"Hopefully in time for Chloe's good." Suddenly Lacy remembered the camera in her jacket pocket. "Listen. I need some time at my computer. We'll talk later." She stood abruptly and left the office.

Swinging into her desk chair, she withdrew the camera. It was a standard setup, though inferior in makeup. Removing the memory card, she inserted it in her computer and transferred the pictures, bringing each up in turn on the big screen. There were shots of Chloe herself that someone had taken, and a picture of a big guy with a cowboy hat standing against a wooden fence talking to a group of other men—some with Western hats, some without.

Another picture was the big man at the fence walking in the direction of the camera. The stems of foliage in front of the approaching figure told Lacy that he hadn't known his picture was being taken. Chloe had obviously taken it from behind shrubbery.

"Got you!" murmured Lacy.

The rest were shots Chloe had taken in the bar on River Road. People drinking and talking.

Lacy's focus went back to the fence scene. It nagged at her memory. Wherever it was, she would remember…maybe if it was bigger?

Lacy enlarged a picture of the advancing man and printed it. Grabbing up the print, she rushed into Jason's office without knocking. "I got this off of Chloe's camera. He was the guy at the bar with her—Jimmy, she called him."

Standing, Jason took the picture. "I'll get this to Quinn…which reminds me. A license report came in earlier on that maroon SUV, the one that fella, Joe Walters, got the number off when they tried to run you down. It turns out to be a dude named James Forner. He worked for the Kerrigan Ranch up to a few weeks ago when he just up and quit without giving a reason. He had a prison record, several counts of assault and burglary. The Kerrigans have seen him around town but have no idea where he's been staying or worked since he left their ranch."

"Well, I can vouch for the fact he was alive and well on that hillside road this morning, as can Quinn's man in the tan pickup. How is he, by the way?"

"His name is Frank Hammond. Quinn said he sounded tired, but fine, not too happy about the situation. He plans to make adjustments in the future."

Lacy nodded and sighed. "Good. Glad he's okay. He was a Godsend on that road."

Jason averted his gaze at the statement. "Let's call it a day. Go home and get some rest, Cottrell. I am." He ran his hands through his mussed hair. "It's been a long two days, and we deserve a break. I'll follow you home." He reached for his jacket.

She shook her head. "I'm going to grab something at the café. Kelly has dinner plans. Don't worry about me. I'll call if I need backup. I'm a few blocks at most from home. Give yourself a night off, Boss." Lacy shifted toward the door.

Jason's hesitation told Lacy he wasn't happy with the arrangement. As he slipped into his jacket, his jaw worked. "Let me know when you get home. If I don't hear from you, I'll come after you…are we clear?"

Lacy raised an agreeable hand as she left the office. Maxine was busy finding a fill-in for Lacy's column this week, and it gave her a new twinge of guilt knowing someone had to cover for her inability to do two jobs at the same time. Thinking of the nickname Kelly had given her, she winced. *Some Wonder Woman I am.* Gathering her things, she carried her briefcase, purse, and the manila envelope to the car and drove around the block to park in front of the café. Keeping an eye on her own safety had become a way of life the last few weeks.

She was surprised to see Wendy still working the café and immediately went to her section on the far left. While she waited, Lacy laid the envelope from Nadine on the booth table, almost too tired to read what was inside. But by the time Wendy arrived with hot coffee, water, and a sheet promoting the specials for the day, Lacy was engrossed in the papers Nadine had printed off for her.

Wendy sat across from her. "If you don't mind my saying so, you look terrible. Deep circles aren't flattering to a striking career woman."

"Never mind the compliments, why are you here so late in the day?"

asked Lacy, turning the conversation.

"Covering for a friend. Besides, I get this Saturday off this way, and Quinn is taking me to an art showing in Detroit. It's an all-day deal, so I'll gladly go home and soak my feet tonight." She cocked her head at Lacy. "I see Morgan Streeter every day. That man is addicted to chicken-salad sandwiches. So tell me. Have you had any more dates with that handsome man about town?" She winked.

Chuckling, Lacy said, "After that sterling first dinner date, not likely, especially with a growling Cindy on the prowl. Though he did whisper a promise when we parted." She gulped her coffee, wanting to change the subject. "I'll order dinner, Wendy. Kelly's out with Jerome tonight. When Eric Greer called and put her on the spot for dinner, Jerome passed her a note that read, *Tell him you've got a date with me.*"

"Well, well," cooed Wendy, "This business with Eric is lighting a fire under our shy Jerome." The women laughed together.

*

By the time Lacy dragged everything in the house and up the stairs to her room, she was ready to do as Jason had advised and get some sleep, but if she once succumbed to her weariness, she'd be dead to the world until morning and there was too much to attend to. Rolling across the bed onto her back, she phoned Jason, assuring him she was tucked in for the night with the bolt on the door.

"Kelly may have to come through the doggie door in the back," she quipped in a vague attempt at humor.

"You're punchy, Cottrell. Good night," he said softly and hung up.

Lacy looked through heavy lids at her phone and hit Quinn's number, wondering if Wendy had any idea the caliber of man she was dealing with. In Lacy's opinion, Gladden Hills' substitute DA involved himself in a wider variety of covert activities than any DA she'd ever had dealings with. When it clicked into answering mode she was ready to hang up, but Quinn answered, sounding out of breath.

"Yeah?" he growled into the phone.

"Maybe I'd better call back at another time." She heard him grunt.

"Hang on, Lacy, while I move to my desk. I was in the middle of grilling my supper."

She couldn't resist saying, "You should have eaten at the café tonight. Wendy was working overtime, and the special was great." He grunted again. It was proving to be a rousing conversation. "Do you have information on Rod Corbin?" she threw out, getting the idea Quinn didn't want to stand around and talk without good reason.

"Get paper and pen." He gave address and phone in precise tones. "He's working for a trucking company, doing their books."

"Doing their books?" She was incredulous. "They obviously don't pay much credence to his indictment for embezzlement."

"He's working for extended family members. Rod has maintained his innocence from the first. I don't know what you'll get from talking with him. He was interrogated extensively at the time of the investigation. "

"That's what you said about Clem Browning's last cellmate, Haden Parker," she reminded him.

"Yeah, I did, didn't I? It's too bad we got to Browning's stepsister too late. Parker should have been followed up on."

Lacy inhaled. "Haden had been badly beaten and warned against speaking with any law. I doubt he would have revealed anything before I spoke to him. Enough time had elapsed to soften the past, and I was a reporter, posing as a magazine writer. Right time, right place."

"Could be. Listen, we're been doing some investigating into the companies and the trust funds that were in Heywood's private files—on the Q.T. of course. Some questions have risen. Nothing concrete, but enough that they're digging into some of the bank's computer files. There was a lot of activity in the areas of those particular files. Funds were being routed in and out around the country, and in some instances in Europe and Asia as well. It was so totally confusing that it caught our attention. More investigation so far has borne out that Eric Greer might be heavily involved in whatever is happening. His name is on all the papers. A big surprise to me. So far, Heywood looks clean. Which is strange, considering those files are in Heywood's possession."

Listening to Quinn talk, she felt a dull ache mounting inside. Her gaze went to the windows where the last light of an eventful day was fading from a partially cloudy sky. Everything within her wanted to cheer at what Quinn was saying. She detested Eric Greer. He was a self-promoting jerk who thought homage was due him on every level. Considering what she'd learned about his aunt's prior position at the bank, it was a possibility the aunt could have set things in motion seventeen years ago. Lacy groaned inwardly. There were too many people with connections dating back to that deadly time. She waited for Quinn to finish before speaking.

"I've got some information that might put new light on that situation.

Give me a minute to get my papers." She laid down the phone. "I have a few resources of my own, Mr. DA," she mumbled. Coming back to the phone with the contents of the material she'd received from Nadine, she fumbled for the right page. "Okay, here we go. I'm sure you've gone over Heywood's background at some point. You know that when Conrad, Connie as he is known to friends, was still an impressionable kid, his uncle, on his mother's side, came to live with him, staying on for several years until his death. The uncle died of lung cancer—smoking, I believe."

"Yes. Yes," replied Quinn, clearly more interested in his waiting dinner.

"There's more. Conrad Heywood's uncle was Franko Ulrich. Apparently Franko spent ten years in prison for fraud and forgery—a master forger. He was considered an artist by many, having degrees in art and business. It took the government a long time to catch up with Franko." Long seconds of silence followed her exposé on Franko Ulrich. She added, "Have you seen Heywood's watercolors, by chance? They are really quite excellent. Now, let me tell you about Eric Greer's family connections..."

"All right, your message is received. We'll bring in an expert in that area when we do a surprise audit. You're sworn to secrecy on that item, Cottrell, in case the reporter in you rears up. Listen, we need to keep alert. From your own words, Heywood wasn't pleased to find you in his house. That doesn't make him guilty, just unfriendly. If he is involved, he's slick. Nothing has stuck to him so far. Keep your eyes open and stay in contact. Someone has been pushed into radical action. There may be more. Watch yourself."

Radical action—like the SUV on that hillside road yesterday or kidnapping Chloe.

Closing down her phone, Lacy continued to muse about what the following days would bring. There were forces in motion that could not be turned back. Tonight would be a good time to spend time in prayer and reading. It would calm her spirit. She felt a little shaky.

She thought of the lies she'd told in the past couple of days and was ashamed. She'd reached a point where lying was no longer acceptable to accomplish her needs, but over and over, she'd found herself resorting to it. Bending the truth had become an integral part of her work investigations. Now it didn't set so well on her conscience. The difficulty was putting truth into everyday working practice. *God, please help me.*

Her thoughts returned to Jason. From phrases he'd let slip, she'd learned Jason had some background in church and a basic knowledge of God. Whether he'd ever accepted Christ's gift of salvation was an unknown factor. He'd clearly had early training. How far it went she had no idea. But there was a real blockage in that area now. Because of her own feelings of anger she'd battled for years, Lacy surmised that could be Jason's problem, but there was a lot she didn't know.

When her mind flitted to Morgan Streeter, her thoughts always ended in confusion. There was no way she could dismiss their mutual attraction, but no other foundation for friendship had been established. There had been no time. His humor was fun and enticing, but Lacy knew Morgan had no leadings in spiritual areas. Any god Morgan worshiped would center around accomplishments and money. He was an ambitious, powerful man. Lacy's heart knew she had no business considering a relationship with someone who didn't acknowledge God in their life, yet she was tempted, unwillingly drawn to this man.

Lacy rested her head on the pillow and drew up her comforter, too tired to ready herself for bed. She slipped into a deep well of sleep until Kelly's persistent pounding on the downstairs door dragged her from her foggy, unconscious state and led her stumbling down to undo the bolt and let her in.

"Welcome home, she said, drowsily, her eyes stubbornly refusing to open all the way.

"Oh, Lacy, you're a mess! Let's get you upstairs, undressed, and in bed."

Lacy allowed herself to be guided up the stairs, too tired to register a protest.

20

Mixed Messages

THE INCESSANT RINGING OF LACY'S PHONE on the night table roused her at 5:00 a.m. even as printed newspapers were being stacked to drive to specific places. "Hello," she managed.

"Lacy, are you awake enough to understand what I'm saying?" asked Jason, his voice strained with tension.

She pushed up against scrunched pillows. "Jason?" Her bleary focus gravitated to the clock blinking rudely back at her. "What is it?"

"I have to leave town, a family emergency. My dad had a heart attack and is in surgery right now. Hopefully I'll be back soon after I know he is stable. I can't believe the timing!" She heard the worried irritation in his voice. "Listen carefully, Lacy. Don't do anything that even seems the least bit dangerous. I mean it! Call Chuck or Quinn. Jerome will come through in a pinch. He's got a good head on his shoulders. Listen, I gotta go to make my flight. I'll call."

"Jason," she said before he could hang up, "I'll pray for your dad."

"Thanks," he said after a slight hesitation.

The phone clicked; then the dial tone resounded.

Laying her head down on her pillows, Lacy closed her eyes but her mind was too active to recapture her lost sleep. She thought about Jason's dad and how she would feel if that was her rushing to be with her father during surgery. She prayed that God's hand would rest upon the ailing man, touching and healing him. She prayed for the doctors and nurses attending him. Then she added, "And somehow find a way to reach Jason's heart; take away the pain that holds him prisoner. Thank You, Father, for what you are going to do. Amen," she murmured, holding Jason within the confines of her heart.

The darkness blanketing the area beyond the windows belied the fact it was officially morning. Many people were readying themselves to go to work. Still, Lacy refused to leave her warm spot in bed. It was in this bed that her grandparents would read her Bible stories and pray with her. Lacy touched the sheets below her. It was as if God had sanctified the area with His presence, and Lacy rested in the quiet peacefulness she felt here and now, unwilling to leave or acknowledge the danger beyond this safe place. She dozed off and on during the next hour, a vague shadow of something forgotten nagging her to remember—something important.

Her eyes snapped open. Had she dreamed about Stevie again? Perspiration dotted her chest and forehead. She threw the covers off. Ever since the notes began arriving, the dreams of Stevie had been coming back. *Notes!* Lacy thought back to the day before, when the big envelope from Nadine had come in at the paper. Maxine had also handed her a note. Pushing up from her warm place, Lacy went to where she'd dropped her purse the night before and carried it back to the edge of the bed.

With fingers stiff and unresponsive, Lacy pulled out the folded paper observing the purple feather fall to her lap. Seeing those feathers never failed to make her heart rate increase. Her eyes went hungrily to the folded paper.

> It's time to remember, Lacy. Think about the day before the bombing. Walk through the afternoon, minute by minute. Everything counts. Be careful who you trust.

Her fingers clutched the note.

Who was sending these? It had been a shock to learn Chuck had taken college classes. She could no longer discount him as her contact. Especially after he'd mentioned Stevie had shared things with him about her. She balked at the thought that it could be him. The note sender had a military type mind. He planned things.

Whereas Chuck seemed so upfront—not the type to be clandestine in his actions. Then again, Jerome hadn't exactly taken a hands-on approach to the investigation. Just like when they were children, he was off to the side, watching. Could it be he was more involved than it appeared? Lacy had sensed a new strength in Jerome. If she called, she had no doubt he would come. Raking her brain was no help. There was no one else who could have known about the feathers. At least none that she knew about.

By the time Kelly stumbled out of her bedroom and followed her nose to the kitchen, Lacy was frying bacon and the coffee was hissing with fragrant steam. "Hurry up, sleepyhead. I've got French toast ready for the pan. We do have syrup, don't we?"

Walking to the coffee pot where cups sat ready, Kelly poured a full cup. "It's in the fridge. What's with Suzy Homemaker this morning?"

Lacy lifted the last of the bacon from the pan and turned toward Kelly, still holding her coffee cup. She filled her cousin in on Jason's emergency flight to be with his father. When they sat at the table after breakfast, Lacy finished by bringing Kelly up to date on the past few days.

Kelly's expression resembled a startled owl. "No wonder you looked like roadkill last night. With Jason gone, I think Jerome should stick with you. Call him, Lacy, if something happens. He's stronger than he looks. He's been working out for over a year. Don't be a hero. Remember what Mr. Darling said about backup. Promise me, Lacy." She pressed her point home.

"If I think something is going to be dangerous, I'll call." Their eyes connected in the same way they had related as children—total trust. Glancing around the kitchen, she gestured toward the mess. "Speaking of help, I could use immediate help with clean-up."

*

Lacy had drained the coffee pot at home into her large thermo mug, which she now balanced carefully in her hand. The cloudiness outside didn't tempt her to play hooky. It was a good working day, proved by the briefcase in her other hand. Setting the briefcase on Maxine's counter, she folded a new copy of the *Gazette* and stuck it under her arm, proceeding awkwardly toward her desk.

Maxine gave her a doubtful look. "You could ask for help, Lacy. If you drop that coffee mug on the floor, it will make a mess to beat all messes."

"I've got it, Maxine, thanks," Lacy called as she labored down the hall. She was determined to work up the column she'd planned for this past week. With any luck, she'd complete it and have it ready before the day was over, leaving her free to begin the following week's column in advance...and available to follow up leads in the investigation. No word had come in about Chloe's whereabouts, and it worried Lacy to no end.

As far as the investigation went, all directions in Gladden Hills were currently at a standstill. She'd mentally made plans to call Rod Corbin either today or later tonight. The Union official accused of embezzling funds seventeen years ago, according to Quinn, was now working for a trucking firm. Her chances for connecting looked better for evening, though she could get lucky during the lunch hour.

When that was accomplished, Lacy would be forced to wait on Quinn's internal investigation on the bank. She paused. Was it this money her contact had told her to follow, the alleged discrepancies at the bank? Money had also come up missing seventeen years ago when the Turner house was bombed. Were the two connected? Unfortunately, no connection had been established between the missing money and the Turner bombing. Lacy's main reason for coming back was far from being accomplished. Still, she would like to be a mouse in a corner when the surprise audit commenced on Heywood's Bank. It would be amusing to see the smugness on Eric Greer's face shocked into oblivion. Suddenly she was worried they wouldn't find enough evidence to convict the guilty. If discrepancies were discovered in bank files, it wouldn't pinpoint the murderer of seventeen years ago. They needed clear-cut evidence.

Lacy suddenly saw an image of Morgan's face. She felt a twinge of sadness that he might learn unpleasant things about his uncle and share in his disgrace. But sensing Morgan was a survivor by nature, she took heart in his resourcefulness to adjust, though she hated the part she'd play in bringing trouble to his life. Morgan had been kind to her—more than kind if she was honest. The longing in his gaze might indicate something deeper than just a romantic conquest…perhaps an inner desire to reach out to someone?

She took a moment to enjoy her coffee while she scanned the newest edition of the *Gazette.* Maxine had found interesting fill-ins to replace Lacy's missing column. Jason was right; the woman was a jewel. The freelance articles from nearby areas were actually quite good and informative. After covering the major columns and newsworthy notices, she folded the paper and laid it aside. She would indulge herself and mull over the remainder of the paper during lunch. Opening her briefcase, she pulled out her outlined subject and the opening draft for the next column. It felt good to be using the craft she'd honed since college.

Lacy raised her hand when a count was taken to send out for sandwiches. She'd planned a stay-in lunch hour. Her eyes checked the clock regularly, wondering where Jason was and how his father was faring. Maxine had shared what he'd told her before leaving. It was much the same as he'd told Lacy.

Maxine plodded through the mechanics of a Friday following the paper's release as every other Friday, but the distant look in her eyes told Lacy that the older woman's thoughts were miles away with Jason, too.

Munching on her turkey on rye, Lacy propped her feet on top of an open bottom drawer. Maxine had put on a new pot of coffee, and as soon as it was ready, Lacy planned to walk over and refill her large thermo mug. The morning had proved productive.

She unfolded her paper and thumbed through it to the classifieds. It was a habit of hers with every release. Interesting new items were often found there. Her gaze went to the third column halfway down to one particular advertisement. In capital letters were the words *REMEMBER THE PURPLE FEATHERS! Meet me.*

She reached for the bottle of water on the edge of her desk, unscrewed the top, and gulped down several swallows to help her get down the bite of sandwich stuck in her throat. She read it again. It was bizarre! What did it mean? Was her contact finally going to set up a face-to-face meeting, using the classifieds as she had done? She took another gulp of water and studied the short, dynamic words.

"Lacy, this came in for you a couple minutes ago," said Maxine, extending a small, light blue envelope toward her. Seeing Lacy's troubled face, she went on to say, "A courier dropped this off at my desk. It looked personal, and I thought it could be important."

Lacy took the envelope, staring at it like it was a snake. As Maxine turned to walk away, she stopped her. "You say a courier dropped this off? Which one?"

Maxine's face puckered into a frown. "It wasn't one of the regulars. The name on his shirt wasn't one I recognized either...Gator Service, Inc.?"

"Thank you, Maxine." Lacy held it, racing to connect the dots. "Maxine, could you find out who placed this classified ad in the paper?" She stabbed the startling worded advertisement, as Maxine bent down to trace Lacy's finger.

Standing erect, Maxine frowned. "That's a weird one. I'll check and get back to you."

"Good!" Lacy said absently, staring down at the small envelope that read *Lacy Cottrell* in bold typewritten words. Her fingers trembled as she undid the back and withdrew the folded note on matching blue paper:

> Remember the purple feathers. You want answers, meet me at the quarry top at 3:00 p.m. today!

The beginning of the delivered note read identical to the classified ad in the paper. Lacy frowned, puzzled. Why had her contact differed in the way he wrote the notes from the previous ones? This note was typewritten. The other notes were all handwritten in a bold, hurried scroll. This note carried no purple feather, yet they mentioned the feathers. Why? One hand went to her hair and began twirling a lock of it.

Although the differences caused her some concern, she knew necessity sometimes called for variances in routine. Her fingers drummed the top of her desk. Could she afford not to show up at this meeting? Lacy didn't think so. She had told no one about her secret contact. Not Quinn. Not even Jason. Only Kelly. There was no one she could take with her, nor did she want to. Her first meeting with her contact would be personal.

Wadding the crinkled parchment that had contained her sandwich, she threw it in the trash, her eyes going to the large clock. Three hours. She would have to keep busy, or she'd be a nervous wreck by the time of the clandestine meeting. Looking at her large notepad, she saw the name *Rod Corbin.* It would be a long shot to reach the man this early in the day, but Quinn had given her Corbin's cell number as well as a home phone.

When the tenor voice of Rod Corbin answered the phone, it took Lacy aback. "Rod Corbin," she asked again.

"Yes. What can I do for you?"

Lacy introduced herself. "Rod, I've read a lot about your case and the crime you were charged with. I'd like to get your take on the matter. I want to be upfront with you. Although I am a reporter, I have a personal interest in what occurred during the time of the Turner bombing. The little boy, Steven, was my closest friend. I'm investigating anything that might bring the person behind that bombing to justice. The more I've read about your case, the more doubts I have concerning your guilt." She allowed a space for Corbin to think about what she had said.

After a long pause, he sighed. "I guess your past is never really behind you, is it? I'm getting on with my life, Miss Cottrell. A big part of me wants to say good-bye and hang up. If everything were to be rehashed in the media, I could end up getting hurt—again. I have a wife and family now."

"Mr. Corbin, Rod. Did you know Mrs. Turner?"

"Yes. I was shocked to the core when she was killed. It was such a brutal death…and her little boy. Mrs. Turner was the only one who believed me when I said I was innocent of stealing those funds. We'd had a private meeting a few days before the bombing. Frankly, I was surprised when she called that meeting. She wasn't the one I usually dealt with."

"Who did you usually deal with, Rod?"

"A Mr. Heywood. I'd only talked with him on the phone, and he kept saying he'd try to get everything straightened out, but I waited and waited. He was the first one who'd alerted me to the difference in the bank records and told me how concerned he was. Him? It was my neck. I was scared out of my skull. Mrs. Turner asked me to bring copies of my accounting sheets to the meeting, said she would take them back with her to the bank. I saw her put them in her briefcase. She promised she would meet with Mr. Heywood and get back with me. That's the last I heard from her, and no one knew about those copies when I was arrested. For all I knew her briefcase was burned up along with everything inside. My accounting sheets were taken into custody and disappeared in the system. My only proof."

"Why's that?" asked Lacy.

"Because the bank had no record of any of the accounting sheets I'd given Mrs. Turner. The only documents in their files differed from mine. There had to be two sets of books. Mr. Heywood told me he'd look for discrepancies, but I never heard back. I tried to tell the police I was set up, but with nothing to back it up..."

"Didn't you tell them about your meeting with Mrs. Turner?"

"I tried. I talked mainly with the district attorney after my arrest. No one contacted me from the bank, not even Heywood. After a while, I kept my mouth shut. I got to thinking about the bombing. How maybe it had nothing to do with the missing Union money, but maybe it did, and whoever silenced Mrs. Turner was still around. I doubted they would hesitate to eliminate a low-level Union employee like me. I was young and inexperienced. Not long out of school, I'd hooked a job with the Union and began working in the accounting section."

Lacy heard the agony in his voice and was sorry she'd made him relive that difficult time of his life. But she waited, hoping he'd continue.

"I worked hard and quickly advanced. Thought I was on my way to a promising career, until I had that unexpected brick wall fall on me. Frankly, I didn't know what to think. The DA first said my record sheets were made up—a ploy, a slipshod way of covering up my theft. He made it sound like I was setting things up to run off with the embezzled money. I tried to tell them I wasn't that stupid, but..."

"Your accounting sheets were mentioned in the newspaper write-up, the fact you claimed they existed, yet they couldn't be found anywhere in the system. Am I remembering correctly?" asked Lacy.

Rod Corbin grunted. "You've done your homework, Miss Cottrell. Yeah. A reporter came by and took my statement all right. They made a big deal of it, implying that either the Sheriff's Department or the DA's office had lost pertinent evidence. Mr. Shaw was terribly embarrassed by it. He yelled at everybody in his office. I know. I was sitting in the outside office waiting for a meeting with him. Suddenly he acted like he might believe me about those statements, even asked me if I had another copy somewhere."

"Did you?"

"I told him I didn't."

Lacy thought about his answer. "But you did, didn't you?"

His silence left Lacy to draw her own conclusions. There were some things Rod didn't trust her enough to share.

She tried a different direction. "What alerted the authorities to the shortage in funds? Did Heywood at the bank call the DA's office or what?"

"The Union manager got an *anonymous tip* that Union funds were being funneled out of the accounts about the same time Heywood called me about it." Rod's tone was tinged with sarcasm.

"Anonymous tip? How convenient," echoed Lacy. "They never found the missing money at your place or anywhere else. Didn't that ring any bells with anyone?"

"They found a few thousand in a newspaper in my freezer and figured I'd hidden the rest of it too deep to find. Every paycheck I collect is relieved of a certain percentage to pay it off. I'll finish paying off that debt about the time my kid is married or they close my casket—whichever comes first. If it wasn't for my wife's job, we'd barely make it. She's a good woman." His voice sounded as if his last statement was one he'd thought a lot about.

"Listen, Rod, thanks. I don't know how this will come out, but I'll get back with you when it's played out. In any event, I appreciate your being honest with me."

"I'm content where I'm at, Miss Cottrell, but if Mrs. Turner's death is solved at some point, I'd like to know. It would give me a certain amount of closure to know they hadn't gotten away with what they did."

"Nobody gets away with anything, Rod. God keeps better records than anyone. Records no one can alter. God's Word says that every spoken word is written down and every tear is placed within His bottle."

"He must have a big bottle, Miss Cottrell." His voice was somber. "There's a lot of hurt in this world."

"I'll call when it's over," she said softly. "Good-bye for now." She hung up and grabbed hold of her extra-large thermo mug. It was time for a refill.

The next time Lacy looked up at the clock, it was 2:15 p.m. She reached for her phone and called Kelly. "Listen carefully," she said in a low tone. "I received another note. No purple feather, but it mentioned them—just a note telling me to meet him on top of the quarry outside of town at 3:00 p.m. if I wanted answers. This is my chance to meet my contact, Kelly."

Isn't this what I've been waiting for? Then why am I so nervous?

Kelly stopped her. "Whoa! Lacy, I don't know…why so far out of town? Are you sure it's from the one who sent you the first notes? You said they all had a feather. I'm worried. That's where Ralph Wagner was found dead. That place is creepy. I'd ask Jerome to go with you, but he left earlier, mumbling something about an appointment."

Lacy had forgotten that the former DA's body was discovered at the bottom of the gravel pit where he'd supposedly driven his car while drunk.

She'd read the report and flipped the pages over to the autopsy report on the back. There wasn't enough alcohol found in his body to have gotten the job done. Not only wasn't Ralph Wagner a stupid man, neither was he a drinker, according to Nicholas.

Nicholas said Wagner had taken an interest in the old files about two weeks before his "accident" occurred. Was the chief of police investigating that crime while passing it off as an accident? She shivered, wondering why her contact had set up their meeting for way out there. Had he found evidence about the unsolved crime of the former DA?

But she didn't have time to think through all the probabilities. The clock was ticking. "That's all right, Kelly. I need to meet my contact alone. I just wanted you to know..."

Just then it struck her. Jerome was out of the office. *Perhaps his appointment is at the gravel pit.* Saying good-bye, Lacy gathered her purse and briefcase and paused at Maxine's desk to give her the completed articles. "I'll be gone the rest of the day. If you hear from Jason before I do, please call me. I've really got to rush. I have an appointment."

"Lacy, Mr. Gardner is more likely to call you before he is me." Her voice lowered. "Are you going to be all right? Do you want company at this appointment?"

There would be nothing more comforting than having Maxine riding next to her this afternoon, except maybe Jason himself. But the purple feathers were between her and her contact. "I'll be fine. Appreciate the offer, though. See you Monday morning, Maxine." Lacy waved, then whirled to leave the building.

An uneasy tension rose with each mile she drove on the back road toward the quarry. As the tires hummed over the uneven blacktop, Lacy rummaged inside her purse until it rested on her trusty canister of pepper spray. She'd carried that old canister for four to five years in areas her mother would cringe to know about, all for a story. Today Lacy was treading territory that could prove unstable, but not for a story. She had to know who knew about the purple feathers besides herself and Stevie. Who was responsible for her being in Gladden Hills? Sending her a purple feather was like sending an engraved invitation.

She took the gravel road to the left after the second main junction out of Gladden Hills. It wound around in a series of S turns winding all the way up to a large flat area approximately five acres across. Slowing her car, the powerful engine strained to be let loose, like a large, black cougar itching to stretch its powerful limbs.

Off to the far right lay a dense thicket of trees and bramble surrounded by scrub brush and loose gravel. Scattered heavy equipment sat quiet and poised, like metal statues in a museum. Lacy found it curious that the quarry would be closed this particular Friday afternoon. It was also strange there was no sign of any workers. Her secret contact had obviously known it would be secluded at this time. She moved her phone next to her pepper spray and slowly coasted onto the main surface of the top of the quarry.

As her tires crunched over the gravel surface, she saw the jagged outline of the precipice. Beyond the edge was the steep drop to the pit below. Lacy put her foot on the brake. With all the rain this part of the country had seen the past few weeks, part of her was curious to see if there was water standing in the bottom of the pit, but she'd go no further. The story of Ralph Wagner's death was too fresh. This was where she would wait.

It was her contact's move. He'd said 3:00 p.m. It was almost that. She scanned the horizon and her rearview mirror. There was only one road to the top and no vehicle in sight. She wanted to believe her contact would keep his word. He had fed her clues like worms to a baby bird, so it stood to reason he knew more than she did. Why did he need her? Was she bait to lure out the killers? She wanted to know his real reason for inviting her back to Gladden Hills.

Two minutes to 3:00. Her eyes continued to rove. They came back to the grader on the left. Was that a dark shadow tucked in behind the massive grader or the outline of a car? Her contact? The low-hanging clouds made visibility difficult.

Easing her vehicle forward at a snail's pace, she stopped a short distance from the back of what was proving to be a rusted-out, old blue sedan. She could see the outline of the back of a man's head tilted forward, a bulky jacket pulled up high around his neck and face. Easing her foot down on the speedometer, she edged her car up on the left of the sedan.

Weirdly, it looked as if the man was reading a newspaper spread out across his steering wheel. The *Gladden Hills Gazette,* no doubt—nice touch!

Surely he could hear the engine of her vehicle. *Why isn't he looking over my way? If this is my contact, he should be looking for me.* A swelling of uneasiness encompassed her. She edged closer to the parked car, now able to see the profile…a perfect, unmoving profile. She knew the answer in a heartbeat. *The man isn't real! It's a mannequin! This whole deal is a setup!*

Lacy's head snapped upward. The grader was roaring to life on the other side of the parked car. The driver was wearing a ski mask and, unless Lacy judged wrongly, he wasn't a construction worker. She slammed the

Challenger's gear into reverse and squealed her wheels, backing up and around across the top of the quarry. It would buy her a couple of minutes. She glanced wildly around for the best route to the exit. Her free hand grabbed the phone and hit Quinn's private number.

She waited until it clicked into voicemail. "Quinn, help! Send someone, the police, hurry! I'm at the quarry, pitted against a backhoe. The message was a trap! Hurry!" Lacy's panic eased some. Quinn would send help. He was never far from his phone. Hadn't he sent help when she and Maxine were in danger on route to the Camry farm? Still, experience had taught her to hedge her bets. Trying 411 got her a busy signal—only in a small town!

Pulling out the private number Chuck Walden had given her, she clumsily punched in the numbers, frustrated she was forced to leave him a message as well. Now she wished she'd told Jason about the notes. Were they *all just a scam* to lure her back to Gladden Hills and her death? It made her sick to her stomach to consider she had been so stupidly naïve. *Haven't I learned anything?*

Flipping Chuck's paper over, she saw the second number listed, the emergency number to use when all else failed. She stabbed at the buttons.

A deep masculine voice asked who was calling. "Lacy Cottrell," she spit out. "I'm a friend of Chuck's. He gave me this number. I can't reach him, and I'm trapped on top the quarry outside of town."

"Describe your situation," said the voice.

With racing pulse, Lacy stared at the backhoe, its engine revving to a high pitch. The monster-sized machine slammed its gears into reverse and backed around, blocking off the only exit road behind her. The mammoth bulk of the construction equipment covered nearly the entire surface of the road, leaving no room for a car her size to squeeze by.

Lacy described the unfolding horror to the patient male voice on the phone, even as a huge road grader to the far right was pushing the rusty sedan with the mannequin over the lip of the quarry.

For my benefit, no doubt, she mused. *If they are trying to scare me...* Lacy heard the plummeting of the wrecked car with the mannequin and the crashing metal against the stones in the deep pit.

Gasping, she hissed into the phone, "Dear God, no! He's coming! The guy on the grader is coming! I've got to keep away from his blade." She threw down the phone and shifted the car into gear. She wasn't pinned down yet, but it didn't look good. The backhoe was in place to keep her from getting off the top of the quarry alive. *If I can avoid the grader, I can buy time. Who is there to come to my rescue? And even if they did...?* With the top blocked, what chance was there anyone could reach her? *Lord, let someone get my message in time,* she prayed.

Lacy didn't know who she'd spoken with at the emergency number Chuck had given her and had no reason to believe she could rely on help from that quarter. Waiting until the grader was almost in front of her, she spun her wheels and sped out around the cumbersome machinery. Her car was powerful and easy to maneuver in an open space. She was well out of the grader's reach by the time he turned around. She knew that evasive action might not work again.

The ear-splitting sound of his engine was getting to her. Only then did she realize the silent remainder of the heavy equipment had been staged in such a way to block off part of the quarry top, reducing her area of movability. This meeting had been strategically arranged. *And I walked right into it!* It looked like her contact in Gladden Hills was working with the bad guys.

The grader was now cleverly positioning himself to herd her in the direction of the quarry lip. The operator was close enough for Lacy to see his large form and his Western hat. She sucked in a breath—Jimmy Forner, Chloe's friend! How would they explain her death? she wondered. What kind of accident could they work up that people would believe? But then again, maybe they were way past that. The gloves were off and the one behind the curtain—whoever it was—was desperate to be rid of her interference, just like Ralph Wagner and maybe Terri Turner had been handled so many years ago.

Managing to out-maneuver the grader once again, she fixed her eyes on the thicket of trees and scrub brush. She hit the gas and spun off, barely missing the grader's blade, turning about on the far side of the thicket. It wouldn't keep Jimmy Forner from eventually getting to her, but she'd try anything to keep out of their grasp for as long as possible—until Quinn could send help.

Hopefully, this counteraction might buy her some additional time. It had been more than twenty-five minutes since this stop-and-go game of cat and mouse began. Every once in a while she heard the nerve-wracking noise of the backhoe making his presence known. They had the advantage, and they knew it. Lacy could only avoid their clutches so long. Already the area for her to maneuver had dwindled considerably.

Before Lacy climbed out of her car, she grabbed her phone, pepper spray, and keys, pushing the lock fob. She would hide the keys in the scrub grass at the base of a tree. If Jimmy and his friend couldn't plant her inside her car, her death would be a hard sell.

Choosing a direction, she dashed to the far right in the thickest part of the bushes between the trees. It occurred to her as she dropped down out of sight, there was a possibility their heavy equipment could uproot these trees. She looked up at the wide girth of the tree and prayed it wasn't so.

The machinery noise was drowning out her thinking. Sticking her finger in her ear, she dialed Kelly's cell phone, noticing her battery was low. On the third ring, her cousin answered, sounding distracted. "Yes?"

Lacy turned her head away. "Listen, Kelly, I'm in trouble on top of the quarry! They are trying to kill me! It's Jimmy Forner! Heavy machinery involved! Help!" Lacy hung up, close to tears. She doubted Kelly had heard anything she'd said. Dropping her phone in her pocket, she clamped her fingers around the pepper spray. Again the irony of the situation struck her. *They've got heavy equipment, and I've got pepper spray.*

At that instant Jimmy doggedly positioned the grader, aiming the massive blade straight at the trees she was hiding behind. Was he going to try and push them over? How long would they hold? She looked beyond the tree line. It was only about twenty feet to the rim of the quarry beyond this thicket. The fact Quinn hadn't called her back was panicking all her senses. *Think, Cottrell!*

She raised the phone to her ear and dialed 911. It rang and rang but finally got through. "Hello, this is an emergency! Send help!"

A high-pitched voice interrupted her. "Hold on, ma'am. I'll get your information in a minute. I'm dealing with another call, an emergency. *Click.*"

"Don't put me on hold!" she screamed, watching her battery go dead in her hand. "Oh Lord," she cried, feeling sick to her stomach.

Grabbing her keys from the grass, Lacy stood and moved off to the far right of the thicket, charging her way through the grabbing foliage almost to the front edge of the quarry. She wanted him to see her, at least long enough to turn the grader far away from her car. She'd stay just long enough to lure him. Once he was turned in the opposite direction at a farthest angle he could go, then she'd dart into the trees, backtracking to the Challenger. And if she was fast enough... *I've got to be fast enough!*

By the time Lacy reached the Challenger, Jimmy had that grader turned in her direction. Had he anticipated what she had in mind? Jumping in behind the wheel, she listened as the engine responded. Would there be sufficient time to get out of his way? Flooring the gas pedal, she sped off, angling out to what little of the quarry top was left to her. It wouldn't be long now. She was almost boxed in.

At some point Lacy became aware of a growing sound, much like a swarm of hornets. Her head snapped to the far left as the sound ascended the quarry road and the hornets roared over the crest of the hill. The first motorcycle tore around the backhoe on the right, another on the left while she stood gawking. A sonic zoom soared over the machinery din and a lightweight cycle came airborne over the backhoe bucket. They kept coming. Lacy counted ten, fifteen, and suddenly there were nineteen motorcycles circling the quarry top. They spun about, tearing around the backhoe and the grader until they completely surrounded the massive machinery.

Jimmy's Hispanic friend on the backhoe climbed down out of the cab. He stood aside with his hands raised high in face of the large number of tough looking cyclists closing in on him. Refusing to surrender, Jimmy Forner squared off against the opposition for a fight. He shifted the huge grader into gear and came roaring at the cycles in front again and again, trying to smash them, but the three in his sights were agile and kept maneuvering out of the reach of his deadly blade.

The staged, unmanned machinery that had been so carefully arranged to hem Lacy in for a fatal attack were now obstacles blocking Jimmy from escape. He could only push the grader so far. Whenever he braked, he was immediately encircled by a mass of cycles. Distant wailing from police sirens grew near. They had to be close to the road leading to the quarry. From there it would be only a matter of seconds before they crested the top of the road where the backhoe sat. Lacy saw a motorcyclist mount the backhoe cab and back it out of the way just as the patrol cars crested and whizzed by to the quarry center.

Jimmy shut off the grader and jumped out of the cab on a dead run between the stationery equipment to the nearest hillside, where he could descend and possibly escape. One of the motorcyclists tore down the hill and cut him off. Two more followed and pinned him to a stop. He backed away, raising his hands in surrender.

As the police cars roared up to the top, Lacy staggered out of her car. The cyclists were taking off their helmets and stood in groups, talking amongst themselves. One brawny black-jacketed cyclist half-pulled, half-dragged Jimmy Forner up the hill in the direction of the first policeman in sight. Lacy forced her leaden legs to join the group. Her eyes flew open when she saw it was Chuck Walden holding a vise-like grip on Jimmy's arm. Jimmy was sporting a bleeding bruise on his right cheek.

After telling the policeman the short version of what had occurred on the quarry top, she turned back to Chuck. "I can't believe all this!" She gestured toward all the cyclists. "What is that emergency number I called when I couldn't reach you?"

Chuck motioned to a cyclist in a gray leather jacket. When the man walked forward, she recalled the man from the bar on River Road. "Johnny Fey," said Chuck, introducing the man with pride. "Johnny's the main man in our club. We train in formation and split-time assembly, like we did today. Everybody was ready to roll in less than fifteen minutes. It would have been ten, but I was just coming in from a towing call. Johnny was special ops. We do special presentations at rallies throughout the state. Mostly it's for show, but once in a while, it's the real thing, like today."

Lacy looked at Johnny Fey. "Thank you! Thank you! I prayed, but I didn't believe. You all should be wearing wings."

The light-haired, well-built man grinned. "Funny thing was, I was outside and might have missed the call. I'd forgotten to wear my cell, something I rarely do. Then I got this feeling that I needed to go inside. I stepped inside the door and heard my phone."

Two tears trickled down Lacy's face. "It's a God thing."

Johnny hung his head and nodded while Chuck looked puzzled at their exchange. Scratching his head, Johnny began backing away. "Glad we could be of help, ma'am," he said, inclining his head. "See you around."

"Count on it. Say, could I interview you sometime?" said Lacy, laughing.

Johnny waved. "We'll see."

Lacy touched Chuck's sleeve. "Stevie would be proud of you, and I-I don't know what to say. The Marines couldn't have arrived at a better time."

He stared down at his feet. A small smile formed. "Does this qualify for another dinner?"

Shaking her head, Lacy laughed out loud. "Dinner? It gets you an extended gift card of meals. Thank the guys for me."

"Is it over, then? Are you safe?" His brow furrowed in concern.

"Not yet. These men are key players, but if we can't connect them to the head man…"

Chuck's face grew somber. "You know how to reach us should another need arise." He gave her a two-fingered salute.

She saluted back.

Lacy was talking with the officer in charge when Kelly and Jerome raced up to them. She assured them that the worst was over, asking if they could talk at home. Giving Lacy a knowing glance, Kelly, with Jerome's help, escorted her back to her car. The adrenaline that had pushed through every panicked limb the last hour and a half was gone, and Lacy was whipped.

At home, the three of them ate an easy supper in a subdued, thankful atmosphere, while Lacy leaked out pertinent parts of the story during the course of the meal. "What I don't understand is why you were up there in the first place?" asked Jerome. His inflection indicated he was hurt Lacy had not called him earlier than she did.

Lacy took a deep breath. "I received a note promising that I would learn some important information if I met with them at the quarry."

Jerome's face was awestruck. "You should have realized it was a trap. I mean, with everything that has transpired…you're brighter than that, Lacy. I've always credited you with common sense."

"Jerome, please!" Kelly interjected. "There were extenuating circumstances. Things we can't share at this time."

His eyes rested on Kelly. "I see."

"No you don't see, Jerome. I haven't even told Quinn or Jason—only Kelly," said Lacy, pushing away from the table. "It was something personal, and Kelly gave her word." Lacy stared at her empty coffee cup. "Let's just say today's events have left me somewhat shaken. When I responded today, I thought I was responding to someone I could trust."

He looked puzzled as Kelly added, "I bet anything that the notes weren't the same, Lacy."

Lacy looked up at her cousin. "Maybe, maybe not. There can't be that many people who know about them." She sighed. "I, ah, asked the officer at the scene if Quinn Darling had called the police, but he said no, the call had come in from an unknown source. Now what do you make of that?" Still staring at the empty cup, she walked over to the coffee pot.

At that instant the phone rang, startling them all. Kelly looked unsure whether to answer it or not. Finally, Lacy moved to grab the phone.

Her hand went to her hairline, her mouth dropped open with surprise. "Speak of the devil." She went back to fixing her coffee, cradling the phone on her shoulder. "I gather you've read the police report and caught up on your phone messages. Believe me! I'm sorry you weren't within phone reach too. It was pretty lonely up there for a while—just me and them, and they had bigger toys," she said wearily.

"How did it happen? My guardian angel worked overtime today. And now that you have Jimmy Forner and his accomplice, do you think you can make him tell where Chloe is, and who he is working for, before an 'accident' happens to anyone else? Look, I'm rather tired. Yes, I know there are things I'm not explaining. We'll talk soon. Okay, tomorrow, but not before noon. Bye."

Shutting down her phone, she looked toward Kelly and Jerome, who were staring at her. "That was Quinn. He's not pleased."

"No wonder," retorted Jerome in a peevish tone. "That was quite a brouhaha today. You could have been killed!"

Kelly raised her brows in Lacy's direction. It was only natural for Jerome to feel as he did, not knowing about the purple feather notes.

As Lacy watched Jerome moodily nurse his coffee at the table, Lacy said pleasantly, "Kelly, would you mind going upstairs to get my heavy cardigan for me? I'm feeling kind of chilly."

Nodding, Kelly left the room. When Lacy heard her footsteps on the stairs, she sat across from Jerome. "Listen, I truly appreciate you watching out for my cousin. I know when she's with you, she'll be safe, and that means a lot to me. It's possible someone trying to get to me might come through her. About today…I called the line of channels I was supposed to call, as I was able. With Jason away, I tried Quinn. He has clout with the police. Then Chuck, which on hindsight was providential. Be that as it may, I then called you and Kelly. That is the way it is, Jerome. Please don't be offended."

"Sorry, was my ego pouting?" He looked sheepish. "I'm glad somebody called the police."

"Me, too. I was counting on Quinn to do that." She patted his hand. "You are being a great help. Just keep her safe for both of us."

Jerome was still smiling when Kelly returned with the sweater. Stopping in the doorway, she eyed them both with a curious glance.

Saying an early good night, Lacy tossed and turned on her bed with troubled thoughts. Was Chloe still alive? And, if so, where was she? Lacy was confused about that classified ad and personal note that had lured her out to the quarry. Had she been betrayed by her secret contact?

Sitting up in bed, she turned on a light, staring at the silent phone. Why hadn't she heard from Jason? What was she going to tell Quinn tomorrow? Could she bring herself to talk openly about the purple feather notes? After the attempt on her life today, Quinn would demand to know everything.

Jason finally called about 10:00 p.m. sounding tired. Lacy decided to keep the harried events of the day to herself; he'd learn about them soon enough. She immediately inquired about his father, knowing it naturally was his foremost thought.

"After a very difficult time in recovery and a bad few hours, my father made a remarkable turnabout." He exhaled wearily. "What's important is, he made it."

"I'm so glad, Jason." Lacy could almost picture him raking his dark hair while talking and wondered if he was wearing his shaded glasses. She clung to his words.

"If Dad's stable in the morning, I'll fly back tomorrow night. Everything all right there?"

She was suddenly glad they were miles apart, and he couldn't see her incriminating expression. "Ah…it's been interesting, but right now I'm tucked in my cozy bed." She kept her tone light, her fingers drumming the bed covers.

"Sorry if I kept you from sleep." He heaved another sigh. "That part about a warm, cozy bed sounds very inviting the way I'm feeling…" His voice faded. Lacy heard his sharp intake of air. "Sorry! I didn't mean…I-I…"

She giggled. "No offense. I know how you meant it. You're like a man in the desert reaching for water. You need to get some rest. I'll pray for your trip back," she said slowly, wondering how he would take the remark.

"Thanks, Cottrell," he said huskily. "If all goes well, I'll see you in the office on Monday morning. Maxine sent me a text saying the paper was received quite well, but several people asked why your column wasn't in this week's paper. She left a copy on my desk to read when I get in." There was a slight pause, then, "Good night, Lacy."

"Good night, Jason," she whispered into the phone as he clicked off. She felt anxious about what he'd say when he did return and heard about the attempt on her life. She had special plans for tomorrow afternoon. It might be the only way to stir her lagging memory.

Hadn't the note with the feather told her it was important to remember back to the day before the bombing? She leaned back against her pillows. Why would her contact tell her to remember, when he was plotting to set her up to be killed? It didn't make sense, but then her senses were too dulled to reason further. The contradictory logic churned her gut in agony even as she recalled Kelly's comment about it possibly being two different individuals…unlikely as that was. By the time she committed her turbulent concerns to prayer it was late, almost midnight. Out of sheer exhaustion, she flipped off her light and drifted into an uneasy sleep.

21

Unmasked

LACY AWOKE SATURDAY MORNING with the nasty beginnings of a headache. Kelly was reading the classifieds in the paper when Lacy walked into the kitchen. As she turned from the counter with a steaming cup of coffee, Kelly pointed to the offending entry in the paper. "So…this is what took you to the quarry?"

"Not just that. A personal note arrived by courier in the morning, telling me where and when to be at 3:00 p.m."

"But there was no purple feather with it, right?"

"Right. There were other dissimilarities, too. Oh, I don't know what to think. I'm not even sure what I'm going to share with Quinn."

"Why?" Kelly pressed.

"It's hard to explain. This thing with the purple feathers was something special between Stevie and me, and I figured whoever was sending the notes somehow understood that—maybe even knew Stevie. At least that's what I thought until yesterday." Her disappointment was stark.

Kelly thoughtfully refrained from further comments.

A short time after lunch, Lacy took the bull by the horns and phoned Quinn. She'd basically told him almost everything the night before. After filling in the remaining blanks, she related her phone interview with Rod Corbin and pressed him for info on his side. Conversations with Quinn were always a little stressful. He had a way of probing, like a doctor with a dull scalpel. Lacy often thought she could use a little of his technique in her own interviewing skills. "How's the bank investigation coming?"

"It's getting close, Lacy. They are following the complex electronic money transfers, but things are beginning to come together. Eric Greer's name keeps popping up and with his background in computers, it would all make sense. Then, of course, he and Heywood could be in it together. The double files kept in Heywood's bank office, as well as his home office at home, are where all the discrepancies lie, but if he's the head man, he's one sly fox. There is nothing with his own signature."

When Lacy tried to interject, he stopped her. "I know, I know, we're investigating the possibility of forgery, but it will take time. The information Corbin gave you last night presents a core of gray areas that will take time to investigate." After a few minutes of silence, Quinn asked, "What are your plans this afternoon?"

Lacy chuckled. "I was thinking of taking a drive within the city limits of Gladden Hills where there are lots of people—people who are good witnesses and great deterrents to would-be attackers."

"Yeah, well, keep your cell phone handy. I'm at the office doing extra work this afternoon."

Checking in with Kelly at the real-estate office, Lacy put a sweatshirt under her windbreaker and poured her thermos cup full of hot coffee before leaving the house. She knew what she planned was the only possible way to bring memories to the surface—back where they happened. She drove slowly through the neighborhoods on the outer fringe of Main Street, enjoying the scent of spring in the air and watching families work together outside, raking away the dead foliage and readying gardens for summer flowers. Lacy had forgotten this little town, but the sights and sounds she'd experienced the last few weeks were putting down new roots. It was going to hurt pulling out those roots when she left.

She pulled in front of the property where Stevie's house had once been. Now a cape cod, double-story, white frame with three dormers stood formidable, like an unfriendly stranger in the exact spot. How was she to bring the memories back when everything was so altered? Sighing, she locked her car and not too bravely walked the driveway to the side door. It was the way she'd always come to Stevie's house. It occurred to her too late that it might have been more appropriate to approach from the front. She rang the bell.

An older woman answered the door, peering out at her. The woman clutched her sweater against the brisk air. Lacy hurried to identify herself, explaining that she used to live in town and her best friend had lived on this land before he died. As she talked, a knowing look crept into the old woman's eyes, revealing she knew about the notorious story. Lacy inclined her head. Coming here was harder than she'd expected. Hesitant, she asked for permission to sit for a while in the backyard where she'd played with her friend so many years before.

The woman's eyes filled with compassion. With her family gone for the day, she explained she was reluctant to say yes, yet the longer she looked at Lacy's face, the softer her expression became. "I'm sure it will be all right for you to go back there and sit for a while. That was such a sad affair. We heard all about it, of course, though the land was completely cleared when my son-in-law bought it."

Smiling back at the woman's encouraging wave, Lacy stuck her hands in her pockets and walked the side drive through the earth-colored fence across a manicured lawn. She paused, glancing to the left. There was a small deck extending from a sliding glass door off what looked like the kitchen area.

What am I doing here? This isn't Stevie's backyard. It belongs to some yuppie family, complete with patio deck and fancy barbeque.

She blocked that area out of her mind and focused further back, where the lawn swing had once stood. It had been made of logs, weathered and strong. Beyond that had sat the rugged picnic table where Stevie and she would map out activities and adventures. Together, their imaginations were unstoppable. Jerome and Chuck had sometimes joined them for brainstorming sessions before they'd run to the park to play ball.

The gnarly old apple tree at the lot line had grown so tall. Lacy followed it with her eyes, her fuzzy brain scanning back through the years. The branch she and Stevie used to anchor themselves to before climbing higher was there, waiting. Was it waiting for two happy eight-year-olds to climb its branches again? The limbs were in the same places, only now their girth had tripled.

Lacy walked toward the tree, pausing on the exact spot where the lawn swing had stood. Tears came unbidden to her eyes. She spun about and tried to imagine the swing still in its original place, and she and Stevie sitting next to one another. It was the day before the bombing, the last time she and Stevie had been together. Closing her eyes, she lowered herself to the damp ground, sitting cross-legged and still, allowing the smells of the damp vegetation to clear the fogginess of that lost day.

Lacy rubbed her arms, recalling it had been blustery and cool. They had been in the house playing a kid game when someone came to visit Mrs. Turner. Lacy remembered how agitated she'd become. She had immediately sent her and Stevie outside to play, scooting them out so quickly, they'd forgotten to take their jackets.

Swinging on the lawn swing wasn't fun like it usually was. The sky was cloudy, and the dropping temperature made the playful wind bitter. Stevie complained of being cold. Jumping down from the swing, he said he'd go get their coats and bring back the new package of cookies his mom had bought.

I waited and waited, she remembered. *My face stung from the wind, and the cold made me want to cry. Why was Stevie gone so long? What was he doing all that time? When Stevie finally came back, he acted funny, and he'd forgotten the cookies.* Pushing the hair back from her face, Lacy was stunned at her recollection. She'd forgotten how odd Stevie had seemed when he came back outside.

Wrapping her arms around her chest, Lacy allowed the tears to fall afresh. She rocked back and forth, clearing away the remaining hurt stuck somewhere between her heart and her mind. A silent scream ripped through her. Maybe if she could let Stevie go, there would be room for someone else? "Take the rest of the pain, dear Lord." Her murmurings were low, for God's ears only. She sat perfectly still with her eyes closed, mesmerized by the quiet around her and the new peace filling her breast.

As if a cloud lifted, Lacy discovered that she'd stopped rocking at some point. Opening her eyes, she remembered the man who had visited Mrs. Turner. He'd come out the side door and turned to stare at them strangely before getting into his car. She saw his face clearly in her mind. He had hard dark eyes. *Heywood had come to the Turner house the day before the bombing. Is that important?* she wondered. Lacy thought how Clem Browning had made bombs with delayed settings. She was afraid to allow her thoughts to speculate further.

Shivering, she was about to get up off the ground when she heard a double clicking sound and looked toward the separating hedge between this house and the Bradford house. A connecting gate that folded perfectly in with the hedge opened and Cynthia Bradford stalked through, disgust blazing on her face. She tossed her flamboyant blond curls. "I couldn't believe my eyes. You sitting out here in the middle of the lawn. What do you think you're going to accomplish? How pathetic can you get? Stevie is dead, Cottrell. Get your head on straight." She raised her hands in a gesture of helplessness.

"Ever since you hit town weird things have been happening, and you're the catalyst! You have caused nothing but trouble—deliberately, I might add. From the time you were a kid you were difficult and strange." She laughed harshly. "I came through the hedge one day after school and there you were, as always, you and Stevie, drying a slew of purple feathers on the picnic table. Yuck! What a screwy thing to do, dye bird feathers purple." Cindy's face was nearly purple with rage. "And another thing, stay away from Morgan Streeter. He's off limits!" she screamed.

Until Cindy mentioned Morgan's name, Lacy remained in a daze. Coming back to herself, she jumped up off the ground, feeling the wetness seep through her clothing. "Hold on there! Did you say you remember seeing Stevie and me drying our purple feathers?"

"Yeah, it looked so stupid, I thought you were weirdos. I never knew what Stevie saw in you anyway. Where did you get the feathers…from those filthy pigeons that always hang around the courthouse?"

Moving toward her with steady footsteps, Lacy narrowed in on her target. "Who all did you tell about those feathers? Tell me, Cindy. Someone who knew about them was responsible for trying to kill me yesterday at the quarry. It's important for you to remember. Being a lawyer, you know what accomplice means, don't you?"

The startled, guilty look was quickly replaced by an indignant glare. "I don't know who all I might have mentioned it to, or if I ever told anyone about the weird feathers, so don't try to accuse me of anything. You and Stevie weren't as important as you always thought. I hardly ever thought of you, let alone talked about you. You're crazy as a loon, sitting out here on the ground where your dead friend used to live." She spit out the words with venom.

The hard glint in Lacy's eyes must have unnerved Cynthia, because she began backing away to the gate.

"Not crazy, Cindy," Lacy said intently. "In fact, I'm seeing clearer than I ever have. I'd forgotten about you barging in that day. You always spied on us but rarely came through the hedge. The day before the bombing, when Stevie and I came outside to swing, were you watching that day, too? Who was the man who came to visit Mrs. Turner? Did you see him? Think back."

Cindy's eyes took on a wild look of uncertainty. Without another word, she whirled about and hurried through the hedge gate.

Lacy cast a longing gaze at the gnarled old apple tree, then turned away from the past. Walking through the backyard gate, she stopped at the side opening to the house and rung the bell. When the old woman pushed open the door, Lacy said, "Thank you, ma'am, for your patience. I had some memories I needed to deal with, as well as some old hurts it was time to lay to rest. I hope I didn't disturb you."

The woman's eyes brimmed with moisture. "I'm Helen, dear. At my age, I know about hurts and memories. You come anytime. And I wasn't troubled at all. Live your life in peace."

"With God's help," Lacy said softly. "Thank you again, ma'am."

Once in her car, she locked her doors and reached for her phone. "Quinn, are you still at the office?" She barely waited for his reply. "I'm driving over."

She paced his office, getting things straight in her head. Quinn's tapping pen on top of a stack of papers belied his surface patience. Stopping, she leaned across the desk. "I saw Conrad Heywood coming out of the Turner house the day before the bombing. He was the one who visited Terri Turner that day. That was why she sent Stevie and me out to play in the backyard." Standing back, she chewed on her finger.

"We didn't have our coats and we were cold, so Stevie ran back inside the house to get our jackets. It took him a long time, and I thought I'd freeze before he got back. Both of us were on the swing when Heywood came out of the house. He turned and stared straight at us before he left. I'd forgotten all of that until today when I went back over to the Turners' old place and spent some time in the backyard."

"So this is exactly what you remembered today?"

She nodded. "After the bombing, my parents refused to drive by and let me see what had happened. I guess they were afraid of how it would affect me." *With good reason.* "But I snuck out and rode my bike one day when they didn't know. I was horrified by the charred wreckage. I kept thinking of Stevie and his mom being blown to pieces inside that house. I had nightmares for a long time. Most everything about that whole time frame blanked out, but I remembered us swinging and kept that picture in my mind so I wouldn't have to think about what I saw."

"Type it out in your own words and sign it," Quinn urged. "It establishes Heywood's presence at the crime scene in the right time frame to have planted the bomb." He rubbed his nose. "Unfortunately, though, that's not enough for a conviction."

"Too bad Stevie isn't here to substantiate my statement."

Quinn dropped his pen and shifted, looking down at the folder in front of him. "Yeah, isn't it? We'll keep looking for more evidence."

Lacy paced several seconds longer. "Something else happened this afternoon that I think you should know about." After Cynthia Bradford's remark about the feathers, Lacy could no longer keep the whole scenario of the feathers and her secret contact a secret.

Quinn's initial reaction to her revelation about the feathers was surprisingly more low-key than she expected…until she mentioned the classified ad and the personal note sent by courier that lured her to the top of the quarry.

He stood abruptly, his gaze freezing her in place. "The police report said you were given a tip about information for a story on top of the quarry…"

"That's true. I was told I would get answers, and since the note said, *Remember the purple feathers,* I assumed it was my contact." She hunched her shoulders. "Cindy's comment has brought up the possibility it could have been someone who'd heard about the feathers from her. Of course, I have no way of knowing. I still don't know what to believe."

"Quite understandable. Call me if you get any more notes, classifieds or otherwise." Quinn's expression was grim.

Then Lacy remembered something else. "Someone called in a tip about what was happening at the quarry. I naturally thought it was you, but the police said the person refused to leave a name. I don't understand, Quinn. Who would know? It wasn't Kelly. I didn't call them until later."

"I honestly don't have any idea, but they did you a favor." His thoughts were obviously on heavier matters.

"I know. Between the motorcycle group and the police, they saved my life."

But it wasn't that simple to Lacy. It was an anomaly that continued to nag the outer edges of her consciousness. Being a reporter had taught her anomalies were important. They were like the string on a kite. You needed to follow them to the end.

*

Lacy was exhausted by the time she returned to the house. It had been an emotional experience walking into Stevie's backyard earlier but worth it. Would it be enough to connect Heywood to the bombing? Time would tell. If they could only get their hands on Clem Browning's client book...but that was in the hands of the enemies. She took more aspirin and flopped on the couch in the parlor, burrowing snugly into its plush cushions. By the time Kelly arrived she was sound asleep.

*

In the morning, Lacy begged off from going to church with Kelly and Jerome. She decided to down more aspirin tablets and take her coffee, along with her Bible to the parlor where a small fire glowed in the grate. The crackling wood took the chill off the old house in the early morning fog.

Kelly asked no questions. Simply placing the phone on the table next to her cousin, she instructed, "Keep it handy. Call if you need us. We'll stop for lunch and bring you back a care package."

Lacy stifled a yawn. "Sounds good to me."

Sometime later, when the fire was low and the coffee almost gone, Lacy laid her Bible aside. Her brain was cluttered with fragments. She laid out what she'd learned since coming to Gladden Hills. The former DA, Ralph Wagner, was killed after researching files dating back seventeen years ago, files dealing with the Turner bombing and a young Union official, Rob Corbin, accused of embezzling funds.

Rising from the couch, Lacy carried her mug to the kitchen for a refill, her mind arranging the puzzle. The preplanned attack on her in the courthouse still caused her to awake in the night. What was it that had struck her about the attacker? Closing her eyes, she thought back, picturing herself positioned on the stairs when those powerful arms had grabbed her. He had been so close she could smell his breath. At the time, the thought had occurred to her, strangely, that he'd just had lunch. She knew the pungent combination of onions and mayo. Her heart pounded at the new memory.

From searching the courthouse basement files, her investigating had led her to Heywood's bank office and, later, his private home files. All of them were currently under scrutiny. From her interview with Haden Parker, Clem Browning's final cellmate, she'd learned about Browning's client list, smuggled out of prison shortly before his sudden death. Haden directed Lacy to Latoya Browning's little known stepsister. From Latoya, Lacy discovered the client list had been confiscated by an unknown man in a Western hat. She assumed it must have been Jimmy Forner, the man from the maroon SUV—the man at the quarry.

Combining all she'd learned from the old files in the courthouse along with the culmination of interviews and the attempts on her life the last three weeks, Lacy added the evidence of her own eyesight the day before the bombing. As clever as Heywood was at keeping his name off incriminating documents, the evidence was gradually stacking up. If the electronic investigation of the files in Heywood's private drawer came to a head as soon as Quinn hoped, the case could be solved by the end of the week. Yet there were so many loose ends.

Quinn hadn't had sufficient time to find out how the quarry came to be closed on a Friday. Lacy, herself, was in a quandary over how that information might fit in the picture. The most puzzling mystery of all was the person behind the purple feather notes. Were there two note writers or just one? There was one remaining week left of her leave from the Chicago paper. Would all her questions be answered by the time she had to leave Gladden Hills? The idea of leaving only brought feelings of depression.

She looked around the kitchen where she and Kelly had grown close while sharing simple kitchen duties and talking about the deep things of the heart. It would be like leaving home and a beloved sister. Lacy thought about the series of articles she had barely begun in the *Gazette,* stories centered on Gladden Hills' residents.

It was warm and friendly being recognized on the street, having her readers stop to talk with her. Never before had she had an opportunity to interact with people who read her column, unless they wrote angry letters to her. To drive away thoughts that increased her headache, she made a list of important things to attend to before she returned to Chicago. First on her list was to buy an Amish quilt to take to Nadine.

Lacy felt much safer, knowing that Jimmy Forner, Chloe's drug-pushing friend, and his accomplice were locked up in the county jail. No bail had been set yet, though an out-of-town lawyer had showed up, surprising everyone with his speedy arrival. Lazy knew Quinn was speculating on who had hired the lawyer. One phone call had reached someone with money.

The next week would definitely be interesting.

When Kelly and Jerome arrived back from church with her takeout dinner, Lacy was ready for a diversion. It was fun sitting at the table with people she cared about, talking and laughing easily. Lacy found herself wishing Jason was there with them.

The fog of early morning had ushered in a temperature change. Summer-like weather was predicted for the coming week. Kelly threw care to the wind and opened up the kitchen windows, allowing the semi-warm breezes to fill the room with the hope of better things to come.

*

When Lacy walked into Jason's office the next morning, the atmosphere was tense. The scowl on Jason's face was like facing an angry wolverine. Her gaze moved to his desktop. The latest edition of the *Gazette* was turned to the classified section. It didn't take a mind-reader to assume Jason had spoken with Quinn before she arrived. She sat down, deciding to wait for Jason to make the first move. She was in uncharted territory.

"What do you think you were doing going alone to the top of the quarry based on this?" His finger stabbed at the classified entry, his voice rising. "And some ambiguous note? Where's that note? I want to see it." Then, almost as an afterthought, he added, "You didn't say one word about this last night on the phone."

Exhaling slowly, she murmured, "Good morning to you, too." She didn't quite understand the reason for all his anger. Was Jason that worried about her? "Quinn told you about all of this, didn't he?" She stood, walked the short distance of the room, then swiveled toward him. "Because I wanted to believe the writer of the note had some connection to my dead friend and myself. It's personal, Jason, something you wouldn't understand...and all the previous notes I'd received had been helpful. Their direction led me into significant areas of importance. The note is in my desk. I'll get it to you later."

Jason rubbed his jaw, which looked as if he hadn't taken much time shaving. She wondered what time he'd flown in the night before. "I see...and this *last note* you received was like the others?" he inquired pointedly, his tone more subdued.

"Not exactly, but I couldn't believe there was anyone else who knew about the purple feathers from our childhood. It's ragged at me since that day. Then I talked with someone yesterday who'd lived next door to Stevie. I'd forgotten how she used to spy on us as children." Lacy shook her head. "Look, I know this makes no sense to you, but it opened a possibility for a second writer. I still don't know if there is one writer or two, and until I do, I don't know if I could ever trust another note."

Jason's face grew pensive. "If you receive *another* note, bring it to me."

"That's what Quinn said."

"Bring it to me first!" His chin was tight.

Lacy saw his hand come up, and she knew he would rake his hair. For a split second, she was mesmerized and charmed by his predictable actions. Coming back to herself, she said, "I'm glad your father is stable enough for you to return. If there is nothing more, I'll be at my desk. I'll bring that note in."

"Don't bother. I'll come by your desk later for it. Quinn told me that questioning those who were arrested on the quarry top hasn't brought any answers about Chloe's whereabouts. Forner and his friend seem to be pretty confident they'll be released soon."

"Wonder why that is?" she asked almost immediately.

His mouth twisted into a wry smile. "Quinn's checking into it."

*

The next couple of days went by slowly, and the few communications she had with Quinn Darling were short. He kept telling her everything takes time. He did mention in an off-handed manner that he'd arranged to have Jimmy Forner and Raman Alvernez transferred to a jail in Lansing. They were charged with stalking, attempted murder, and kidnapping. "It might be a tad overkill, but it'll keep them behind doors until we need them. Kidnapping puts them under federal jurisdiction, at least for the present."

Word reached her through Vicky, Quinn's secretary, that Judge Shaw had stormed into Quinn's office, ranting about Quinn's strong-arm tactics with prisoners. He claimed Quinn didn't have enough evidence to keep them on kidnapping and would leave the city open for a law suit.

When Lacy and Vicky accidentally met in the grocery store, Vicky was livid. "Shaw demanded they be returned to Gladden Hills. I want to tell you, my jaw dropped a mile. I hope Mr. Darling isn't in a lot of trouble. I've never seen the judge so angry!"

"What did Quinn say to all that?" asked Lacy, unable to help herself.

"He said it was out of his hands. That the lady in question had made out the charges with the chief of police."

"Lady in question," Lacy said slowly. "Guess that would be me."

The women laughed together, but Lacy sobered after leaving the store, sensing the mounting of a big storm that she was squarely in the middle of.

The weather had been incredibly warm, teasing people into thinking an early summer was on the way. When Lacy arrived home after work, a surprising phone call came in from Morgan Streeter. "How about a picnic lunch tomorrow at River Park, completely on me? Daffodils are blooming, and the ducks and swans are setting up housekeeping. The park is officially open as of last week. All we have to do is show up."

"I don't know, Morgan. Things are pretty crazy. A lot has happened lately."

"Yeah, I heard about that nastiness at the quarry. Girl, you're going to have to change your profession. I worry about you."

"I worry about me sometimes too," she said, chuckling.

"It's lunch, Lacy...maybe an hour and a half at most. If you don't tell your boss, he won't even know you're gone. I'll come by and pick you up about 11:30 a.m. If we hurry, we'll get a good table before the squirrels. It will clear out the cobwebs of the last week." His humor was infectious.

"You know, Morgan, going on a picnic might be what I need about now," she added, remembering Jason's scowling face.

"I guarantee it! Tomorrow at 11:30 p.m. Wear something comfortable. Good night, Gorgeous."

Lacy walked into the kitchen where the opened windows allowed the illusion of fair weather to continue. A cold front was reported on its way. Everyone in town was rushing to take advantage of every sunny moment. It had been a rash move, agreeing to share a picnic with Morgan, but the pressures of the investigation, added to the fear of attacks, had brought her almost to the breaking point.

The continued tension between her and Jason since their confrontation on Monday morning had a bearing on her impulsiveness. They passed in the hall with barely a nod, giving Lacy a feeling of isolation. Her sense of belonging was falling away. Maybe it was good she was planning to return to

Chicago. Confusion plagued her. Was Jason offended because she hadn't told him about the quarry incident when they'd spoken that night on the phone? She couldn't discern what his problem was, but the tenuous situation was suffocating her. She needed some space. Morgan's invitation offered a respite, and she'd grabbed at it without pausing to consider much of anything.

On hindsight, she now wished she could have a redo. Lacy wanted God's best for her life, and she basically knew Morgan was not of the same mind. Where had her thoughts been? Was she flirting with disobedience just by having lunch? And she didn't want to lead Morgan on and give him the wrong opinion. She sighed. *I know I want someone in my life to pray with as well as laugh.* It was time to set her priorities. If only the case would break.

When Lacy arrived at the office, everything was humming with the printing of the paper. In a new world of technology, the people of Gladden Hills still wanted their small-town newspaper. Maxine was overseeing everything like a mother hen. The one element missing was Jason.

When Lacy questioned Maxine, the busy woman looked around. "He was here earlier…I don't know, Lacy. He must have gone out at some point. Usually he checks in with me."

Frustrated, Lacy heaved a sigh. She had planned to talk to him about how stressful the workplace had been of late. She was determined to get some answers. She'd never been the type of person to allow things to simmer. A lack of patience, her mother had often said, "That's your trouble." Whatever it was, their conversation would have to wait.

"Maxine, I'm leaving early for a luncheon date with Mr. Streeter. I might be a little late. My phone's on."

Someone approached the major general about that time, and Lacy waved and turned away.

Attired in dressy jeans and a colorful jacket, Lacy flipped her rich, mahogany hair outside of her collar and grabbed her purse before hurrying through the front lobby. Morgan was parked out front waiting. He jumped out of the car and rushed around to open her door. She grinned up at him. "Where did you learn to open a woman's door? I thought that was something in my grandmother's day."

"Not according to my mother. She tried her best to civilize me, poor woman." He laughed. "Maybe if she'd lived longer…"

When Lacy was situated, he pulled gently out into traffic as if he thought she might break if he lurched the car too fast. Morgan's mood was bright and shiny like the weather. He talked more than she had ever heard him. He talked about funny situations with some of his clients. He even made her laugh at a story about Cindy, how she had embarrassed herself by snubbing a wealthy, would-be client because she mistakenly took him for a janitor.

"He was dressed in clean, but shabby, comfortable clothes and Cindy assumed wrongly about his station in life." Morgan's laughter was full and free. "Cynthia practically ordered the poor devil out of the building until she discovered he was a billionaire. The man was waiting for an appointment with me. It took me fifteen minutes to convince him to stay. Cynthia slobbered all over herself. It was beautiful!" He brought his fingers to his lips.

Lacy bit her lip to stay her laughter. Cindy had always been a snob. Lacy knew it wasn't nice to gossip and tear someone down, no matter how much she disliked the woman. But it didn't matter. Morgan was full of stories today, and he bridged one to another. Lacy wondered if he'd been drinking prior to picking her up. His next statement caused her more concern. "I brought some chilled wine...just in case you should decide to join me." He shot her a sassy look and grinned.

It was no more than a couple of miles to River Park. It was such a beautiful area with early flower beds radiant with color. Weddings and senior pictures were often staged within the park area. The last time she had been here, Stevie had been with her and her family. Her head swiveled from side to side, devouring it all with her eyes.

"Nice, isn't it?" said Morgan, his mellow voice blending with the rustling wind in the trees branches. They'd lowered their windows to drink in the freshness of spring in its grandest display.

The place Morgan chose was somewhat secluded. There weren't many picnickers this early in the season. They parked on the road and loaded up with bags and drinks before navigating the steep incline down to the valley area around the river. Its wild beauty took Lacy's breath away as they neared the table, a perfect setting for their picnic.

Morgan set their food on the table. Lacy watched, amazed to see him lay out a plastic tablecloth. "Hurry, use the bags to anchor the cloth before it blows away," she cried.

They rushed, grabbing things as the wind tried to carry away plates and lighter objects. By the time everything was grounded, they both were laughing at their frantic actions. It felt so good to let loose and laugh freely.

"Thanks for asking me, Morgan. This is fun. I love picnics."

"Then we shall do our best to make sure there are many more of them," he said, reaching for her hand. Discreetly she withdrew her fingers from his grasp, reluctant to respond to his comment. She refused to lie to the man about their chances for further interaction and vowed to enjoy this short time, then put it behind her. There was no reason to spoil the nice lunch Morgan had gone to so much trouble to plan.

When the sandwiches were laid out, she bowed her head, fully expecting Morgan to silently mock her. Surprisingly, he bowed his head in a respectful gesture and waited for her to say a simple blessing. She shot him an approving glance. Perhaps there was a chance of Morgan becoming a Christian. That would drastically alter their chances for a relationship.

"Let's eat while everything is fresh. I've coffee in the thermos and cups and fixings in the bag," said Morgan, his excitement matching that of a little boy at his very first picnic. He took three sandwiches out of the bag. "When I ordered the picnic lunch, Wendy told me you liked the fresh turkey and the Rueben, so I bought both. Take your pick." He placed the remaining sandwich on his weighted-down paper plate. The wind tossed their hair and voices playfully back and forth.

Every bite was pure nectar. Lacy had forgotten how good it was to eat outside after a long, confining winter. Her ringing phone was an irritant—definitely an unwelcome intrusion. "Sorry Morgan. It's an occupational hazard, especially on press day." She laughed, trying to make lighter of the situation than she felt.

"Hello," she hollered into the phone, to be heard over the wind. She stood and walked a good distance from the table and stuck her finger in her ear in order to hear. As she listened, her face contorted into various expressions. "It's happening right now?" Her heart raced in excitement. "Warrants for both the bank and his house. You are going to arrest who?" she whispered so Morgan couldn't hear. "Well, that's a shock! How does he fit in?"

Although surprising, it made sense as Jason carefully explained to her how Judge Shaw was implicated up to his eyebrows. The money trail led from Heywood to him. "He was the connection to the courthouse, taking a percentage to keep the law away!"

Lacy had had her suspicions but never found any proof. Evidently Quinn had. Shaw's involvement would account for the missing evidence during the Turner investigation, not to mention criminals being released too quickly. She wondered if Shaw had any actual part in the Turner bombing.

Without additional evidence, she knew neither Shaw nor Heywood could actually be tied to the bombing. Unfortunately, a belated memory of an eight-year-old kid wouldn't carry much weight. "No kidding." Her face blanched in shock. "Shaw arranged for the quarry to be deserted on Friday a week ago?" She repeated the spoken words slowly, careful to keep Morgan from seeing the anger in her face until she could gain control.

Turning back, she shot Morgan a smile to reassure him everything was fine, which it wasn't. She continued to listen, debating whether to tell Morgan about his uncle's arrest. *Perhaps he would take it better from me.* Silently, she mourned for their lost picnic. Things would never be the same after this day. She almost wished Jason had waited to call her.

His demanding question irritated her.

"Where am I now? Didn't Maxine tell you?" She covered her mouth, whispering. Looking around, she told him about her picnic lunch. "Yes, I said I was with Morgan. Yesterday, he asked me out on a picnic." It gave her pleasure to tell Jason she was out with someone who appreciated her.

Sensing Morgan coming up behind her, she raised her voice. "Okay, boss, I'll take care of that as soon as I get back to the office." She spoke the words for Morgan's benefit. "Now, can I get back to my picnic?" She listened to Jason's noncommittal comment. "Good-bye." She closed down her phone and took one half of her sandwich from Morgan's extended hand. "Thank you," she said, wondering if she should hold off telling him about Heywood and Shaw.

"We can't let it get stale," he said. "Wendy would never forgive us. She thinks the sun rises and sets on you. I don't blame her. You caught my eye as soon as you hit town." He walked over next to the tree, only a few feet from the raging river.

"From what I hear, every woman catches your eye." She laughed.

Morgan spun about. "That's not true, at least not in the way most people think. I've dated a lot. That's no secret. None were worth a second date except Cynthia. She is smart and ambitious, like me. Together we made a good team."

"I believe she thinks a lot of you, Morgan. She may even love you. At first I thought Cindy was only being possessive, but now I believe it's something more."

Morgan lowered his head. She couldn't see his eyes, but she waited. Something told her that Morgan was dealing with his own emotions.

"Cynthia and I have a unique business relationship, and for a while had something deeper. That was before you returned to Gladden Hills." Their eyes met as he raised his head. "You're one of a kind, Lacy Cottrell."

Trying to determine if he was sincere, she said, "Come on, Morgan, everyone is unique or special in some sense. And, as you should know, looks are strictly short term and surface at best." She stared off in the direction of the river while finishing her sandwich.

"I'm not talking about appearances, Lacy. Your drive for integrity caught my attention. Why do you think your first article moved an entire town to rally around a family in danger of losing their farm? They could see that family through your eyes. They saw that you not only cared, but you were trying to preserve their dignity. It's rare that a reporter will consider the feelings of others over a more sensational storyline. That's what began drawing me to you. I need someone like that in my life." A bitter line formed on his mouth, as if something unpleasant had filled his thoughts.

She frowned. "Morgan, I don't understand your thinking. Your Uncle Heywood took you under his wing, so to speak. Seeing the potential in you, he sent you to law school, then helped you become established in Gladden Hills." Whatever else Conrad Heywood was, Lacy gave him kudos for helping a young boy fulfill his dream. It was commendable, and she hated that very soon Morgan would hear about his uncle's arrest.

Morgan's face twisted into an angry expression. "Oh, yeah, dear Uncle Heywood saw potential in me all right. I was the leader of a street gang, robbing and maiming kids my own age." Morgan inhaled swiftly, as if he'd caught himself from saying something he shouldn't.

Lacy interrupted. "But he took you out of all that."

His expression turned dark and thoughtful. "Yes, he took me out of all that." Morgan walked away from her. "And here I am in Gladden Hills, where I had the good fortune to meet you. There is real goodness in you. I've seen it. Goodness that is rare. My mother had it, but she died when I was still young. I think she might have been like you. You reach out to people just for the sake of helping them, not for any gain."

Embarrassed, Lacy swallowed the last bite of her sandwich, feeling it stick in her throat. She walked back to the table to take a drink. How could she respond to Morgan's sterling description of her? Swiveling back to him, she prayed for wisdom in her words.

"Stop it, Morgan. It makes me feel like such a hypocrite. Any goodness you *believe* you have witnessed in my life is due to my relationship to Jesus Christ. And, up until a short time ago, those qualities weren't evident, at least to my family. Coming out of college, I tunneled my sights straight for the top. Achieving a position on a big name newspaper, I worked around the clock and bought a fancy car."

She crossed her arms and looked up at the trees bulging with buds. Any day they'd burst out in full leaves, their green bright with the freshness of new life—a lot like the turn her life had taken.

She turned toward Morgan. "Of course, I had little time for my wonderful parents or cousin. Ask Kelly. She and I had become almost strangers. In my time off, I was lonely, miserable, and thought only of myself.

And like you, I came here—invited, so to speak, where God had a wake-up call waiting for me. He gave me a clear look at what I'd become. It wasn't pretty. I discovered Jesus was what was missing in my life." She fidgeted. This was personal stuff she was sharing.

She locked onto Morgan's gaze. "It wasn't until I repented of my selfish living, and yielded the controls of my life back over to Him, that God began to form the good things in my life that you claim to have noticed. So don't put me up on a pedestal, Morgan. I'm a sinner saved by grace—nothing else." She expected Morgan to scoff.

His face went passive. It was hard to tell what he was thinking. Morgan inserted his hands in his pockets, forcing a laugh. "I haven't heard anything like that since my mother used to preach to me in grammar school. Later my father beat any thoughts of a loving God out of my mind. I learned my lessons well on the street." He rose up and down on the balls of his feet.

"Then along came Conrad. He talked my dad into letting him be my guardian. A case of booze and a little money slipped on the side and Dad would sell his own mother, but hey, it kept me out of jail." He chuckled at this statement. Lacy felt awkward, hearing the underlying sadness beneath the sophisticated amusement in his tone. "So you see, two years in military school, then college and law school made me into the man I am today," he said. Suddenly, he smiled brightly, the kind of smile that normally would have drawn her into its warmth. Instead Lacy felt chilled to the bone.

She turned to the river and walked to the tree, where she could feel the stiff breeze emanating from its raging force. As every year, the spring rains swelled its banks.

The light mood of their picnic was now only a memory. Morgan's openness had revealed a darkness in his life that had shaken her. Was it possible that he might turn toward the Lord? He had reached a plateau of success in his profession and was wishful for something better. The thought gave her hope.

"There's a stimulating feeling of power in that river," said Morgan, standing behind her. His voice held an element of rising excitement, as if he was personally drawing from the river's power. It bothered her on some level of consciousness. They were several feet from the river, but too close for Lacy's comfort. She tried to back up, but her foot faltered on the uneven ground. Morgan stepped up quickly to steady her, his strong hands grabbing her shoulders.

Morgan's breath was warm on the back of her neck. It was filled with all the fragrance of his recent sandwich—the onions, the chicken, mayo…chicken salad! The pressure of Morgan's vise-like hands gripping her shoulders and the overwhelming odor of chicken salad threw her emotions back to the stairway in the courthouse and her attacker.

Lacy gasped out, "It was you! You tried to kill me at the courthouse!"

Morgan spun her to face him, and his horrified expression loomed close. "No! Don't you see? I saved you that day. I didn't throw you over the railing."

Lacy recalled how his brute force had at first propelled her toward the railing. Then he'd stopped and almost, as an afterthought, pushed her off to the side, down the stairs.

"I was supposed to kill you, but I couldn't. You've got to believe me! I wanted you to live—for me. It was me who called the police to save you on top the quarry. He wanted you dead, not me." Morgan wagged his head helplessly.

Lacy's brain raced to connect the dots. She was remembering, months ago, the mysterious death of the former DA. "Did you kill Ralph Wagner?" she screamed out.

Her accusation took him aback for a second. He looked down on her as if she'd asked a ridiculous question. "I had no choice. He holds my past as leverage, and I had my orders. Wagner had been prying around in the old courthouse files. He wouldn't tolerate that."

His face twitched. "Remember, I warned you to leave Gladden Hills. I was trying to warn you away from him. He has been behind everything, but nothing can ever be proved. You see that, don't you, Lacy? He's much too clever. He's so sure he's covered all his tracks. So clever he is. But I've finally got something on him—something that will give me power. Power to live my life like a normal person, not like some mafia family Don," he said bitterly.

Is he talking about Heywood? Lacy wondered, trying to wrest away from him. But Morgan's hands held her firm with a steel-like grip. His thumb was pinching her arm almost to the bone. "You do see, don't you? You have to!" He shook her so hard her head hurt. His features were like stone.

"Let me go, Morgan!" she screamed.

"Not until you tell me you understand. That's why I told you all these things. So you would understand. I care about you, Lacy. You're the first woman I've ever…"

Lacy tore one arm free. "Let me go, Morgan. Please! If you care about me…" Her panicked words carried on the wind as Morgan grabbed her free arm.

"Let her go, Streeter!" Jason's voice roared from the top of the incline where their cars were parked. His revolver was directed at Morgan's head.

Pulling Lacy around in front of him, Morgan backed up to the edge of the muddy, swollen river. "Hold it, Gardner, I'm not hurting her. We were just talking, having a nice picnic," he shouted, continuing to back up. "There's no need for any guns here."

Lacy stared up at the road. Beside Jason was Frank Hammond, driver of the tan pickup, his cowboy hat giving the illusion of a scene from an old Western. They stood, legs apart, with pistols in hand. Behind them to the side was Jerome. He looked nervous but determined to do whatever was necessary.

Jason started sidestepping down the steep incline, the revolver now in his right hand, still aimed at Morgan. "Streeter, Mr. Hammond is from the FBI, and he has a warrant for your arrest. Your uncle, Conrad Heywood, and others were arrested earlier on forgery and embezzlement charges. It seems you were on the payroll as well. Step aside from Miss Cottrell. Put your hands up, and we'll do this nice and neat."

Lacy wanted to scream out that Morgan was a murderer, but she was afraid of making matters worse. He hadn't released his grasp on her arms and kept pulling her closer to the rim of the river. Whenever she attempted to brace her feet, he'd jerk her, dragging her across the rough ground.

"Listen up! I'll toss her in, Gardner. Don't push me. Just back up," he threatened. "All I want is time to get to my car and I'll let her go. It was never my intention to harm her, but I will do what I have to do to get away. Do we understand one another?"

"It's not my call, Streeter. Mr. Hammond here is in charge. I'm only along for the ride. But just to let you know, I'm a whale of a good shot. Let her go. It ends here. You can't get away." Jason's features hardened like granite, his voice smooth as cold steel. "Think about this, Morgan. The instant after you push her in that river, you're a dead man! Weigh the odds."

Morgan quit pulling her. He stood still and glared back at Gardner. "I like to make my own odds, Paper Man. Now back up, or your ace reporter takes a spring dip. You better hope she's a strong swimmer. That river has an iron current, and the twisted limbs beneath the surface are lethal. Deaths are recorded every spring." He laughed harshly. "I don't figure I have much to lose." Morgan was making his stand a challenge.

Lacy's vision blurred for an instant. She forced herself to concentrate. This was her life! Feeling his grip loosen on her arm, she noted Morgan's focus center on the two men. In that instant, Lacy saw her chance. Yanking her right arm away, she stamped brutally hard on his instep and jabbed her turned-in elbow straight back in his chest. Defensive instruction from the old correspondent in Chicago was serving her well.

The surprise of her actions and the sharp jab to his chest disengaged his firm grasp. Lacy jerked away from him and ran toward Jason and Frank Hammond. Morgan looked around for a direction to escape until he saw an armed officer coming across the park from the left. The officer's presence had gone unnoticed during Morgan and Jason's confrontation. Morgan was blocked in and out numbered.

Inclining his head, he raised his hands in surrender. When Frank Hammond pulled his arms behind him to handcuff, Morgan grunted, his mouth twisted in suppressed fury. Jerking his head toward Jason, who was moving toward Lacy, he called out, "Are you on the level about Heywood? Did you really get the goods on him?" Morgan seemed more interested in Heywood's arrest than his own.

After cinching up the cuffs, Hammond nudged Morgan in the direction of the incline toward the cars on the upper ridge. He was reading him his rights as they passed Lacy, who was now standing with Jason and Jerome.

No one talked. The air around them was charged with a torrent of emotions. Lacy was having a hard time absorbing everything. As one thought rushed to the surface, she broke away from Jason and Jerome to race across to where Hammond was marching Morgan up to the vehicles on the rim.

Jerome reached out in an effort to stop her, but Jason stayed him with a shake of the head. They watched her with interest.

"Frank, wait up a minute," she called, her breath coming in short puffs as she reached their side.

Hammond jerked Morgan to a standstill.

Morgan's eyes drank in her features like a drowning man. "Hi there, Beautiful. Forgive the theatrics. I would never have thrown you into that river." He flashed his cocky smile, and Lacy thought of the little boy whose mother had died and left him with an abusive father, only to have Heywood turn him into a professional killer.

"Morgan, I need to know. Did you mean that part about having something solid on Heywood? We need evidence to connect him to the Turner bombing seventeen years ago. If you've got something—anything?" she pleaded.

His laugh was chilling. "That was supposed to be my ticket to freedom, isn't that a kicker? But if it will stick it to the old boy, hey, it will be worth the show. Why not? Come closer."

When Lacy shot Hammond a questioning glance, he nodded.

Stepping next to him, Lacy tilted her head near his. Morgan lowered his mouth to her waiting ear and whispered a series of instructions.

"Good luck, Beautiful," he said, softly brushing her cheek with a kiss. "Guess I won't see you for a while. You were never in my league anyway." He looked up toward Jason, who had walked up behind her, and aimed a devilish grin his way. Straightening, he allowed Hammond to move him forward.

When she turned away, she became aware of Jerome and Jason by her side. Lacy was dying to know why Jerome was there but decided her curiosity had to wait. "We *have* to get to Cynthia Bradford's house."

Eyeing her quizzically, Jason looked to Jerome. "Take Lacy's keys and drive her car back to their house. You and Kelly can wait for us there." He turned to her. "You ride with me to Cindy's."

They raced up the hill and down the park road to Jason's Durango. "We had to park away so Streeter wouldn't see the cars drive up."

Once they were on the road, Lacy rubbed her arms. The warm, spring day was growing damp. Either that, or the disappointment of finding out Morgan was her attacker was having a chilling effect. "You know, he really had a bum rap most of his life," she said in Morgan's defense.

Jason's face hardened. "Quit making excuses for him. He could have killed you, Lacy. All of us have dark places in our past and difficult choices in our life. He made the wrong ones. What happens when we get to Cynthia's house?"

Lacy nodded, knowing he was right. Still, she experienced a special sadness for Morgan. She forced herself to think of the task ahead. "Morgan hid something in her backyard. It's in a place she wouldn't easily find."

Wondering how they could retrieve the hidden package, Lacy asked, "If Cindy happens to be home, what do you think our chances are of her willingly turning the evidence over to us?" Seeing his grimace, she chuckled. "My sentiments exactly!"

Jason exhaled. "We could get a warrant, but it will take time, and Hammond is busy dealing with Streeter. Quinn is tied up with the arrests from this morning, and Shaw is under arrest. I could try asking her nicely."

Lacy grew thoughtful. "No, don't ask her for anything. You go to the front door and talk to her as the owner of the *Gazette.* Ask for her reaction upon learning that her partner, Morgan Streeter, has just been arrested for his part in illegal dealings in Gladden Hills. I'll take care of the rest."

"Do I want to know what you're planning?" he asked, bringing heat to Lacy's face.

"No," she replied softly.

As it worked out, it proved to be much simpler than they expected. When no one answered the door after repeated tries, Jason walked back to the

Durango, and Lacy moved out silently from behind the car into the driveway next door where she had visited a couple days earlier.

Walking boldly to the side door, she rang the bell, relieved when Helen answered the door quickly. Lacy smiled. "Helen, I need your help. I have to go into your backyard just one more time. I wouldn't ask if it wasn't terribly important. I promise to only be a very few minutes."

The old woman seemed to sense this time was different. "That's fine, dear. I'm sure it's important," she said with a curious look.

Lacy felt like hugging the woman. As soon as the door closed, Lacy hurried to the wooden fence and through to the carefully sodded yard. Edging over to the hedge dividing the lot line between the two houses, she came to the vine-covered gate, hoping she could access it without notice.

Lacy touched on a latch that gave way when pushed. As the gate swung open, she maneuvered slowly into the Bradfords' backyard. She stood in place, listening for unfriendly sounds, like protective dogs or shrill yelling from former childhood acquaintances. Gaining a small amount of confidence, she tiptoed further, each step with trepidation. Seeing the overgrown path to the garden, she kept her footfalls light and moved swiftly.

The Bradfords' flower and vegetable garden was in shambles. Without Mrs. Bradford's loving hands tending and pruning, the perennials had grown wild and entangled, causing her to recall Morgan's words, *"Cynthia never goes near the garden."* Lacy stared at the daisies, a lump forming in her throat. Memories of Stevie picking her a bouquet from this very garden hit her like a mallet. She'd always said daisies were like sunshine on a cloudy day. They made everything bright.

Pressing her thoughts back to her mission, she cautiously moved through to the angel birdbath and knelt at the base. Pushing the cement structure free from its muddy base, she lifted a black vinyl case from beneath, allowing the birdbath to fall back to its resting place. Standing, she made her way back, wiping her shoes and the vinyl case on the wet grass. Although confident the yard bushes provided good coverage, Lacy kept a sharp eye on the path.

Slipping the vinyl case in the back of her slacks, she pulled her jacket over the top and stepped carefully back down the path toward the hedge. Her gaze went to the back door of the Bradford house, where the heavy curtains kept their own secrets. Lacy prayed they would keep hers as well. Spinning on her heel, she dashed back to the hedge gate and leaped through to the other side. When she turned to retrace her way from the backyard, she spotted the small face of Helen watching her from the window. She waved, and Helen waved back.

Opening the window, Helen gestured with her finger. "You better hurry, Miss Cottrell. She comes home about this time every day."

Lacy laid a finger to her lips and Helen nodded. Hurrying through to the driveway, Lacy darted across the street to the Durango and hopped in the front seat. "Let's get out of here. Helen says Cindy will be home any minute."

"Helen? You have an accomplice in the next-door neighbor?"

"She's a sweetie. She won't say a thing. Go!" She wasn't anxious for another encounter with Cindy anytime soon. As Jason drove, Lacy pulled out the black vinyl case and opened it. Inside was a type of journal. She leafed through the pages, afraid to believe what she was looking at. Staring over at Jason, she said hoarsely, "It's Clem Browning's client book! If Heywood's name is in here..." Her mind raced like a runaway colt.

Jason's foot pushed his gas pedal to the floor. "We've got to get this to Quinn. Call Kelly and Jerome and tell them we'll be late."

Lacy had been running on adrenaline so long, it was inevitable she would crash at some point. But she'd ignored all warning signs that it was near. They reached Quinn's office at a dead run. Vicky was just collecting her things to leave for the day. She announced they were waiting and bid them good night, her curious look lingering on their backs even as she closed the door. Lacy supposed that Vicky could write a book on what she'd heard over the time span she'd worked in the DA's office.

Quinn thrust open the door and gestured them inside. His hair looked as if his fingers had ravaged it more than once, and his shirt sleeves were badly wrinkled. "What do you two want? I heard you rounded up Streeter. Frank Hammond told me he came like a lamb. I wouldn't have figured that. I'd measured him more of a fighter. I guess you can't tell with some of them."

Lacy kept her thoughts to herself and waited for an opening.

"All right. What do you have for me?" Quinn looked from one to the other impatiently.

Lacy handed over the book. "Clem Browning's client book. Morgan told us where to find it."

Quinn worked his mouth. "Morgan Streeter told you where to find it? I have to wonder why he gave it up without trying to work a deal for a shorter sentence. Especially with him being a lawyer? It doesn't figure. It's an anomaly that doesn't fit." His fingers attacked his nearly black hair.

Lacy sighed, feeling completely played out. She leaned on Quinn's desk. "I don't think Morgan cares what happens to himself. Things he said to me at the park gave me some insight. He despises Conrad Heywood! I believe that it is more important to him that Heywood gets punished. It seemed to rankle him that Heywood was so proud of covering his tracks in his illegal transactions. Morgan is dissatisfied with his life." She walked the distance of Quinn's office and stood staring at his picture on the wall.

Quinn eyed her strangely. "He shared all that?"

She answered without turning. "In one way or another."

Jason and Quinn exchanged glances. Quinn rubbed his chin. "Streeter got to you. They said he has a way with the ladies."

Lacy didn't rise to Quinn's bait.

Strangely, it was Jason who commented, "Morgan has a fixation on our lady here. I heard some of the comments he made about the stairs incident at the courthouse. He went against Heywood's orders to kill her. The guy's conflicted, definitively unbalanced, and more dangerous than she realized. Her heart is too soft." When he glanced in Lacy's direction, she swiveled to meet his angry eyes. "At some point Lacy should be debriefed." His glare never wavered from her gaze. She dropped her eyes to the gray-flecked carpet.

Lacy wasn't ready to be interrogated. She was exhausted, and her emotions were raw. Seeing the real Morgan at the park was so sad, it had weighed her soul with a depression she couldn't shake. Her prayers would center on him for a long time.

"We'll set up a time in the next two days for a debriefing, so stay flexible, Cottrell. Is that all?" Quinn drilled them with a piercing gaze.

She met him eye to eye. "Not really. What about Chloe? I haven't heard a word about finding her yet. Did they search Heywood's complex?"

Lacy had visions of the poor girl lying dead somewhere, meeting the same fate as Clem Browning in prison, or the former DA, Ralph Wagner. Why hadn't they found her yet?

"The searching will continue. They searched Heywood's home, his guest house and the barn, as well as all the outbuildings, and found nothing but those files you took pictures of in his private office."

Lacy rubbed her neck. What had she heard that was troubling her now? What couldn't she remember? "Tell me where they searched again."

Quinn studied her with interest, repeating what he'd just said until she halted him.

"That's it. The other guest house. They searched the guest house behind the main house, right?" Not waiting for a reply, she raced on. "Did they search the second guest house? There are two of them," she said excitedly.

"I wasn't aware there were two. Where is the second one located?"

"Morgan told me there was a cabin back somewhere in Heywood's woods. If there's even a chance she could be there, Quinn…"

He wrinkled his nose. "Don't count on it, Lacy. If nothing else, Heywood was careful about protecting his image. It would be pretty stupid having that girl confined on his property. It's out of character for him. He always lined someone else up for the fall. Look at what he did to Eric Greer. At face value it looked as if Greer was the one doing the embezzling, just like seventeen years ago when he set up Rod Corbin for the Union fund shortage. I don't think so."

She walked toward him, her hands balled into fists. "Desperate people do rash things out of character. They don't think clearly. We've been putting pressure on him lately. Where else could he stash her? This is a small community where people notice comings and goings."

Quinn sighed and reached for the phone. "Okay, it's worth a try, but I hate to make this call. My guys have been at it all day and are dead on their feet. It's been a long day. If a life wasn't involved..." He looked over at Jason and jammed a thumb toward the door. "Take her home, and both of you get some rest. I'll let you know how this turns out."

Jason nodded. "How long do you think you'll be here at the office? I may call later."

Quinn yawned. "Hopefully not long. I'd like to start packing a few things in advance. It'll help me get ready to leave without all the frantic last-minute details." He waved them off. "Get out of here."

In the elevator down to the first floor of the new legal building, Lacy asked, "What did Quinn mean about getting ready to leave? Is he taking a trip after everything is wrapped up?"

The door opened on the elevator. Jason sidestepped the question and ushered her out. "We better hurry, or Kelly and Jerome will be frantic."

One step outside of the building and they were bracing the strong breezes of a playful spring day turned cold and vindictive. The entire distance to the Durango, they found it difficult to keep their footing. Lacy forgot her question about Quinn in the battle against the fierce wind. All the way home, she prayed that somehow, somewhere, they would find Chloe still alive. If not the cabin in Heywood's woods, then perhaps Heywood would bargain for a better deal with Chloe's life. Lacy tried not to worry but to trust God.

When Lacy and Jason stepped through the threshold entering the warm kitchen, Lacy noticed that all the windows were closed up tight. The inviting aroma of some kind of soup simmering on the stove was like a welcome home hug. Kelly placed a dishrag on the counter and turned to stare, as did Jerome, who was nursing a cup of coffee at the table. The silence was like a wall that Lacy found hard to break through. But she needn't have worried, because Kelly dashed across the room, flinging her arms around her.

"When I told Jerome you were lunching with Morgan at the park, both of us were uneasy that there was no back-up for you, so Jerome went in search of Jason." She gushed everything out in one sentence, causing Lacy to chuckle. She held her cousin an extra second longer than normal.

Then, pulling away, Lacy said, "As it turned out, that was a good thing. I guess it was another of those God things, huh?" She was so tired, her legs began to buckle.

Jason grabbed her around the waist until her legs steadied. "Let's get you to a chair. A cup of that coffee wouldn't hurt either."

Kelly dashed to the coffee counter and filled a waiting cup. Over soup and warm bread, Jason filled Kelly and Lacy in on what all had occurred. Jerome had already told Kelly about the scene at the river in the park.

"What did Morgan say in his defense? It's hard to believe he was actually in cahoots with Heywood on the embezzling." Kelly looked doubtful.

Lacy clasped her hands together in front of her plate. "I think Morgan had other duties than the accounting end. He may have benefited from the thefts at the bank, but Heywood had singled him out for a specific purpose." She couldn't think on the anguish of it now, instead choosing to dwell on Conrad Heywood's treachery.

"It was Heywood who actually planted the bomb. It had a delayed mechanism. After I went back to Stevie's old place and roamed the property, I recalled seeing Heywood at the Turner home the day before the bombing. That established Heywood at the scene of the crime in a time sequence to have planted the bomb. Stevie and I were in the backyard swinging when Heywood arrived, and he stopped and stared right at us when he left." She shuddered. "Quinn says it gives him an eyewitness against Heywood, and Browning's client book connects him to the bomb maker."

"You were a forgotten witness," mumbled Kelly. "When your family moved, it minimized the possibility of your ever remembering. No wonder the attacks began right after you returned. He couldn't afford to have you recall what you saw as a child. It gives me the creeps. Such a horrid man! And from what you've said about Morgan, like they say, the apple doesn't fall far from the tree! All that evil in one family…"

Lacy pressed her lips together at her cousin's accusing words, thinking back on all Morgan had told her about his difficult past, but she held her tongue, uncertain if she should share.

But her inquisitive cousin stared at her, as if realizing there was more to the story, but that Lacy was finding it difficult to discuss. But as seconds passed, Lacy slowly unraveled what she knew about Morgan. "Morgan was

Heywood's personal assassin—that's true. He was carefully molded for the job. Heywood became Morgan's guardian during his teen years. It all happened very quickly. Heywood made arrangements to become the boy's guardian and whisked him away to some military school out east. Morgan indicated that he'd previously been a gang fighter. I got the feeling Heywood had something on him from that period of his life."

Jason looked thoughtful. "Morgan could have killed a kid in a street fight, and Heywood got wind of it. By getting him out of town and into military school, it probably kept Morgan out of the clutches of the law. He hasn't said much since he was taken into custody. He sits off by himself, brooding."

"Jason, get ahold of Quinn!" Lacy said with alarm. "They should put Morgan on a suicide watch. The kind of mood he was in when he left wasn't normal. He didn't seem to care about anything except Heywood getting convicted. He hates him with a passion!"

"Really?" exclaimed Kelly. "He always seemed so friendly whenever the two were in the same room. Since Heywood is his uncle, I just figured they were a close family."

"Morgan told me he and Heywood were actually cousins. Heywood wanted people to think he was his nephew." Lacy reached for another slice of bakery bread, remembering the sandwiches at the park. "It was the chicken-salad sandwich that clued me in," she said, more to herself than anyone at the table.

"Chicken-salad sandwich?" Jerome questioned before Kelly could speak.

Swallowing the bread, Lacy related the chicken-salad connection to the attack at the courthouse. "It was the one thing I remembered about my attacker—he smelled like chicken salad. Morgan was eating chicken salad in the park today. More than once, Wendy has made comments about Morgan's obsession with the sandwich. I just never made the connection until today by the river. When I smelled chicken salad on his breath, my memories all fell into place and I…well, I accused him on the spot, and everything came apart."

"Morgan was the one who attacked you?" Kelly's tone made it sound like an incredulous statement. But—but he really liked you," she stuttered.

Sheepishness crept across Jerome's face. He glanced at Jason, explaining, "I didn't mention the part about what happened at the river to Kelly. I knew she would freak if she knew Morgan had threatened to throw Lacy in that swollen river. Thought it could wait for later when she saw Lacy was safe and sound with her own eyes."

Lacy smiled over at him. "Thanks, Jerome. You did right." Turning to Kelly, she lifted another piece of bread to her mouth, mumbling, "Morgan did care for me—in his own sad, peculiar way. That's why he didn't throw me over the railing. Remember when I couldn't understand that brief hesitation on the landing during the attack. In essence, he saved my life."

"Oh, yeah! He could have broken your neck," said Kelly.

"To him it was the lesser of the options. He'd been told to kill me—Heywood, I presume. That way Morgan could say he failed. He was also the one who called the police, telling them to hurry up to the quarry top if they wanted to save a life. And that threat at the river was just that…a bluff."

"What about the purple feathers?" Kelly challenged.

Lacy shrugged. "Cindy knew about them. She could have spouted off at some point, but who knows? I'd like to think there were two writers, but I may never know that, either."

Kelly regarded her with tenderness. It appeared as if she wanted to say something but had no words to comfort.

Lacy was unwilling to bear her wounded heart. She'd trusted the writer of the purple feather notes until the episode at the quarry. Now she was afraid to trust him again. Her eyes followed Jason as he rose from the table and went for more coffee. "Jason, what did Quinn mean when he said he was getting ready to leave?"

The corners of his mouth twitched at the ends. He carefully sat back down and sipped an overly full cup. "I was afraid you wouldn't let that comment by Quinn pass." He sighed, acting as if he dreaded what he was planning to say. "I guess you might as well know what will become public knowledge in the days to come. I just ask you to keep it quiet until a public announcement is made by his office. The *Gazette* will get that exclusive," he said, holding Lacy's gaze by the sheer intensity of his own.

Even through the shaded lens, the force of his will gave her pause. Something important was up. "What is all this, Jason?" Her voice rose, sensing an announcement of epic proportions—something that would alter everything important to her. She tried to shake off the heavy feeling of foreboding.

Jason looked at the tabletop still cluttered with supper dishes. "It's been widely stated that Quinn Darling was a temporary District Attorney appointed by the governor of Michigan. In truth, he is a FBI agent investigating the death of Ralph Wagner, the former DA. There were also some unanswered questions dealing with his honor, Harold Shaw, that were under scrutiny. For anyone's information, Quinn did pass the bar a few years back, and was in fact a lawyer before joining the Bureau. While he was here, he planned to look into the cold Turner case. When everything is wrapped up, he'll be heading back to Washington." Jason set his cup down, resting his elbows on the table.

"Who will be the new DA?" asked Kelly.

"A new appointee, I suppose. No one has said." But his answer was evasive, and he didn't meet her eyes.

Lacy studied Jason's placid features. "How long have you known?" *And why did Quinn feel the need to keep me in the dark when we were working so closely together?* Her suspicions mounted as fast as her questions. One thing she knew...Jason was deliberately avoiding looking at her.

He glanced her way only briefly. "About the time I took ownership of the *Gazette.*" His features were locked in stone, like a sphinx.

Leaning across the table, she demanded, "What *aren't* you telling us? How did you come to know about the FBI's plan? They don't usually inform the new owner of the town newspaper, do they?" Little things were beginning to make sense to her. Like why Frank Hammond, later identified as an FBI operative, was working under Quinn. Quinn had called Frank his man.

"As it turns out, I will be leaving town, too," Jason announced. "My real name is James Calhoun." He let the name lay in the air like a suspended balloon with no anchor. When no one spoke, he continued, "Up until a few months ago, I was the assistant District Attorney of Columbus, Ohio. I had been investigating the Turner case on my own time. It caught my attention a few years back as a high-profile case. I knew it would certainly be a big career boost for the one who solved it, so I hired a private investigator to do some work on the side, told him to see if he could stir up any new information. It ultimately got him killed, and I don't take that lightly!" he said tersely, glaring up at no one in particular.

Lacy sat in the closest chair as if lightning had struck her. "*Jake Gibbons*, the P.I. who uncovered Clem Browning as the bomb maker for the Turner home—he worked for you." Her anger fired to explosive proportions. "You knew about this when I came to you for help about the Turner case and never said a word?" She pushed away from the table, rose from her chair, and stalked around to where he sat. "All the time I was trusting you, you couldn't trust me enough to share that important information?" Her eyes spit sparks.

"I had to keep confidences close. As a reporter, you know that!" His hand smacked down on the table. "You came to me for back-up, and that is what I provided! It just so happened we were working on the same case and were able to help each other, Lacy. It accomplished a common goal. Isn't that true?"

Her chest heaved in angry frustration, but she couldn't speak one word against his logic. They *had* both achieved their goal. But inside she felt betrayed, and the trust between them was crushed. "Yes, Mr. Gardner...excuse me, Mr. Calhoun...we both achieved our goal. My reason was personal—a debt fulfilled to a friend. For you, it was *professional*—something to stamp closed on top of a folder. I have to give you credit. You did all that and still fulfilled your commitment. You get a 'well done'!" Her words were sarcastic and sharp. She clapped her hands in applause.

The room turned deathly still as Kelly and Jerome watched in dismay.

"If you feel I owe you any further compensation, please send me a bill. Under the circumstances...I believe it would be better if I considered this my last day at the paper. My month is up in a few days anyway, and next week's column is already in Maxine's hands. It works out well for both of us. You can send my last paycheck to Chicago." As she gazed at his hardened features, tears streamed, unbidden, down her face. "Good-bye Mr. Calhoun." Turning, she fled the kitchen for the comfort of her bedroom.

Rising from his chair, Jason called after her, "Lacy...*Lacy!* We need to talk!"

22

The Exposé

STUMBLING UP THE STAIRS AND DOWN THE HALL, she flung open her bedroom door and slammed it behind her. From the darkness of her mind the word *betrayed* kept spinning in her brain. That was the only word for it. In his everyday silence, Jason had perpetrated a relationship built on a lie. Lacy didn't know this James Calhoun. Had she ever known Jason Gardner? Her deep feelings for him were caught in a turbulent whirlwind. This wasn't the kind, considerate man she'd known—the *trustworthy* man named Jason.

Hearing the front door close, Lacy made her way through her blackened bedroom to the window and peered through the partially opened blinds down at James Calhoun opening the door to his Durango. When he paused and stared up toward her window, she stepped back until she heard the roar of his engine, listening as it disappeared down the quiet street.

Had the gentle touches of his hand upon hers and the occasional longing she'd thought she'd seen in his features been lies, too? Had she only imagined them because of her own longings? It was suddenly blatantly clear: she loved him! She loved Jason Gardner! The awareness alarmed her. *How could I let this happen?* Jason had, for all practical purposes, vanished in the space of a few spoken words, leaving in his wake her brooding anger.

Turning away from the window, she threw herself across the bed, her face wet with the constant drain of tears, her sobs uncontrollable. Hearing a soft knock at the door, she answered with a hiccup, "Yes?"

"Do you feel like company?"

"Not now, Kelly, maybe later. Thanks." She didn't have the will or energy to talk.

Kelly spoke softly. "Jason—James—said he will get with you later. He wants to straighten things out, Lacy. He feels really bad that you were hurt by his deception. Even though he was technically undercover, he was there when you needed him. Remember that, Lacy, and try to understand and forgive."

Lacy could almost hear Kelly's breathing on the other side of the door waiting for a response—a response Lacy couldn't give. Seconds later she heard her cousin's gentle footfalls down the hall and stairs. Lacy rolled over, unable to stop her sobbing.

It was almost 11:00 p.m. when the phone rang, dragging Lacy's sleep-drenched mind to the surface of a heavy fog. She groped for the phone and pushed up against the pillows. Realizing she'd never undressed for bed, she pulled the wrinkled sweater around to the front and groaned, "Y-es. Who is this?"

"Quinn. We found Chloe! Good call, Cottrell. She was in the cabin, drugged, but still alive. She was alone, lying across the bed. Would you believe that not one of the servants in the main house knew anything about that poor girl being kept out in that cabin? The fire was cold, and it didn't look like anyone had been there for hours. They probably ran like rats when the cops arrived to search the estate. Anyway, she's back in the hospital. The doc says she has a good chance of coming around, given time, but she'll be in the hospital for a week or so and then into a rehab center following that. Her real family has been notified."

Lacy awakened enough now to grasp the meaning of his words. "That's wonderful, Quinn! I just had a feeling she was still alive. Thanks for letting me know."

"Yeah, well," he said gruffly. "Actually I asked Jason to call you, but he said it would be better coming from me. What in the heck happened between you two, anyway? He sounded like he'd lost his best friend."

"Don't you mean James Calhoun, Quinn?" she replied stiffly.

"Oh, oo—o," he said slowly. "You know?"

"I know."

"Yeah, well, keep all of this off the record until you hear from James or me and nothing about the Turner case until Saturday, understand? By then we should have things on the way to being wrapped up. There is so much to deal with, and so many people involved. I've talked to the governor. The chief of police has known at some level, but none of his men had any inkling. James will tell you what is on the record and what isn't tomorrow."

Lacy didn't bother telling him that she wouldn't be there tomorrow. Maybe by Saturday, she'd feel up to cleaning out her desk and saying good-bye to Maxine. Tomorrow she only wanted to sulk by herself. "I understand. Thanks again for calling."

"Listen, Lacy. I haven't talked to Wendy yet, and it's too late tonight. I'll call her in the morning. Until then…?" His meaning was clear.

"Don't worry. I won't say anything to her until I know she's spoken with you. Good luck. She's sure going to miss you, Quinn."

There was a moment of silence. "Maybe not," he said, his tone ringing with a mysterious hint of humor. "Good night, Lacy Cottrell. It's been an experience working with you and a delight knowing you. I'll see you before I go, but I have to tell you that I couldn't have put all this together without your help. You're a great investigative reporter! You made the hair on my head raise a few times, but you sure came through. You should be thrilled that the guilty party for the Turner bombing has finally been caught. With eyewitnesses who can vouch they saw Heywood at the Turner place the day before the bombing, and Clem Browning's client book you brought to me, we've nailed him!" There was triumph in his voice.

After her phone call with Quinn ended, Lacy rolled back across the bed, pondering his plural remark about eyewitnesses. Perhaps Cindy had come forward after hearing about Morgan and Conrad's arrest. It would be just like her to try and cover her backside and come out a hero. Instantly, Lacy felt convicted about her peevish attitude. "Forgive me, God. I don't like feeling hateful," she whispered.

Forgiveness was a precious thing, the feeling you've been made right and have peace. Grabbing the comforter, she turned over and went back to sleep. Her clothes would hit the laundry in the morning. She hoped the weather would be as gloomy as her spirit. She had lost more than a friend when James Calhoun had walked out of her house. She'd lost her heart.

Kelly had left the house by the time Lacy stumbled out of bed the next morning. She glanced at the clock in passing toward the bathroom. She could count the number of times in the last year she'd slept until 8:00 a.m. on one hand, and three quarters of them had occurred right here in Gladden Hills. This case had aged her in body and spirit. A long hot shower soothed her tight, aching muscles.

With a towel on her head, she was clad in no more than a huge bath towel when the phone rang. "Hello," she said, slightly irritated to be dripping on her bedroom rug.

"Lacy, Maxine. The boss told me to tell you to hustle in this morning. I'm also to inform you that you've got a special-edition exposé to put together for a Saturday release. That's not much time. How soon can you get here?"

"Maxine," Lacy countered, "you'll have to do it without me. My one-month contract with Jason is up. You also have that advance article for publication this coming week. Hasn't he told you? I'm going back to Chicago." She didn't want to have to explain things to Maxine this way, but she was pushed into a corner. What was Mr. James Calhoun thinking, calling her in like this after last night?

She heard a big sigh issue from Maxine. "I'm sorry to hear that, about Chicago, I mean. I really am. I'd hoped…" Seconds passed. "The thing is, we need you *now*, Lacy. I don't know what this exposé is all about. I've heard rumors, but that's all. I don't have the facts or information. Jason did say that in case you balked at coming in, I was to remind you that your contract stipulates in the case of a special edition or exposé piece, you are *required* to put in extra time, and your contract isn't officially up until the middle of next week—legally speaking," Maxine added, expressing another heavy sigh. It was clear she wasn't happy being the "heavy" in the situation.

Lacy held the phone away from her and stared at it, feeling like she could scream. *Unbelievable!* "Listen, I'm just out of the shower. I'll be in as soon as I can get dressed. You better tell *Jason* that, according to Quinn Darling, he has to lay down the perimeters of what we can print and what we can't print in the exposé."

"I'll tell him, Lacy. See you in a few minutes." Maxine sounded like one confused and nervous major general.

*

When Lacy pulled her car into the back parking lot of the Gladden Hills Gazette building, she saw Maxine standing at the rear door. *I get to use the special door today…my, my!* Maxine appeared anxious for her to arrive. Lacy hurried in, carrying all her notes and research in her briefcase.

Following Maxine through the hallway, she felt excitement building for the assignment. Even her irritation at Jason paled next to this opportunity. Lacy knew it was in her blood to write news like this. News that would right the wrongs done to so many people. Her steps quickened as she neared the offices. Pausing at Jason's office, her hand came up to knock, but Maxine swiftly interrupted.

"He's not in there, Lacy. Mr. Darling called him over to his office for some kind of emergency meeting. He left a few minutes ago, but he told me to give you this. It's your parameters." She looked at Lacy with curiosity. "What's going on with you two? What's wrong, Lacy?"

"Nothing—and everything—is the only way I can describe it right now." She patted the older woman's arm. "It will be okay, Maxine. And now we have a paper to put together in a few hours. Something tells me the presses are going to be running late tonight. I'll be at my desk. Give me a couple minutes before we get started. I need to read this and assemble my notes. Thanks for your help."

She turned to the left where her quiet desk waited for her. It was a desk she'd grown accustomed to and would miss in the weeks to come.

Her eyes strayed to the area where Chloe had sat, deciding she would take time to visit her before leaving town. Had Maxine heard the good news about Chloe? It was a silly question. Jason would definitely have let the woman know. He was considerate in that way.

Swiveling in her chair, Lacy opened the legal-sized envelope and withdrew the folded paper. Flipping it open, she read:

> Lacy, my identity is to remain classified at this point. The governor is going to appoint a new DA this morning. That name will not be released for another week. Center the headlines around the solving of the Turner case. I trust you. Those are your perimeters! Good luck. Jason.

I'll keep your secret, Jason. I don't like it, but I'll keep it. She wondered how Maxine would react when she learned Jason's true identity. Through pressed lips, she considered the way the dear woman adored the new owner. Maxine wouldn't like the fact she hadn't been allowed on the inside of the important case, but she would forgive him. It was different with Lacy.

Deeper, more personal.

Lacy stood and pulled over a long table to lay out her notes. "Maxine, let's get going." She threw the words over her shoulder, surprised to see the woman standing on her left holding a steaming cup of coffee. "Good start. Now help me lay out the headlines, and we'll build the main article around that. There were multiple offenses that Heywood and Shaw were arrested on yesterday, along with Morgan Streeter, " she added somberly.

Neither she nor Maxine stopped for lunch until 1:00 p.m. Lacy offered to walk over to the café to pick up the orders. She wanted to see Wendy. Sliding into a counter stool on the left side where Wendy waited tables, she waited until the perky blond leaned across the counter and set her bag of lunch orders in front of her.

"Working today, I see." Wendy grinned mischievously.

Lacy inclined her head. "Quinn called you." It was a statement.

She lowered her head in a conspiratorial way. "Oh, yeah, that was a call to remember! I liked to fell off my chair. My boyfriend is a G man—imagine that! Whew!" She rolled her eyes, laughing.

Lacy's smile was strained. "I'm sorry about his leaving town. I know the two of you became quite close."

Wendy checked around for listening ears. Her eyes were as bright as Blue-Bonnets in Texas. "Are you ready for this? Quinn wants me to move back to Virginia with him and live with his sister. She has an apartment in her large home. He says I can look for a job there and keep up with my classes. He loves me, Lacy. He wants to marry me." The color rose to her neck and face.

Stunned, Lacy stared at her friend. "Whew is right, girl. I'm speechless!" Laying out the money for the order, she rose slowly from the stool. "I am *so happy* for you. Though I shouldn't be totally surprised after seeing the way Quinn looks at you."

She pulled out a slip of paper. "You already have my cell phone. This is my email. Please keep in touch. You've been a good friend. I don't want to lose you. Friends are important. I wish you every happiness, Wendy." Treasuring friendships was a lesson she was still learning.

Wendy grabbed Lacy's hands. "I'll stay in touch." Her countenance shone with her happiness. Lacy bit back a flash of envy and hung tight to her friend's hands.

The rest of the day was grueling and long. Hour after hour, Lacy wrote and rewrote. She alone knew the nuances of this complicated case—she and Jason, who'd been conspicuously absent for most of the day. He rushed in about 3:30 p.m. looking haggard, as if he'd gotten little sleep. Rushing straight to his office, he closed the door with only a passing nod in her direction.

Forty minutes later he came out of his office and went directly to Maxine, handing her two pages of printed material. Maxine scanned the material and returned her focus to Jason's sober face. She nodded curtly, as if she understood what he wanted. Lacy viewed the incident from across the area, curious and somewhat irritated that she'd been excluded from the conference, but then Jason had proven last night that he had a habit of doing just that. Considering he'd put her in charge of the exposé, why was he now bypassing her on selected material? *Suck it up, Cottrell.* She reminded herself he still owned the paper.

She grimaced and turned back to her computer. When this column was finished, the exposé would be completed. She'd had Maxine pull out pictures to accompany the articles. The hardest picture to deal with was an old family portrait of the Turner family. There was Stevie standing between his parents, Terri and Matthew.

Tears brimmed in her eyes. That off-center grin of his, that special look that told the world, as well as his friends, that he could be counted on, that he had that unusual something extra that God doled out to very few. Stevie stood beside her when she had to explain the purple dye they'd mixed up and spilled in their laundry room. Biting her bottom lip, she placed the picture with the others and moved on.

It was almost 6:00 p.m. when Lacy reached for her coat. She stopped by Maxine's desk, noticing the lines or exhaustion in the woman's face. "Go home, Maxine. Everything's in the works. You've been amazing! I will miss you." Her voice quivered. Her tiredness was showing as well.

Maxine took off her glasses and locked her eyes on Lacy. "You belong here, Lacy Cottrell. You may leave, but a part of you will always remain right here." Her hand rested on Lacy's shoulder. "You come back, you hear?"

Lacy walked from the building feeling as hollow as the sound of her shoes on the tile floor. The thudding of the door closing behind her exit affected her more than she would have ever thought. Would this be the last time she'd ever cross the threshold of the *Gladden Hills Gazette?*

With a heavy spirit Lacy drove home. She and Kelly observed a quiet evening dining on leftover soup. They both knew that this was one of the last several days they'd spend together for quite a while. Lacy planned to return for frequent visits, but it wouldn't be the same, and clearly Kelly felt that as well. Their conversation was light, except for the moment Kelly told her Jerome wanted them to date regularly.

"He told me he was a methodical person who needed to feel as secure in the decisions they would make together as humanly possible. Jerome wants us to know each other in good times and bad before making any serious decisions."

Lacy smiled into her cousin's face. "And what kind of serious decisions might the two of you be considering?"

Kelly turned away, her tell-tale blush telling more than she intended. The quiet night was savored by both women. The next few days would be full and emotional, but they were in no hurry to rush toward them. They watched the embers die slowly in the fireplace and shared more of their childhood moments. Neither wanted to ever forget the strong bond they shared.

*

Aware that the exposé would be distributed all over town by early Saturday morning, Lacy made plans to stay at home. Except for a quick trip into town to pick up the Amish quilt for her coworker in Chicago, Nadine, she spent a quiet Saturday organizing her packing. She would leave by midmorning on Monday if all went well. Taking time out to call Chuck Walden, she found he'd already read a copy of the special edition.

"The thing is, Chuck, I'm heading back to Chicago the first of the week, but I'll be back around Memorial Day. How about a picnic at our place? Bring Johnny Fey and some of your friends. Sorry, there won't be any liquor. Think you can last the day?"

"Good company is sufficient stimulate," he said, laughing. "I'm glad it's finally over…that nasty business about Stevie and his mom, you know. It's bothered me for years. A guy doesn't get many friends like Stevie."

"I know. Without your help, Chuck, I might not be around to celebrate. If it wasn't for you, Johnny Fey, and your friends…" Memories of that frightening time threatened to overwhelm her. For personal reasons, none of the motorcycle group wanted their names mentioned in the paper, and Lacy had honored their request.

"That was quite the editorial write-up about you on the front page, Lacy. Your boss gave you credit for being instrumental in uncovering events that recently came to light. I think that's the way it was worded. He also said you were a great investigative reporter, and the town should be proud of its hometown girl. I gotta tell you…it made me proud to know you, Little Ellie," Chuck said, sounding pretty pleased with all in general.

Lacy could hardly wait for Kelly to come home with a copy of the paper. She pored over the articles, astounded that Jason had written such a sterling write-up of her participation in solving the cold-case murder of Terri and Steven Turner. As Chuck said, Jason had credited Lacy with uncovering key information leading to the embezzling discovery at the bank.

"James Calhoun is quite a writer himself, isn't he?" asked Kelly with a tongue-in-cheek tone.

With her elbows resting on top of the closed paper, Lacy mused on Kelly's comment. It was surprising how well Jason did on the editorial.

"It definitively isn't the first article he's ever written. I find that curious. Tell me, Kelly, why would a district attorney, who takes on the solving of a seventeen-year-old cold-case murder as a cause, go so far as to quit his prestigious job to buy a small-town newspaper as a cover to investigate the case? Can the professional benefits be that high?"

Kelly stared at her. "I don't know. He's obviously good in the paper business. Maybe it's what he's secretly always wanted to do?"

"But he's not staying. He said he was leaving, remember?"

Kelly frowned. "I don't know. Maybe he didn't quit his job in Ohio, but only took a leave of absence like you did? From what Jason said, he and Quinn had already had an understanding before they arrived."

Lacy shrugged. "Maybe…"

"Look, why don't you quit being a detective for long enough to give the guy credit for the wonderful things he wrote about you. If you're curious about those other matters, ask him." She lifted Lacy's elbows off the paper. "Now, if you don't mind, I'd like to finish the rest of the paper. It's your turn to fix supper."

"I know. I'm picking up carry-out from the rib place in town in a half hour." She left the kitchen and went back to packing.

The questions about Jason—James Calhoun—still nagged. She didn't like unanswered questions. Kelly had told her that life was full of them, and she needed to make peace with that fact. It was bad enough leaving Gladden Hills without knowing who had sent her the notes with the feathers, but having to carry the knowledge that only someone close to her and Stevie could possibly have known where the feathers were hidden rankled against her nature. That person was still out there, and the image of Cindy Bradford didn't quite fit the mold. However, stranger things had happened.

She had come to the point of accepting the possibility that the last note might have been a fake. Her small voice kept whispering, *All the others contained a feather from the lunchbox.* Yet it looked as if Lacy would leave without knowing who her secret contact was.

She checked her watch. It was time to pick up the ribs. She'd been half listening all day for the phone. Hadn't Kelly told her that Jason promised to get with her and explain? Maybe he felt his editorial was the best he could do at trying to make up for his deception.

Several people in town had congratulated her for her part in solving the Turner bombing. They all felt as if they had a special interest in that particularly tragic case. It had happened to one of their own families, and the next best thing to having their friends back with them was seeing the guilty parties punished for their deaths. In spite of what Lacy had written, they also seemed to think she had more to do with the arrests than the substitute DA and the FBI agents. Then again, Lacy was one of their own. She thanked them for their kindness, while trying to explain everything was a joint operation. They'd all worked together, including her boss, Jason Gardner.

By bedtime, Lacy had not yet heard from Jason. She reasoned with herself that nothing he could say would erase the feeling of betrayal she'd felt through his deception, yet her personal emotions desperately wanted him to care enough about her to try and explain. It was a fitful night's sleep.

*

Sunday morning she awoke feeling unrested. Lacy rode into church with Jerome and Kelly, but it didn't seem the same going to church without Jason. Purposely late, the trio entered the sanctuary about the same time the choir took their seats behind the podium. They'd timed it perfectly, trying to reduce the amount of opportunity for people to approach Lacy concerning the exposé in the paper the day before. When Lacy turned to adjust her coat comfortably behind her, she spied James Calhoun, alias Jason Gardner, sitting in the last line of chairs in the church. Their gazes locked briefly before the congregation stood as one to sing a hymn with the choir.

When she sat down, her mind whirled. *What is he doing here? He only came to church with me under duress.* She paused to consider the one occasion when Jason had showed up unexpectedly at the house to accompany her and the others. *The threat of danger was still high,* she reminded herself. Lacy stole another glance to reassure herself Jason was really there. After a second confirmation, she continued to ask herself why.

Her gaze wandered out the window. A couple weeks ago, Jason had been aware of every car in the parking lot, in case they might prove a threat to them. Today the threat was over, still Lacy found it hard not to scan for would-be attackers wherever she went. The night before she'd felt vulnerable just driving to pick up the takeout dinner. Her eyes lingered on the top of the cemetery wrought-iron gate, her emotions going beyond to the graves in the last row.

By the time the closing prayer had been offered and the benediction music soared in the auditorium, the congregation spilled out into the aisles. Many of them spoke with friends as they walked slowly toward the exit. Lacy's focus shot to the back of the church, but the seat Jason had been occupying was glaringly empty. He was gone.

*

"Why aren't you going out to eat with us?" asked Jerome. He peered at Lacy in the rearview mirror as he maneuvered his vehicle out of the church parking lot.

Lacy beamed a huge smile, knowing she was being viewed. "Appreciate the offer, Jerome, but there's plenty to eat at home. Besides, I have much to do before leaving tomorrow. Just drop me off first when you go through town." She knew that Kelly would explain to him later that Lacy planned to run up to the hospital to see how Chloe was doing.

*

Forcing herself to down a bit of lunch, she stopped at the front mirror in the hall for a last minute evaluation before leaving the house. Her peach tweed sweater was a favorite that brought her a small measure of comfort to wear when her spirits were down. It was balmy enough outside for her to grab her white windbreaker to slip around her shoulders.

Her eyes still scanned her surroundings wherever she went. Would that habit remain with her forever? It wasn't the habit per se, it was the fear that motivated it. When she reached the hospital, she found Chloe was restricted from having outside visitors. The police guard outside her door gave evidence that Quinn was carefully guarding his witness. Recognizing Chloe's family, Lacy spent some time talking with her mother.

She asked the family to let Chloe know she'd been by to see her and left. Walking away, Lacy felt some of their pain and confusion. Some paranoid, greedy man had manipulated their vulnerable daughter to achieve his own agenda. She left the building with a heavy heart. When the Camry family let it slip that the *Gazette* owner himself had stopped by earlier to ask about Chloe, Lacy had offered a wan smile.

Inwardly she was perplexed. Who was this man of contradictory actions? He'd come to church but not bothered to stay around and talk to her. He was clearly avoiding her. So much for his promise to try and explain his actions in her respect. Her feelings didn't seem to matter much to him, yet he'd made an extra effort in the midst of the whole Heywood-Shaw disclosure to stop by and talk with Chloe's family. Without meaning to, Lacy drove around to the back parking area of the Gazette. The lot was empty. Had she hoped to find his car here?

In truth she actually knew little more about James Calhoun than Jason Gardner. In this whole month of interacting with him, he'd never once mentioned where he lived. Had he rented a house outside of town or a room somewhere within the city limits? Gunning the engine, she headed for home. Tomorrow would close the chapter on whatever relationship they'd had. She'd told God she'd committed every area of her life to him, and asked Him to guide her. Then why did she think everything was wrong with the way things were?

Where is my faith? Have I learned so little?

Yes, the goal had been reached, but she'd lost something important to her in the effort. Was that the price? Her heart told her God wasn't like that. Yet she couldn't get over the hurdle of Jason. She'd finally let down her guard and allowed herself to care about a man, and the result was heartbreak. She was miserable, yet there seemed little she was able to change. It was like a strong tide dragging her down the river.

I'll trust You, Lord. I don't understand, but I'll trust you.

Trudging up the steps to the house, Lacy spotted the envelope sticking out between the doorframe and the screen door. Her pulse raced as she walked in a daze to the door and withdrew the envelope with her name written in that familiar scrawl across the front.

"Why now? I'm leaving tomorrow, no matter what this note says," she muttered. Ripping into the seal, she withdrew the folded paper, catching the feather in her waiting hand. She read the words with trepidation: *Come tomorrow where it all began. 10:15 a.m.*

Lacy closed her eyes.

23

The Final Note

LACY HAD THE CAR PACKED BY 8:30 A.M., leaving her and Kelly time for one final cup of coffee and a chance to say good-bye. They made preliminary plans for the big Memorial Picnic with Chuck Walden, Johnny Fey, and their other motorcycle friends.

"I'll be thankful if the neighbors don't take up a petition forcing me to sell this house by the end of the day." Kelly chuckled. "Lacy, I'm going to miss all the excitement that seems to follow you." Her voice held sad affection.

Lacy worked to hold down her rising emotions. Everything within her screamed that she belonged in this sleepy little city. She belonged sharing a place with the only sister she'd ever known. "The neighbors know who the rowdy one is. Don't kid yourself," she said, laughing. "And you can count on Jerome being there to keep everyone straight and respectable. Besides, several of the men will have their families present, so it should be tame enough to pass muster. Now…the food bill is going to be a shocker!"

"I'll help you," offered Kelly quickly. "If it wasn't for them showing up on that quarry top, I hate to think…" Her face clouded. "I know the Lord had them all lined up to be there for you. I certainly don't begrudge them a good meal. How many did you say will be there?"

They laughed together like a couple of schoolgirls.

Lacy clung to those last moments as she drove away from the neighborhood. She experienced a hollow, sinking feeling in her stomach. She'd not had any say when her parents moved away years ago, though she'd cried and carried on. This time she was leaving on her own. Some people were homebodies at heart, and Lacy had never felt at home anywhere except this tiny place tucked in the heartland of Michigan. It was silly, really. Her hand rubbed her eyes, and she forced her thoughts ahead. She had one more stop before putting Gladden Hills behind her.

Pulling in across the street from the courthouse, Lacy locked the door and adjusted her sunglasses before heading for the old impressive steps. Stopping briefly at the front desk, she found Dede all "gaga" over the exposé.

"Just to think about all that happening right here in our little town makes me sick." Her hand went to her heart. "That Mr. Heywood at the bank was never that friendly, but who would have thought…and Judge Shaw. Well, he should be ashamed of himself, and him being paid to keep our town safe. I'm glad you came back to Gladden Hills, Lacy Cottrell. You're a credit to us. You did it for your little friend, didn't you?"

Lacy choked back the emotion threatening to gag her. She had to get away from this loving woman who was only trying to compliment her. There was no way she could tell her that she was leaving Gladden Hills. Nodding, she backed away in the direction of the elevators. It took all three floors to compose herself after the door closed behind her.

When the elevator door opened, she came face to face with Nicholas Cooper, her file room conspirator.

"Well, howdy, Miss Cottrell. Say, that was a nice thing you did, mentioning my name in such an important manner. I didn't do all that much and you know it." He shook his gnarled finger at her.

Walking over, she embraced the old man. "I know nothing of the kind. You were my pillar of encouragement. You guided me toward the right sources on more than one occasion. I just came to say good-bye before heading back to Chicago. My time here is up. I'll miss you, Nicholas. Perhaps people will have the courtesy to call you Nicholas now that you're such an important man." She smiled fondly, watching his eyes crinkle in mirth.

He chuckled. "I don't mind people calling me Coop all that much. It's not the name; it's the man, or so they say." He raised his eyes to meet hers. "You shouldn't ought to be leaving town like this, Miss Lacy. You belong here. People love you in this town. They took to you like a baby chick coming home to the nest."

Lacy bit her lip to keep from bawling like a baby. She should have listened to her better sense that told her to keep on driving and not stop, but she felt Nicholas deserved a personal good-bye. "I don't really have an option, Nicholas. I thought there was something for me here, but it disintegrated into thin air, so to speak. I don't even have a job anymore. I have to go back to Chicago. I came here on a month's leave of absence from my old position." She embraced him again and turned away before she totally lost control.

Past the city limits, Lacy pushed the pedal down and sped away, tears coursing down her cheeks. When she reached the junction, she turned right on the road that would take her to the interstate, her lips pressed in determination. There was no way she was going back to that cemetery and those graves. She'd done everything within her ability to find Stevie's killer, and now it was time to leave. The bad guys were behind bars, and justice had been done. *I'm done playing hide-and-seek with someone who hides behind a childhood memory...whoever they are.*

What difference did it make at this point? Listening to messages from someone who claimed knowledge of those feathers had almost gotten her killed. There was no way to know the intention of the writer of the note. Her trust level was at its lowest ebb. What if there was still someone in Gladden Hills who meant her harm? The purple feathers had been responsible for bringing her here. Was it so Heywood could eliminate her? Her mind was running crazy. She fought the fear.

The ramp to the interstate was under the overpass less than a half mile away. Her hands tightened on the steering wheel as if she were fighting an unseen force. She drove under the overpass and approached the ramp.

Then, without truly knowing why, Lacy sped up and drove past the ramp, turning around at the first side road heading back to the junction. That's when she realized she was driving to meet whatever was waiting for her in the cemetery. *God, I don't understand. I feel like I'm flying blind.*

Whipping into the parking lot behind the church, Lacy slammed her foot on the brakes, scanning the area for other cars. Her heart pounded. She was tense as a violin string. *Something monumental is about to happen! I feel it.*

She was early. It was not quite 10:00 a.m., causing her to wonder why Pastor Jaminson's car wasn't sitting behind the church at this time of day. Then she recalled it was Monday, his day off. Too edgy to remain in the car, she decided to head for the back of the cemetery and see if there was another note. If there was, she'd take it and leave.

There was something different about being here today. The abrupt change in weather made her turn her collar up against the wind. Even so, Lacy felt perspiration form on the back of her neck. Her fear level was higher at this moment than a month ago, when she'd crept through the wrought-iron gate at 11:30 at night.

Closing the gate, Lacy winced at the loud rusty squeak that had developed in the recent wet weather and began picking her way along the outside path. The grass was still soggy from the rains. She'd chosen to wear jeans and her favorite peach sweater for comfortable traveling on the long highway miles ahead of her. Clutching her coat tighter, she pushed windblown hair from her face.

Lacy shivered as the chilling dampness penetrated her clothing, even as her eyes searched the wooded area beyond the ancient stone wall. Should anyone walk out of those woods, she didn't want to be taken unaware. The last half of the cemetery was of lower ground and the earth was spongy, oozing moisture in places. Stepping around small puddles, she turned down the last line of headstones to stand in front of the graves that had brought her all the way from Chicago.

After everything that had transpired in the last month, she felt these graves should somehow look different, but the granite headstones bearing the names of Terri and Steven Turner were no less cold or permanent.

"Stevie, I did my best, but I still miss you so terribly. Knowing who did it couldn't bring you back," she murmured. Her heartfelt emotions reached toward the heavens.

Stooping down, Lacy felt in and around the long, thick foliage growing at the base of the headstone, frustrated not to find an envelope. Surely something was here. Her fingers moved further out in her frantic search, discovering a plastic bag trapped beneath a patch of sodden oak leaves. Holding her breath, she pulled out the bag, withdrawing the familiar white envelope with a shaking hand. She carefully opened the note, catching the purple feather in her hand. Even the handscript was the same as the first notes, yet old fears overrode her initial joy.

Her head shot upward, scanning the area for any would-be attackers. Once assured she was alone, Lacy focused on the enclosed message:

> I brought you here to explain. Remember, "Love is patient" and "Love always protects."

She scrunched her brows in confusion and distrust. The note writer had quoted the Bible. What did that mean? What was she to expect? Who was going to explain?

Her eyes lifted to the empty front gate and traveled slowly around the exposed area, lingering on the path leading into the forest beyond the stone wall, almost as if willing someone to emerge from the shadows. She was totally alone, and it was creepy waiting here for the unknown. Her flesh felt prickly and instantly cold. *I should leave now!*

Once again Lacy recalled the trap set for her on top of the quarry. She swallowed and checked her watch: 10:30 a.m. Lacy stood, preparing to hurry away from the graveyard, anxious to be safely inside the confines of her car heading for the open road. She heard the loud creaking of the front gate and whirled forward to stare back through the cemetery.

A lone male figure was closing the wrought-iron gate. As he turned to walk the outside path of the cemetery, Lacy stood momentarily fixated on his progression. If he didn't turn aside into one of the midway off-shoot paths toward older headstones, the visitor was squarely headed in her direction. She could see part of a light-gray jacket, but most of the upper half of his body was hidden by two large, long-stemmed full bouquets of colorful flowers. As he clutched them protectively inside his right arm, his left hand held tightly to the felt gray hat pulled low on his head. Finding it difficult to see past the flowers and hat, Lacy studied the rhythmic manner of the man's walk and frowned in consternation.

I know that determined stride. Her heart pounded like a trip hammer while she frantically tried to recall the man behind that walk. Was it friend or foe? Considering her options, there was no way she could leave without bypassing him on the path unless she chose to retreat to the woods.

Perhaps the visitor was here on a legitimate mission. If not, those flowers were a well-chosen decoy, and that would make her a target. Her next few decisions depended on whether she could afford to trust his intentions, or her own whimsical belief it could be her note writer. But now it no longer mattered; her safety was the main issue. The man's long strides were quickly eating up the distance between them.

Lacy looked to the woods in terror. She and Stevie had tramped those woods. If she had to, she could lose a pursuer. *If I could just reach the tree line...*

The reality remained that it was possible not all of the bad guys had been rounded up. Quinn and Frank were still combing through the evidence, and there was a good possibility Heywood, at least, had far-reaching connections within the criminal element. Witnesses were expendable, experienced by Clem Browning and Jake Gibbons.

Perspiration now ran freely down Lacy's jacket collar. Hadn't Kelly prophetically pointed out that Lacy was the forgotten witness?

Lord, tell me if and when to act. Her ears echoed the pounding of her heart. She deftly transferred her pepper spray to her coat pocket next to the last note. Yet something held her in place, even as her mind flitted to the woods behind her for refuge.

The rows in the cemetery were narrowing fast, bringing the man closer at an alarming rate. A powerful breeze rattled trees and nearby shrubbery. Lacy watched the visitor grope fiercely to hang on to the fast shifting flowers and still keep his hat from flying off.

She placed her feet in readiness to run...then saw his face.

"Jason! Wha—what are you doing here?" she gasped out, momentarily forgetting his name was James.

"Lacy," he murmured. Opening his mouth, her former boss paused, ill at ease, as if whatever he'd planned to say had flown.

Had seeing her unexpectedly thrown him off kilter? She was probably the last person he'd expected to encounter on a Monday morning in the cemetery. Waiting for him to answer was awkward. She stared at the flowers with wonder and question.

Jason attempted to adjust the two bunches of disheveled flowers, laughing nervously at his own awkwardness. "Now that the case is near completion, I-I just figured it was only appropriate that I bring these to the graves of the victims."

"Very appropriate." Lacy felt a sharp twinge of guilt. Why hadn't she thought of that? She was Stevie's best friend. She stared at the large bouquet of mixed tulips in his arms. It spurred a vision of large beds of tulips in Terri Turner's backyard. They'd flooded her yard with color in the spring. "It's very nice of you," Lacy added as the tension between them grew more strained.

This was just more evidence of Jason's consideration—to everyone but her.

When he didn't reply immediately, her gaze wandered anywhere but his face. Finally she pushed herself to state what had been on her mind since the paper first came out. "Jason, I really appreciate that tribute editorial you wrote about me in the *Gazette,* though I didn't feel worthy of all that praise."

"As far as I am concerned, you are. You risked your life more than once for the truth." He now looked as uneasy as she felt. "Listen, Lacy…"

She hurried to fill in any gaps of conversation. "Honestly Jason, ah, sorry, James, I was quite impressed, and I have to say amazed at the writing quality of the article. Perhaps more so, now that I know you're a lawyer." She stared off into the woods.

"Don't be. I graduated with a second minor in journalism and ran the school newspaper two years in a row. It's come in handy several times. Lacy, I meant to call to talk, but it has been so busy. And, ah, truthfully, I'm here for another reason as well. I think we…I mean, I really want to…"

Cutting off his words before he could say something personal and make both of them feel increasingly uncomfortable, she raced on, her words jumbled. "Yes. Yes, I'm sure you do, but…," she said hurriedly. Just being near him was making her ramble erratically. She tried to gather her thoughts and return them to his writing. "Your writing skills obviously served you well for your undercover work in Gladden Hills the last few weeks."

Seeing the frown cross Jason's features, she winced, feeling regretful she'd mentioned it. She hadn't meant to send him that sharp jab, a reminder of his deception. Without giving him time to respond, she added quickly, "I was also surprised to see you at church yesterday. You know, -considering your previous attitude." Instantly, she heaved an inward groan. It was almost like her mouth was on auto self-destruct and she couldn't stop herself.

Her focus veered in the direction of the stone wall, remembering the note she'd found in her door yesterday and the most recent note nestled this very minute in her pocket. Was the fact Jason appeared in the cemetery keeping the note writer from making contact with her? If so, maybe that was a good thing, considering her fearful doubts. She was fast wishing more and more that she'd taken the ramp to the interstate and avoided all of this.

Jason stared down and seemed to remember the flowers in his arms. "Yes, about that. The events of the last several weeks have shown me I have some things to clear up with God. Pastor Jaminson and I had breakfast this morning to discuss some of them. It's a start."

She couldn't help her shocked expression. That was the last thing she'd expected him to say. "Yes-ss, I'd say a *very good* start." She wished he had elaborated more, but Jason had always been short on explanations. Watching him move toward the Turner headstones, she was mesmerized by his movements as he kneeled to lay the tulips gently across Terri Turner's grave.

Jason turned his head with a look that was hard to discern. "Did you come by the graves to say good-bye to your friend?" he asked, studying her.

She sighed, feeling the chasm separating them from meaningful conversation. It mentally hurt Lacy to continue making small talk with her emotions ready to explode. This man she cared for so much was never so far beyond her reach than at this minute, yet she could think of nothing that might change that situation.

"In a manner of speaking, I'm here to say good-bye," she said stiffly, observing the careful way he distributed the arrangement of tulips. Jason seemed visibly moved by what he was doing, tenderly patting the irregular ground around where the flowers lay. It was almost a loving, personal act. Lacy's hand rubbed her arm nervously, suddenly aware how his movements strangely tugged at her memory, bringing forth new shadow suspicions—suspicions that didn't make any sense and confused her even more.

The second flower bouquet was a wild arrangement of white daisies, just like the ones Stevie had cut from the Bradford flower garden seventeen years ago. Cindy's mother had been livid at his actions, and when Cindy found out Stevie had given them to Ellie, she was hateful for weeks.

Lacy was afraid she was mentally losing control. Why else would she relate the flowers and Jason's movements to past shared experiences with

Stevie? It was past time for her to leave the area. As she turned to walk away, Jason's deep voice caused her to turn back.

"You know the truly sad part about all this? For the longest time *the soul* of that little boy lay buried beneath this cold ground." His sober tone caused her breath to catch.

Feeling a sudden shiver, Lacy frowned down on his bent head. "That's a curious thing to say." Everything she knew from God's Word told her a child's soul went immediately to be with the Lord.

He pushed up from the grave to a standing position. She noticed the bouquet of daisies was still clutched within the confines of his arm. "Why didn't you place that bouquet on the graves with the others?"

Jason's features grew heavy with emotion. "Because that grave is empty, Lacy."

Tilting her head, she stared at him strangely. His shocking declaration saturated the dense air, holding her immobile. As their eyes locked, Jason strolled over and placed the bouquet of radiant daisies in the cradle of her limp arm. Gently closing her fingers around the stems, he tenderly held on to her hand. "These are for you, Ellie Cottrell." His voice was as soft as a nestled bird. "I remember someone telling me many years ago that daisies were like sunshine on a cloudy day. They make everything bright."

The words sent chills through her body and her emotions reeling through seventeen years of grief. "*Daisies are like sunshine on a cloudy day. They make everything bright.*"

Jason drew her focus back by gently squeezing her hand. "It was my soul that laid in the empty grave for years on end. And, up until recently, I would have added that only the hollow form of what was left merely went through the motions of living by losing himself in work. Even that form was empty and damaged. But, I repeat, that grave is empty! I'm Stevie—Steven Turner." He shook his head in overt frustration at her unresponsiveness. "I've been trying to tell you, Lacy. It's been so hard all this time!"

The image of the flowers and his words stung deeper than a bee, electrifying her senses. Still, it seemed she was looking through a haze. "I said those very same words about daisies to Stevie." Her free hand flew to her head as she fought to process every movement and word conveyed in the last several minutes. But she couldn't put it all together. It was like a mind blackout in a time of dire distress.

"No! That can't be!" she retorted, pushing him away. Her whole body trembled in shock. Shaking her head, she backed away, staring at the armload of daisies, like they'd morphed into a snake. Past images were strong and pushed to the surface. She'd stood at Stevie's grave in the rain and placed daisies on his tiny casket before they'd lowered it down into the earth.

Lacy stared at this man trance-like, as if she would a stranger, withdrawing into the safety of her memories. His words still failed to register as logical in her organized thinking. Hadn't she stood next to his grief-stricken father when the pastor had talked about the tragedy of Stevie's young life being snatched away too soon? Had it all been a sham, as Jason claimed?

Vaguely aware of movement in front of her, she noticed him brush off his dirt-flaked hands and move backwards until he stood close to the stone wall under the shading of the overhanging oak branches.

She watched him with compelling magnetism as he removed his shaded glasses. Lacy slowly advanced, finding she was unable to help herself. His dark brown eyes appeared to have those same amazing red highlights that always fascinated her in Stevie's unusually colored irises. She swiped at the gathered moisture in her eyes, her gaze roaming the contours of his face and features, trying to compare them to her memory of the child Stevie.

Jason squinted against piercing shafts of light penetrating the tree limbs, allowing her to continue to gawk. Not yet able to accept the meaning of his words, she fought against the ring of truthfulness that resounded in her ears—truth linking his admission with her previous suspicions.

But how could it be? She started to reach toward his face, but stayed her hand.

Everything battled her numbed senses as she watched him replace his sunglasses, becoming Jason once again. She felt like screaming, but instead she heard herself demanding more proof. "All right, enough role playing! Who are you? What are you? Some kind of chameleon that changes skin color to whatever he stands next to? First, you're Jason Gardner, newspaper owner. Then you're James Calhoun, DA from Ohio. And now you claim to be the long-dead son of Terri and Matthew Turner. Well, I'm not buying it!" she shouted angrily. Wanting to escape, she paced the length of the stone wall.

Frustrated, she quickly reclosed the gap between them to remove his glasses a second time, peering at him like an insect under a microscope. Only then did she notice the tiny burn scars around his eyes. Continuing to stare, she offered no apology. "What caused those scars?"

"My eyes were affected in the blast and remain super sensitive to light. I also have scars from flying debris across my back and neck. I escaped the main blast of the bomb, for which they told me I should be thankful. Thankful," he repeated scornfully. "With my mother lying in this graveyard, and me under the knife on and off for over a year, I was supposed to feel thankful." He heaved a sigh, as if reliving the events from those horrible days. Lacy saw such pain in his twisted expression, she could hardly bear to witness it.

"Actually I felt guilty," he continued. "I keep reflecting on the scenario, thinking if I'd only told my parents about seeing Heywood in the basement on that ladder…" He winced. "Afterward, I reasoned what I'd seen away. The fact I didn't understand is reasonable. But if I'd just told them!" His agony was revealed in his eyes. "Maybe my parents would have found the bomb, and my mother would be alive today. Amazingly, I was spared to remember that moment for the rest of my life. I couldn't deal with that kind of sparing. "His words held subdued anger.

Did he think living was a curse? Lacy found her tongue. "You should be thankful! Your life was a gift from God! What makes you think that you were in charge of what happened that day—an eight-year-old kid? If you do, you've greatly overestimated your abilities! God is in charge of life and death," she accused. "You weren't thinking straight. It doesn't sound as if you're thinking right yet." She wasn't in a mood for coddling this man.

His laugh was tinged with sarcasm as he replaced his glasses. "You have such a gentle touch, Ellie—Lacy—Cottrell! Maybe I wasn't thinking straight, but those were my thoughts for a long time, and Pop was hurting too badly to notice at the time. Later I happily shared the blame with God, which was the attitude you noticed that first Sunday in church. Until lately, that is. Recently, I've had a change of heart in many areas. You played a part in that, Lacy," he said softly, lifting his eyes to watch the scudding, dark clouds before continuing.

"I trusted Heywood was doing something good for my mother that day we spent swinging in the backyard. Mom was his mentor at the bank and helped him over the rough spots. I didn't suspect he'd done anything wrong until after the blast." Jason rubbed his brow as if trying to eradicate a headache.

Making her way to the stone wall, Lacy sat down, staring back at this man as if she was having a hallucination. She didn't know how to think of him: Jason—James—Stevie? Her world was out of focus, foggy with the desire to deny everything she'd heard.

Suddenly her insides felt like they were strung so tight she might be sick with the shock of Jason's declaration. Her whole life had been spent mourning this man. Even with her eyes glued to his face, she still found it difficult to connect him with the Stevie of her youth. While struggling to make a transition, Lacy tried to picture that ghastly moment and him living through it. Slowly, she said, "Tell me about the blast."

Following her to the wall, Steven sat a couple stones away, still working to get the rest of the dirt from the palms of his hands. His words flowed as if someone turned a page in a book, and he was back reliving that horrific time. "The day of the bombing I'd forgotten my homework in the car. When Mom sent me out to get my backpack, the bomb went off. I was in front of the car when the blast ripped through the house. For an instant, the world was brilliant white. The force propelled me into the hedge across the drive, where I remained unconscious for quite some time, basically out of sight.

"It was Pop who found me later, as he was stumbling around in a daze. All the firemen were too busy putting out the blaze, so he raced to get the police chief, who in turn called an ambulance from Wellington. They whisked me away in the night to some hospital in Lansing, where my identity was carefully concealed." The corners of Stevie's mouth turned up in a quirky attempt at a smile. Revisiting his horror was taking its toll on his nerves.

"This is where the big deception came into play. The chief kept quiet about me, not knowing if I'd live. Then the FBI arrived and took over the show, ordering everyone to keep the fact I survived hush-hush until they knew who was responsible for the bombing. Of course, that never happened. They arrested Pop, and their interrogators turned him inside out for days. He was a wreck by the time he was cleared and released. After the funeral, he hurriedly packed up what few things remained, arranged to have me transported from the hospital, and we left Gladden Hills for good—or so he thought. "

Lacy sat wooden-like, listening, all the while feeling like she was existing in a cocoon. Her stony silence encouraged him to share more.

"Pop stayed at my aunt's house for several weeks while I received treatment for my wounds. Shortly afterward, the Bureau moved us to Ohio and gave us new names—Anthony and James Calhoun. Pop kept maintaining that Heywood had something to do with the bombing because Mom told him about irregularities in Union files—files that were under Heywood's supervision. But it was his word against Heywood, and the bank files proved Heywood right."

"Heywood's altered files," she interjected and Jason nodded.

"Right. When you photographed the file names in Heywood's private office, and identical files in his house, it gave us a direction to focus our investigation. Mom had told Pop that she and Heywood had a meeting that day at the house before the bombing, but Heywood denied it, having a convenient alibi to back him up. He thought everyone was dead who saw him there—except you, the forgotten witness." Steven looked at her tenderly.

Still stunned, Lacy said, "No. You're the forgotten witness. Heywood thought you were dead! He thought I was neutralized until I returned to Gladden Hills."

Stevie countered, "But that's it. Don't you see? Your remembering that day before the bombing gave credence to my recollections. I was so ill and bewildered I wasn't much help initially. It was almost a year before my thinking sorted out enough to remember anything worthwhile, and the Bureau figured a slick lawyer would take me apart on the stand, so we waited."

"Discovering Clem Browning was the bomb maker was your big break, wasn't it?" Lacy asked. It helped to delve into a realm she felt was solid ground—thinking like a reporter. She recalled how excited she'd been when she'd heard the news about uncovering Browning's involvement. "I read it in the paper and remembered seeing your name, wondering why a DA in Ohio would become involved in a cold case in Michigan."

"Yeah, that was Jake Gibbons' collar. He was the best private investigator I ever knew. We didn't see that attack coming." Stevie's features pinched in emotion. "I figure I basically got him and Browning killed. I should have remembered Heywood's prison connections through his uncle." Steven's gaze darkened. "Just like I almost got you killed. When I think of all those close calls, I get sick inside."

"What are you talking about? Those attacks on me weren't your fault." She stared at him incredulously.

He raised his hat, and his fingers raked his disheveled curls. "I sent you those notes with the purple feathers—the notes that brought you back to Gladden Hills. Just like today. I wanted you here so I could explain, but then I didn't know how to begin. Everything was so tangled." He heaved his shoulders, appearing suddenly vulnerable.

"Of course—you sent the notes!" She shook her head at her own stupidity, feeling dumb as a toadstool. When she heard he was Stevie, that fact should have been obvious, but she'd been too distracted to think on it. "But why bring me back?"

"Because I needed you to remember that last day when we were in the backyard, and to remember Heywood coming to the house." He deferred his gaze to the woods. "And I wanted to see you. It had been so long." His focus snapped back, as if he couldn't bear not watching her reaction. The intensity of his body language held her immobile by sheer will.

"Then why did you keep deceiving me? All of it was a continuing lie—every moment we were together, at the paper during work, or church that entire Sunday afternoon. All that time we were on the road to Indiana and back. The motel. You had plenty of opportunities." She stared at him. "Stevie?" she barely whispered, with hesitation and question, trying to reconcile everything she now knew about this man. She was unsure why she couldn't quite state the name out loud. Perhaps she was afraid it would make it real?

Her gaze moved slowly over every inch of his face. Yes, his hair was the same, maybe a mite shorter, curling around his ears. Her first glimpse of his eyes had stunned her—their color and shape hadn't changed. Yet he was changed. Where the joy and innocence of life had once shined, she now saw sorrow, remorse, and a fiery anger. It was Stevie; yet it wasn't. Her emotions were a wreck. Part of Lacy was still furious with him for deceiving her, but she longed to reclaim her friend and heal his unseen wounds.

Even as her heart reminded her that only God could do that, Lacy was at a loss to know where to go from this point. They had reached an impasse. She stood abruptly and strode blindly toward the cemetery path.

"Wait, Lacy!" He jumped to his feet. "Stevie doesn't exist anymore. Let him stay that way. He has to stay buried!" His voice was firm. "Trust me. It's better that way. Please understand. I felt I had to tell you before you left. I refused to allow you to leave thinking as badly of me as you did. Don't go yet. There's more." His face twisted in emotion.

Lacy took several steps back toward him and slowed. Unsure of herself, she waited there to hear him out. "More?"

He stopped. "Look, I thought I had everything planned until I saw your face that first morning when you rushed in late to the office. Everything changed in that instant. My emotions became involved. I-I couldn't tell you the truth. My faked death was not my lie, but I was forced to keep it until the case was solved. Dad's life, as well as mine, was at stake." He paced a little, then stopped. "I did some research and discovered you'd been investigating the case on your own. When I made my decision to come to Gladden Hills, I decided to use your interest for dual purposes—God help me." His hand extended upward in her direction.

"Ellie…Lacy…I've loved you since I cut those silly daisies from Bradfords' garden to give to you.. I just didn't have the guts to tear your insides out again, to tell you I've been alive all these years and my life was a sham. It would also have destroyed our working relationship and most probably tipped Heywood off prematurely. But after your close call on the courthouse stairs, I lived in constant dread morning and night, hating myself for bringing you back. I thought the only thing to do was protect you the best I could. Quinn and I worked together on that. It was the only reason I consented to go to church with you that first time. You were more important to me than all my frustrated opinions of God."

"Why didn't you tell me then?"

"I couldn't!" He averted his eyes. "As Jason Gardner, I'd seen the attraction that was developing between us. I was caught in a hard place. I couldn't encourage you knowing that I wasn't who you thought I was. Lacy." He raked his hands through his thick hair. "Didn't you hear me? I said I love you! I don't want you to leave thinking of me the way you did. I don't want you to leave at all! " Lifting his head, he removed his glasses, his strained eyes brimming with moisture.

"But you're leaving. Why would you want me to stay?" She was thoroughly confused.

A mischievous smile spread. "As it turns out, it seems I won't be leaving after all." His eyes held such longing that her pulse started to race like a runaway train.

Lacy wrinkled her nose. "But I don't understand." She slowly closed the distance between them. "Are you planning on staying and running the *Gazette* after all?"

The edges of his mouth tilted upward. "No-oo, I have someone else in mind for that. I've been offered the position of District Attorney of Gladden Hills. A representative from the governor's office met with Quinn and me yesterday. Quinn recommended me for the job without my knowing. I guess he feels I belong here." Steven's grin was infectious. It reminded her of the old Stevie.

Her jaw dropped. "You got the DA job? Wow! The *Gazette* needs to get out a special edition right away! Wait until your readers learn their editor is their new DA. How are you going to handle that transition? You can't change jobs until the town knows you are a real DA and not just an editor."

Steven laughed. "Like I said, I have someone else in mind for writing a second exposé, as well as running my newspaper. Are you open for a permanent position?" He was clearly enjoying himself. "Technically I'll still own the paper, but I'll maintain only a cursory interest in the week-to-week operation."

"Run the paper? You want me to run the entire paper?" She froze in disbelief.

"Well, yes, that is my hope. Naturally there's a pay raise involved, and Maxine will be there to help. Is there any problem?" Clearly, he was a man who studied reactions. He closed the remaining gap between them, causing Lacy to have trouble concentrating.

"A slight problem...I was scheduled to return to Chicago by Wednesday morning and I don't feel a phone call is appropriate. They've been good to me, and I respect my former boss too much for an email resignation." She chuckled nervously, still slightly bewildered by his offer. Everything was happening too fast, and her head was swimming. In fact, her entire world was off kilter.

When his hands lifted slowly and rested lightly on the outsides of her arms, Lacy caught her breath. Steven's firm chin lowered toward her face. "Personally, as an editor, I agree with that professional attitude. I'll hold up the announcement of my appointment until you return from Chicago and can handle the carefully worded explanation of my career change. Is that acceptable?"

"Ye-s-s," she answered, struggling for air.

"Something else?" He tilted her chin upward with a gentle hand.

Lacy's breathing was now almost nonexistent. "Yes. What do I call you?"

His laugh was husky. "Not Stevie! I will continue to use the name the Bureau gave me—James Calhoun, DA from Ohio. The story will be that I was undercover, working with Quinn Darling in Gladden Hills. It will be less confusing that way now that I'm planning to stay. They will accept the fact I was a former DA in Ohio because it's on record. In time it will seem natural for the town to call me James. Only Quinn knew my true identity when I came, but I'll tell you about all that later." His lips lowered, trembling, toward hers. "I'll call you Lacy, and you call me Jason, James—anything but Stevie."

His face was so close, she could feel his warm breath on her cheeks. His next words came out in an intimate whisper. "In our hearts we'll always be Ellie and Stevie...will that be okay with you?"

At that moment, she felt the gentle touch of his lips on hers. It sent her swimming in a sea of emotions, emotions that both consumed and empowered her to believe she and this man who had been a part of her since childhood could have this special, electrifying love. When their lips at last parted, they stood, their eyes caressing each other's features as if they were seeing one another in a new light.

"I've never kissed a girl in a graveyard before," he admitted. "It's quite a rush."

When Lacy looked around aghast, her reaction brought an instant roar of laughter from James. He steered her toward the path that would lead them out to the gate.

They walked slowly, their arms entwined. James paused, casting one last look back to the graves before facing forward. He squeezed her arm. "You know, when I called Dad to tell him Heywood was under arrest, he cried. I think he'd lost all hope that it would ever happen. I've told him about you too." James smiled down at her. "But Dad never lost his faith, Lacy. He's been praying for your safety. I should have been, but I forgot how."

"And now?" she asked softly.

He exhaled. "I've been to the place where God never fails to show up—my knees. The deep hurt I'd brought to you these last several days was the catalyst that brought me to that decision. I couldn't tell you I was sorry, until I told God I was sorry." James reached down and took her hand, cradling it in his own. "And I am sorry for the hurt I caused you, Lacy." She applied a gentle pressure to his hand in response, not feeling the need to reply.

They sat in Lacy's car quietly together. As he leaned his head against the headrest, James appeared more relaxed than Lacy had ever seen him. She watched his features soften, fascinated that her childhood friend was sitting beside her. Would she ever get over marveling at the way God had worked everything out? She doubted it.

She turned her head toward him. "Tell me about the strange connection between you and Quinn. You said that he knew about your identity?" Lacy wanted to know the whole story so she could set it aside and go forward.

James took his time answering. "I'll give you the shortened version. The Bureau already knew of my existence and the situation, so when I contacted Quinn and told him of my plans to return as editor of the paper, he was able to establish a working relationship between us for a two-fold goal. I informed him about you, but he wasn't expecting the zeal with which you jumped into the case. You also worried him. I'd get phone calls asking me to call you off, but there was no way to do that with you. I knew that better than anyone. You never could back away from a challenge." He grinned at her.

When it came time for Lacy to leave, she and James Calhoun stood outside in the church parking lot to say their good-byes.

James held both her hands. "Look. Don't panic about getting back. Quinn will be most of the week tying up loose ends before he'll be able to leave town, so an announcement can be held back until that time."

She nodded. "Good. I have a few responsibilities to follow through on in Chicago. We'll meet back in Gladden Hills by the end of next week." When she would have turned away, he drew her back into his arms, so tightly she had trouble breathing. His lips enveloped hers with a banked passion. "Think on that while you drive back."

She watched him stride across to his Durango with all the energy she remembered seeing in Stevie Turner. Climbing inside the vehicle, he rolled down the window and stuck his head out. "Whataya say we go to the park for a swing when you get back, Cottrell?" His smile blazed in the sun as he wheeled out of the lot. She sighed, clinging to the last vestige of dust from his tires as his vehicle disappeared down the road.

"Is it possible, Lord, that I will have the joy of sharing my life someday with this man—a man of mystery, with secret identities? Like old Nicholas at the courthouse said, "It's the man, not the name," she reminded herself.

As a child, Stevie had devised the plan of communicating with the purple feathers—their secret connection. He'd been gifted with special love and responsibility for those around him, like Chuck and Jerome. Lacy would have much to think on as she drove back to Chicago to resign, before turning her life toward Gladden Hills. Coming back to live was a dream come true, but then God was a God of delightful surprises.

Speeding out toward the interstate, she clicked her cell phone, dialing a well-used number. "Hello, Kelly. Don't rent out my room. I'll be coming back home in a few days." She had to hold the phone away to avoid the ear-piercing squeal emitting from the phone.

Coming home had a nice sound. Ellie Cottrell and Stevie Turner had come home.

Epilogue

LACY'S HEAD WAS STILL ABUZZ with all of the arrangements she'd put into place before leaving Chicago: the boxes shipped to storage in Gladden Hills, the apartment sublet until the lease ran out. She hated the good-byes to Nadine and J.T. Goff. She was going to miss them, but her heart was pointed toward Gladden Hills. James' phone calls to her in Chicago always left her with wonder and expectation. On one occasion, he reminded her of her obligation to redecorate the editor's office at the *Gazette.* "The least you can do is fulfill your promise," he chided.

"Hey, at least give me time to get moved in. Is this what it's going to be like if I continue to work for you?" she asked playfully.

"There are compensations to be considered," he replied, and they had laughed together, filling Lacy with a sense of excitement. She couldn't wait to get back.

The last phone call she'd received from James began with a different feel. From the first she'd noticed a tense uneasiness, as if he was unsure how she might respond. He'd begun slowly, revealing yet another aspect in the unveiling of his complex undercover work in Gladden Hills.

"I know I've never mentioned before who I've been staying with in town. Please don't think of this as another deception. There have been too many secrets between us, and I want to change that."

A large lump had formed in her throat. It was always a new surprise with James, alias Jason Gardner, alias Stevie Turner. "Just tell me, James!" she'd spit out. "Enough of the theatrics!" She'd heard his unsettled laugh.

"I've been staying with a great uncle who lives outside of town. His place is fairly secluded and fit my need for privacy. He's a great old guy, thinks the world of you, Lacy…and generous to a fault. He loaned me his car on several occasions. I felt terrible about shocking him the way I did. When I first showed up on his doorstep and told him who I was, it was pretty overwhelming for him. But he welcomed me with open arms—even said he understood the reasoning behind the sham." James' earnest tone begged for her to understand as well.

Lacy was getting the gist that his uncle was someone she knew. "Who is it, James?"

She heard the hesitation in his voice. "Nicholas Cooper. He works in the courthouse file room."

"Nicholas Cooper is your great uncle?" She inhaled, remembering all the things Nicholas had said to her—little hints she never picked up on. As James' revelation gradually filtered through her grid, one statement in particular hit a rough spot. "Wait a minute. You said Nicholas loaned you his car on occasion?"

"Ye-s-ss." He slowly drew out the reply.

"What kind of car was it?" The wheels of her mind churned.

"Nothing elaborate…just a little gray sedan," he answered with a hint of laughter.

"A gray sedan!" she shouted in the phone, thinking of all the anxious moments that gray sedan had caused her. All the time it had been James watching out for her. "Honestly, James. We need to have a long, long talk. I want to know all the surprises at once."

She heard him chuckle quietly. "That's all, really. You've got my word. But we will have that long talk. I have everything arranged. Stop by our meeting place on the way in tonight. Your instructions are there." She'd heard his delighted laugh just before the phone went dead—so much like Stevie. Was this the same man she'd thought grim and austere when she'd worked under him at the paper?

*

Lacy checked her watch as the endless ribbon road stretched out before her. Great…it would be almost 10:00 p.m. by the time she reached the graveyard. "You're right, James Calhoun. We are going to have a long talk someplace where you can't hang up on me. These graveyard meetings have got to stop."

The moon was bright when she pulled up close to the wrought-iron gate and checked her surroundings. Everything looked clear. If James knew the lingering fear it brought, he wouldn't ask her to come here alone at night. But then, Lacy had never wanted anyone to know the extent the fear had touched her. She walked through the gate. The path to the graves had become familiar—too familiar. She made her way quickly, standing over Steven Turner's grave with her flashlight moving across the base of the headstone. There it was, a glint of white envelope reflected from the flash of her light.

Lacy stooped to a kneeling position and retrieved the plastic bag with the encased envelope. Laying the flashlight on the ground, she opened the bag, hearing a hoot owl in the woods beyond the stone wall. A purple feather fell from the center. James had informed her that she should have known the earlier note was phony without the feather. "The feather was our special signal," he'd reminded her.

> Ellie, call me after you get this. We'll meet near the park swings at the fountain. I want our first date to remind you of all the wonderful times we've shared together as children, and to start our new relationship with a focus on the great things we will share in the future with God as our guide. I'll take care of all the arrangements.
>
> Your forever playmate, friend—and love…Stevie

A picnic and swing ride at midnight.

"Oh, yes, Stevie, life with you will definitely be interesting," she murmured. She turned and made her way to the car, her heart joyful and ready for adventure.

uncharted STORM

PATRICIA L. STEBELTON

A motorcycle roared up. She stared as the rider set the stand
and stepped off the cycle. "What do you want?" she demanded.
"Leave immediately before I call the police."

Removing his black helmet, the tall rider stepped forward.
Curiosity glinted in his eyes. "If you greet everyone
with this degree of civility, Miss, you must have a host of friends."

Before dawn, Shelby Rawlins creeps through her dark apartment to part the front window curtains. There, in the street beneath the city light, is the same dark car, always watching. Flattening herself against the wall, she thinks wildly through her escape. *What if I fail? What then?* She never could have dreamed that her now deceased husband would have become involved in anything illegal, but that was before….

Now Shelby is the only person her three-year-old daughter, Anna Elise, has to count on. They have nowhere to go, almost no money to live on, and her beloved nana is in the hospital. Then a ray of sunshine intrudes when she finds lodging near the hospital with the kind Emily Thornton, who also enjoys Anna Elise's company. But a frequent visitor to Emily's home is Reed Montclair, a motorcycle-riding pastor who seems to unsettle Shelby's life, ask questions she's afraid to answer, and niggle at her heart. Dare she risk trusting Emily and Reed with her secrets? And just why does looking into Reed's eyes unnerve her so?

WATCHED!

PATRICIA L. STEBELTON

Ginger's nightmares are now coming more and more often.
But what if there's truth to her troubling dreams?

Ginger has lived in the small town of Collier all her life, where everybody knows everyone else. So why does mystery still surround the death of her aunt, and why was her house robbed after her mama's death? And why is someone stalking her now?

Then Ginger finds some mysterious old journals while helping out at a local book shop. She's convinced that Lisbeth, the owner of the shop, knows more than she's telling. But secrets swirl around Lisbeth, too. Why did she leave town, and then suddenly come back a short while ago?

Ginger is up to her ears in too many surprises…and her confusion over the handsome Houston, the first boy to ever be interested in her, isn't helping.

SUSPENSE. MYSTERY. ROMANCE.
A keep-you-on-the-edge-of-your-seat
mystery & detective thriller with a twist of satisfying romance
www.oaktara.com

INHERITED DANGER

PATRICIA L. STEBELTON

The black Jag sped head-on toward Ginger and switched to her lane.
The driver was going to ram her.

Ginger thought her nightmares were over after she and her boyfriend Houston had explored Garnett Manor's long-hidden secret. But now, after visiting a controlling relative she's just discovered she had, things start happening to her. Crazy things, like two cars in one night trying to bump her off a dark stretch of highway into a deep ravine. Clearly, somebody is trying to kill her, but why?

Just as Ginger is starting to put the pieces of her life back together, the old, unanswered questions about her past and a potential large inheritance rear their heads. But all is not what it seems. Will Ginger be able to uncover the dark deception in time to save herself, and a dear friend, from their deadly enemies?

The exciting, not-to-be-missed sequel to Watched!

SUSPENSE. MYSTERY. ROMANCE.
A keep-you-on-the-edge-of-your-seat
mystery & detective thriller with a twist of satisfying romance
www.oaktara.com

The Sleeping Matchbook

Patricia L. Stebelton

A yellow Mustang.
A maroon and gray jacket.
A mysterious matchbook.
They all lead to murder.

Samantha Westhoff will never forget the night she waved good-bye to her crazy-in-love best friend, Amanda Griffin, as she jumped into her boyfriend's yellow Mustang to go to a birthday party. The next day Randy's gunshot body was discovered behind the wheel of his car in an empty parking lot. Amanda hasn't been seen since.

Now, four years later, as seventeen-year-old Sam is helping to sort out Amanda's room, she finds the jacket she's sure Amanda was wearing the night she disappeared. *But then, how could it be in her room now?* Sam wonders. When she discovers a matchbook hidden deep in the lining of the pocket, Sam knows she might be holding the one clue to what really happened that night....

SUSPENSE. MYSTERY. ROMANCE.
A keep-you-on-the-edge-of-your-seat thriller
www.oaktara.com

Acknowledgments

To Paul Marks, retired police crime scene investigator and friend, for his technical help on several occasions. To Ramona Tucker, my editor, who patiently deals with my penchant for many words, and the entire OakTara crew for their work and creativity. As always, my faithful readers.

About the Author

Patricia L. Stebelton, a masterful romance-suspense and mystery-detective writer, began by writing poetry when she was young. Now she is the author of six not-to-be-missed novels: *The Sleeping Matchbook, Watched, Inherited Danger, Henri's Ghost, Uncharted Storm,* and *Forgotten Witness* (all OakTara).

She has also published numerous other writings, including a real-life love story "A Night of Destiny" in *Falling in Love with You* (OakTara); a devotional in *Love Is a Verb,* compiled by Gary Chapman with James Stuart Bell; a short story in *Angels, Miracles, and Heavenly Encounters,* compiled by James Stuart Bell; a short story in *Whisperings in God's Ear,* compiled by Wayne Holmes; and short stories in Guideposts book series *Unexpected Prayers* and *Desires of Your Heart.*

Patricia and her husband live outside a picturesque, small town in the heart of Michigan. They have three children and six grandchildren. In the midst of raising a busy family, Patricia took courses in writing and art, attending seminars whenever possible. Presently she works at her writing and commissioned art projects, enjoying activities with her family such as summer cookouts and camping trips.

Patricia enjoys hearing from her readers: **plstebelton@yahoo.com.**

www.oaktara.com